Proof of Life
The Untold Story of Christ's Resurrection

A NOVEL BY
PASTOR BLAINE MacNEIL

Proof of Life

The Untold Story of the Resurrection of Christ

The Trilogy of the Cross Part Three

Meet Me On Facebook

Macneil Publishing

A Novel by
Pastor Blaine MacNeil
Copyright © le2018 Blaine MacNeil
MacNeil Publishing

Proof of Life

Pastor MacNeil's Bio

Pastor Blaine MacNeil has specialized in small town and rural church ministry. He spent his career in parish ministry including seven years working as an interim pastor for churches throughout his home state of Minnesota. He has also worked as a hospice chaplain, helping others to prepare for their journey home to heaven.

Pastor MacNeil holds a Master's degree (2001) in Counseling Psychology from the Adler Graduate School in Richfield, Minnesota. He graduated from Luther Seminary in St. Paul, Minnesota with a Master's in Divinity degree (2004). He furthered his educational experiences by completing the chaplain residency program at the Veterans Administration Hospital in St. Cloud, Minnesota (2013-14).

He also served as a Major in the United States Air Force Auxiliary/Civil Air Patrol as the chaplain of squadrons in the Minnesota and Wisconsin wings. In his service to our nation he has earned two Commander's Commendation awards for his service. He has served in search and rescue missions as a ground team member, and as a flight crew member. He is a graduate of the North Central Region Chaplain's Corp College and was the Minnesota Wing and North Central Region Chaplain of the year in 2012.

He and his wife Melanie love spending time with their grandchildren.

Thanks

A great word of thanks is due to those three people who have helped along the way to make this book possible. Thanks to my proofreader, my wife Melanie MacNeil. Her technical expertise completed what my creative writing skills lacked. Her help and encouragement has gone a long way to help me in the completion of this novel.

Introduction

As has been my practice in this series, I have written overlapping chapters from the previous novel and its sequel. This continues to be true in this final novel in the series, The Trilogy of the Cross.

There is no resurrection without the crucifixion, but there could be a crucifixion without a resurrection. There was no guarantee given that the Father would raise his Son Jesus from the dead. How could there be? There was only the promise of it. This promise was made in several prophecies and it was given to Jesus directly from the Father. The promise required the man Jesus of Nazareth to have faith and to trust, that God the Father would be true to do what he said he would. Relationships are built upon trust and by their very nature they are personal. With his death the disciples acted as though their relationship with the Lord had died. When he reappeared as their risen Lord it required them to know him in a new way.

In this novel the promise comes true. The challenge is no longer about the Lord suffering and agonizing about going to his death. This story is about the challenge of believing in his resurrection. For as wonderful as the news is about him rising from the dead there is a lot of resistance by those who believed in him the most. Following those early reactions of doubting and disbelieving the story really comes to life as Jesus visits with his many followers.

Chapter One
Morning Dark Mourning

Just the evening before some of the women had prepared more aromatic spices. Mary Magdala had been planning to do this since that Friday when they had hastily placed her Rabbi into Joseph's newly sculpted tomb. She could not live with the idea that they had so quickly prepared the Lord for his burial. This was a part of her way of saying goodbye to him. In preparing his body, she regretted that she and the others hadn't had more time to do all that was necessary. They had a need to carefully and painstakingly prepare his body for its eternal rest. If they had been allowed to do this the process would have been full and meaningful to them. It was the limits of time that would not allow them to carry these preparations out. So, when all that was needed did not happen, she determined to return and complete these rituals in the morning after the Sabbath's end had come.

Mary Magdala had been joined by Joanna, Maria, and Salome who worked with her in the pantry at Joseph of Arimathea's home. Together they had selected the spices they would use: myrrh, frankincense, cloves, cinnamon, dried flowers and other spices too. They had also made dressings for his wounds and bandages so that they could wrap his injuries again. The bandages would also be used to rewrap his arms and legs so that they would lay in proper alignment in resting positions. The women worked quietly and it was a very difficult time for them as they ground everything together with mortar and pistol. Their emotions were very tender, almost to the point of being raw. They did not say much to each other and in silence they shed their tears.

As Mary Magdala's tears rolled down her face some of them made their way on to her lips. Their saltiness reminded her of the bitter herbs she had dipped in saltwater before eating them in remembrance of her ancestors at the Passover feast. This made her experience doubly unpleasant. She was reminded of the life of her people from long ago and how they had suffered so greatly in Egypt. It made her call to mind the terrible pains her Lord suffered under in his death. He died, not in the fullness of the years that comes with a good and long life but as a victim of vicious brutality. She feared that just as he died wounded and on the cross so would her heart remain wounded for all the remaining years of her life.

It all seemed so natural, so automatic, that as they prepared the fragrant spices for his body the women were also able to live in the midst of their grief and sorrow. The compounds they had ground were mixed with the sacred tears they shed. When they had completed their tasks, all of their supplies were put into cloth bags and then placed in baskets. The women hardly made eye contact with each other during this whole time. They simple glanced at each other peripherally and noticed how reddened their eyes were from the many tears they had shed. Their faces were long, drawn and tired. Their broken hearts they could not hide. They were very tired and worn which made them look and feel as though they had aged many years older in the two days that were now all but past. Soon they left for their rooms and fell off to sleep but it was a fitful sleep for the women as it was for everyone in the household. No loss in death of anyone before had affected them so deeply as this one.

It was early morning, not even hardly first light when Mary Magdala rose. She trimmed the oil lamp in her room so that it would give more light and then she washed and dressed before going downstairs. Though she was very quiet the other women in her room woke and joined her in silence back in the pantry where they had left their supplies the night before. Joanna lit a lantern and carried it for their journey and they all carried a basket of spices and bandages. In silence they left the warmth and safety of Joseph's home.

The servant who kept the door was surprised by their insistence that he let them go out alone and at that hour. They would not be deterred by his offer to wake some of the men who could accompany them. He knew better than to stand in the way of these very determined and highly emotional women. He did not want to raise his voice and get into an argument with them that would have woken the others who were still asleep. Therefore, he opened the door for them as they had so insistently badgered him to do. Then he went and woke up John and Peter and reported to them what had just happened.

As the women made their way out into the darkness they walked at a determined pace. At that early morning hour it was very cool and so they hurried all the more to arrive at their destination. Because first light was yet to come there was nothing out there in the city streets for them to see along the way. Even if they had left in the light of the day their vision would have still been solely focused on getting to the tomb. Had the day been underway even the fulness of the city's busy activities would not have been able to offer them a single distraction that could have captured their attention away from what they were doing.

This was the first day of the week. It was the day when God first began his creation. In the beginning it was dark and then came the light by his creative voice. So also, they were walking in the rhythm of God's creative work. Every stride they took was part of their sacred task that they must see fulfilled even if it was still dark. Their devotion to it could not have been any deeper or greater. These few women were the first ones in the city to embrace the new day and begin their work. Step by determined step, they made their way to the Garden of Jerusalem which was the name of the cemetery where Jesus had been entombed. It was a sacred pace that the women's footsteps took, each step one by one, as they planted their feet in unison and moved forward in an unrelenting forward roll. They too moved with all of creation, moving with the pace of the heartbeat of their Creator and his sustaining work in the world he had made and set in motion so many ages before.

Each one of the women walked closely with the others and together in the darkness of the early morning they each privately shed their own tears. Soon they came near to the garden cemetery. All was still heavily cast in the shadows of the night and first light had only just appeared as they left the home. There was an early morning midst that had begun to form. It was a fog of white clouds that hovered just inches above the surface of the ground and rose only a foot or two into the air. It added a certain mystical feeling to what they were doing. Mary Magdala thought to herself, *'It appears to be like the Spirit of God hovering over the ground just as it did over the waters on that first day of creation.'* The air was cool and the mist that had formed was a cold vapor that touched them deeply and make them shiver.

As they approached the stone wall surrounding the garden, they slowed and took notice of what was just ahead of them. It was a dim light that was cast by a lantern. They had not known that Roman soldiers had been posted to guard the Lord's tomb. They hesitated about continuing and then came to a stop. Joanna turned down the wick of the lantern that she carried because she did not want them to be seen by the Romans. As they looked on they could see by the light of the soldier's lantern the imperial seals and ropes that had been place over the stone that covered the entrance to the Lord's tomb. One of the soldiers sat there with their backs against the wall of the tomb and were sleeping. The other three were standing only a few feet away from it. They were night weary and their eyes moved slowly, drooping as they stood their night watch keeping guard over the tomb. They both stood but in their weariness they leaned heavily on their spears using them like walking staffs to help steady their weary stance.

The women feared that the plans they had made would not be fulfilled. They were fearful for their own safety as they thought about what it would mean if they approach the soldiers at that hour. Their hearts were again breaking as they quietly whispered to each other. They wondered if they were going to be denied access to his body and kept from completing what was lacking from his burial on that past Friday. Their weeping hearts grew increasingly emotional as they feared what the presence of the soldier meant for them and their intensions.

Mary Magdala wept again but covered her mouth to muffle the sound of it for fear of alerting the soldiers to their presence. They still wanted to carry out this small measure which would bring some closure to their need to honor their Lord fully in his death. It would be much like reliving his death all over again, but they needed to do it. On that fateful day in their haste they had not been given the time to sing him a funeral dirge. They had not recited a lament or been allowed enough time to be with his body before the tomb was closed to them. They had been robbed of this by the onset of the Sabbath and now they were being robbed again of their needs by this new setback. They wrestled within themselves. Each one longing to go to their Rabbi this one last time but fearing the presence of the soldiers who stood where they longed with all their hearts to be. In their minds they were near to the idea of setting their own safety aside and going up to the tomb in spite of the soldiers. They worried that the soldiers were there to arrest any of the Rabbi's followers who might come to visit his tomb. They all knew that they were willing to die for him while he lived, but now in his death they were uncertain of what they needed to do.

The women all peered over the wall that surrounded the garden and they made their decision. They were going to approach the tomb even though there might be a great danger to them in doing this. As they entered the garden and turned to walk to the tomb there was suddenly a great earthquake that violently shook the ground below their feet. Their eyes quickly darted about in a fearful panic and they saw the soldiers they had feared knocked around like rag dolls and thrown down hard to the ground. The women themselves quickly laid on the ground for fear of falling down. They screamed out in fits of rage because they were worried that the tomb where Jesus' body lay might be disturbed or that the tomb itself might collapse. They were absolutely overwhelmed by their worst fears and they held their hands to their hearts and beat their chests in deep felt protests.

As the earth continued to shake the soldier who had been sleeping was tossed up and down continuously. They were all shaken hard about until they had been bounced some distance from the tomb that they guarded. Their weapons were also tossed about and were now nowhere to be seen. Then the four of them crawled together but were helpless to stand or search for their weapons and shields. To their shock and horror, the great stone covering the tomb was lifted out of its place in the grooved channel that held it in place. It was no longer touching the ground as it slowly moved outward from the tomb as they screamed with great fright. Along with this there were suddenly great flashes of bright light one upon another, each one brighter than the last. They flashed outward from within the tomb and lit up everything around them so that not a shadow was left anywhere. The light was far brighter than any lightning they had ever seen, and it momentarily blinded all of them. In fear, the soldiers covered their eyes and tried to act as though they were dead.

All the women bowed their faces low to the ground and prayed to the LORD God Almighty for deliverance. Mary Magdala wept aloud, "This is absolutely dreadful! Why has this happened to our Lord? That he should suffer so greatly in life and now in his death to have such a tragedy befall his body!" As she wept she hit the rocky ground with her fists in rage as her sense of helplessness overflowed.

Chapter Two
First to the Tomb

The frightened women watched his tomb from just inside the wall to the garden cemetery. At his tomb there was something far beyond their wildest imaginations that suddenly and violently unfolded. The women looked steadily and the stone that covered the tomb's entrance was violently loosened from its track. The imperials seals that had been placed on it had exploded and the ropes that crisscrossed over it were shredded and were thrown everywhere. The massive stone door had been lifted up and was being carried away from the doorway. As this happened, there suddenly flashed a light brighter than the sun. It was more striking than the brilliance of lightning they had seen, and it nearly blinded them completely. The women shielded their eyes from the light and tried to see what kind of terrible thing that this was that could cause all this to happen. From inside the tomb, where the flashes of light came from, there came an angelic being of great size who was carrying the massive stone in his hands. He set it off to the side and leaned it against a stonewall near to the tomb. Though its weight was great he was able to carry it with ease. He was a glorious person with a very winsome appearance. His garments were whiter than the purest of white wool and they glistened intensely. When he came out of the tomb he stood tall, as tall as the height of two grown men. So great was the sight of him that the women dropped their baskets and their contents spilled onto the ground at their feet.

Now the angel completely ignored the soldiers who continued to lay on the ground and were now hiding their faces from him. His voice was clearly one of authority and might yet the sound of it was a caring one as he stated, "There is nothing for you to fear. I have been sent from heaven with these men to meet with you here. We have come to give you wondrously good news!"

Then from within the tomb there appeared three men. Two came out and stood to the right and to the left of the angel. One of them spoke to the women, "You are looking for the body of Jesus of Nazareth who was crucified and died. Please, go inside the tomb and see that he is no longer here."

The women left their baskets where they had fallen and timidly went into the entrance as they had been instructed. Inside they were greeted by a young man. Even though the tomb would have been very dark the man's appearance was extremely bright. By his presence he cast light everywhere and left no shadows anywhere. He spoke to them saying, "Do not be afraid. You are safe in here I assure you. I know that you came to this tomb to visit the body of Jesus of Nazareth who was dead."

All of the women thought to themselves why did he say, 'Was dead?'

The man continued on uninterrupted, "Look at the bed where you had laid his body to rest. See, he is no longer here. He is no longer dead! The Father has sent his Holy Spirit who has raised him from death and he is alive again!"

The women stood speechless and gripped by fear. They were frozen in their thoughts and neither believing or disbelieving what had been told to them. In their fright, they did not dare to do or say anything because of the presence of these great heavenly beings.

Then the young man spoke to them again, "You must remember how he told you and his disciples that he would be betrayed: into the hands of sinners, that he would be rejected by the elders, suffer many things, be crucified and that on the third day he would rise again. Now, do not linger here. You must go to Peter and all of his apostles and tell them this good news! Tell them that Jesus will return to all of you and be with you again today."

Then, just as they had first boldly appeared to them, there were great flashes of light and the angel along with the three men simply vanished from their sight. The women had been so very frightened from all that had happened to them that they stood frozen in place. Yet it was out of obedience to their instructions that they soon left to return to Joseph's home. As they turned to leave to the garden, the soldiers remained with their faces glued to the ground, silent and still as though they were dead men. As the women left the garden they ran as swiftly as they could.

As they made back to Joseph's home Mary Magdala could not keep herself from weeping. She continued to be overwhelmed with sorrow over her Lord's death. She did not cope well with not having seen the Lord's body and she worried that it was stolen. Neither the words of heavenly men or the mighty angel had persuaded her mind to believe that he was risen. Having been weakened by a poor night's sleep and overcome with weakness she found a secluded place and fell to the ground. There she continued to weep and lament his death and now the added loss of his body.

Chapter Three
Soldiers at the Tomb

It was early in the morning just barely first light and the Roman soldiers were guarding the tomb that Pilate had ordered sealed. There were four of them and three stood at their post while the other one slept. They were very tried from their turn on the final watch of the night. Their day prior, and all through the night, was without incident. The soldiers knew the circumstances surrounding their duty assignment and they felt like their time was being wasted there. They knew their commander, Pilate, did not concern himself with the worries of the chief priests who had insisted on them being stationed there. The governor had only posted them there to pacify the priests and get them to leave him alone. The only thing that the soldiers took relief in was that they were able to alternate turns standing watch and sleeping. As the night drug on they slept harder and those standing grew increasingly worn by the long hours of boredom. They were looking forward to the changing of the guards that would come sometime after sunup. Once their replacements had been fed breakfast they would march to the tomb and relieve them. Until then they endured their time as dutiful soldiers of the empire.

Now suddenly there was a terrible shaking of the earth that continued to vibrate the very ground the three soldiers stood on. They were extremely frightened and while they tried to stand their ground the quivering of the earth under their feet jostled them violently about like mere ragdolls. They were excellently trained, and they were able to remain standing initially. Oddly enough it was very humorous to watch their frightened faces and see them trying to remain standing while they were jittered about. Finally, as they realized it was a vain effort to try and fight off their inevitable fall they yielded and were thrown hard to the ground below.

The two soldiers that were asleep awoke in a great fright and as they instinctively reached for their shields and weapons the agitation of the ground around them kept them and their weapons apart. They tried to hold their helmets on, but they were wiggled loose by the violent shaking of the earth. As they struggled in vain against the earthquake they were rolled and bounced around on the ground like dancing fools.

The soldiers who were in tremendous fear for their lives crawled toward one another and eventually were able to lock their arms together. Their lantern had burned low during the night watch and had now been knocked over and put out. The early morning light had grown just enough so that everything was dimly visible to them. Their fears were focused on two things, surviving the earthquake alive and guarding the tomb with its imperial seals upon it. Should the seals be broken, even though there was an earthquake, they could be severely punished though it be no fault of their own. The nature of the Roman army was a very unforgiving one when it came to soldiers who failed in their duties. The ground continued to rumble and increasing so. The men were tossed about more than before, and their fears only grew with each passing moment as they wondered how long this earthquake would last. Though they tried to stay close to the tomb they were being bounced and tossed further and further away from it.

One of the soldiers named Novis said, "There God is angry with us. That is why this earthquake has come."

Then the great stone that covered the entrance to the tomb began to move forward and away from the entrance.

The soldiers feared that it might roll over to them and crush them. They screamed as they saw the imperial seals with Pilate's own name embedded in them explode and in shreds fly hectically everywhere. They feared again for their lives. They worried that the earthquake might kill them or that Pilate might have them executed because the tomb was now disturbed. They worried that the Judean's angry God might take their lives.

As the earthquake continued nonstop, they suddenly saw great and powerful flashes of light that shone outward from inside the tomb. It was much more brilliant than lightning and its peculiar glow was much longer lasting. There was a strangely unique quality to this light, one that was a colored shade of light that they had never seen before in all the earth.

The soldier named Aulus was the first to see that a magnificent being was emerging from behind the stone and from inside the tomb. He was a being of light and very large in stature, greater than that of a giant. Fearing for his life he cried out, "It is one of the gods!"

Then the soldiers could also see three men in the brightest white robes they had ever seen.

Helvis, another soldier, shrieked out, "We are all dead men!"

The soldiers feared for their lives and wondered why these people had appeared from within the tomb of the dead man. They dared not reach for their shields or even for their spears for fear of provoking them. They simply laid with their faces to the ground like dead men as they trembled in fear. Once the great stone that covered the entrance was fully out of the way the magnificent being carried it to the side and leaned it against the stone wall. Though the ground shook with violence the soldiers were amazed that the being and the three men were not shaken by it in the least.

Now the angel ignored the soldiers entirely but spoke to the four women who had now entered the garden. His voice sounded to them as one of tremendous authority. It was a voice that was greater than any voice of the earth. They heard him speak and listened to all the things he told the women which were fantastical to their minds.

When it was all over, when the great being and men had gone and the women had left, they stood to their feet. They straighten their uniforms and body armor and regathered their weapons. None of them spoke because they were all still recovering from the shock of what they had gone through. Eventually, they began to discuss what they should do.

Trebellius said, "One of us needs to go in there and see if the body is still there or not."

The other three with him froze in place over the fear of the idea of going into this man's tomb. They said nothing and Trebellius looked them over wondering if any would volunteer or even agree with him.

As he looked at the others he shook his head and called them cowards. Then he ventured in and saw that the tomb was empty. He looked everything over thoroughly two and three times to be certain that he was not missing anything. He pushed on all the wall and looked for a hidden passage but found none. He came out of the tomb shaking his head and then said, "Empty."

Aulus worriedly said, "If we return to the Praetorium and report this to our officer he will accuse us of failing to perform our duties. Pilate will have us beaten and executed."

Helvis added, "If we remain here until we are relieved they will arrest us and we will be severely punished. They will accuse us all of sleeping."

Then Trebellius reminded them, "We are soldiers of Rome. We must report this to our officer. We have a sworn duty."

Novis was near to a panic attack as he said in anguish, "They will never believe our report. We hardly believe it happened to us as it is."

Helvis' voice shook as he said, "What can we say that will not make us look entirely guilty? The officer will accuse us of making up this story."

Aulus said, "These people here in Judea have their own notions about the gods and the other world. If we say that four of their gods appeared from inside the tomb and broke the four seals, they will not believe us."

Trebellius reasoned to the others, "Listen to me and do not let your thoughts get out hand. I know that the only reason we were ordered to be here was to satisfy those chief priests. The governor could have cared less about their affairs with their own people over this. If we return to the Praetorium it will go badly for us. We will be made to suffer and for no good reason. If we go and report this to those chief priests who went to the governor, it may go well for us. Who knows? If for some reason the chief priests believe us, then they will not hold this against us. They were the only ones who were worried something might happen. Then if they will speak to Pilate to excuse us from this, he may be more lenient to us."

Together they all resolved it was best to go directly to the chief priests that had insisted on them being there in the first place. So, they gathered up their shields and spears and rushed off to the Temple in search of Rabsaris and Elamadad.

Chapter Four
Peter and John

The doorkeeper on the night watch knew that he should not stand in the way of the determined women who left the house so early that morning. If he had resisted them they most certainly would have simply left after pushing him aside. He also was smart enough to go and wake Peter and John and report to them what they were up to. He went upstairs and at the door to the room where Peter and John were sleeping he knocked lightly and said, "Master Peter? Peter you must wake up."

Peter stirred without much difficulty, "Yes, what is it?"

"I am so sorry to wake you at this early hour of the morning."

"Yes?"

"Some of the women of your company have ventured out into the city with the intentions of going to Rabbi Jesus' tomb."

Peter was disturbed by the report. Not that he was objectionable to the idea of them going to the tomb, but that they went alone without a male escort and at this hour. He sat up and then stood to his feet. John had woken up too and overheard what was said. The two of them went to the kitchen to find some bread to eat to hold them over until breakfast. Then they set out from the house and made their way to the tomb to meet up with the women. Their pace was a casual one because they both knew the women would not be able to enter the tomb without them to move the stone away from the entrance.

As they made their way to the garden where Jesus was buried, the city showed no signs of coming back to life yet. The Sabbath had been fulfilled and the first day of the week was a working day for everyone. Soon the people would awaken and feel rested from a good night of sleep. They would find themselves especially refreshed from their festival. Once first light came upon the city, energized people would be found everywhere busying themselves with their tasks and moving about with bouncing strides.

Unlike the women who were anxious to get to the tomb Peter and John walked slowly. They were in no hurry to get to there. All of them, the women and the men, were in mourning and disillusioned with the death of their Rabbi. Though the women walked at a hurried pace to get to the tomb because of their sorrow, it was for the same reason that Peter and John walked slowly. They were in no hurry to bring more sorrow into their lives.

The sun had only just begun to brighten the day and it would be some time before it would appear over the mount of Olives. The cool night was only beginning to feel warmer and this was a welcome feeling to both Peter and John. As they grew nearer to the tomb Joanna, Maria, and Salome came running toward them. Their faces revealed a strange mixture of fright and delight. Peter worried about what it could have been that frighten or threatened them so. It appeared as though the women would run right past the two apostles and that they did not even recognize who they were. They were running as fast as their legs could carry them. As they neared Peter they seemed to be steering clear of him and so he urged them to stop.

Peter asked them, "Women! Stop! It is Peter and John is here with me. What in the world is going on? First you leave Joseph's home while it is still very dark, and you set out without a man to accompany you? Now, what has you running in fear in this way? And where is Mary Magdala?"

The women were surprised to hear that she was missing from among their numbers. They looked back to the way they had come. They had no idea that she had stopped because she was so very overcome with weeping. The women were hesitant to tell Peter and John what they had seen and heard because they were too frightened by what they had been through. Yet mingled with that was a new hope that their Lord was raised from the dead. They had not taken any time to discuss among themselves what that exactly meant.

Maria spoke but she was out of breath, "When we arrived at the wall around the garden we saw Roman soldiers. One was sleeping and three were standing watch in front of the Lord's tomb."

Peter's mind went to work worrying that the worst may have happened and that the soldiers may have done something to Mary Magdala.

Then Joanna spoke in turn, "There were imperial seals on the stone covering the entrance. Then there came an earthquake that knocked the soldiers to the ground."

Peter looked at John and wondered why she said there was an earthquake. The two apostles had not felt an earthquake or anything like that. He told the women, "I felt no earthquake this morning. What are you talking about?"

Joanna continued, "There was an angel and men there. Three of them," but she could not go on.

Salome spoke, "There was the earthquake and we saw the stone being moved away from the tomb. There were flashes of blinding light like no other on earth that anyone has ever seen."

Maria continued, "We were told that Jesus isn't dead anymore. They said he is alive again! He has arisen from the dead and is alive! That is what they told us. But we did not see him. We did not see Jesus."

Joanna shared, "They invited us into his tomb and we saw the place where he had been laying. But he was not in the tomb. We saw his shroud, but it was empty. The heavenly man said to us that we had to tell you and all the disciples about it."

Maria then spoke, "There were more flashes of blinding light Peter! And the angel and the three men vanished from our sight."

Salome added, "We left there running all this way because we were so afraid and because they told us to. And now somehow Mary Magdala is missing."

Peter and John were highly alarmed by everything they said. They listened with all intensity not knowing what to make of their incredible story. It was all too much to believe. John stood there in utter silence unbelieving everything the women said. Peter turned his head sideways and looked at them out of the corner of his eyes as he scrutinized them. He shook his head questioning everything they said and how they were saying it because their reports were so chaotic and farfetched. Even though they were all telling him the same things and they did not disagree with each other he still did not believe them. He wondered what would make them tell him this wild idle story of things that were simply not possible to have happened. The women, however emotionally they may get, simply do not go from the depths of sorrow and bereavement to this highly charged up state. There was nothing about it that made sense, not the story and certainly not their wide sweeping emotional moods.

John looked at Peter to see what his reaction would be and based his own on it.

Peter simply responded to the women insisting of them, "You must calm yourselves and try to settle yourselves down. This story of yours is very concerning. I want you to return to the house and stay there until we get back and can talk to you again."

Then John asked them, "Do you have any idea what has become of Mary Magdala?"

The women's thoughts returned to that concern and they worried about her, but they did not know what to say. They simply shook their heads and smiled as if it was of no great concern.

Peter sharply told them, "Now, get back to the house without delay and wait for our return, please!"

Both the men thought independently that there was too much to their tale for it to be true. Given the presence of the soldier there, they were very worried about the safety of his tomb and his body. Or perhaps there were grave robbers who stole him away or even Temple authorities who took his body into their custody. It could even be that the Romans had done something. Their worries seemed to multiply unceasingly and that gave way to panic and in their panic they ran wildly to the tomb.

Chapter Five
Seeing Jesus

The women were faithful to Peter's instructions about returning to Joseph's home. They had calmed down quite a bit since they talked to him and John about their encounter. After all that was what they were told to do by the visitors from heaven, to tell everyone about Jesus' resurrection. Their pace was no longer a hurried one of panic because their fears were subsiding. As their joy increased so also their step took on a certain merriment that was almost dance like. As they walked along the quiet and lone street there was suddenly a man who appeared in front of them. The hood of his robe was draw up over his head and it veiled his face. His hands were withdrawn into the sleeves. They were frightened about who he might be because he was concealing himself so. They stopped where they were because they were worried that he might mean to harm them. They considered turning around and running away to safety. Then he slowly raised his arms and turned his palms outward revealing to them the scars that had been made by the nails. The women both stared intensely at him sharpening their focus and they could clearly see the newly made scars. They looked to his feet and he raised his robe enough for them to see the marks of the nails there too.

All of their fears subsided and a growing faith began to rise in their hearts. They lived in the expectation that this man would show them his face and that it would surely be their Lord. Now the man lifted his hands and pushed his hood back and showed them who he was. Immediately they knew it was their Lord. Spontaneously and in unison they spoke out, "Jesus! Our Lord and Master! You are the Son of God!" Then Jesus walked over to them and they fell with their faces to the ground. As he stood before them they touched his feet and worshipped him with joy overflowing in their hearts.

Jesus spoke softly to them, "You must no longer have fear in your hearts or doubts in your minds. I have been raised from the dead and I am alive again. Go and tell my disciples that you have seen me and tell them that I will come and visit them soon." Then Jesus bent down and took them by their hands and helped them to stand up again. He affectionately touched their faces and stroked their cheeks wiping away their tears and hugged each one of them. "Be of good cheer and rejoice for once I was dead but now I am alive as you can see." As the women heard those words their sorrows and doubts were wiped away and as they smiled at their Lord he simply disappeared in front of them.

The women looked at each other and laughed in joy uncontrollably. They could not contain themselves because they knew the greatest comfort a person could ever know. This was that the Son of God had come to them and showed himself alive. Soon, as the revelation they had come into settled into the depths of their hearts and minds they knew that they needed to share this news with Jesus' disciples and with everyone in Jerusalem. Even still they could not help but join arms and celebrate in a circle dance as they sang praises to God.

"Shout and sing praises to our God and King.
He has triumphed over the grave.
Great is the LORD and greatly to be praised.
He rules of all creation.
He is victorious over death and the grave.
The Son of God he raises.
The bonds of death he destroys.

Sing praises to our God, sing his praises everywhere.
Sing loud praises to God, sing his praises everywhere. "

Soon there were other people who appeared on that street. They stopped to wonder what it was that would make these women rejoice so greatly at this time of day and in such an obscure location. The women's spirits were so captivating that these people were filled with a certain warmth and contagious joy. It was overflowing from them like the refreshing strong current of a river in the springtime. Their joy was so contagious that it kept the people watching and some even joined in as they clapped their hands and danced in circles near them. After all it had just been a festival and a high one at that because it was paired with the Sabbath. Now after they had rejoiced for a while the women noticed the others around them and how profound it was that their celebration had captivated the others who had gathered there to watch.

One man who had just come by asked, "Women the festival and the Sabbath have passed. Why are you dancing in our street? Have you been drinking wine this early in the day?"

The women each bore witness to the Lord telling the people that they had seen Rabbi Jesus who had now been raised from the dead. Salome told them all what had happened. "We are followers of Rabbi Jesus who is from Nazareth. He was a prophet strong in the word of God and mighty in miracles, signs and wonders as all of Jerusalem knows. He taught regularly in our Temple and was known throughout all of Judea. He was arrested by chief priests and condemned to die by them on the day of the Passover. They compelled Governor Pontius Pilate to crucify him and he died on a cross on Friday. Today when we went to his tomb where he was placed we saw a mighty angel and men from heaven. They told us that Jesus is no longer dead. They said that our God, by the power of his Holy Spirit, has raise him from the dead and that he is now again alive. This Jesus who you know, we have seen him just today with our very eyes, we have heard his voice and touched him with our hands. Therefore, know that God's prophet, Jesus of Nazareth, was wrongfully accused and condemned. Even though they put him to death to silence his message he has overcome death and the grave and has appeared to us."

The people who heard their testimony found their words so compelling that they took hope from it and many more believed that Jesus was risen from the dead and alive again. One of them called out, "What must we do?"

Maria shared with them this time, "Women and men of Jerusalem, as our Lord Jesus preached he called on everyone to repent of their sins and believe in him for their salvation. Know that this Jesus who was crucified on Friday, God has raised from the dead this very day. He is both our Messiah and God's only Son. Turn away from your sins and turn to faith in Jesus so that you may be forgiven and have new life in him."

Some of the people there scorned the women and then left. Those that remained confessed their faith saying that they believe in Jesus of Nazareth as their Messiah and as the Son of God. Then they all rejoiced before the LORD with loud shouts of thanksgiving and high praises.

As the women prepared to leave Joanna shared, "Watch for his apostles. They will come and teach you all that you must observe as believers in Jesus." And then the women returned to the home of Joseph of Arimathea.

Chapter Six
Race to the Tomb

All that the women had shared with them created much anxiety in the hearts of these two men. Neither Peter nor John thought that the women's story had made much sense. Their report was confusing and jumbled. The very idea that Jesus' tomb had been disturbed was a fearful thought though. It was a terrible crime and an abominable sin to rob a grave or disturb an entombed body. It was nothing that their own people were likely to do. Perhaps the Roman's might do such a thing they thought. The women had been there while it was still dark. Peter reasoned in his mind that they may not have been able to see anything clearly. John imagined that if there were Roman soldiers there they may have threatened or hurt the women. They may have in their godless ways told them these tails that they had repeated to Peter and himself. Whatever it was that was happening it demanded their immediate presence and investigation.

Energized by the strong emotions that had now been put into play, the two men raced with all their might to get to the tomb. John had the favor of his youth and easily outran Peter and arrive at the cemetery first. He looked over the wall and saw no one inside the garden. At the entrance to the garden he quickly looked around for the presence of Roman soldiers as the women had reported. However, having seen none he continued inside and arrived at the tomb first. He saw that the stone that had once covered the entrance was moved away from the tomb. It was curious to him that it was not rolled to the side and in the grove that was carved for it to rest in. It appeared to have been lifted or drug straight out and away from the entrance and was now several yards away. As he approached the tomb's entrance he thought about going in but stopped and only looked inside. In the shadows of the morning he could see Jesus' empty linen grave clothes laying on the bed where they had placed him to rest on Friday. Along with the shroud were the bandages that had been place on his many wounds. The special cloth that had been wrapped around his head was there on the bed. It was folded very neatly and on the edge by itself. Then he believed some of what the women had said about the Lord no longer being in the tomb. This was all too much for him to be comfortable with and he did not want to venture inside alone. It was in there that he had known the greatest sorrows of his life. In there was the place where he experienced his own worst sorrow and the sorrow of Jesus' mother Mary when he was with her on that day. He did not want to relive those terrible fresh wounds of grief and loss.

Now as Peter arrived, he was out of breath and he was huffing and puffing hard. He took quick notice of the stone and where it had been moved to. He saw the open tomb and he had the look of shear horror on his face as he looked at John wondering if he would say anything. But John was silent as he struggled to grasp what he was now witness to. Peter looked around, but he did not see any Roman soldiers. What he did see was the remains of some of the shattered imperial seals that had been placed on the tomb's door. He picked up a few of their crumpled remains and worried what this meant. He feared that the governor might have reason to suspect his Lord's followers of carrying out a conspiracy or of attacking his soldiers and stealing the body away. He feared that all of Jesus' closest followers might have to go into deep hiding and escape from the city if Pilate or the Temple authorities were making plans to arrest them.

Peter felt so utterly helpless and completely vulnerable to the circumstances that were being laid upon him. His face grew sadly long, and his present worry was that soldiers might appear at any moment and arrest them. Nevertheless his focus returned to the tomb and in silence he peered inside. He ventured to put his head inside and he looked around before bravely venturing inside. Because he was now seeing things for himself he also believed parts of the women's story. Clearly there were Romans involved in this. The stone covering the entrance was moved away from the tomb as they had reported to him. It was not in the channeled grove that it was meant to be held in when the tomb was opened. Worst of all the body of his Master was indeed missing. There were scattered randomly about the remnants of the many spices that had been used to prepare his body for burial with. As he cautiously inhaled their aroma, he also noticed that the smell of a decaying body was strangely absent. He also found it very strange that the burial shroud was still there. He picked it up and quickly noticed that the stiches that held it shut were all still intact. Yet outside of it were dressings that had been placed on his Lord's wounds. The bandages that had held them in place were also found on the bed. The rolls of gauze that had held his arms and legs in their resting positions were also outside the sealed shroud and placed on the bed. Lastly, the wrap that had been placed around the Lord's head was also resting on the stone slab. It was neatly folded up and laying there by itself at the top of the bed on the west end.

Then Peter softly said to John, "Look at this." He showed him the shroud that he was holding and pointed to the intact stiches. They both shook their heads not knowing how they could still be unbroken. Peter took his time to view everything thoroughly. John watched and waited not knowing what to think about any of it. He wondered why and how the women would have made up that outrageous story. Peter continued to look at everything two or three times over and carefully inspected it all. As he went over the shroud one last time he studied the bloody stains that had formed when they wrapped the body of his Lord in it. By their markings he could see that undoubtedly this was Jesus' burial shroud. But neither he nor John could make any sense out of what they were seeing. All the evidence was there for them to see and touch, but they could not add it up and come to believe in his resurrection. That thought was still very foreign to them. They only believed that his body was indeed missing. Peter and John stood outside the tomb and looked about for anything else that was worth noting. As they lingered outside the tomb and pondered what could have happened, the sun rose above the Mount of Olives. Its brilliant rays of light aligned directly into the tomb and for a few minutes everything inside was clearly seen. For Peter and John, that moment did not reveal anything new to them. Then they searched the garden for Mary Magdala. Not finding her they returned to Joseph's home.

Chapter Seven
Mary Tarried

It was when the women left the tomb that Mary Magdala became very distressed and being overwhelmed by his empty tomb she fell behind. In exhaustion, she collapsed in a quiet recess on a narrow street. Then in solitude she wept. As she regained her strength she took measure of her situation. It was after Peter and John had visited the tomb when she decided to return there. Again, her weeping returned, and her tears were without measure. She had hoped that the angel or the heavenly men would still be there or perhaps return to visit her. Their words to her earlier were not understood by her and even now they did not persuade her thinking. If they returned she could talk with them and hear their words again, but they were gone. As she approached the entrance to his tomb she could not bear the thought of going in and seeing his empty grave clothes. As she came near she smelled the sweet scent of the aromatic spices. The remembrance of them overwhelmed her. She collapsed in front of the entrance to the tomb and fell into sobbing without measure. The ground there was dusty and cold which left her with a deepened sense of abandonment in the death of her Master. She was so deeply sorrowful that she did not notice anything around her but was swept away into a deeply hopeless despair. She travailed in grief over the lost body of her Lord and she feared that she would never be able to stop her weeping. Her heart felt like it contained more sorrow in it then all the stars in heaven.

Eventually her tears began to subside, and she looked into the tomb again and saw two angels waiting there. They had taken seats in the tomb on the bed where Jesus once laid. They were waiting to speak with her. They were dressed in gowns that were whiter than any she had ever seen. They were without wrinkle or imperfection of any kind. One was at the head of the bed and the other one sat at the foot which was on the east side and closest to the entrance. They spoke with each other, but their words were not distinguishable by Mary. They were not in any distress, but they were happily content and joyous to be there. They looked at her and seeing her dreadful state one spoke directly to her with a soft and concerned voice, "Mary Magdala, why do you continue to weep so on the morning of this first day of the new week?"

Now when they spoke to her she stood before them and then bowed low to the ground to honor them. As she answered them she sobbed so much that words were riddled with crackling sounds, "Some people have taken away my dear Lord Jesus' body! And I don't know who they are or where they have taken him!" She burst into weeping again because it was so painful for her to say these words.

Just then, she heard the soft footsteps of someone who came up and stood beside her. She rose from the ground and turned to face him as he spoke to her. "Women, why do you weep? Are you looking for someone? Who is it that you are looking for?

Mary imagined he was the one who took care of the garden. She was thinking that this man for some reason believed that Jesus' body was mistakenly place in Joseph's tomb. She sobbed as she answered him, "If you have carried his body away from this tomb then please tell me where you have placed him. I will take him from there for you." She again broke down weeping and she hid her face to the stranger.

It had been a long dark night of grief and mourning which was only worsened for her by the earthquake and the great things that happened there that early Sunday morning. She had seen and heard the men from heaven and the angel as well. Still, she did not understand much of what they said or believe their report that Jesus was raised from the dead. Rather, it only drove her deeper into a bottomless depression. She simply wanted to be near her Lord's dead body, but what God wanted was for her to be near his Son the risen living Lord. The man's face showed deepest compassion and even sorrow for the loss that Mary Magdala was expressing. Then she believed that he could help her somehow.

Now the man spoke to her simply calling out her name, "Mary Magdala!"

Suddenly Mary's face was transformed and grew joyous as she turned to face him directly. She happily screamed out, "Rabbi Jesus! Rabbi Jesus!" Then she overflowed with insurmountable joy. The worn and worry appearance that her face carried, her tear dampened eyes, and her voice were all transformed. She quickly grabbed Jesus and hugged him continuously like she was never going to let go as she sang out, "My Jesus, dear Lord, my Jesus, dearest Lord of mine." As she hugged him tightly she swayed slightly and found the greatest comfort in his arms. He was warm and soft and he hugged her back. This was very healing to her and took the pain away that had haunted her since she had last seen his cold and lifeless body.

And Jesus knew that this was what she needed for now because she was so greatly devoted to him as her Master. But soon, after several minutes had passed, he said, "Mary, Mary, listen to me. You must let go of me for now. I must still ascend to my Father who is waiting for me in heaven. I must go to my Father and your Father now too, to my God and to your God as well."

Mary let go of him though it was with great reluctance and then she stepped back and looked at him with a new depth of heart felt love. She bowed to the ground at his feet and honored and worshiped him.

Then Jesus spoke to her again, "I need you to do something special for me right now."

She stood again to her feet and eagerly nodded and waited in great expectation of what he would ask her to do. Whatever it was going to be she was sure that she would do it. He only needed to say what it would be.

Jesus reached out and held her shoulders in his hands saying, "Please go to my disciples and tell them everything that you have seen and heard this morning. Tell them, 'I have seen the Lord and he is alive again.'"

Then, before she could say anything, her Master simply vanished before her very eyes. She was overwhelmingly filled with a joy that she could not contain inside. Even though such a tragedy had befallen her Lord, now in his resurrection she felt like no sorrow on earth could ever hurt her so much again. She felt like a young girl and was renewed in her strength and fancy free. She danced and worshipped the LORD, raising up her hands as she sang for joy.

'My soul lifts up the name of the LORD
I will sing to the LORD with all my heart,
I will declare his glory to his disciples.
For the LORD is great and greatly to be praised.
He has worked marvelously among his people,
and has brought again from the grave his risen Son.

All honor and majesty are his,
glory and strength are his alone.
For I have seen my Lord and worshipped
him in the beauty of his holiness.
May all the angels of heaven be glad
and the people of the earth rejoice.
Let it be said among all the peoples
the Lord is risen to day
and he has brought salvation
to all who will believe."[1]

Then Mary Magdala took to the street outside the garden and ran with the speed of a gazelle as she hurried with all of her might to bring word to the apostles and everyone at Joseph of Arimathea's home. She absolutely could not wait to tell all of them that their Lord was risen from the dead. On the way, she recalled the anguish of her mind and the sorrow of her heart, and the depth she had sunken into. Now, she found that as she remembered those long hours that were in the frightening recesses of her memory, her grief was transformed by having seen and touched her risen Lord. For this great spiritual healing that had come to her and she could not wait to bring this word of hope and faith to the others, especially to Jesus' mother, Mary.

---

[1] Based on 1 Chronicles 16:23-35

44

Chapter Eight
Rabsaris' Coverup

The four soldiers rushed toward the Temple as if they did not want to be late for worship, but worship was the last thing on their minds. They knew they could not go inside. They could not even step near to its entrances. That was the strict order of Rome that had been put in place to help keep the peace. So, they stopped a Temple worker who was headed inside and asked him to summon Chief Priest Rabsaris for them.

The unofficial leader of the soldiers was Trebellius. He moved in close to the worker and in a demanding voice whispered into his ear, "And tell him it is an emergency."

Soon, Rabsaris along with Elamadad, appeared at the entrance to the Temple. Their eyes scanned the streets below as they looked for the group of soldiers. They followed the Temple worker, but kept their distance from him. They did not want to appear rushed, so at a leisurely pace they followed the worker who had brought them the urgent message. They approached the soldiers not knowing what to expect, though they did recognize them from when the tomb was sealed shut. As the two chief priests approached the soldiers, they dismissed the Temple worker. Then they walked closer to the Romans and appeared as if they would walk right past them.

Trebellius spoke under his breath not wanting to be overheard by anyone else, "There had been an incident at the tomb. We must go somewhere and speak with you privately."

The hearts of the two chief priests sank as they feared what this might be about. Rabsaris said to them in a stern and harsh voice, "Quiet you fool. Come with us, all of you.

We will go someplace more secluded where we can talk. Follow me, but not too closely." He quickly led them to a small café that hosted gentiles. It was a very strange setting for the two groups to mix socially. For chief priests and Roman soldiers to be seated and talking together was unheard of. They drew looks from everyone. Some people left. They did not like having armed soldiers in their presence. Others did not like the idea that the religious authorities were there for fear of being judged publicly by them for their heavy drinking and sordid company.

Rabsaris looked at the soldiers and turned his head to indicate that he was waiting for one of them to speak. The soldiers all seemed very anxious and looked about distrustful of the situation and the place they found themselves in. They did not initiate any conversation for fear of where it would lead to. "You said this was an emergency? So, I recognize the four of you. You were there when the tomb was sealed shut. What is this all about?"

Trebellius spoke for the others, "Forgive us sir. Something dreadful has happened." He and the other soldiers were very tense and trembled in their seats because great fear continued to grip them.

Elamadad was much more composed, but Rabsaris was very alarmed though he spoke calmly to the soldiers, "I understand and I see how very frightened you are. But I am grateful you have come to me. Now, please tell us what has happened?"

In hushed voices the soldiers told the story to the two chief priests. It was clear to see how upset they were over the incident and their fears only continued to grow with every detail they shared. Their version of the story was mixed with their pagan points of reference. The men that appeared at the tomb were referred to heavenly born children of the gods and the angel was referred to as a god himself. Rabsaris and Elamadad were able to set aside the soldiers distorted interpretations and make some clear sense of it all. Other than that, they did not doubt what was being told them. Even, as corrupt as they were as religious leaders, they believed that angels did exist. However, as Sadducees they strictly did not believe in the resurrection of the dead under any circumstances. They did not question the truth of any of it. The truth did not matter to them. They simply did not want to let this situation to become known to anyone.

Rabsaris' mind worked quickly and he thrived on a crisis. The soldiers that had worried about incurring his wrath now heard him say, "Here, let me get you something to drink. It will relax you." And then the four of them began to calm down a little knowing that the chief priest was not angry with them.

Rabsaris raised his hand and the waiter quickly brought them strong wine to drink. As they were served he said to them, "I will work with you if you will work for me and do what I want." His mind pondered for a moment about what he would devise and how he would explain it to them. "I want you to say to everyone who asks you and testify saying that you had all fallen asleep during the late hours of the night. That his disciples came and opened the tomb while you were sleeping and removed his body. If you will do this simple thing for me and tell absolutely no one otherwise then I will go to Pilate for you. I will go to him and I will have you forgiven. After all, I was the one who insisted on you being posted there. I manipulated him to get just what I wanted from him. He wanted nothing more to do with this man after his death. I will tell him that if he does not punish you then the entire matter between myself

47

and him will be over. I know the governor. He will be so relieved that he will be glad to excuse you from any wrong doing."

Novis was not so assured by his words, "How can you be so certain?"

Then in a fearful and whimpering way Helvis said, "Don't you know that a Roman soldier is punished for not doing as he has been order to do regardless of the circumstances."

Trebellius told the chief priest, "You are asking us to take a huge risk. We are ready to go into hiding to save our lives. But if we do we will be outlaws. We have been marked with the tattoos of the legion. We will have no pension and no one will take us in. If we are caught, we will be put to death for deserting."

Rabsaris cunningly added, "I will give you each a sizable amount of silver if you will work with me as I have instructed you. If you choose to go into hiding this sum will be generous enough to support you for a long time to come. But first I must meet with some of the treasury officials and get them to agree to this."

Trebellius pointed out the danger saying, "And what if Pilate discovers that you have paid us this bribe? He will have us severely flogged. How can we trust you about any of this?"

"It will not be the first or the last time a Roman soldier takes a bribe will it?"

The soldiers were embarrassed over that and then their objections ended.

Now Rabsaris worked to build their trust and create good will with them, "I am the one who must beg your forgiveness. I was the one who insisted that the tomb be sealed and guarded by you. I was the one who put you in this awful position and I feel just terrible about it. This is why I am doing it for you. It is my penance. Surely you can see that this is all being done for you in good will and not for malice. If you have better ideas on securing your future, then share them with us now."

The four soldiers looked at each other but remained silent.

Trebellius questioned him, "So, what do we do in the meantime? Pilate will learn shortly that we are missing from our post and that the tomb has been opened. He will send soldiers to find us."

"Give me a moment."

Rabsaris walked over to the owner of the café and spoke with him. Then he returned to the table. I know this man. He had agreed to let you stay in a room in the back. It is very private. You can stay there for the night if needed. He will feed you and if you need to escape he has agreed to give you clothing and food for your journey. You can trust him."

A distrusting Novis asked, "How soon can you put the silver in our hands?"

Rabsaris nodded and then gestured to show them he was optimistic about how soon it would be. The truth was that he had no idea of how soon it could take place or if it would take place. He wasn't even sure he could obtain the money from the treasury. Still he did not want to let his doubts cast a shadow on these soldiers hopes in him.

Trebellius inquired, "How soon will you go to Pilate?"

"I will go now and see about the silver immediately. Wait in the back and do not worry. I will be able to make my plan work. I won't abandon you. Once I have secured your money, Elamadad here will bring it to you. I will return once I have met with the governor and secured his good will for you." Then with an extra measure of calm assurance in his voice he added, "Do not worry yourselves further. Stay here and enjoy yourselves. I will pay for your bill. When I return I will be bringing you word that it is safe for you to return to the Praetorium."

The two chief priests got up and went outside. There Elamadad stopped and pondered for a moment while Rabsaris waited impatiently.

Then Elamadad shared his thoughts, "The verdict we rendered on Friday was actually supposed to have been delayed until today. That was because it was a capital case. Even though we condemned him to death it appears that he may be alive again. Now the testimony of these soldiers and whatever the followers of the Rabbi may have come into knowledge of, seems to be unraveling all that we thought we had accomplished. Ironically, if he has been raised to life on this day then our verdict and sentencing him to die has been overturned by it. As the Roman's put it, *Ipso facto,* it is by the very fact of resurrection that our verdict of blasphemy and condemning him to death has been reversed. That is if I believed in the resurrection of the dead of course."

Then in an angered voice Rabsaris cursed the day as he stormed away to the Temple.

Chapter Nine
To Tell the Men

The women rushed back to the home of Joseph of Arimathea and were welcomed back inside. The doorkeeper took notice of their state which awkwardly appeared to be one combined with shock, delight and impatience. This did not at all seem to be in tune with his expectations as their house was in mourning. They were supposed to appear like women filled with sorrow who had just returned from the grave of the Rabbi where they prayed and wept for him. Furthermore, Peter and John who had left the home to find them were absent from their company. While he was just the doorkeeper he believed that things were not as they should be. As the person who was responsible for those who came or left Joseph's home he found it all very unsettling. Being perceptive to these marked inconsistencies he wondered if they had been drinking wine or even strong drink. He worried that they had slipped into a delusional state of mind from the extremes they had been enduring with the terrible suffering and death of their Rabbi.

Maria told him with the strangest sense of elation, "We have all seen the Lord and he is alive." Her eyes shone with an almost sparkling light as she said this. It was nearly irresistible to him. He found that he had to pay attention to her. The first time she spoke her words did not touch him and conveyed no meaning. But once he got over the glimmer in her eyes the words settled into his thoughts. He found they were all that he could think about. That they had seen the Lord and he is alive. The other women all stared at him with their eyes wide open and smiles almost larger than life and told him that it was true.

Then he backed away from them and was unsure of what they actually meant. He knew that he must bring their state of affairs to his master's attention. He wanted to keep them in the house and occupy them with some activity, "May I suggest that you all go to the dining room for some breakfast? I'm sure that you must be very hungry. My master will meet with you there."

Then the women spoke privately to each other. Salome spoke for them saying breakfast can wait. Mary needs to hear about her son's resurrection from the dead. That cannot wait. We will go to the dining room later.

The women with gladness overflowing made their way upstairs to Mary's room. The three of them stood at the door to Mary's room. Joanna softly called out her name, "Mary?" The resonate tone in her voice carried with it such a beautiful melody that Mary was soothed by the sound of her words.

Mary peacefully said, "Come in. I am just brushing out my hair."

Then the ladies entered in. They noticed that Mary was calm but moving slowly which often comes with mourning and grief. Her window to the courtyard was open and the sun shone in with a soft and renewing light.

Mary asked them, "Are you back from the tomb this early?"

Maria spoke out bursting with joy and rising onto the tips of her toes as she said, "Mary you must be the very next person that we tell. Your son Jesus has been raised from the dead and is alive. We have seen him. He spoke to us and we touched him and worshipped him at his feet."

As she spoke, Joanna beamed with joy that was brighter than the sunlight that shone into the room. She nodded in affirmation the entire time and could hardly stand in one place as she nearly broke out dancing.

As Mary heard Maria's testimony, she grasped her heart and sat to her bed. Her thoughts and emotions ran wildly within her. Imagining that is was true and also impossible to be true. She was feeling a new hope and still the sense of dread over the greatest loss of her life. Her eyes moved about dashing as her mind tried to conceive of what the ladies had been telling her. In her mourning she was inwardly telling herself to simply not accept it because it could not possibly be true. Mary knew that all that they were claiming was very out of the ordinary. She worried that they were trying to convince her of this report because their minds had gone astray over the unrestrained grief they had over the great tragedy of her son's death. Therefore, she kept her responses constrained. "This is all too wonderful to think about alone," Mary said. "We must speak with Peter and John and see what everyone thinks about it." While her word reflected her doubts she secretly pondered the possibility of him rising from the dead.

When the ladies had gone to see Mary, the servant quickly made his way to Joseph. "Sir, the few women who went to the tomb have returned, all but Mary Magdala. But Peter and John were not with them."

"Good," Said Joseph.

His servant was struggling with finding the words to tell him what they said about the Lord being alive again. He didn't want to have to say anything at all and would not have, except that it was so outrageous that he could not leave it unreported.

Joseph could easily tell that he was in distress and worried that there might be a concern about the condition of those women. "What else is there that you are not telling me? Are the women alright?"

"Sir? Yes. No. I mean they, they were not themselves at all. They were not women in mourning. Not at all. They told me something. I'm not even sure if I heard them right. It sounded like one of them said that she or all of them had …" He stumbled over his choice of words and held off saying more.

Joseph was kind and compassionate with his doorkeeper and he patiently said, "What was it that she said then?"

"Word for word sir. She said, and all those with her nodded in agreement, she said that, 'We have all seen the Lord and he is alive.'"

Joseph's mouth dropped, and his hands began to shake a little. He put one hand to his forehead and held it there. The servant could see by his master's darting eyes and the movement of his head that his thoughts were racing wildly. Joseph shook his head from side to side slightly. He was worried that something terrible must have happened when they left his home unescorted and then visited the tomb so early that morning.

He told his doorkeeper, "Thank you, that is all for now. I will meet with them shortly."

His servant told him that he saw them go Mary's room but now they had all gone into the dining room. Then he bowed and left.

Joseph worried about his guests. Their care was his responsibility while they were staying under his roof. He could not make sense of why the women would have made such a claim as was reported to him. Then, half panicked, he rushed to find his wife and told her, "The women have returned alone but Mary Magdala is missing. Please come to the dining room with me. Our doorkeeper has said they are claiming to have seen Jesus alive this morning. I am very disturbed by all this. Please come with me and meet with them." Then they both rushed to hear what was being said by them.

Joseph and Ziphorah arrived in the dining room a few minutes after Mary and the other ladies had. As they entered, they found that most of their servants and household members had gathered there too. They were all listening to the ladies as they shared their testimony of what they had seen and heard, and how they had touched the risen Lord. This was in sharp contrast to the emotions that clashed within Joseph's heart. He was still in mourning but now he was confused. His sorrow was not converted to joy as the ladies each took turns speaking and retold their early morning adventure. He was offended by them and ready to rebuke them all for their far-reaching, fantasy filled old wives tail that they had conjured up.

As his anger rose to the surface, his wife who knew him so well could detect his intentions. She whispered into his ear, "Darling, do not be offended so quickly. Remain calm and hear everything they will say. Peter and John will return soon and then we will hear more from them as well."

Joseph accepted the wisdom that his wife guided him with, and in it he found that calm he needed to counter his heated reaction.

Now as the ladies told all that had happened to them, everyone listening was stirred and had many different reactions. Some, especially the men among them, did not want to believe them. Some of them even left the room scoffing and calling them crazy. Some of them wept as they remembered anew how much Jesus had suffered. Others focused their attention on Jesus' mother Mary and wondered how she was responding to all that these ladies had to say.

The story they told was began by Maria, "We went to the tomb very early this morning and we saw a magnificent angel and some men from heaven. Their robes were vividly whiter than anything I have ever seen, and they shone with light."

Joseph looked at the other women and they all smiled and nodded as she continued to tell him their story.

Maria was so joyous that she could hardly contain herself, "They told us that Jesus is no longer dead, but that he has been raised back to life again!"

Joseph raised his voice, "What!" He nearly rose to his feet as he said this. His wife quickly took hold of his hand and looked calmly into his eyes and he relaxed and remained seated.

The other ladies approved what Maria was saying as she went on, "That is right. Though he was dead he has risen from the dead and it alive again."

This strange report was still sinking into Joseph's thoughts and his mind began wondering how these women could have come up with such a story. He abruptly asked them, "Peter and John left here to go to the tomb and find you. What has happened to them? Did they find you?"

Joanna now spoke, "Oh, we met them as we were returning from the tomb and told them everything too. They were in shock and would not believe us. But when they heard our story of what we have been witnesses to they raced to the tomb to see it for themselves."

Joseph's reaction was one of anger and bewilderment. He was very angry to the point of being outraged. Though it was not so much about the women that he felt this way. It was also because the tomb he had offered to bury Jesus in had been opened and the body was missing. Whether angels or men from heaven, or Roman soldiers were involved or not, none of this was acceptable to him. It was his tomb, his private tomb for the use of him and his family. His mind busily rolled out theories on what may have happened. He wondered if one of the women had dreamt this during the night. He imagined that the others had been beguiled into believing in it too. He suspiciously wondered if they had conspired to do this because they were not able to accept Jesus death and the end of his ministry. The fact that one of their companions was missing, Mary Magdala, only made his reservations more firmly implanted in his mind. He ordered his chief servant Gamalah, "Bring three men with you and go at once to the tomb where we laid Jesus' body and search for Peter and John. When you get there carefully observe everything you see and then return to me."

Chapter Ten
The Makings of the Morning

The morning's news at the home of Joseph and Ziphorah was so tremendous that almost all work had come to cease. The guests, which were many, was a quickly growing number as the word was spread throughout the city. All were glued to every word of the ladies as they told and retold their story. Many believed their report, but those who doubted were double that number.

Before an hour had passed, Peter and John along with Gamalah and the others with him returned. Now their testimony was something that Joseph felt he could rely on fully.

Peter shared, "It is true what the women are saying about the tomb. We found the tomb just as they said. The stone had been moved away and it was not in the track that was carved for it to roll in. It had been moved from the entrance and it was many feet away from it. Sadly, the body of the Lord is missing but his grave clothes and the spices remained there. There were remnants of the Roman's imperial seal scattered about. The rest we don't know. We saw no one else; no angels, no heavenly men or soldiers and we did not see the Lord. We have no reason to believe the rest of their story."

Then John shared too, "We found the tomb itself to be perfectly intact other than it having been opened as Peter said. If there was an earthquake as the women reported it did no damage to anything there that we could see. The most curious thing was his grave clothes though. Peter showed me the stitches that closed it. They were all still perfectly intact. The threads had not been broken or even stretched."

Now Joseph's interest was keenly stirred. He listened to what was being told him by the men because the women had said nothing about it. He asked, "What do you make out of that?"

Peter responded, "I don't know what to make of it. I don't know what to make of any of it. If we had the report of just one man who could refute these women or report that he saw and touched a risen Jesus, that would be helpful."

Just then Mary Magdala returned to the home and she was quickly ushered into the dining room. As she appeared, the other women who had been at the tomb with her rushed to her side and greeted her with giggling delight. They said nothing to each other. They didn't have to. The quality of their overflowing mood said it all. Then Mary Magdala went to Jesus' mother and bowed before her. "Mary, I have seen your son. It is true that he is alive again. He has been raised from the dead. He appeared to me at the tomb and he held me in his arms! It was wonderful. He urged me to return here to you and to all of his followers and tell everyone, 'I am ascending to my Father in heaven, to your Father, to my God and to your God.'"

Then they held each other and wept for joy. It was because of this lady's report that the Lord's mother Mary doubts were put to rest. Now Mary, the mother of the Lord, believed her. It was so healing to his mother. To know and believe that her son was a live and had appeared to this Mary. That he spoke with her and that she was held in his arms too. Together they rocked from side to side and many in the room now believed because of what they just saw and heard and felt in their hearts.

Having heard the full report of the women and the additional report of Mary Magdala, Peter motioned to John and Joseph that they should leave the room so that they could meet privately. Joseph invited them into his office. There he realized that his doubts were softening thanks to the cautions his wife had spoken to him. As he reflected about it all he said to the two apostles, "I was just remembering that the court that condemned him to die on Friday was supposed to adjourn without pronouncing a verdict. The Law required them to wait a full day so that they could ponder the merits of the case, both pros and cons."

Peter and John listened attentively.

"They were supposed to reconvene today and continue the case. This day, Sunday, was the day they were supposed to make their verdict and if he was found guilty then they could sentence him to die."

Peter said, "What is it that you are saying Joseph?"

Joseph nodded and said, "If Jesus is risen from the dead, it would have to be by the power of God for that to happen. And, if what the women are saying is true, perhaps it is God's verdict we are hearing about. That God has declared him innocent by our laws by raising him from the dead. Maybe God has revoked their verdict, declared him innocent, and annulled their sentence of death."

Some time passed and then Peter spoke out, "I think that John and I must meet with the other apostles as soon as possible. They must all hear from us what these women have said. We need to discuss it among ourselves. And for all we know they may know of other reports being made like this one."

John nodded in full agreement.

Now Joseph issued them both a word of caution, "You must be very careful. We don't know what the Roman's involvement in all of this is. There may be dangers waiting for you in the city. Use every caution and do not go about openly. I think the women should stay here for now for their safety."

He went to a chest of draws and returned. "Peter here is enough money for you and the rest of the apostles to travel back to Galilee if you find it necessary to leave the city. Send me word of your situation when you can." Handing him the money he nodded heartily and hugged Peter and John both. Then the two apostles headed out to the street where they quickly mingled in with the other people who were going about their day. They went to the home of Zechariah where they had sometimes lodged when their Master was in Jerusalem.

Chapter Eleven
The Regathering of the Apostles

On Sunday, a few the apostles continued in fellowship in the upper room provided for them by the Lord's patron. They did not venture out into the city for fear of being arrested by the authorities. Though it was the first day of the week of ordinary days, there was a deliberate slowing of the work that took place at Zechariah's home. He was having everyone who came to the door carefully but discreetly screened. He had instructed his household servants and all of his family to speak to no one in the city about the presence of the apostles. He insisted that all the first-floor windows and doors to his home remain securely locked. The doorkeeper was instructed to keep it locked at all times other than to only let household members in or out. They were to receive no guests that day other than the apostles who were not already there should any of them show up. He also posted a lookout on his roof and gave him the instructions that he was to see but not be seen. He was a man of wealth and prominence in the community which afforded him a certain sense of security in the city. Still, he worried that because of the extremes the chief priests had gone to in arresting and killing Rabbi Jesus that he and his family could be at risk for hosting the Rabbi and his disciples.

It was about midway through the morning when Peter and John arrived at Zechariah's home. Their patron was glad to host the Lord's apostles as well as a few of his closest followers that were among them. This included James and Jude the Lord's own brothers. Zechariah had generously offered them the use of his upper room for the foreseeable future. There was much about their situation that they all needed to considered. There was much that they needed to contemplate about what their futures might hold. Of the original twelve, already there was Peter's brother Andrew and John's brother James, along with Thaddeus, the other James and Philip.

Some of the apostles had fled further away from the city retreating to the village of Bethany and were staying with Lazarus and his sisters Mary and Martha. This group was made up of Bartholomew, Nathanael, Matthew and Simon who had been a Zealot.

The Lord's followers were suffering with sorrow and grief over his death. Added to that they were also feeling very demoralized about the loss of their lives as they had seen their futures. They had expected that their Messiah was going to war with the Romans and restore the Kingdom of David to their nation. Then they would reign together with him. Instead the worst thing possible had happened to them all. They no longer saw a future for themselves other than returning to their prior occupations. Most of them felt it was for their best if they were to live out quiet lives and seek to remain unknown for fear of being put to death themselves.

When Peter and John arrived, the doorkeeper announced their presence to his master. Zechariah rushed out to welcome them into his home. There was little to be said but as was their custom nothing needed to be said. All was assumed about how the other person might be doing. Heartache and despair were overflowing in their lives.

Zechariah spoke somberly to them, "My friends, some of the other apostles are here in my upper room. I have set this place aside for your exclusive use for the time. I have stationed several servants there to attend to you needs. Do not be shy about asking for anything at all. While you are my guests, I have secured my home and taken extra precautions for your safety."

Peter was feeling the fatigue of a man in mourning as he was slow to speak to his host. He nodded and then said, "I cannot thank you enough for all that you have done and are continuing to do for us Zechariah. There is so much about this that I cannot put into words right now. I must go up and speak with the other apostles. There are things that I must tell them about."

Zechariah answered him saying, "Of course." Then he motioned with his hand to the staircase that would take Peter and John to the upper room.

There were a set of double doors that led into the great hall. The room was well lit with candles. Its elegant stone pillars with their decorative carvings were impressive. The floor was inlaid with a mosaic pattern of decorative stones. The eminence of the high ceiling and its supporting arches gave to the room a sense that it was larger than it actually was.

Peter and John stood in the doorway but their focus was not on the elegant room that was provided to them. It was on their worries and the disturbing reports given to them. As they entered into the upper room, their mood was very different from the rest. Their emotions were compounded by what they knew from that morning. They had a great and disturbing mystery that they brought with them. It was one that they only hoped could be unraveled from its tangled web of wild reports made by those few women.

As those present joined together to hear what these two would say, Peter was shaking as he said, "Here, it is time for you to hear what has been reported to us by some of the women and about what John and I are witnesses to." Then he and John took turns and told the apostles exactly what the women said to them. They could only confirm that the tomb was indeed empty, and their Lord's body was missing.

It was then that Peter said they must send messengers out to Bethany to have the other apostles join them in the upper room. Zechariah himself made the arrangements. He took elaborate precautions because of the prevailing fear among all the disciples that they might be arrested. The servants he sent carried with them robes for the apostles to wear that were made in Jerusalem. This way the style and fashion of their clothing would not reveal that they were from Galilee. Everyone seeing them would simply assume they were from Jerusalem or Judea at the very least. That was of course as long as they did not speak to anyone, because they all had northern ascents. When the servants returned with the other apostles they went to the marketplace. There they purchased food, firewood, and other supplies for the home. This way when they arrived it would appear as if they were simply servants returning from their assigned tasks.

As they gathered again in the upper room, the only apostle that was unaccounted for was Thomas who had not been seen or heard from since the time of Jesus' arrest. Then it was time for Peter and John to relayed to them the entire story of what had happened that morning. The other apostles were very reluctant to believe any of the reports that they had just heard given that the information was from those four women. The fact alone that Peter and John did not believe the women was more than enough to persuade them not to believe. They did accept the dreaded news that the Lord's body was missing, and this was greatly disturbing to them.

Nathanael was very agitated by all that he had heard. He got up from his couch and paced the floor. He spoke out first from among the other eight apostles. "We are just simple tradesman and fisherman! What can we foresee if we try to make some little sense out of these women's tales? This is a terrible mystery and our women are of no help in solving it, none at all I tell you. Their involvement has clouded everything and now I can't imagine how it will be unraveled. That doorkeeper over there is to blame. He should have known better than to let them leave the house alone and at that hour no less."

Bartholomew turned his head attempting to follow Nathanael's pacing, "I agree. There is no proof of their claims. They should not have involved themselves in this way in the first place. They should have left well enough alone. His body was prepared on Friday for burial. They did not need to do more."

James the Lessor was also very critical, "These stories are too much for us to believe. These women have concocted this great story because they have become hysterical over the death of our Master."

John made a point in their favor though, "It is a fantastical story, but I will say this for them. They all agree on every single point."

Then James countered him, "Perhaps so, but this story about an angel and heavenly men that were seen, but seen only by women. It is all too good to be true. Women are too easily confused which makes them quick to be given to such superstitions and magical thinking. Their thinking does not mature much beyond that of children who live in a make-believe world."

Andrew speculated about the reason for their delusions, "Think about it; it was dark, they had not eaten, they were

66

suffering from a loss of sleep and were in terrible sorrow. That is why they became delirious and their wayward minds fashioned these stories for them to believe in."

Matthew spoke to Peter asking him, "How much of all this are you certain of?"

Peter asserted, "We are absolutely certain of this; an imperial seal had been placed on the tomb after it was closed. It probably was guarded by the soldiers but we did not see any of them. The stone was many feet in front of the tomb. It was not in the grooved track that was carved for it to rest in. It had been moved many feet away from it. He was removed from his shroud without breaking a single stitch and his body is missing."

Nathanael inquired, "How did the stone get moved so far from the entrance?"

Matthew questioned, "Could Roman soldiers have moved it there?"

John answered him, "Why? What reason would they have to do that? It would have been easier for them or anyone for that matter to simply move it in the channel cut for it."

Peter answered, "The women said that after the earthquake an angel moved the stone."

Then Nathanael's eyes circled the room as he asked everyone there, "Is there anyone among us who felt an earthquake at first light today?" The room fell silent and he said, "I didn't think so."

Matthew conjectured, "The stiches could have easily been cut out and replaced. Perhaps someone may have done this to deceive us. It was one of the women who sewed it shut in the first place wasn't it? They could have easily done this thing. They went there with all they needed to do this along with the spices and other supplies."

John shook his head hard, "Why on earth would the women do that?"

Thaddeus' voice quivered as he spoke fearfully, "There is another possibility here. I wonder if the women have seen his ghost and that is how this is possible. If in his death he has been lingering near to his body in these early days, then it is possible. Many believe this happens. I have heard claims to it. Perhaps these women have disturbed him by their plans to further prepare his body with additional spices and such. This would keep him from his rest? Is that why he appeared to them?"

John countered that possibility saying, "But then how do you explain the women's claim that they touched him, and he hugged each one of them?"

"Well," James the greater spoke up, "If he was not a ghost but was a man then it wouldn't make sense that he was near his tomb. He would have quickly gotten as far away from it as possible. If he was there, then I have to wonder why you and Peter didn't see him when you were both there? It just seems too impossible to accept that the women's stories are even remotely possible. And if Mary did see him, risen and not as a ghost, then why didn't she bring him back to Joseph's home or even here to us? I would have insisted on it. Why didn't she?"

Thaddeus continued, "True, but the only ones who claim to have seen Jesus are these few women. And I find it very hard to believe that if Jesus were alive that he would visit with women first. They are not apostles as we are."

Peter said, "The one thing that I continue to wonder about is what Mary Magdala said. That she saw the Lord, that she touched him and spoke with him. He told her that he needed to ascend to his Father in heaven. What does that mean?"

Nathanael objected to that saying, "Of all the women in the world she is the one I would doubt the most in the first place."

Peter didn't respond to his comment but went on, "I cannot make sense of it. Why didn't she recognized him when she first saw him? Then when he called her name how was it that she recognized him then? Why would she make up a story like that?"

Nathanael continued to criticize her, "What if she did see the gardener and her mind lied to her? I think that is a more likely explanation. What if she just made it up because it was too difficult for her to accept the truth, that our Master is dead. No one else saw a gardener. Do we even know with any certainty that there is even a gardener employed to care for the cemetery?"

Now Simon stood to his feet, raised his arms and forcefully spoke out, "There is a greater concern here for us than all these speculations. There is a danger that looms about in the city for us all! Think about it! One or two soldiers could have guarded the tomb. There were four of them. That was more than they needed. Perhaps they were there to arrest any of the Lord's followers who came there. We must go into hiding immediately! Spies from the Temple or even from the governor may have even followed anyone of us here and they could be watching the house even now. This could all be a terrible plot to flush us out from hiding, get us all into one place as we are now and arrest us too."

Peter countered him, "None of us have been arrested yet Simon."

The alarm in Simon's voice was growing, "What about Thomas? He is missing. We don't know if he was arrested or not."

That put a greater fear into the apostles as they sat in dumbfounded silence. They felt hopeless, helpless and confused.

Then Simon continued on, "What if it was the soldiers who opened the tomb?"

Peter asked him, "Why would they seal it shut and guard it only to open it this morning? That cannot be the case here. I believe they were simply there to guard the tomb not to arrest anyone who came there to visit."

Simon sharply asked, "How can you be so certain of that?"

Peter reluctantly said in a calming voice, "If they wanted to arrest us, they would not have been out in the open for everyone to see. They would have been hiding and laying a trap to catch us." He paused and then went on to say, "Then it is best for us to remain here. With any good fortune Thomas will come here looking for us. Our host is able to provide for our needs and perhaps over the course of a few days we will better understand what we are to think."

The apostles continued to meet together, and other followers joined in with them throughout the day and into the evening. The reports that Peter and John had received from the women were shared and shared again as they pondered all that was told to them. Oddly enough, none of the women who had seen the Lord were present among them. None of them had been asked to come and no one requested to hear from them directly. There was a very important question that every one of them should have been considering but didn't. That was could Jesus have actually been raised from the dead somehow? It remained unasked by them all because they were unwilling to believe the women's testimony of what the Lord told them to say. Now as the end of the work day in Jerusalem was coming, the city streets swelled with people traveling home. The apostles hoped that Thomas might use the crowded streets to conceal himself in and show up. But he did not appear and their worries about his fate worsened.

Chapter Twelve
The Emmaus Road

It was the first day of the week and the end of the workday had come. Cleopas and another disciple of the Lord who was called Simon of Emmaus were walking home. The walking distance was about an hour and a half from Jerusalem where Cleopas had a home and there the two would spend the night. It being Sunday they were living in the immediate shadow of the Sabbath and were not as tired as they might be on a Thursday or a Friday after a long work week.

The narrow road they traveled on was barely wide enough for a cart to pass on. It was only about three persons wide. The road was well beaten and had a smooth surface. There were occasional rocks and debris along the way that had rolled onto the road. They took time to kick these off to the side. Though most of the countryside around them was grassy, there were a few trees as well as some scrubby areas. The road itself was sun bleached and it did have a few rough and rocky spots to it.

As they journeyed along, the two men were discussing what they had learned about the mournful circumstances beginning with Jesus' betrayal and execution. As they made their way home Rabbi Jesus came alongside them and joined with them in their discussion. But the Lord prevented their eyes from recognizing who he was for the entire length of their journey.

Having listened to their discussion and seeing how they could not reconcile the terrible events to what they perceived as the will of God he asked them, "What is this that you two are discussing among yourselves as we are walking?"

Now the two men both stopped and looked at each other with puzzled looks on their faces. Then they looked at Rabbi Jesus and Cleopas said, "Stranger, are you the only person in Jerusalem who has not heard about the tragic things that have befallen Rabbi Jesus?"

"I suppose I am," he replied.

"Haven't you heard about Rabbi Jesus from Nazareth? He was God's prophet who was proven by many powerful signs and wonders. He performed countless miracles: healed the sick, cleansed the lepers, gave sight to the blind, and even raised the dead. He came into Jerusalem one week ago today to the warm welcome of the city. Everyone hailed him as the son of David because he was a descendant of our ancient king. We had hopes that he was the promised Messiah. But then the chief priests conspired to arrest him by bribing one of his disciples to betray him. They tried him in their courts and condemned him to die. Then they turned him over to the Roman governor to be crucified." Cleopas was near to tears as he recounted the events. He looked at the stranger to see what his reaction was and waited for him to respond.

As an apparent stranger to them both, all that Jesus did was to show that he was listening carefully to him and nodded for him to say more.

Simon continued on, "Everyone who followed him had the hopes that he was going to set us free from Roman oppression and reestablish the throne of King David. We welcomed him into the city with high praises.

We called out to him saying, 'Blessed is he who comes in the name of the LORD and called out Hosanna to the son of David.' We had hoped that he would do many great things among us by reestablishing our former glory among the nations. This is the third day since his death. Now today, just to make matters worse for his followers some of the women among us astonished us with a wild tail. They told Peter that when they went to his tomb very early this morning they had a vision of a heavenly angel and some men telling them that Rabbi Jesus is no longer dead but is alive somehow. They found the tomb where he was laid empty and some of them said they even talked with the Rabbi and touched him as well. But none of the men among our numbers were there to witness this claim of theirs. Peter and John went to the tomb and they found that the stone covering the tomb was rolled away and it was indeed empty as the women had said it was. But they did not see any angels or Rabbi Jesus' body. We don't believe what the women said they saw. We don't know what to believe now. We are very perplexed about the opening of his tomb and we fear that his missing body may have been stolen away."

Now the stranger walking with them responded to all that they had said. "How foolish it is that you have not remembered what the Prophets have foretold in the Scriptures. They tell of a coming Messiah and that person is indeed Rabbi Jesus, of that have no more doubts left in your minds. You and everyone else were expecting him to come to deliver you from the oppression of the Romans, but the Writings of the Prophets do not foretell anything like that. The Scriptures tell of his coming to suffer and die to deliver you from far worse things like death and the grave, and from bondage to sin and the devil."

Cleopas and Simon looked at each other and questioned in their minds whatever could this stranger be talking about? Cleopas spoke out, "How can that be true? Where do the Scriptures bear this out?"

Then from the Books of Moses, the Prophets and the Writings he began to explain to them exactly what the prophecies were and what they meant. He connected them all to the events of Rabbi Jesus' life and his death. He began with the very first record of his promised coming. "Do you remember that story about the temptation and fall of Adam and Eve into sin?"

Simon responded, "Of course we do. That is essential for every child to learn and know."

"Good. Moses wrote that the LORD spoke to them saying, 'I will put enmity between you and the woman, and between your offspring and hers; he will strike your head, and you will strike his heel.'"[2] On the very same day that they fell into sin there was the first prophecy that was given to them of a Savior who would redeem them from their sins. It means that the Messiah will strike the head of the devil who was the serpent and would disarm him. It means that when the Savior would strike him it would be like a mere bruise to his own foot."

Cleopas said, "I'm not sure that is connected to Rabbi Jesus' death."

The Lord continued, "The devil and his agents crucified Jesus, that is the bruise to his foot."

Simon scoffed over what he was told, "But that is not a mere bruise, he suffered greatly and died."

Jesus agree with him saying "Yes, and that is every bit as terrible as you can imagine. What I am saying is that compared to the great suffering and death of the Messiah it is as if it was a bruise to his foot compared to the devil's far greater injury to himself.""

Simon and Cleopas thought hard about what he said. It was not easy for them to grasp what the Lord had explained to them. They had doubts and each of them wondered privately if this stranger knew what he was talking about.

---

[2] Genesis 3:15

His explanation was perhaps as farfetched as stories that they had heard about from the women.

The stranger was not put off by their reluctance to believe what he was saying to them. None the less, he continued speaking to them as one with knowledge and authority on the matter. "Now remember when God told our father Abraham to take his only son Isaac into the wilderness and sacrifice him? And Abraham went to the land of Moriah and prepared wood for the fire for the burnt offering. He had already bound the arms and legs of his son and placed him on the altar."

Cleopas answered him, "I remember learning this when I was just a child. My own rabbi taught me. It was very frightening as it was first being told to me. I was worried that if that was possible for him to kill his son that it could happen to me or any other child among us. I worried that I might have to run away from home."

"Indeed, and it was meant by God to be just that so that Abraham and all who would hear about it would understand what the terrible cost of sin is. Abraham held in his left hand a flaming torch to start the fire with. In his right hand was the knife which he was going to use to take his son's life. His son was very trusting as he asked his father, 'Where is the lamb for the sacrifice?' In faith, Abraham said that God would provide the lamb they needed."

Then Simon added, "I remember how very frightened I was as a child when the story got to this part. I almost ran away from home for fear something like that could happen to me."

Jesus continued, "As Abraham lifted the knife, God called out to him from heaven saying, 'Abraham, Abraham my dear servant! Don't do anything to your promised son

Isaac, your son of the covenant. Now I know that are my faithful servant in all things because you were willing to give up your son in obedience to me.' Then God showed him a ram that was caught in a thicket for their burnt offering. And just as he offered this sacrifice in the wilderness, so also the Son of God needed to die outside of the walls of Jerusalem for the sins of the world."[3]

"Pardon me for asking, but what does that have to do with all that has happened here in Jerusalem in the past few days?" asked Cleopas.

"This is a prophetic message that foreshadows and parallels the events that would come to pass. This story from Abraham and Isaac's life prophetically foretells of the life of the Messiah. Just as Abraham offered his son of the covenant to die as a sacrifice for his sins, so also in the same pattern God would send his only Son to die for the sins of the world."

Then the two men marveled at this stranger's mastery in understanding the Scriptures. Even still, their minds were questioning him, and their hearts were not yet believing. What he said and the manner in which he told it burned in their hearts and they could not think of anything else as they continued homeward to Emmaus. They were enraptured as they heard him quote from memory the long texts of Scriptures and then tie them in so well into the details of their Rabbi's life and death. They thought it was as if he had been a constant follower of the Lord because of all that he knew so well. If what he was saying was true, they wondered how big of fools they were for knowing some of the Scriptures he talked about and yet they had failed to see their fulfillment in his life and death.

---

[3] Genesis 22

As they neared the village of Emmaus the man indicated that he was going to continue on to a further destination. But because he was so helpful to them Cleopas and Simon did not want him to leave their company. Cleopas insisted that he come to his home and be his honored guest. "There are already a few stars in the evening sky and darkness will fall shortly. Please come to my home and have supper with us. You really must also stay the night. We both want to hear more from you and those at my home will be delighted with all that you have to say too."

The stranger, whose name they never did ask, stopped and thought about the offer.

Simon urged him, "You must be weary and hungry as well. There will be freshly baked bread and much food for us to enjoy. We will all be honored to offer this hospitality to you."

In their custom, it was a great honor to be offered this kind of hospitality and it was improper to refuse. So, the man nodded his head and followed with them to Cleopas' home. As they came in the door, Cleopas' family rushed to his side and welcome him home and they greeted Simon and the other man too. By his presence inside the door they automatically knew that they were going to be hosting the stranger for their meal and lodging for the night. The whole house smelled wonderful from the aroma of freshly baked bread and roasted lamb. Soon everyone was seated on pillows around their humble table and Cleopas, knowing that their guest was a man of great faith, offered to let him call upon the Name of the LORD for the blessing of the meal.

The stranger asked them all to hold hands then he looked to heaven and sang,

"Blessed are you, O LORD our God,
Ruler and King of the universe.
You have created the fruit of the earth,
the fruit of the vine and given us wheat for
our bread, and meat for our tables.
By your mercy you have provided us with
all things that are necessary for life.
Amen"

Now the stranger took bread and broke it and distributed it for everyone to eat. They were so captivated by him that all of them were solely focused on what they might hear from him next. Then a miracle unfolded before their very eyes. The stranger was transformed and it was as if he had a hood over his head and lifted it back. They suddenly saw that this man was Rabbi Jesus himself. They saw on his hands healed wounds with scars from the nails that had pierced his skin. Then to their utter amazement he suddenly disappeared from their sight.

Now a moment passed as their minds realized what had just happened to them. What delight he had brought with him into their home. Their hearts had been deeply warmed by him and all that he did and said among them. Their joy and faith was made complete when he revealed himself to them for that briefest of moments. In sadness they felt a true shockwave had reverberated among them as this sudden revelation was made known to them. As it subsided, they began to talk among themselves.

Cleopas was the first to speak after he disappeared, "Simon, this is why our hearts burned within us as we walked home with him. Our minds were so amazed, and our thoughts were going wild with all that he revealed to us from the Scriptures about his life."

Simon excitedly replied, "I had no idea that he was the Lord! He spoke so clearly and was more knowledgeable in the Scriptures then all of the scribes. The way he explained things now makes complete sense to me now that he is gone. Oh, how I wish he was still here so that I could ask him some questions."

As their conversation continued to flow they resumed eating their evening meal which miraculously was delicious beyond any they had ever had thanks to the Lord's blessing upon it. They continued to reflect on all the fulfillment of the prophecies he had revealed to them until their meal was over.

Then Cleopas spoke to Simon saying, "In the morning we are going to need to get an early start and return to the city to tell the apostles what has happened to us. This is something they must know."

Simon looked at him with a smile and said, "I think that this is something too fantastic to wait until morning. We must leave now and tell Peter and the other apostles what has happened to us. We must return to Jerusalem right away."

Another member of Cleopas' household said, "But the sun has already fallen and to journey in the dark is difficult."

Cleopas agreed with Simon, "Yes, it can be difficult, but Simon is right. This news is too wonderful to simply wait until the morning. We must bring this to them now."

Chapter Thirteen
The Upper Room

As the day rolled into evening and the evening gave way to the night so did an endless and fruitless discussion by the apostles. They did not believe what the women reported to Peter and John even though these two apostles continued to repeat their story countless times throughout the day. The apostle's speculations about what might have happened did not help them come to any consensus of the truth either. Because of the hardness of their hearts they were more willing to believe in their own misguided assumptions than the reports of those who had actually seen and touched the Lord. In vain they continued on in restless conjecture into the late hours that followed the setting of the sun.

They were a very nervous and frightened bunch. The upper room's door to the street was securely locked as it had been all day. That was because many of them compulsively inspected the bolt that secured it and pushed on it to be sure it was not going to be opened from the outside. They feared being arrested and mistreated by the Temple guards. They feared being turned over to the Romans and their barbaric ways. The windows to the upper room were also all secured shut which made the room smell a little congested with a stale and flat air to it. They felt this was necessary given the extremes their Master had suffered under. They were physically tired, mentally exhausted and emotionally downhearted. All that their lives and their three years of dedicated service to their Rabbi's cause was lost to them and what their future would be was equally bleak. In their fatigue and fright it would not have taken so much as an unexpected sneeze to set them all off into a wild panic attack and send them running aimlessly into the nighttime streets of the city.

It was about two hours past the sun's setting and all of the eleven apostles save one were present. Thomas was not among them and no one knew anything about his whereabouts which only added to their worries. His absence gave them too much to worry about and their thoughts of what had become of him were horrible. It was during the night hours that their Master had been taken under arrest. Therefore they feared that if they were going to be sought out and arrested it would most likely happen during the dark of the night.

Peter looked at the wall where the two swords had hung. Those were the ones he and John both drew in the Garden of Gethsemane on that night. John noticed him staring at that place and he looked at the wall too. They worried the most about being arrested because they were the ones who had drawn their swords during the arrest. And of these two, Peter feared it the most because he had cut off the ear of the high priest's servant.

Because of the circumstances surrounding Jesus' arrest and the illegal trials where he was condemned to die, they all feared that if they were captured there would be no justice for them, none at all. This was especially true because in the end, even though Jesus was ultimately found innocent by Pilate, he was still sent to be executed.

Among the many precautions that Zechariah had taken were included having set a lookout on the roof of his house. There in the darkness that blanketed the city he watched carefully for any movement, any change in the silhouette of the landscape or any noise that was out of the ordinary. Then he spotted the outline of two men coming down the street. He rushed down three flights of stairs to alert the doorkeeper and his master. Quickly there was a quiet sense of alarm that came over everyone one in the home. The entire household was quietly awakened, and the apostles were alerted to this approaching threat. The lookout returned to his station and keenly watched for any other signs of danger in the streets below.

At the door the two men softly knocked.

Zechariah himself answered because he wanted to use the utmost caution in talking to these strangers of the night. "Yes, who is it?" he said.

Cleopas spoke for the two of them, "I am Cleopas and with me is Simon of Emmaus."

Neither Zechariah or the doorkeeper knew these men. "We do not know who you are. Why are you at my door? Come back in the morning when it is light."

Simon now answered them, "We are followers of Jesus of Nazareth."

This was very a worrisome answer and Zechariah's heart dropped in fear thinking that this might surely be a trap. Immediately he sent the doorkeeper up to the apostles to the alert them of who the men at the door said they were.

Zechariah questioned them further from inside the locked door, "What is it that you want? What are you doing here at this hour of the night?"

Simon of Emmaus continued on, "We are searching for Simon Peter or one of the other apostles. We have urgent news for them."

Zechariah worried that these men might have been sent to his house as spies by the chief priests.

From the upper room Peter rushed quietly downstairs to the door and listened in. In a whisper he asked Zechariah, "What are their names?"

"They say they are from Emmaus. They claim to be Simon and Cleopas."

Now the apostle relaxed a little but still feared it could be a trap. Peter knew these men, but he needed to hear their voices to be certain it was them before the door could be opened. He told Zechariah what to say so that he could hear their voices for himself.

Zechariah asked them again, "Who do you say you are? Tell me your names again."

"Simon of Emmaus."

"And Cleopas."

Then Peter recognized their voices and he breathed a hard sigh of relief as he said, "I know these men, it is safe. You may open the door."

Now as they came in the doorkeeper stepped outside and took time to see if there might be anyone else out there. Seeing no one hiding in the shadows he quickly returned inside and shut the door. Then he and another servant attended to their custom of washing the two men's feet.

As they rose from their seats, Peter offered them a sober greeting. The smiles on the men's faces revealed their joy, but Peter simply dismissed it thinking they were glad to have arrived and been received inside. As they entered the upper room, the two men from Emmaus could see about twenty or so men including the Lord's brothers James and Jude. They were mainly gathered around the dining table. Some were standing others were on the couches. They were conversing with each other in small groups. Simon and Cleopas were a little surprised to see that many of the men had kept their sandals on their feet, their coats on or near by, and wore their headwraps too. Some even had their traveling bags strapped over their shoulders and their staffs in hand. In their anxiety, they were prepared to make hasty exits if the authorities should come to arrest them. It reminded Simon and Cleopas of how they did this as part of the Passover observance. There was some bread, fish, and wine on the table. It appeared to be left over from their evening meal.

As the two men from Emmaus were seated the table lamps revealed their joyous smiles. A few of the others noticed that they appeared rather refreshed even though the hour was very late. They privately wondered to themselves how this could be since they had traveled over an hour to get to the city. Some took mild offense at how the two were wearing such smiles. This was a very sobering time of mourning and their grief was complicated by the disturbing reports that had been given to them by the women who had visited the tomb earlier that day.

Then Peter spoke to them in a perplexed voice, "What could have moved you to travel all this way and in the dark no less? Why didn't you wait until morning to come?"

The two looked at each other and grinned widely. They even had to hold back their joyous laughter not wanting to appear too insensitive to the apostles and their somber mood along with their very worn appearances.

Simon spoke first and shared in some detail, "I must have everyone's attention if you please. If you could all just stop whatever you are doing and listen to Cleopas and myself, thank you." Then he announced, "We have both seen the Lord. He is risen from the tomb and alive. This evening as we made our way home he appeared to us as a stranger and he journeyed with us to Cleopas' home. As we walked together, just the three of us, he explained in the most fascinating way, from Moses, the Prophets and the Writing all that was foretold of the Messiah. That it was God's will that he should suffer and die for the forgiveness of our sins. That he would be raised from the dead on the third day. Our hearts burned within us as he spoke because the Word of God was at work deep in our hearts. As we came into Emmaus, he looked like he planned on going further but we urged him to join us for bread and to stay the night. As we sat for our meal, we asked him to bless the LORD for our food. Then he took bread and broke it in front of us for all to see. Suddenly, the veil of his illusion of appearing to be a stranger among us was lifted and we saw him as he truly is. It was Jesus of Nazareth. We saw in his hands the scars from the nails and our hearts were amazed. Then before a single word could be spoken he simply vanished from our sight and the sight of everyone in our home." Simon spoke with all conviction and he detailed for the apostles some of the prophecies that Jesus fulfilled and explained to both Cleopas and himself.

The apostles who were standing then all took heart and sat in stunned silence. This was the first report that they had heard from men rather than women. These were good men who they considered fully reliable.

Simon said to them in conclusion, "We heard his wisdom and our hearts burned within us. We hugged this man as we welcomed him into our home. We saw him with our own eyes. He is our risen Lord; it was Jesus of Nazareth. That is why we came to you at this hour because this kind of news could not wait until the morning. It demanded that we come to you tonight."

Now all of the apostles struggled with what they heard from the two men. They knew the Scriptures well. They knew all that Jesus had taught them. They knew all that he had done among them. However, this news that these two men brought seemed to be in direct contradiction to all that they thought about Jesus' death.

Then Peter struggled to his feet and looked up to the top of the high ceiling that was all but hidden in darkness and sighed bleakly, "Your story is very ... well ... I don't know what to say about it." His voice grew worn and weary, and there was a touch of anger added to it. "I am worried that you have heard a secondhand report of the wild and outlandish claims of the women. I am worried that you have been taken in by their hysterical reactions to all that has befallen us with the loss of our Lord's body. I spoke to those women at length. I believe that they became senseless in their thinking because they did not have the strength to accept the truth. Terrible things like this play on our minds which are already filled with grief. These kind of compounded tragedies, well I wonder if your minds are deceiving you by imagining this illusion too."

Cleopas defended their testimony, "We have heard about the testimony of the ladies who were at the tomb. I have to say that from the sound of things I may be the first man among us to say that I personally believe them."

Then Simon of Emmaus defended their own testimony, "He was with us both and others in Emmaus also saw him. How could all of us had the same illusion and agree on it? I also believe what the ladies have testified too. I join with them in saying that I have seen the Lord and I cannot do anything but believe. My life has been forever changed by this day."

Peter conjectured, "Maybe this man you two say you walked with was someone who also heard the report of these women. Perhaps he just wanted to believe them because it took away the pain of his sorrow. I think that sometimes when so great a tragedy has befallen us that we cannot accept it fully. At least not at first. Our minds deny the pain of it and struggle with the truth of it. Its pain is too great and so our minds give us these imaginings so that we can have something to ease our sorrow and give us a hope that leads our minds into this crazy thinking."

Cleopas exclaimed, "No! My mind is sound. My thoughts are certain. Mine and all those with me in my home. I know he died. I do not deny this, I confess the horror of his suffering and crucifixion. Now to that I also add my belief in his resurrection."

Peter and the other apostles rejected their testimony. Then they all broke into small groups continuing in their discussions and trying to make sense out of what was being reported to them. They also began to speak harshly to Simon and Cleopas.

Then James the brother of the Lord reacted strongly to the rude way the apostles were treating their guests. He stood tall among them and said, "These tales that the women have reported may be too much to give consideration to. But the men, Cleopas and Simon of Emmaus, their testimony we may need to give further consideration to. I know them, and they would never seek to mislead us for any reason on earth or in heaven." Though he was not an apostle his word carried considerable weight among everyone there. Then the room was silent as those present reconsidered how they had treated these two men.

Chapter Fourteen
Peace and Forgiveness

The apostles and everyone in the room were clearly on edge. They had worked themselves to exhaustion and frayed their nerves by their never-ending debate over the reports of their Lord's fate. To their discredit they had failed to ask the right question amongst themselves. It was almost as if they were avoiding that very simple question which was has the Lord been raised from the dead? That was because they did not want to believe the testimony of the women. Worse they did not want to give up their hardened position that Jesus was dead and that was the final word on the matter.

As their fruitless discussions rolled endlessly on, Peter stood up to say, "Everyone, I think that we should give up on our discussions for the night. What we all need to do is let this day come to its end and get some rest."

Then at that moment when they all were giving up on their efforts to understand what it was that had happened Jesus appeared in the middle of the room and stood among them. It was as if he was there the whole time and was just waiting for them to give up their futile attempts to reconcile the day. Some of the apostles saw him when he first appeared before their very eyes and their voices fell silent. Others soon noticed him there in the middle of the room and they motioned for the rest to stop talking and look at him too. They were stunned into utter silence and motionless as monuments. None of them spoke a word. Most of their fears were amplified and a few were still not believing what they were seeing. Some of them thought that it was his ghost that they were seeing.

As the apostles and those with them were stunned by the revelation of their Lord's appearance, Jesus was himself very composed and spoke to them, "Shalom. My peace be with you all, my friends." Then he smiled as wide as a man could and he opened up his arms to them all. "Why do you fear? Your eyes are not deceiving you. It is me and you see me clearly as I truly am. Touch me all of you and see that I am a man of flesh and bones just as you all are." He pulled back his hair to reveal the puncture wounds he received from wearing the crown of thorns. He lifted the palms of his hands to show them his wounds from the nails and said to them, "See the healed scars on my hands and feet." Then he pulled back his robe to reveal to them his wounded side from where the soldier had pierced his chest with his spear. "See my wounded side. This too is healed. See the scar with your own eyes so that you may know it is me and let all of your doubting stop. See me and know that I am alive again. I am risen from the dead and will never die again." Then he went to each of the men and hugged them warmly as is their custom. Looking each of them in the eyes he greeted them by name and he showed them his good will toward them saying again, "Shalom. My peace be with you." As he did this he blew his breathe on them and said, "Receive the Holy Spirit."[4] Each of his disciples and followers felt the very presence of God's Spirit move upon them, in them and through them. It was a stunning experience. It was an experience of new birth and it filled them with awe.

Now because some of them continued to disbelieve and thought that he was a ghost he asked them if they had anything to eat. Then he sat on the side of a couch at the table with them. They gave him some broiled fish, bread

---

[4] John 20:21-22

and wine, and he ate and drank as he talked with them. "Do you remember how early on when you first traveled with me and we made our way to Bethsaida? You all argued intensely on the road about who was the greatest? I know you did though you never admitted it to me when I asked you. Then I taught you by taking a mother's young child and giving you a lesson by example. I posed a question to you for your consideration. I asked you how do you become the greatest one among the rest? I shared with you that in my Kingdom you must become humble like that child, in order to become great. Then I went on to say that if I was to send that young child to you in my name you must welcome him in my name and receive him as if he were me. So then if you were to welcome anyone, including that child, who I have sent in my name, you would be welcoming me. And when you welcome me you are welcoming the one who sent me, who is my Father in heaven."

Now some of the apostles began to believe because they remembered that day just as it was retold to them.

Jesus continued on, "My Father sent an angel to the tomb along with the three men from heaven. They announced my resurrection to the ladies: Mary Magdala, Joanna, Maria and Salome and they believed. I appeared to them all and they believed in me again. I also walked with Cleopas and Simon to Emmaus. They have been my faithful witnesses and you have not believed them. The ladies and these two men are like the example of the child sent in my name for you to receive. You must believe their testimony now. And as I sit here with you, believe in me your risen Savior and Lord."

Now the full room confessed their faith and there were no more doubters counted among them. Then Jesus stood in the middle of the room and instructed them saying, "I give to you the Keys to my Kingdom to possess. When you forgive the sins of anyone in my name they are truly forgiven them. If you have reason for them to remain in their sins, their sins will remain with them and they are unforgiven.[5] Having said that the Lord vanished before their very eyes.

The men were tired from the exhaustive pondering over the reports that had come to them that day. Now the one thing they needed to know, they knew. Their Lord had been raised from the dead. Little was said among them and they all turned in to get a restful and good night's sleep.

---

[5] John 20:23

Chapter Fifteen
Telling Thomas

It was not until the second day of the week, on Monday, in the early morning that the last apostle reappeared. Thomas had been hiding in the Garden of Gethsemane. It was easy for him to blend in there because of the thousands of pilgrims that were camping there for the Passover. With his Galilean ascent and clothing he blended in quite well with most of the people there. They were glad to extend hospitality to him even if it was out of their tents instead of their homes. But, as the festival was over, so also, they were leaving. Thomas worried that if the religious authorities were seeking to arrest Jesus' followers that he would be easily found in the garden when all the pilgrims had left. So, he made his way back into the city of Jerusalem by blending in with the crowds who were going there. He mixed in with some merchants that were entering the city to sell their farm produce and other goods in the markets there. As a means of caution, he offered to help ease a merchant's work by helping him carry a load of firewood through the gate. He was very observant for any sign of danger, such as Roman soldiers, or even Temple guards who might be watching for him at the gates. Then in vigilance he took an indirect route through the city streets as he made his way to the home of Zechariah. He stopped at several merchant's booths and appeared to be looking at their produce but purchased nothing. He was really looking about to see if he was being followed by anyone. Then he slowly made his way zigzagging through the streets until he was within sight of home where he had celebrated the Passover. From a distance he stopped and tried to appear as if he was merely resting as he searched the area with his eyes to see if anyone was spying on the home. As the infrequent flow of people walked down that street he waited until he recognized several of Zechariah's servants returning from the market with baskets of food and he simply followed closely behind them wanting to appear as if he was accompanying them.

From inside, Zechariah and his servants were continuing to take every precaution about who was coming to the door and entering this home. Doors and windows were locked and lookouts took their turns watching for the least sign of danger.

As the servants approached the house he spoke very anxiously to them, "Please, I am a disciple of Rabbi Jesus. My name is Thomas. I must speak with your master if I may."

They simply nodded and continued the short walk to the entrance where the servant keeping the door recognized him immediately and warmly welcomed him in.

Thomas was nearly out of breath because of the great fear that he was hardly able to manage. He asked, "Is it safe for me to come here? Has anyone else been arrested?"

The servant closed and bolted the door. He made a point of his deliberant actions for Thomas to see but he said nothing to him. He let Thomas gather for himself that things were still very worrisome and what precautions were being taken. Then he left him to tell the other apostles that Thomas had just arrived while another servant washed his feet.

Peter, along with James and John, soon appeared at the entryway and greeted Thomas wholeheartedly. While the three apostles were enjoying their newfound joy, Thomas in contrast was very worn and in considerable distress. They all went upstairs into the upper room where Thomas was welcomed by all the other apostles and many other disciples who had gathered there.

Peter invited Thomas to join him at the table. Some of the others looked on as Peter shared with him the news of Jesus' resurrection. "Thomas, have you heard the news about our Master?"

Thomas was near to tears as he shared in his distress, "I am so overwhelmed with sorrow that I can hardly speak of it. I cannot believe what has taken place and of how they crucified him." Then tears welled up in his eyes and his voice became weak.

Peter was patient to listen to him and then shared again, "Yes. We all know. It was very sorrowful."

Thomas nodded his head.

"But, there is more that has happened," Peter said gleefully.

Thomas looked around at the other apostles and saw their joyous faces too. He was suspicious about why in the world they would look so happy and content when their Lord had just been tortured and executed. He could not reconcile in his mind what was going on. "Would someone tell me why you are all so happy? What is wrong with you?"

Peter could not contain his joy and broke out in laughter as he shared, "Thomas, our Lord has raised from the dead and he appeared to all of us last evening, right here in this upper room! It is amazing!"

Thomas was speechless. He thought, *'Have they all gone mad? This claim of theirs is simply impossible!'*

John came over and set a plate of food down for him to eat. Then he told him everything. Beginning with the report of women who went to the tomb early Sunday morning.

Thomas sat, stupefied, uncertain and distrusting of what to make of it all.

Thomas was very bold as he spoke out to everyone, "This is all so very hard to believe. How can I accept what you have said? Such a thing has never been heard of before. If he has risen from the dead, why isn't he here among you right now?"

John smiled, "We don't know! It's all part of a great divine mystery that is still unfolding before us."

Thomas said, "I'm going to need some time to think about all of your claims. Now, tell me everything again, from the beginning on Sunday as the women approached the tomb."

Then the apostles all shared in telling him everything in greater detail. They explained very carefully everything they knew, had heard and experienced. Thomas listened to every word and watched everyone carefully as they spoke studying their faces as he asked them questions along the way.

An hour had passed as they shared with him every single detail, including many of the prophecies that foretold of everything too. Still in the end he spoke to them saying, "This is all so very interesting, and it is very thrilling. But as an apostle just like all of you I cannot simply accept what you have said. I want to believe you but there is a problem."

The others were very disappointed with Thomas but still he held his ground with them and explained his reasons for not believing. "I am not saying that I don't believe you or that I do believe you. And I don't doubt the truth either. I simply don't know what the truth is. But I must know, I am an apostle too. I do not understand but I must understand all this. I remember when Jesus did not travel openly for fear of his enemies, but he never disguised himself either. I cannot understand why he would disguise himself to the brothers from Emmaus or from Mary Magdala. He never did that before. As an apostle, as are all of you, if I am to be a witness to the life of my Lord, I too must have the same experience that you have had. Just as you can testify to saying, 'We have seen the Lord and he is alive.' I must be able to do this too, I insist on it."

Then Thomas stood to his feet and turned to see everyone. Making eye contact with them all he asserted very strongly, "Like you I must see his face and know that it is in fact him and not someone else as he seemed to be to some of you. I must carefully and thoroughly examine the scars from the nails in his hands and feet, and the spear wound in his side. I cannot serve as an apostle of our Lord and tell others, 'I was told he is risen from the dead and that he is alive by all the other apostles.' That would not be right. Then I would not be serving with the full authority that has come to you because you are witnesses to these claims that you are making."

Peter, having been recognized as the spokesman among them, responded to him, "I cannot say that I am not disappointed with your position because I am. I have listened to all that you have said. In part I agree with you and therefore we must all pray diligently that our Lord does appear to you and shows himself alive to you. At the same time, I must remind you that all of us here were reprimanded for not believing the testimony that the ladies gave us. The Lord himself told them to tell us that he was raised from the dead just as we are sharing it with you."

Then Thomas raised his hand high above his head and moved it about as he forcefully said, "I am an apostle of Jesus of Nazareth, who is the Son of God. Of that I have no question in my mind and let there be no doubt remaining in your minds either. He empowered me to perform miracles and heal people in his name even to cleanse the lepers. As an apostle, if I am to believe in what you say, then I too must be witness to the resurrection. For me to serve with the same authority and power as the rest of you, I must also experience what you have experienced. Accept this, don't accept it, I don't care. I must see him for myself! Until then I will reserve my confession of faith in this report of his resurrection."

Peter, having considered his point said this, "I will grant you this, that you make a good argument Thomas. But when the ladies who were the first witness to Jesus' resurrection having seen and touched him came to us and shared their story, we did not believe them. When Jesus did appear directly to us he chastised us for our disbelief and doubt. Then he showed us that he was not a spirit or a ghost. We ate broiled fish with him, we touched him, he breathed on us and said receive the Holy Spirit. We even felt his breath upon us and it was the Spirit of God. We live in the hopes that he will return to us, but we don't know when that will be. He instructed us to share this good news with everyone. Everyone Thomas. It is by the word of our testimony that many will believe because not everyone will be visited by him. That is why we are urging you so. Believe in him and that he is raised from the dead."

Thomas carefully considered his words and said, "Just as you are taking certain precautions here with the locking of all doors and windows so also my heart is locked shut from this for now. But I will continue in fellowship with all of you and we will talk more about all that has happened. My prayer is that our Lord will return to be with us again. When that day comes, then I will be able to examine him myself. Then I will believe. Until that happens I cannot believe." So it was that Thomas continued to share in fellowship with the rest of the apostles. He stayed at Zechariah's home and did not leave for fear of missing the next visitation of the Lord.

Chapter Sixteen
James, Jude, and Nicodemus

It was on Monday at about midmorning when Nicodemus learned about the reports that Jesus had been raised from the dead and appeared to the apostles. The Lord's own brothers, James and Jude, came to his home and shared this with him.

Nicodemus told them, "When I first heard about your brother's teaching I was absorbed by the reports I was hearing. So, I went to hear him teach the people and I saw him performing miracles without measure. My mind and my thoughts were stunned that he was able to do such wonders: sight to the blind, opened the ears of the deaf, made the lame to walk with bounding strength in their legs, and even cleanse the lepers. I myself investigated the lives of these people whose lives he touched so wondrously. His teaching was also, well what can I say, it was beyond anything I had heard of before. I'll admit to you two that I was at first a little jealous over what he knew about the Scriptures. But I was so happy to learn from what he had to say that I got over that quickly. Everywhere he went, the scribes, the Pharisees, and the Sadducees were infuriated by him. He drew their followers away from them and oh how they love an audience and the praises of men. They were fuming mad over his influence. It served them right to lose their following. As your brother Jesus righty put it, they were blind leaders of the blind. When I had finished sizing up the situation, I had no questions remaining in my mind. Your brother was undoubtedly a prophet sent by God to us. I knew that I had to talk to him myself. For my own interests I wanted to learn all that I could from him. I went to visit him one evening so that we could have a discussion about his ministry."

Jude asked him, "But why at the close of day when you would not be able to talk for very long?"

The venerated teacher explained, "For a couple of rabbis in a deep discussion we were not limited by the lateness of the hour. We could have ended up talking until the sun came up. The evening is the perfect time for us as the night unfolds and the blue dome over the earth begins to roll away and the stars first appear. That is a mystical time and place for us. One that opens up to us only if we will enter in."

"What do you mean?" said the other brother James.

"When the dome that covers the earth lifts away and the veil that separates our world from heaven's vastness and its unending display of stars, there comes a certain state of mind to us. It is one that gives us the opportunity to ponder the greater things. Then we can consider the deeper and weightier secrets of God and his creation. It is when the endless stars of heaven are revealed in the vast darkness of the night sky that there are no bounds to what the mind can consider. Our thoughts meld with the limitless expanse of what we can see. It is a time for opening our minds to consider the mysteries that God holds for us. It is in those hours that we can have a daring spirit that reaches out and questions what do the Scriptures mean for us. Then we can ponder the creation and the greater things of God as we seek to know him.

It was at that time of the night that I came to your brother to visit with him. Except I did not share any of my wisdom with him. It was him who shared his wisdom with me. It was your brother, the younger Rabbi, who passed on to me the old rabbi words from God that I had never considered before."

James asked, "What was said?"

Jude also nodded to indicate his eagerness about hearing what his brother the Lord had said.

"I came to find out what I could from him. I wanted to believe in him. I knew he was a prophet sent to us from God. But a man in my position and as a leading rabbi I needed to do more than simply go with assumptions. I needed to examine him and what he was teaching in light of what Moses wrote. I had to see if he was a prophet in truth. Moses required the examination of a prophet to see if he was genuine or not.

I have to back up in my story to say that it was because of John the Baptist and his followers that I was alerted to the coming of the Lord. John was the predicted forerunner to the Messiah. The scrolls of Malachi[6] and Isaiah[7] told us that God's messenger will be a voice calling out in the wilderness who would go before him to prepare his way."

James interjected, "They were cousins, my brother and John. Cousins on their mother's side each of them. They were both the same age too. Well John was a little bit older by a few months."

The old rabbi continued on, "How very remarkable." He chuckled as he said this. "When I came to visit I told the Lord that I believed he was a true prophet from God. I initially based that conclusion on the great extent of the signs and wonders he was preforming. But I also wanted to base my evaluation on what he was teaching. I told myself that I must know how his messages compared to what Moses and the prophets wrote for us."

---

[6] Malachi 3:1
[7] Isaiah 40:3-5

Nicodemus was giving a very thorough explanation of his work surrounding their brother but he had not said anything about the actual visit yet. This foundation that he was laying was typical of academics and the scholarship they do. This was what his life was made up of. The pursuit of knowledge and understanding, wisdom and the truth. But it was not that interesting to James and Jude. They wanted to hear about the visit the two rabbis had together.

Jude asked him, "So what happened when you visited him? What was said between the you two of you?"

"Jesus warmly accepted me into his company that night even though I came without an invitation or announced. Then he taught me things that I knew nothing of."

James inquired of him, "Like what?"

"One of the greatest things he told me was that just as we born into our earthly life and have our bodies of the earth, we need spiritual birth too. He said that in order to enter into heaven and live we must also be born from above. We need a second and spiritual birth. He said we must be born again.[8]"

Nicodemus and the brothers reveled in joy as they giggled together while he taught them this lesson that Jesus had given to him.

The rabbi continued on, "Now I was puzzled by what he said. He taught me a tremendous thing, but I had even more questions that came up as we talked together. It was like nothing I had ever thought of. It was like nothing I ever heard from anyone else and I didn't understand him at all. I asked him 'how is it that a man such as myself who is old can be born of his mother a second time as you say?'"

---

[8] John 3:7

James and John looked at each other with blank faces and shrugged their shoulders. Then James said to him, "I agree too. I don't understand what he said either."

"He explained it to me and with patience. Being born as a body of flesh is only physical. Being born of our heavenly Father by the Holy Spirit gives us spiritual birth. Our physical body functions for our earthly life. As children of God in heaven we need a spiritual body which only comes from this second birth and being born again. Born of heaven."

Nicodemus looked at the brothers who were still thinking about the idea of being born again but they posed no more questions about it, so he went on. "I was having a great deal of trouble understanding what he was saying. I was astounded beyond all that I had ever thought or imagined. I have read and studied all of the Scriptures, Moses, the Psalms, and the Prophets. I have heard many of the ideas and philosophies of men. I have read and studied all the manuscripts written by men trying to explain and expound on what the holy writings mean. But I had never heard this message before. I asked him how can this be? How can a man be born of the spirit? He said in certain words that it was an elusive thing like the wind. He said 'The wind blows where it will. We cannot see it, but we can hear it and feel it. Where it comes from and where it goes is unknown to us. So it is with being born of the spirit.[9]' He was right too. There is an intangibility that everyone who is born again has in their lives. I believe it is because they live by being guided by God's Holy Spirit."

Jude asked him, "What did you think of all that rabbi?"

"It was a far-reaching teaching that made me rethink many things. It reverberated through my mind and all that I

---

[9] John 3:8

believed to be true. I am not a prophet, but I tried to imagine what it was like for them when the Spirit of God came upon them and inspired them to preach God's message or write holy Scripture. I tried to imagine what it was like for them to be inspired by the Spirit. Your brother the prophet could see what I was thinking, and he told me flat out that while I knew about the things of this world, I knew hardly anything at all about heaven. He explained that there was much that was beyond the limits of my powers of deduction and what I could discover by my pondering.

I want you to know that of all the things that he told me about, there was one thing that I now see clearly today because of the news you have brought me of his resurrection. I struggled endlessly with it until today"

The brothers simultaneously spoke out, "What was that?"

"From the forth book of Moses, Jesus reminded me of the wilderness days when our people sinned by grumbling against God and poisonous snakes came and bit them. Many of them died. Others we've made terribly sick and suffered. When they repented they begged Moses for help. He prayed for them and God told him to make a serpent out of bronze and lift it up on a stick. Then everyone who would believe in God and look to the serpent would be healed.[10]"

Jude said, "Yes. I remember that lesson."

"Then Jesus said what seemed like the strangest thing to me."

James was anxious to hear more as he asked, "What was that?"

---

[10] Numbers 21

"He became very serious and then told me, 'Just as Moses made a bronze serpent in the wildness and the people were healed, I too must be lifted up so that whoever believes in me may life eternally.'[11] Until today, I did not know what he meant when he said that to me."

James wanted to hear the rest and impatiently asked, "And what did he mean by that?"

"He meant that the salvation of our ancestors in the wilderness was dependent on them looking at the bronze serpent that was lifted up among them. Their death was caused by its bite and their healing came by looking at it as God commanded. Our salvation from our sins comes from looking at Jesus on the cross where his life was sacrificed for our sins. God put our iniquities on him when he was hung on the cross. We must look at him and remember him there as he bore our sins on his body."

James was speechless as the revelation of this set in. He did not want to say anything but only to savor the moment of this new understanding that had come to him.

As it was nearing the noon hour, Nicodemus extended an invitation for the Lord's brothers to join him for lunch. They spoke more about Jesus' life and continued to ponder what the resurrection of Jesus would mean for them in the coming days and years.

---

[11] John 3:15

Chapter Seventeen
Mary's Visitation

Mary was busy in her kitchen that morning. She was taking the time to make bread from scratch. It was a joy for her to this. She had been raised that way. Her mother made fresh bread for her family when she was young. It was that way in the home she made with her husband Joseph too. She had never grown accustomed to purchasing bread at the marketplace. It didn't taste the same. It didn't taste as good as the recipe her mother had given to her, the one she had gotten from her mother before her. When her son entered into public ministry she missed making her own bread and seeing him eat it. This brought her a warm sense of joy to nurture him in this way. In his ministry they were traveling constantly and rarely returned to her home in Nazareth. On the road they ate what others provided or what they purchased locally. When they stayed with others it was the custom that their hosts did all the food preparation.

John had found a home in Jerusalem and he was able to pay the rent with some of the money Joseph of Arimathea had given to him. His brother James also lived there with them. This was preferable to Mary for now with the loss of her son and with the more recent reports of his appearances. It was just too unsettling. She needed to have her own home again and enjoy a less pubic life. It was not that she wasn't glad for all the recent events that had occurred since Sunday morning. She was very happy and also dismayed. She believed that he was raised from the dead, but he had suffered and died, and that did not merely wash away the torrential flood of emotions that had just uprooted her life.

As the Lord's mother, she was told of every report about his appearances beginning with those about the angel and saintly men from heaven at his tomb. But that joy was overshadowed with the loss of not being with her son on a daily basis anymore. She was feeling a great loss because he had not come to visit her yet and she had no assurance that he would. She was his mother. She loved him and served him. Why shouldn't he come to visit her too? This mixed joy and sorrow continued with every waking moment of her life.

Now the kitchen was still sparsely furnished because they had not lived there but a few days. There was a shabby wooden table for preparing food on. It came with the house and the men hadn't had time to purchase a new one yet. There was a shelf that was hung on the wall with some bags of wheat and barley flour resting on it. She had a few vegetables that were tied in bunches and hung from a wood beam. There were some reddish grey clay vessels with wine in them and others with water in them. There were two with olive oil. One was for cooking with and the other one was for burning in the oil lamps. She had a large bowl that she had just washed after having mixed bread dough in it. The walls of the house were made of stone with mortar joints between them and some of them had plaster over them. In the corner of the kitchen was her stove. It was made of stone and had three holes carved into its top. Pots could be put on these for heating water and cooking food. Next to the stove was an oven which she had put to good use. It was baking bread and its pleasant aroma was just beginning to deliciously fill her home.

The morning had been cool but about midmorning it started to warm up with the new day. Her kitchen had grown warmer still as the bread baked. About then, as the bread was nearly done, there came through the doorway a gentle, refreshing and fragrant breeze that passed in through the house and into the kitchen. It got her full attention, not only because it was a wonderful relief from the heat but because it also passed right through her as well. She knew the presence of her son, it was so familiar to her, and that is what she felt after the breeze waned. It truly was a fresh breath of air from heaven. Now the daylight that had been shining into her home gave way to the brilliant light of heaven that shone in and she could see the silhouette of her son who walked through the doorway and into her kitchen. Tears of joy streamed down her face and she smiled brightly as she reached out her arms to embrace him.

Jesus reached out his arms to take his mother into his embrace and hold her in his loving arms. She rushed to him and kissed his cheeks and wept, wept for joy and for sorrow remembered. And in his arms she found a profound miracle. Her grief and mourning, her wounds from when the sword pierced her soul and broke her heart because of all that she suffered was beginning to mend. In her tears she said, "Jesus, my son, my son, my son. O, how I love you so!"

Jesus held her for a long time in silence while he too was overcome with tears. He held his mother until by the power of his lifegiving resurrection she was fully healed from all her sorrows over his suffering and death. This was the one gift above all others that he wanted her to have. In faithfulness she had suffered the most of all as she faithfully endured with him at the cross.

After some time passed, Mary let loose her tight grip around her son and she stepped back. She knew that her wounded heart was healed, and she knelt low to the floor before him and kissed his feet and worshipped him as her God.

"In my distress I called upon the
LORD and he answered me.
He has heard the cry of his
maidservant and saved her from the pit.
My Son has been brought home to me
and he has healed my broken heart.
All blessing and praise to the Holy One of Israel."

Then her dear son knelt down and took her by the hand and lifted her up. He looked into her eyes and before he could speak she said, "You are the Son of God. This I knew more than anyone. When the angel Gabriel came to me I was just a young woman then. He said, 'Blessings chosen one, for the LORD our God is with you.' But I was overwhelmed with fear and I hid my face from him. I didn't know who this person was or that he was an angel. But he said I had nothing to fear. He told me that I was favored by the LORD among women and that I would have a child by the overshadowing of God's Holy Spirt. He said you would be the holy Son of God and that I was to call you Jesus."

Her son looked at her with kindness in his eyes and shared, "Yes mother. That is how it happened. Just as you said. Forgive me for the pain that has come to you from my life."

Mary gently put her hand to his mouth and with her other hand she covered her mouth to show that he should be silent because she did not need him to say anything more. With streaming tears running down her face she said, "I do my son. I do forgive you. But you should not have to ask me for forgiveness. This was your Father's will that you should suffer and die for the sins of the world."

"Then it was not too much to ask of you? You were so young to become my mother and the difficulties you faced then were great."

Without a moment's hesitation Mary resolutely said, "No. It was never too much to ask of me. I found favor with God and he helped me then as he has helped me all this time. Through everything he has helped me. He helped Joseph too. Some days I miss him very much."

"He was a good man, a good husband to you, and a good stepfather to me too. I have missed him also."

"Yes. He was all that and more."

Mary did not want him to leave too soon so she said, "And now you must let me prepare something for you to eat so that we can enjoy each other's company a little while longer."

"Yes. I can stay with you for a while."

Mary went to the oven, took out her bread, and then she spread olive oil on it. She poured two cups of wine and set them in front of her son on the old table. She also brought over a bowl of fresh charoset that she had made earlier that day. It had roasted crushed almonds, finely diced up apricots and apples, along with dates and raisins in it. At the table, she mixed in honey and cinnamon.

They sat on some old stools and joined hands as Jesus blessed the LORD for their food.

"This is like all the old times when you were a child and when you were a young man. You had no wife to care for you and I was glad to look after your needs. I so enjoyed hearing about your day and how your work went."

"Yes, I remember them too. After a long hard day of work I would come home and you always had food ready for me."

"At the end of those days you would sleep so soundly every night. In the mornings you were always up so very early and ready to work again." Mary paused and became weepy for a moment before she spoke, "You will be leaving after this won't you." It was very hard for her to imagine this.

"Yes. I cannot stay. I have to return to my Father."

"Somehow I knew that you would come to me. As your mother I just knew you would. But I did not want to imagine that it would not last."

"You're right and it is true. It was necessary for me to come and visit you. It was necessary that I should come because of all that you had to endure. So that your heart could heal. So that you could care for me again as my mother and so that we could be together again. Even if it is only for a short while."

Mary loved to cook and even more she loved serving her son. She took a small loaf of bread while it was still warm and smelled wonderful. She used a wooden spoon to spread the charoset over it and then placed it on her son's plate as she smiled with delight. "This reminds me of you as a child when you were first able to feed yourself. And oh, how you loved bread prepared this way."

He nodded gratefully and said, "Thank you, mother." He nodded again as he took a bite and in his thoughts he reminisced about his childhood days and how he enjoyed his mother's cooking.

"How are James and John? Are your needs being cared for?"

"James is good. John is fine. What a man he is growing into. And yes, I am well care for by him and all your followers too. Joseph came to John and gave him a generous gift. It is enough money to support us for some time to come. And your followers. Oh, they would treat me like a queen if I let them. I lack for nothing, but I insist that in our growing community of believers that I share equally in the work. I share in your example not wanting to be served but being a servant to all."

Jesus laughed, "I bet you do too. I suppose they are continually reminded that you are a woman who works hard and doesn't expect to be waited on."

"They do. They want to treat me like someone who is extraordinary because I am your mother. But I show them that I am just like the rest. I have made friends with them all and I let them see that I am human and won't be put up on a pedestal."

Jesus laughed again, and his mother joined in too.

"It is so wonderful to be together again. Isn't it?" he said.

"Yes my dear son. More than words can say."

Mary hesitated to say what was on her mind, but she remembered her son's first miracle. When at her request he made water into wine for the wedding. Then she asked him, "Will you visit your brothers James and Jude for me? They are faithful disciples and I know how much they miss you. They are your family and you three always shared such a special bond together."

Jesus could not answer her immediately though wanted to grant her request. First, he silently prayed for an answer from his Father and when he heard that answer he honored her, "Yes, I will be able to visit them soon. I cannot say just when, but it is given to me from my Father that I should visit them too."

His mother smiled and took heart knowing that what was important to her as a matriarch over her stepchildren was also important to her son, the Son of God.

Their food, which tasted so very good as they cherished each other's company, was almost gone and Mary realized that he would leave her soon. "Before you go, please give your mother another hug. One that I will remember you by forever."

They both stood to their feet and Jesus went to his mother and she nestled warmly in his arms. He slowly swung from side to side as he held her so gently. She hummed a lullaby that had comforted him as a baby. Then he was simply gone from her arms.

Mary sat down at the table where they had just eaten together, and her thoughts returned to their visit as she meditated over all that he had said and done. It was so very healing for her. When her son suffered, her life was torn from her. When he died, she felt as though she had too. Now her life was fully restored because he brought her this wonderful visitation.

Chapter Eighteen
Joseph's Sabbath

In that hour leading up to the sun's setting Ziphorah had bathed her sons and dressed them in their finest robes. As she prepared them for the evening of the Sabbath she schooled her children so that they would better understand why they did these things, "Caleb and Levi, Saturday, our Sabbath day, is unlike any of the other days of the week. This day that will begin very soon for us is a day that is Holy to the LORD God. It should not feel like any other day of the week for us because it has its very own purpose. You must remember that God created the heavens and earth and all they contain in the first six days of the week. Then on the seventh day he completed his work and rested from all that he had done. Therefore, he shares with us and we share with him in his life by entering into his rest on this day."

Her children listened attentively as she explained more to them, "This is why we bathe. So that we may be clean and pure before the Lord on his day. This is why we wash and put on our finest clothes for this day. This is why we work so hard on Friday to prepare all of our food in advance for the Sabbath. And it is our favorite foods that we prepare because this is also a day of celebrating. We do all the work that is necessary in advance of this day so that we can have no interruptions or distractions to keep us from sharing in the LORD's Sabbath that he brings to our lives. By this we can have abundant time in our lives to reflect and appreciate what God's purposes are for our lives that he has given to us."

It was exactly one week since Jesus' death and as the sun was setting in the west Ziphorah sent her two sons outside to watch for the appearance of the first star of the night sky. When nighttime began the first meal of the Sabbath was eaten. This was the point in time which ushered in and welcomed their day of rest and brought to an end the ordinary days of the workweek. It was her place as the wife and mother of their home to call her family to the dinner table. There she would lead them in their rituals to close out the common workdays and begin the celebration of the Sabbath day of rest.

It was not long before the two young children excitedly reappeared and went directly to her announcing together, "Mother, we have seen the first star of the evening in the sky and so nighttime will soon come to us again." The young children beamed with joy to be able to do this task because their announcement told everyone that the Sabbath was at hand. Officially it began when there were three stars seen in the night sky. Now they would close out the workdays, welcome the holy Sabbath and consecrate it with their meal.

Her boys loved to do this, and they so very much enjoyed celebrating the Sabbath. As very young children they did not understand all that had happened on the prior Sabbath. On that fateful day their routine was interrupted by the tragic death of Rabbi Jesus. Their observance of the Passover festival was scaled down from what it was to have been and it became a sad occasion for Joseph and his wife Ziphorah. Their very young children had been so excited by all their parents had told them in advance. They had shared in the preparations for the festive night of dining and remembrance. The letdown of the Lord's death was the greatest disappointment they had suffered within their young lives. When that evening finally arrived, the children did not understand why their parents were so reserved as the Sabbath meal was celebrated by them in their private residence. They did not understand why their many guests that were residing with them did not join with them in the meal either. That following morning on Saturday, the children were overcome with a sadness that they did not fully understand. That was when their mother and father told them of Jesus' death. Then in the days that followed their entire week was one filled with erratic experiences. This was the first death of anyone that they had personally known and at their young ages it was a harsh experience for them to come into. They did not know what to think when on Sunday morning the women returned to their home with their reports of an angel, an opened tomb, and saying that Jesus was risen from the dead. Then there were the reports that Mary Magdala saw and touched him which was followed by the report of the apostles saying they had seen him too. The young children didn't know what to make of all of it. So when the Sabbath rituals began that evening they found comfort in the feeling that things were finally returning to their normal routines in life. This was one of the important things in their lives that had some regularity to it.

The Sabbath table in their dining room was set with two candles and two specially prepared loaves of bread made with a honey, butter, and salt glazing over them. Now their family had gathered: Ziphorah, Joseph and their boys, Caleb and Levi.

The ritual meal was led by their mother who lit the two candles and shared their meaning with her family, "These we light to fulfill God's commandment to us; one candle reminds us to remember the Sabbath to keep it holy. The other candle that we light reminds us to observe the Sabbath by resting and observing it. By doing this we close our workweek and bring it to its end. By lighting these candles we proclaim that our Sabbath has begun. The warmth of their light kindles peace in us and brings joy into our home. By their light we remember that in the beginning of creation God said, 'Let there be light!' and there was light on the first day of creation. And so, we begin our celebration with the creation of this light in our home."

Now as she lit the candles, she waved her hands over the top of their flames and welcomed in the holy Sabbath. Then she covered her eyes and blocked their light from her sight. This was to show the passing of the sixth day and entering the seventh day according to the words of Moses. Then she sang this blessing.

"Barukh atah Adonai, Eloheinu, melekh ha'olam
"Blessed are you, LORD, our God,
sovereign of the universe,

asher kidishanu b'mitz'votav v'tzivanu
who has sanctified us with his
commandments and commanded us

l'had'lik neir shel Shabbat. Amein"
to light the lights of Sabbath. Amen"

And everyone at the table quietly said, "Amen."

At the conclusion of the blessing she uncovered her eyes, and this was the moment in which the Sabbath day began for them. Her children followed in her gestures, covering and uncovering their eyes too. It was then as they all uncovered their eyes that the Lord appeared before them at their table and was sitting on a couch with them. They were silent for the moment not knowing what to say or do or even think.

Then their child Caleb spoke, "I know who you are. You are Jesus who was dead but now you are alive again just as the women have been telling us."

Jesus grinned large and nodded his head as he joyfully answered him, "Yes. I am Jesus and I was dead. But this past Sunday my Father who is in heaven raised me from death and made me alive again."

Now the two children got up and went over to the Lord. Caleb said, "We remember when you said to your apostles, 'Allow the small children to be brought to me. I am glad to lay my hands on them and pray. I will bless them with my Father's blessing. And everyone must know that to such as these little ones belongs the Kingdom of God.'[12] We were there and you blessed us then."

Then the two children looked at their mother with questioning eyes. This was the time in their Sabbath meal when the parents bless their children. But on this occasion, with their very special guest in attendance, their mother knew that they were asking her if Jesus could bless them tonight instead. She hesitated for just a moment and as her head relaxed and turned slightly to the side she smiled warmly and approvingly nodded.

The two children looked into Jesus' eyes and in simple faith asked, "Lord Jesus, will you give us the Sabbath blessing tonight."

Then the Lord placed one hand on each child's head and recited the age-old blessing.

"May God make you like Ephraim and Manasseh.
May God bless you and guard you.

---

[12] Based on Matthew 19:13-15

May the light of God shine on you and be gracious to you.
May the presence of God be with you and grant you peace.
Amen"

The children along with their parents, quietly said, "Amen".

Their meal continued on as Ziphorah instructed her children, "Our week has been filled with the work that God has commanded us to do: to be fruitful and multiply. That part of the week has ended and now our Sabbath day is a time of rest and a time to consider all that God has done and is doing in our lives. As the vessel of wine is raised we make something physical to become something spiritual and we lift up not only the vessel but also our Sabbath unto the Lord. With the Kiddush of our wine we are sanctifying the Sabbath." Ziphorah poured full her chalice and raised it in celebration and as a toast to the day of rest.

"Vay'hi erev vay'hi voker yom hashish.
'And there was evening and there was morning, a sixth day.

vay'khulu hashamayim v'ha'aretz v'khol tz'va'am.
The heavens and the earth were finished,
the whole host of them.

vay'khal elohim bayom hash'vi'i m'la'kh'to asher asah,
And on the seventh day God
completed his work that he had done,

vayish'bot bayom hash'vi'i mikol m'la'kh'to asher asah.
and he rested on the seventh day
from all his work that he had done.

Vay'varekh Elohim et yom hash'vi'i vay'kadeish oto
And God blessed the seventh day and sanctified it

ki vo shavat mikol m'la'kh'to asher bara Elohim la'asot
because in it he had rested from
all his work that God had created to do

ki vo shavat mikol m'la'kh'to asher bara Elohim la'asot.
because in it he had rested from all
his work that God had created to do.

Barukh atah Adonai, Eloheinu, melekh ha-olam
Blessed are you, LORD our God, sovereign of the universe

borei p'ri hagafen. Amein
Who creates the fruit of the vine. Amen

Barukh atah Adonai, Eloheinu, melekh ha-olam
Blessed are you, LORD our God, King of the Universe

asher kid'shanu b'mitz'votav v'ratzah vanu.
who sanctifies us with his commandments
and has been pleased with us.

v'shabat kad'sho b'ahavah uv'ratzon
hin'chilanu zikaron l'ma'aseih v'rei'shit
You have lovingly and willingly given us your holy
Sabbathas an inheritance in memory of creation

ki hu yom t'chilah l'mik'ra'ei
kodesh zeikher litzi'at Mitz'rayim
because it is the first day of our holy
assemblies in memory of the exodus from Egypt

ki vanu vachar'ta v'otanu kidash'ta mikol ha'amim
because you have chosen us and
made us holy from all peoples

v'shabat kad'sh'kha b'ahavah uv'ratzon hin'chal'tanu.
and have willingly and lovingly given us
your holy Shabbat for an inheritance.

Barukh atah Adonai m'kadeish hashabat. Amein"
Blessed are you who sanctifies Sabbath. Amen"

Everyone at the table quietly said, "Amen".

Then everyone at the table passed around a pitcher of water and aided each other in washing their hands. The water was poured first over the top and then the bottom of their right hand followed by their left. The water ran off their hands into a bowl that was also passed. As everyone's hands remained wet Ziphorah led everyone in this traditional blessing.

"Barukh atah Adonai, Eloheinu, melekh ha-olam
Blessed are you, LORD our God, King of the Universe

asher kidishanu b'mitz'votav v'tzivanu
Who has sanctified us with his
commandments and commanded us

al n'tilat yadayim.
concerning the washing of hands."

Their meal continued with the blessing and sharing of bread. The two special loaves of bread that had been set there were to remind everyone that during the days of their ancestors' desert wanderings God gave them a double portion of mana bread on Friday so that they would have bread on their Sabbath day as well. They were covered with a cloth until this time. Their glazed topping was there to reminded them of the honey flavor of mana. The salt was there as a preservative reminding them that God provided not just during the forty years they spent in the wilderness, but that he provides for them for the entire length of the lives.[13]

Ziphorah lifted the cloth from the two loaves, lifted the plate, and allowed everyone to touch it. Then she said, "It is by this bread from God that we are sustained in life. This is food for the body and love and nurture for our family." Then she said this blessing over it.

"Barukh atah Adonai, Eloheinu, melekh ha-olam
Blessed are you, LORD, our God, King of the universe

hamotzi lechem min ha'aretz. Amein
who brings forth bread from the earth. Amen".

Everyone at the table quietly said, "Amen".

Then their meal began. The food for this special day included their favorite foods: soup, roasted fish, barbequed lamb, more honey glazed bread, fresh fruit and vegetables, and lots of all of it.

---

[13] Exodus 16:22

Chapter Nineteen
A Rich Man's Tomb

Once the Sabbath meal was over, their servants cleared the table and brought out desert which was eaten during a time of conversation about the Scriptures. Commonly it was from the portion called the Torah, but it could also include the Psalms and poetic writings, or the Prophets.

As the conversation progressed Ziphorah took notice of the scars on Jesus' hands. He held them out for her to see showing her one side and then other. As she looked at the well-healed scars from where the nails had pierced him, she raised her hands to cover her mouth. It was sorrowful for her to think about his suffering. "My Lord!" Tears began to well up in her eyes. "Should I be sorrowful for all that you suffered? You are well again and risen to life but what am I to think about what has happened?"

Jesus listened to her and was a little surprised by her question, but it was a very good question. "Yes, I am well. There is no more pain for me and I am no longer suffering. Not in my body or in my mind. That is an amazing thing about my resurrection. God has taken away every pain and tear of sorrow from my suffering and death."

Ziphorah had been holding her breath for fear of not knowing what he would say, and she worried anxiously that he was still in suffering or pain."

Then the Lord spoke to her and Joseph both, "There will be times and seasons for you and for all believers to remember my suffering and all that I endured for the world to be forgiven their sins."

The couple listened intensely as the Lord continued to explain this to them. "It was necessary for me to suffer, die, and be raised as the prophets foretold. The judgements of the Law say that sinners shall die for their sins. There is no way around it. But my Father, in his love and righteousness, was not willing to let that judgement be carried out against anyone. Therefore, he sent me to die for the sins of the world. Though one man cannot die for the sins of another, as the Son of God I could die for all. On the cross I became the atoning sacrifice for all the world which only I could do. As the Son of Man I could die and as the Son of God I could die for the sins of the world. But what I really want to share with you is what the Scriptures say about my burial."

Joseph and Ziphorah now listened more intensely.

"Did you know that the prophet Isaiah made mention of your gracious gesture to me when you buried me in your own tomb?"[14]

Joseph and Ziphorah were doubly surprised by this. They did not know if it would be polite or proper for an after-dinner conversation to speak about his death. And they did not feel that it would be proper for them to bring up the use of their family tomb with the Lord either.

With eyes wide open and being a little faint of voice Joseph cautiously inquired, "How is this possible my Lord?"

Jesus chuckled as he reassuringly told him, "Yes, it is true. This is the reason that I have come to visit you tonight. Well, one of them anyway. I know how you and your household were inconvenienced on your Sabbath day and how your Passover celebration was interrupted following my death. For that reason I wanted to come to your home tonight and bless your Sabbath by my presence. I also wanted to remind you of the words of the prophet

---

[14] Isaiah 53:9

Isaiah who foretold of me when he wrote, 'And they made his grave with the wicked and with a rich man in his death.'[15]"

The couple were speechless not knowing how they should respond to this. They did not yet understand that it was to their commendation that they had provided the tomb to Jesus. They wonder how this could be a blessing or even a good thing in that circumstance. They wanted nothing to do with those who had condemned and put him to death.

Jesus did not mean for this knowledge to be anything but a blessing to them and he could not let them have thoughts about it any other way. "You must not allow yourselves to worry about what you did. You provided this one thing that was necessary. Your generous provision in burying me in your tomb was necessary for the words of the prophet to be fulfilled and I thank you for it."

Now the couple relaxed and both breathed a sigh of relief.

Jesus continued on, "Isaiah spoke by the Holy Spirit saying that my grave would have been with the wicked in an unclean common grave. Instead, by your generosity I was buried in the tomb of a rich man, that's you. And there is more to it. It was necessary for me to be buried in a new tomb, one that had never been used. That way it would not be an unclean place. By your placing my body there I have sanctified your tomb by my death and by my death I have sanctified all the resting places of the faithful dead who believe in me."

Joseph looked directly into Jesus' eyes and said to him, "My Lord, I had no idea then and I could not have imagined this even now. Thank you for sharing this with us."

---

[15] Isaiah 53:9

Jesus smiled warmly and was very glad to bestow this blessing on Joseph and his family by telling him, "Joseph, thank you for all that you have done and endured through by defending me in the courtroom and asking Pilate for my body. You must also know that Moses wrote that none of the bones of the sacrificial lamb may be broken. [16] When you went to the governor you prevented them from breaking my legs. I do not want you to be unware of how necessary and vital a role you have played in my life so that the Scriptures would be fulfilled in me. I have come to your home to lift the veil that covered these mysteries of God."

Joseph and Ziphorah were left speechless by the news that they had been part of the prophet's words and that they were used by God to provide for their Lord in these ways.

Then Jesus rose to his feet and held out his nail pierced hands to them, "Before I leave, thank you both for the love that you showed to my mother and all of my followers when you opened up your home to them following my death."

Joseph responded, "My Lord, there is no need to thank us."

"Still, what you have done for them you have done as unto me. And I will bless you for your sacrifice and service.

May our heavenly Father
bestow rich favor upon you both,
and in your marriage, to your sons, upon your home
and all the members of your household.
May my Father bless you in all that you do,
as you rise, as you go out, and when you come home
and when you lay down to sleep. Amen".

---

[16] Exodus 12:46

Joseph and Ziphorah had been looking into Jesus' eyes as he said these things. And when he said his amen he vanished from their sight.

Chapter Twenty
Nicodemus and Jesus

That evening after the sun had set and the first three stars of the night sky appeared to announce the end of the day and the beginning of the next, Nicodemus sat outside in his courtyard. This night he was alone. He had not invited his students or colleagues to join with him even though this was his common practice. He was in need of his solitude. James and Jude had told him what they could about their brother's appearances and what the apostles were learning about his resurrection. The old rabbi knew the holy Scriptures and he knew them very well. But for as well as he knew them, he realized that he did not have the foresight to see how they were being fulfilled in the Lord's life other than a very few of them. This left him feeling very inadequate as a rabbi. It reminded him of his very first visit with Rabbi Jesus when he went to him by night. The things he was taught then were very new to him and so were the new understandings he was coming into about the ancient words of the Law and the Prophets.

Nicodemus needed this time to be alone so that he could contemplate all that was told to him. He needed to meditate on the Scriptures and consider them in the light of Jesus' death and resurrection. While it was a great relief to him to know that Rabbi Jesus was raised from the dead, somehow it had not brought to him the great joy that others were experiencing. He was a man of much thought. He was a rational man with an excellent education. He reasoned and deducted, conjectured, speculated and made his conclusions. His life was one centered on logic and the mind which did not leave much consideration for his emotions. The intellectual pursuits of his life he enjoyed but he was very constrained about expressing his feeling. He believed a rabbi of his stature should be seriously minded and conservative about his showing his emotions to anyone. That included even admitting them to himself. For him to be recognized as one of the foremost rabbis' of his nation he had long ago sacrificed that part of his life. This allowed him to excel as a man of greatest understanding and wisdom.

At Jesus' time of suffering and death he came to know the immeasurable depth of the most sorrowful emotions a person could experience. This was for him something of a first and this introduction to his emotions was a very adverse one. It was for him a baptism unto excruciating pain, suffering, death, and the great tragedy of it. Because those emotions were so very unbearable for him he suppressed them, and he emotionally fled to a safe place for himself after that day. He retreated into his intellectual mind set. He worked to reason out his experience with all that Jesus endured in the vain hopes that this would help him avoid the overwhelming feelings that were stirring his troubled soul to its greatest depth. He was certain that if that was what emotions could do to you then he had just experienced more of them then he wanted to for the entirety of his life.

As he quietly sat in his home the night had already set in and he found himself sinking into a deep depression. He was hardly prepared for this and he could not even put a name to the reason he wanted to weep. He did not understand that by turning away from his emotions they would not simply go away. He had bottled them up and they would eventually burst from within him. He reminded himself that Jesus was raised from the dead and healed of his wounds, but to his surprise this knowledge brought him no relief. Then the powers of his mind remembered the story about the serpent and he knew what he needed to do to find healing for his suppressed emotions. He needed to return to that thing that he wanted to avoid the most. He knew that he needed to remember and mediate on the image of Jesus as he hung from the cross that was burned into his memory on that Passover day. He needed to live in the remembrance of it which meant that he needed to relive it as though he was there again in those hours.

As he did this, tears welled up in his eyes as he felt his pain and he cried out in anguish. "It is not supposed to be like this! Lord Jesus save me! I am looking to you in your pain and hoping that you can help me in my pain!" As he opened up, the floodgates of the feelings that he had held back over his lifetime, his emotions opened up flooding out and overwhelming him. He grimaced in pain and grabbed at his heart as they all poured out in one deluging tidal wave. He felt very helpless as those memories chaotically swept over him. Finally, as his thoughts returned to Jesus' passion and his burial, he fell to the ground at his feet and screamed out for God to have mercy on his soul.

From his anguish Nicodemus had called out to the Lord and his pain was also being swept away. He found strength and comfort as never before from the presence of the Holy Spirit. He also felt a tremendous sense of relief, and then in joy and happiness he wept and laughed in relief. Subtlety the Lord appeared just in front of him. Nicodemus felt his presence and then saw his form from the corner of his eye. Slowly he let his vision focus on him and he did not fear. Even though the room was dimly lit by an oil lamp, as he looked at the Lord he could see him as clear as if he was lit up by the brightness of the sun. He noticed the scars made to his feet when the nail was driven into them. Not only had his long-suppressed emotions been set free but now the burden of a life lived avoiding his feeling was gone, healed, and transformed. He was miraculously able to show his emotions freely. From where he was sitting he bowed his face low to the floor and worshiped the Lord in awe and reverence.

Jesus knelt down and took him by the hand and with a little laughter in his voice he said, "My friend, rise up and let me greet you!"

Now the two men exchanged the warmest greetings with hugs and kisses to the cheeks. Nicodemus lit several lamps and brought up the light in the room and said, "What do we do now?"

Then Jesus looked at him with a particular smile on his face. Grinning widely, he lifted his arms up into the air and began to dance and sing a familiar melody which Nicodemus also knew. As he moved in a large circle around the old rabbi, he nodded his head to the rhythm of the song and motioned for Nicodemus to join in with him. For Nicodemus this was awkward at first, he had not danced since he was a teenager. So, it was with his newfound emotional freedom that he was also able to raise up his hands and he joined in dancing too. Though it was difficult for him at first given the many decades of his life he had spent living so conservatively. Now as he followed in Jesus' example, he became completely at ease with it. As Jesus continued to sing the words to this song, Nicodemus quickly joined in too.

"I will sing of the glories of the Lord forever,
for his hand has triumphed gloriously over my enemies!
His horse and rider he has thrown into the Red Sea.
The LORD is my strength and my song of salvation.

The LORD is my God and I will ever praise him.
He is the God of my fathers and I will exalt him forever.
The LORD is victorious in war,
his right hand has glorious power,
with it he crushes his enemies.
He is majestic in the beauty of his holiness.
He is powerful, preforming wonders beyond compare.
He has redeemed his people
and brought his salvation to us this day.
The heavens are your sanctuary
and the stars tell of your glory!
I will sing of the glories of the Lord forever,
I will never cease to rejoice in him!" [17]

When they were done, the two men faced each other and laughed for joy. It was more than clear that the years of emotional repression and denial in Nicodemus' life had simply vanished from him because of the Lord's doing. The two men sat on cushions and began a discussion.

Jesus spoke to him in a riddle. It was based on the question that he had posed to the spies who had come to test him as he taught in the Temple during the week of Passover.[18] "What do you think? The Messiah, whose son is he?"

Nicodemus grinned because that was a simple answer for him, "He is the son of David, for God promised to him that he would establish his descendants forever and that his throne would be for all generations."[19]

Jesus smiled back at him as he continued to ask another question about that verse which would lead to new insights

---

[17] Based on Exodus 15
[18] Matthew 22:42-46
[19] Psalm 89:3-4

for Nicodemus. "Yes! Yes, that is right! But then how is it that by the Holy Spirit, David wrote calling him Lord, 'The LORD Yahweh[20] said to God Adonai[21] sit at my righthand side until I put your enemies under your feet for a footstool.[22] So how can David call his descendant his Lord when he is one of his sons?

Nicodemus smiled with joy and laughed as he put the great powers of his mind to work on this mystery. "You are my Lord. You are David's descendant, thus his son." A moment passed and then he said, "He calls his son his Lord because he, you that is, you are both Lord and the Son of God. Though David is our greatest king and your ancestor, you are far greater than him as the Messiah and as the Son of God." Then Nicodemus waited for Jesus' answer.

"That's exactly right! Now you understand that great mystery that has been hidden from the day it was written until now."

Then the two men laughed almost hysterically as joy overflowed in their hearts. Then they settled in for a late-night discussion about the greater things found hidden in the Scriptures.

Jesus quoted a Psalm, "Incline to me your ear my people and heed my teaching, listen to the words of my mouth. For I will open my mouth to give you a parable, and I will share with you sayings from ancient of days."[23]

Nicodemus said, "Psalm seventy-eight verse one."

"Yes, and the prophet was speaking about me."

"And your many parables are unmatched."

---

[20] God's proper name in Hebrew
[21] The Hebrew word for God
[22] Psalm 110:1
[23] Based on Psalm 78:1

"I spoke to many people this way because of the condition of their hearts which were hard and because of their necks which were stiff. So that as Isaiah had said of them, 'Go to these people and say, '"keep hearing but do not come to understanding, look but do not perceive what is set before you, making their hearts dull, their ears deaf, and their eyes blind so that they will not understand and turn to be healed.'""[24]

Nicodemus nodded his head in acknowledgement of what Jesus said. He wanted to order in his mind some of the timetable of Jesus' ministry, "Why didn't you begin your ministry in Jerusalem by teaching in the Temple?"

"There are two reasons. I began to preach in Galilee to fulfill a certain prophecy." Jesus tilted his head and lifted his eyebrows. He looked at Nicodemus in this way to challenge him. He wanted him to search his own mind and come up with the text that predicted that.

Now Nicodemus and Jesus grinned again and chuckled in laughter as they waited. Nicodemus' great knowledge of the Scriptures was put work as he searched his mind. But he was not able to find a passage to answer Jesus with.

Then Jesus began to recite Isaiah, "'But there will be no gloom for her who was in anguish. In the former time he brought into contempt the land of Zebulun and the land of Naphtali…'" he grinned larger and larger as he went on until he was joined by Nicodemus who remembered the text that they both recited in unison, "…but in the latter time he has made glorious the way of the sea, the land beyond the Jordan, Galilee of the nations. The people who walked in darkness have seen a great light; those who dwelt in a land of deep darkness, on them has light shone."[25]

---

[24] Isaiah 6:9-10
[25] Isaiah 9:1-2

135

Then they both laughed heartily again.

There was a silence as Nicodemus waited to hear what Jesus' second reason for beginning his ministry in Galilee was. Then he asked, "So, what was the other reason?"

Jesus laughed, "You will find this hard to believe but it was for the simple reason that I was obeying my mother."

Nicodemus roared out in laughter and his belly shook as he said, "What?"

"That's right. My mother had been invited to a wedding in Cana of Galilee and I went with her. It was a terribly frightful thing that happened, but early on they ran out of wine for the celebration."

"Unbelievable."

"Well yeah it was. So, when my mother learned about it she came directly to me and said, 'They have run out of wine.' I knew what she was implying but I did not want to do anything about it. My time to begin my public ministry was not here. Then she gathered up the servants who were charged with pouring the wine and right there in front of me she told them, 'Do whatever he instructs you to do.' Then she crossed her arms and stared at me. What was I to do? She is my mother and it was a wedding. I knew that running out of wine at a wedding was a bad foretoken upon the marriage. If the wine ran out at their wedding you had to wonder what else might go wrong in their lives together? I worried that could be a sign of worse things that might come. It was out of obedience to my mother's wishes and for the sake of blessing their celebration that I turned six large stone jars filled with water into wine."

Jesus and Nicodemus looked at each other and broke into hysterical laughter together.

Nicodemus stopped laughing long enough to say, "You're a good son. Do you know that?"

As the two continued to laugh together Jesus nodded. Then they continued to talk until dawn and as the mornings first light came Jesus stood to his feet and vanished from his sight.

Chapter Twenty-One
Upper Room Doctrines

As the week passed the apostles had more time to consider all that they were eyewitnesses to. They took time reviewing what the Scriptures were telling them about God plan of salvation. That first week there were no arrests made by the Temple authorities or by the Roman governor. Their fears nevertheless continued to run high. More and more disciples and followers of the Lord were hearing about the Lord's victory over the grave and his glorious resurrection from the dead. They, in turn, spread the word to everyone they knew and soon all of Jerusalem knew about the resurrection of Jesus of Nazareth.

A week had passed since the day when the tomb was open by the mighty angel and Jesus had appeared to the ten of his disciples in the upper room. Throughout that week the apostles continued to meet daily in private with followers throughout the holy city. In the evenings they routinely gathered again in the upper room and continued to ponder the mystery of his risen life.

Though all of the apostles had spoken to Thomas who was not there on that first Sunday evening, he would not believe. Some said that he doubted but that was not true of him either. He doubted nothing. He affirmed and strongly that he was not going to confess that Jesus was raised from the dead. Not until he had seen the risen Lord for himself just like the other apostles. He insisted that this was necessary because the Lord had made him an apostle too.

That afternoon some of the apostles were working hard to formulate what they would teach about the salvation God provided through the death and resurrection of his Son Jesus.

Matthew reminded the apostles, "According to Moses, being hung unto death on a tree brings God's curse upon a person. [26] But the Temple authorities would not have hung him. They would have stoned Jesus to death."

Simon added, "The Roman governor has ordered that the Judean court could not practice capital punishment themselves. They had to turn those criminals sentenced to death over to him for that sentence to be carried out."

Peter said, "So, are we saying that God foresaw that the time would come when the Romans would rule in our land? Then he sent his Son to us so that his death would be by hanging on the cross so that he could become accursed under the Law?"

Matthew responded, "I have come to believe that it does seem to fit the nature of the things. The timing needed to be specific to this time of their occupation."

Simon questioned how this could be, "But the Son of God? How could he become a curse?"

There was a pause and then having pondered it Matthew said, "As God, he could not become a curse. But as a man he could."

Simon threw out another difficult question that he was struggling with. He was hesitant to even ask it because he was not sure there was an answer for it. "Jesus is the Son of God. He is God with us. How is it that death overcame him?"

Matthew thought hard about that question, it even frightened him a little. He whispered a prayer and called on God to reveal the answer to them. He was tense but then relaxed and in a moment of time as it dawned upon him, "Not as God. God cannot die. But, by being born a man and

---

[26] Deuteronomy 21:22-23, Galatians 3:13

being the Son of Man as he called himself sometimes, Jesus of Nazareth could therefore die."

Then Peter grew excited as he added, "And being both God and man he could die and be raised from the dead because God cannot stay dead."

The three of them thought reflectively about their conversation. They looked at each other for the moment with a mixture of concern and reserved affirmation over what they had formulated. They all took a little time to rethink what was just said in their minds and nodded to the others showing that they believed their statements were true and consistent with the Scriptures.

Peter raised the next question for them to ponder, "A man can only die for his own sins. It is not permissible for a child to be held accountable for his parent's sins. Neither can the parents be punished for their child's sins. That is what the Prophet Ezekiel has said.[27] So then how is it possible that our Lord has died for the sins of the world?"

Neither Matthew or Simon were anxious to try and answer that question. Instead they sat somewhat dumbfounded over it. Then John and James came over and joined in their discussion. Peter put his question forward to them and then they all sat in silence as they contemplated it.

Then John put forward this idea, "It was John the Baptist who called the Lord the 'Lamb of God who takes away the sin of the world.' So, just as a sacrificial lamb is substituted for the death of a sinner so Jesus took our sins away from us and took them upon himself as he died for us."

Peter reapplied the words of Ezekiel to the discussion, "A parent cannot be held accountable for a child's sins and

---

[27] Ezekiel 18:20

a child cannot have its parent's sin held against it. How then can Jesus be held to account for our sins?"

Matthew saw this question as being very similar to one they had just worked on. He quickly jumped in offering the same insight in his answer, "As a man he could not die for even one other man's sins. He couldn't. But, being God with us he could do the impossible and added to that as a man he could die for another's sins. Being God and a man, he could die for the sins of the world. Like John said he is the Lamb of God who takes away the sin of the world."

Peter felt a wave of revelation come over him and without a moment of hesitation he shared, "Yes, that is it. That is what Isaiah was saying. 'He was pierced for our transgressions' and 'the LORD has laid on him he iniquity of us all.'[28] So, it is just like when we have gone to the Temple to offer a lamb for our sins. We lay our hand upon that lamb and confess our sins. They are removed from us and placed upon the lamb who then dies for us because of our sins. Only in our Lord's death God has placed our sins upon his Son Jesus when he died accursed upon the cross for us! We don't need to place our hands on him like the lamb. Our sins are transferred from us and placed on him by our faith in him. We know that this was his plan because the prophet said, 'it was the will of the LORD to crush him with pain.'"[29]

Simon added a late thought on his understanding about the curse that comes from being hung. "What do you think about this? Moses wrote that anyone who is executed by hanging must not remain on the tree into the night but must be buried on the same day. That is why Jesus had to be crucified on a Friday, so that the Romans would oblige our

[28] Isaiah 53:5-6
[29] Isaiah 53:10 NRSV

customs and not leave him on the cross overnight. That would have been a great sacrilege to the Sabbath."

The four of them broke off their discussion as other apostles and followers began to arrive for their evening meal. Then they shared in fellowship with each other and broke bread according to their new practices following the Lord's resurrection.

Chapter Twenty-Two
Sharing in Our Lord's Suffering

It was Sunday evening, the second Sunday after the Lord's resurrection. When the night began the doors to the house were shut tightly and locked. Although the disciples had been discussing Jesus' death and resurrection for a week, the Apostle Thomas remained closed off to believing that Jesus had been raised from the dead. He neither confessed that it was true or denied that it was possible. He maintained that he needed to see Jesus for himself so that in his apostolic authority he would be able to say that he had seen the risen Lord just like all the rest of all the other apostles.

It was not long into the night when in the heart of their discussions that Jesus suddenly appeared in the middle of the room. As he was seen, the great hall was filled with a special ambiance. It was heavenly and reverent. There was a certain divine sense of peace that radiated out from him to everyone in the room. The apostles and all those with them were in awe and all the conversations in the room fell silent.

Jesus turned about to show everyone that it was him and he raised his nail scared hands for them all to see. As he faced each person he looked directly into their eyes as he said, "Shalom. My peace be upon each of you."

All of the apostles and the others warmly said in return, "And peace be upon you as well."

Then Jesus looked directly at Thomas who was perhaps the most amazed of everyone in the room. Then the Lord smiled with delight in his eyes because he knew that he was going to be bringing this apostle to faith, faith in his resurrection and renewed faith in him. Thomas smiled gleefully as he saw his risen Master and he bowed his head before him.

Jesus called his name, "Thomas" as he walked directly to him and their smiles only grew larger.

Jesus said to him, "Remember what I have taught you. Ask and it will be given to you. Seek and you will find. Knock and it will be opened to you. For everyone who asks receives, and the one who seeks finds, and to the one who knocks it will be opened.[30] Thomas, no longer be without faith but believe in me and in my resurrection from the dead."

Thomas eagerly nodded and showed his newly born faith.

Then Jesus looked around at all the apostles and he waved his hands motioning to them that they should gather in closely and look on. He instructed Thomas, "Look at the wounds that I suffered. See my hands, and my feet, and my side."

Thomas looked at them all. Jesus showed him his hands so that he could observe for himself the scars on the palms of both of his hands. He turned them over and Thomas carefully looked at the other side as well.

Then Jesus said, "Now take my hand into yours and examine my wounds more closely this time." Though Jesus's wounds were healed and there were scars there somehow his wounds were freshly open again though they did not bleed. Jesus took Thomas' right hand and told him, "Place your finger inside my wounded hand and see that it is real."

Although Thomas was reluctant to do this, and he began to shy away from doing it, Jesus gently guided him.

---

[30] Matthew 7:7-8

He said, "My Master, I do not want to bring you pain by doing this to you."

But Jesus reassured him, "You won't hurt me by doing this. There is no more pain there. Now watch and see. I will have no pain as you do this."

Then Thomas consented, and Jesus guided his finger directly into his wounded hand so that he could see and examine it thoroughly. Thomas was cautious at first and as his finger entered the wound he watched Jesus' face for fear of hurting him. But Jesus show no sign of pain as he did this. Then Thomas became giddy with joy and his finger reached through Jesus' hand and the tip of his finger came out the other side.

After this examination of his hand, Jesus pulled his robe to the side and revealed to Thomas his wounded side. This was located right next to his heart. Again, Jesus guided his hand to his side. Thomas became reluctant about examining this wound directly especially given the large size of his chest wound. Jesus gently persuaded him to go ahead. He took Thomas' hand and said, "Just as the soldier pierced my side with his spear to assure that I was dead, now you must examine my wound to see that it is me and that I am alive and have overcome death."

The wound was closed over with a scar but as Jesus guided Thomas' hand to it somehow it was mysteriously opened to him. There was no bleeding and Jesus was not in pain. As he tenderly guided his hand into the wound, Thomas held his breath for fear of what might happen. But Jesus' calm and assuring presence helped him to overcome his fear and reluctance. As Thomas felt his wound, he first noticed the warmth of Jesus' body. Then as his hand entered the holy wound he felt the rhythm from the rise and fall of his chest as he took each breath. As his hand went deeper into his wounded side he felt the exchange of air passing through as it entered and exited his lungs. Finally, he reached in far enough and he could feel the gentle beating of his heart. Then Jesus looked around to ensure everyone there came in close enough to be a witness to this unique miracle. The many people in the room looked on and marveled awestruck at what they saw.

There was also a certain mystery that came upon everyone there. The Holy Spirit touched them personally and they were able to sense the wonderful experience that Thomas was having. Though they did not all see it up close, they all were able to see from wherever they were with rich incredible detail what was happening. Thomas' experience was also imparted to the others as the Holy Spirit moved among them all. They could not actually feel the warmth of the Lord's body or the rising and falling of his chest as he breathed nor the beating of his heart as Thomas did. Even still, they did have a certain special inner sensation of it. The fellowship of the moment in the Holy Spirit was profound upon them. More than words could possibly describe. They were truly enraptured by the experience and there came upon them the sense that they were also joined to and one with the body of Christ their Lord.

Thomas' appearance was changed to the point of being transformed by his examination of the wounds. Then as he stepped back he appeared to be almost angelic in his appearance.

Jesus said to him in the kindest way, "There Thomas. Believe in me again as you believed in me before. Do not be uncertain about my resurrection any longer."

Then Thomas fell to his knees and lifted up his hands in worship and declared to him, "Master Jesus, you are my Lord and my God!"

"Is it because you have seen me that you believe? How blessed you are but how much more blessed are the ones who will not see me but believe because of your testimony about me."

Once Jesus said this he turned to view everyone again and then there were flashes of great light and waves of reverberating power that spread out across the room and touched everyone. Then the Lord vanished from their sight. All the members of the apostles and all the members of believers that had gathered in the room dared not move. They were so held by their new experience that there was a feeling of sacred fellowship and communion in the Holy Spirit among them. It was as if they all somehow had touched the Lord's wounds for themselves just as Thomas had. There was a great sense of quietude that they all shared in. It was a peaceful and restful mood that is rarely known among men.

Minutes passed before the apostles began to move about again. They regathered within the room and reclined at the dining table on the couches and began to talk about their common experience. Thomas, who was also called Didymus because he had a younger twin brother named Samuel spoke first, "I have never felt so close to anyone before, not even my own brother. I have never felt the presence of God so strongly as I did then."

Then the apostles looked at each other to see what the others might say. They all seemed to be saying the same thing as Thomas. That this was also how they felt.

"When I stepped back and saw him there, it was as though a revelation from heaven passed through the Lord and encircled me inside and out. It was his Holy Spirit speaking to my spirit and somehow I knew, in my heart of hearts I just knew it. Not only that this is the Lord but that he is indeed risen from the dead. But I knew that I had touched the very heart of God when I touched Jesus' heart."

Now all of the other apostles were also greatly touched to hear Thomas share what this wonderful and intimate experience was like for him. Some had tears running down their faces and others held their hearts because the depth of this experience was so healing to them. Their wounds from over a lifetime were mysteriously healed in this experience. Their grief and bereavement over their Master's suffering and death was also comforted, and they came into a new understanding of it. It was the kind of experience that they could not explain with simple words. It was too profound for that. Their experience was a spiritual one that was a divine revelation filled with the feelings of the mystery that came over them.

Chapter Twenty-Three
Nicodemus and Mary

Early in Jesus' ministry people were wondering if he could be the long-awaited Messiah. But there were those who were opposed to the idea and they spoke against it. This was because they believed the Messiah must be from Bethlehem, the town of David.[31] Nicodemus, the great rabbi of their day, even challenged the religious authorities about their hasty conclusion and suggested they conduct a more thorough inquiry. But the authorities would not hear of it even at the urging of Rabbi Nicodemus. They told him that the Scriptures do not foretell of a prophet arising from Galilee of all places. Then they insulted him and said he was from Galilee. The Judean's felt that they were better than the others of their nation who were from Galilee in the north. The had developed a sense of elitism because their province was the home of Jerusalem and the Temple. They mockingly called the Provence of Galilee, *Galilee of the gentiles*.[32]

There was a man sent from God, John the Baptist, who did identify Jesus as the Messiah. John spoke clearly about Jesus saying that he was the Lamb of God who would take away the sin of the world.[33] He also said that Jesus was the Son of God because it had been revealed to him by God.[34]

It was the role of the Great Sanhedrin court in Jerusalem to have investigated the life of Jesus of Nazareth when he presented himself in the holy city. It was their job to judge if he was the Messiah or not. They failed in this

---

[31] Micah 5:2
[32] John 4:40-53
[33] John 1:29
[34] John 1:33-34

calling that they had been charged with. They were there to examine him about his teachings to ensure that everything he said was true and consistent with the Prophets, the Writings, and most of all with Moses. The court members needed to see if what was foretold of the Messiah was true in his life. Their examinations were always short lived and prejudiced by their own bigotry against Galileans. They had hoped to trick him into saying something that would discredit himself or something against the laws of the Romans. In their final examination of his life they failed to see that they convicted him of the one crime that he of all the people of the earth could never have possibly been guilty of. They convicted him of blasphemy for claiming to be the Son of God which he was.

There were certain concerns such as the one the religious authorities raised saying that the Scriptures did not foretell of a prophet or the Messiah coming from Galilee. It was in those early days following Jesus' resurrection that Nicodemus visited frequently with the apostles. He wished to know the whole truth, everything there was to know regarding the life of Jesus of Nazareth. He wanted to resolve the lingering concerns that were floating around among the people. Therefore, he issued an invitation to Mary and the Apostle John to come to his home to discuss some of those matters with him.

Nicodemus' home was a modest one for a man of such prominence in Jerusalem. But then he was not corrupted by the greed that had infiltrated most of the other religious leaders who took advantage of their positions and accumulated great wealth and property.

When Mary and John arrived, he was there to meet them at the entrance. "Welcome my guests, welcome!" He was joyously excited to have them come into his home. A member of his household washed their feet and then they all went into his living room and sat on cushions. One servant who was his cook brought in fresh fruit and bread for them to eat and another poured fresh water flavored with slices of fruit for them to drink.

John came along with Mary simply to accompany her and planned to listen to the conversation most rather than be a part of it. He wanted to learn what he could about his Master's life but did not want to distract from the other two's interactions.

The rabbi spoke to Mary, "I am so glad that you have come. I have longed to meet with you and hear you talk more about the life of your son. You can imagine how eager I am to learn more about him and if possible, I would like to find more prophecies in the Scriptures about his life and work."

Mary politely smiled and calmly said, "I know many things of significance, but they are significant to me as his mother. I don't know that I can offer you very much that you will find to be of value to your interests."

Nicodemus nodded in agreement with her and then said, "Yes, but I would love to know what treasures you have stored up in your heart as well Mary. The Holy Scriptures are such that they reveal a great many secrets if you know what you're looking for. It is when you talk things through that these connections to the Word of God can be made."

"Where do I begin? What would you like to hear about first?"

"Why don't you begin with the days when you were first carrying him."

"I was just a young girl and an angel appeared to me. I was scared to death by his presence. But he said to me that

I did not need to be frightened because I had found favor before the Lord our God. I was uncertain why he was there talking to me of all people. He told me that his name was Gabriel and he explained that I would conceive and have a son. I was just a young woman then and I had not been with a man though I was betrothed to Joseph of Nazareth. I was very puzzled by his visit and all that he said to me. I asked him, 'how could this possibly happen?' He went on, 'the Holy Spirit would come and overshadow me.' He told me therefore my child would be holy, he would be the Son of God, and that I was to name him Jesus. Gabriel promised that our God would give to my son the throne of our great King David who is my ancestor."

Nicodemus listened intensely as she spoke. He did not want to miss a single word or turn away from seeing how she relived the memory of every word that she shared.

"Rabbi, sometimes men bring paper and write down notes, or have their scribes record what is said. But you are not writing anything down."

"No. I have been blessed with a bright mind. I remember things very well. Typically, I remember them word for word. It is a gift from God."

Mary nodded.

Now as she finished that part of her story Nicodemus pondered her words over in his mind and then recalled, "The ancient prophet Isaiah had written a prophecy that I believe is about you. His scroll says, 'Therefore the Lord himself shall give you a sign; Behold, a virgin shall conceive, and bear a son, and shall call his name Immanuel."[35]

---

[35] Isaiah 7:14 KJV

Mary and John were both surprised at how the rabbi was able to just that simply and quickly make the connection and quote verbatim the words of Isaiah.

Mary asked him, "Do you know the Holy Scriptures this well?"

"I am well read in them."

Now Mary's eyes grew excited to hear such a wonderful thing and she was very delighted with what the rabbi shed light on.

Nicodemus was a brilliant mind and it was very busy as he searched his memories for other references in the Scriptures that were fulfilled in what Mary shared about her son. Again, he shared, "The second Psalm also comes into my mind, which reads, 'I will declare the decree: the LORD has said to me, you are my Son; this day have I begotten thee.'"[36]

Mary twisted from side to side a little in her excitement, "How exciting to know these things. I wished I had known them sooner, but it is more than enough to know them now. There must be more prophecies. Don't you think so?"

"I certainly expect there to be more. Why don't you go on with your story?"

"I was engaged to be married to Joseph. He was a man full of faith and a servant of God. When he learned that I was expecting a child he had planned to quietly divorce me, thinking I had been unfaithful to him in our betrothal. But God intervened, and he took me as his wife after I delivered the child. Oh, the birth of my son! That was something. That year Emperor Augustus ordered that a census be taken of everyone in the empire. We had to travel from Nazareth to Joseph's family's hometown to be registered. That was very difficult. I was well into the final month of carrying

---

[36] Psalm 2:7 Modified from the KJV

my child. We had to go all the way to Bethlehem. Not Bethlehem in Zebulun though. That would have been easy. It was only two hours from Nazareth. No, because of the emperor I had to travel five days to Bethlehem of Judea. As soon as we arrived I went into labor. It was awful. That little town was packed to overflowing with all of the people who were ordered to be there for the census. There was no room for us anywhere and the people there felt terrible about it. All they could do was rush me to a stable where I could lay down and give birth to my baby. Their midwives were summoned but they did not arrive in time." Mary laughed making light of her experience now even though it was a very harrowing experience for her back then.

Nicodemus joined in laughing with her but for his own reasons. He was joyous because as she continued to tell her story he found another prophecy that revealed whose family line the Messiah would be descended through. "Mary, the Prophet Micah foresaw this. He wrote that your son would be of the clan of that little village. He wrote: 'But you, Bethlehem Ephrathah, though you are small among the clans of Judah, out of you will come for me one who will be ruler over Israel, whose origins are from of old, from ancient times.'[37] He went on and explained, "The religious leadership from the Temple did not believe in your son because they said there were no prophecies about the Messiah coming from Galilee. They wrongly assumed that he was born in Nazareth. But I see now by your words that he was actually born in Bethlehem of Judah. And the prophet also spoke by the Spirit and specified which Bethlehem. It was not the larger and better-known Bethlehem of Zebulun, but the smaller Bethlehem of Judah. Isn't that amazing?"

---

[37] Micah 5:2

Mary held her hands to her face in such joy that she could not contain, "Oh, the mercies of the Lord never cease do they?" Having paused to relish in the moment she went on, "Well after a few days in Bethlehem magi arrived and gave great homage to my child. They worshiped him and gave him gifts: of frankincense, gold, and myrrh. But I am still wondering how they knew that my Son would be born a King? And how did they know to come?"

Nicodemus knew the answer, "It was because of Daniel that they knew about this. When our people were in captivity in Babylon he shared the hope of Israel with many people there. The magi were around then. They were a society of scholars and sages who from that time on also waited for the coming of the Messiah."

Mary continued on in her story, "But then our newly blessed and happy lives were filled with terror. An angel of the LORD came to my husband by night and warned us to flee to Egypt because the Governor Herod the Great was going to search for my son. He wanted to murder him because he saw him as a rival to his throne. We left immediately while it was still dark and told no one where we were going. We had to leave the country, so we fled to a Jewish settlement in Egypt where we could live quietly. We told no one in those days that we had been in Bethlehem or that Joseph's family lived there either. The magi's gift of gold was what we survived on while we lived there. My son wasn't yet two years old when we heard the news of Herod's death. This was a great relief to us for we knew that he would have gone to any length necessary to take the life of my son if he could only find him. We learned that after his death they divided up his territory and his sons then ruled over them. We lived in the fear that one of the governor's sons might also want to carry out his murderous plan. So, then we returned to Nazareth and told no one about any of this for fear that this information could somehow be passed on to one of his sons."

Nicodemus already knew of another prophecy that was fulfilled in Jesus' young life as Mary told him these things. "Hosea did rightly say, 'When Israel was a child, I loved him, and out of Egypt I called my son.'"[38]

Mary sighed as she remembered the history of her ancestors, "Our people were forced into slavery in Egypt. They suffered much under the Pharaoh. He had our baby boys murdered there. He was a horrible tyrant.

Nicodemus nodded knowingly, "That would be Ahmose the First.[39]" The rabbi gave this more thought and then he shared, "Herod the Great was much the same as that pharaoh when he learned of your son's birth. Jesus was born a descendant of David and born to be King of the Jews. Herod made his plans to murder him because he saw your son as a rival to his throne.[40] And when he couldn't find him he murdered all the children near to your son's age in Bethlehem."

Tears came to eyes of them all as they mourned for the loss of those children. Mary felt an inexpressible emotion, that her son survived when so many other women's sons did not.

Nicodemus saw by her expression how deeply distraught she was about this and he comforted her saying, "Mary, that is how Satan works against God's people. You are not to blame for any of it."

Mary nodded and wiped away her tears.

---

[38] Hosea 11:1
[39] (1550-1525 BC)
[40] Matthew 2:18

Neither spoke for a short while and then Mary hesitantly asked him, "Those religious authorities said once that there are no prophecies about a prophet arising out of Galilee. What does that mean for my son?"

The rabbi nodded and laughed. "Don't let them worry you. Most of them are blind to the significance of the Scriptures. They know them, but their many biases and prejudices keep them from perceiving the truth of what has been written for our benefit."

Mary simply nodded and wondered, worry-full of what the answer to her lingering question might be.

Nicodemus understood that Mary still hoped for an answer to put her mind at rest. "They said that no prophet arises out of Galilee. But the scroll of Isaiah says otherwise: 'Nevertheless, there will be no more gloom for those who were in distress. In the past he humbled the land of Zebulun and the land of Naphtali, but in the future he will honor Galilee of the nations, by the Way of the Sea, beyond the Jordan, the people walking in darkness have seen a great light; on those living in the land of deep darkness a light has dawned.'"[41]

Now Mary breathed a sigh of relief and felt like she was supported in her concern that was put to rest by what she had learned from the rabbi.

"Mary, the Holy Scriptures also tell many times about a ruler arising out of Nazareth."

Mary's heart took a certain delight when she heard that, and she waited for the rabbi to go on.

"Nazareth gets its name from our Hebrew word Netzer, meaning a branch or a shoot from a tree."

Mary couldn't wait to hear more, "Yes, go on."

---

[41] Isaiah 9:1-2

"There is a reference from Jeremiah about it but the one I love best is from Zechariah, 'Tell him this is what he LORD Almighty says; 'Here is the man whose name is the Branch, and he will branch out from his place and build the temple of the LORD. It is he who will build the temple of the LORD, and he will be clothed with majesty and will sit and rule on his throne. And he will be a priest on his throne.'"[42]

"What about the other prophet, Jeremiah, rabbi?"

"Well, let me recall Jeremiah: 'The days are coming,' declares the LORD, 'when I will raise up for David a righteous Branch, a King who will reign wisely and do what is just and right in the land. In his days Judah will be saved and Israel will live in safety. This is the name by which he will be called: The LORD Our Righteous Savior.'"[43]

Their time went by quickly and both Nicodemus and Mary were thrilled with what they had learned from each other during the visit. Then as Mary and John prepared to go the old rabbi lifted his hands and blessed them,

> "The Lord bless you and keep you;
> the Lord make his face shine on you
> and be gracious to you;
> the Lord turn his face toward
> you and give you peace."[44]

---

[42] Zechariah 6:12-13
[43] Jeremiah 23:5-6
[44] Numbers 6:24-26

Chapter Twenty-Four
The Disciples of John the Baptist

When Jesus first began his ministry some of John the Baptists disciples left him to follow the Lord. Andrew, Simon Peter's brother, was among those. Later, when John the Baptist was decapitated by Herod the Tetarch many, but not all of his followers, then followed Jesus. Those who did not follow Jesus continued to live life as John had taught them.

John's father served in the Temple as a priest. During his service there an angel named Gabriel appeared to him and announced that he and his wife would have a son. This child was born to serve the Lord the angel told him. He was to take the vows of a Nazarite. This meant that he would be living a very devout and stringent life of ministry to the LORD. He would eat a very strict diet, one that excluded consuming anything from a grape vine in any form. This lifestyle he was called to practice was to begin on the day of his birth. It was also forbidden of him to cut his hair and in his infancy he was dedicated as Holy to the LORD. His lifestyle was one of great denial, great devotion, and great service to the LORD their God.[45]

When he was brought into this world both his parents were well advanced in years. They were both descendants of Moses' brother Aaron. This made his father eligible to serve in the Temple as a priest according to the order of Abijah.[46] This made John eligible to serve as a priest in the Temple also. But God had called him into a very different ministry. He served as the forerunner of the Messiah who announced his coming. Then as Jesus began his public

---

[45] Numbers 6
[46] Luke 1:15

ministry he authenticated him when he announced that this man from Nazareth was the Lamb of God who would take away the sins of the world.[47]

When word of Jesus' arrest and death reached John the Baptist's followers they were filled with sorrow and fear. They too had expected that he would rise to power and reestablish the ancient Kingdom of his ancestor David. That was a time of golden years for their nation. With Jesus' death many of John's followers went into hiding as they worried that the authorities would also seek to arrest and put to death not only the Lord's disciples but them as well. Then when the word of the Lord's resurrection came to John's remaining followers they sent some of their leaders in secret to find Andrew and the other apostles to speak with them.

Samuel and Elias came into the city of Jerusalem by mixing in with a large crowd that had congested the city gate. Their hair and beards were long and unkept therefore they stood out among the others around them. Long before they neared the city they had braided their hair and tucked the length of it into the back of their tunics and they concealed the length of their beards also by tucking them inside of the front of their tunics. They avoided all unnecessary contact with everyone there. As they passed by a marketplace, merchants called out to them trying to entice them to purchase their goods. Other sellers came and stood directly in front of the two hoping they would make a purchase. But the two men blazed through there ignoring all of the distractions that were placed in front of them. Their lifestyle called for them to lead simple lives and not to be tied down or bound to unnecessary worldly attachments.

---

[47] John 1:29

These two devout men were on a mission but they did not know how they would find any of Jesus' followers. They hoped that they might see some of them at the Temple where Jesus had frequently taught when he was in Jerusalem. They felt it would be especially fortunate that if by God's providence they might see some of John's former disciples who had left their company to follow Jesus. And so, as they were outside the Temple searching the crowds that they recognized Andrew as he was leaving the Temple after morning worship. Along with him was Philip and some other men who were followers of Jesus. They approached Andrew and stood beside him before they called out his name for fear of the Temple authorities.

Elias spoke very quietly and directly to the apostle not wanting anyone to overhear them, "Andrew of Bethsaida we mean to talk with you."

"Elias? And who is this with you?" He peered around to see that it was Samuel. He knew both of these men very well at one time several years ago.

Samuel cautioned him, "We don't believe it is safe for us in the city, but we must talk with you. Will you meet with us later, outside the city?"

Andrew understood their fears very well. Over the past almost two weeks he had been living in the same fear. When no one else among the Lord's followers were arrested some of them began to resume their activities more freely in the city.

The followers of John the Baptist were very zealous for their cause and they had become even more devout following his death. They were something of outcasts for their practices. He understood their need for secrecy and great precautions. He did nothing to bring undo attention upon any of them and said, "Here walk with us. These are followers of my Master. You may trust them." They all walked together and turned down another street. They walked quite a ways until they were not mixed in with the crowd. Once they were more alone they felt like they would not be overheard.

Andrew was glad to see his old friends and he was also anxious to share with them the news of his Lord's resurrection. He imagined that was why John's disciples were there to visit with him. "There is a place not far from here where many of the apostles have been staying. We can meet there if you wish. It is a safe place for us to gather. We have been meeting there daily to discuss all that has happened and what is still taking place."

Samuel looked at Elias and he gave him a slight nod to approve this plan. Then Samuel quietly said, "We will go there with you."

Nothing more was said on the way to Zechariah's home. They were men of the country and both lived the life of a Nazarite. They were not accustomed to the well-furnished and large home that they had been welcomed into. As was the practice in providing hospitality, the kitchen was alerted to these guests but then Philip also sent word to them about what food to bring and place before them, water rather than wine, along with simple flat bread and figs only. Then they were taken to the upper room where Matthew and Simon were found. The food was served and they shared in fellowship together, breaking bread and drinking the water.

Elias spoke first, "We have heard many concerning reports from pilgrims journeying north after celebrating Passover. Some have said that Jesus was crucified by Governor Pontius Pilate just as our master John was beheaded by Herod the governor in Galilee."

162

Both Elias and Samuel were very emotionally reserved as has been their natural temperance. In addition to that they were exceptionally somber as they sat. They both wondered about the apostles and the other follower's cheerfulness. It did not seem to be consistent with people who had just lost their leader. Yet in their conservative lifestyle they did not question any of them about it.

Philip answered Elias, "Yes, this is true. He was crucified on the day of the Passover."

He would have gone on to share more of the story, but Elias spoke up and with all seriousness said, "Now other pilgrims are saying amongst themselves that your Master has been raised from the dead."

Philip quickly and eagerly said, "Yes, this is true too and it is wonderful!"

Samuel interrupted, neither he or Elias were much for the slower pace of a social conversation given their lifestyle. "That is a grand claim you are making. We had hoped that Jesus was the Messiah. But his fate is the same as John's. How can anyone believe that the great resurrection of the dead has already come? It has not been the last day that the prophets had foretold has it? And if he is raised why aren't we meeting with him here too?"

Now the rustic manners of the two were wanting. They were not accustomed to interacting with others outside of their restrictive community. They were themselves oftentimes enduring vows of silence as they pursued their spiritual disciplines. Among their own members their words were few and to the point. This way of theirs Philip understood as he had even practiced this lifestyle himself once before. He understood that their manners could be somewhat offensive but were not intended as such and he was able to extend to them a measure of understanding for their lack of social graces.

Philip offered to them, "Here, I am sure we have answers for many of your questions. But, we have found that rather than simply share the short version of his story that it is better if we share the experience of it. This way you can see the context it is set in too. There is much more that is understood this way."

The two disciples of John looked to each other and seemed to come to some agreement on it. However, it was clear that while they would listen to everyone's story they did not appreciate having to indulge in this extravagance of what they felt were unnecessary details.

Andrew was going to call on Mary Magdala to share first. But he struggled in his mind. He knew the two men would be resistant to hearing the testimony of a woman. Yet in light of this he believed that Mary should still go first. Just as the disciples had been reproved for not believing their testimony so also John's disciples needed to struggle through their prejudices over the role of a woman and come to a transforming faith in the resurrection too.

Mary Magdala told them her story beginning with their preparations on Saturday night when they mixed spices to bring to the tomb. She shared about the soldiers and the imperial seals, of the mighty angel, and the three heavenly men who told the women that Jesus was raised from the dead.

The two men were not thrilled with having a woman telling them these things. They sat quietly looking very skeptical in their impatience with her. They truly wanted to know the truth and therefore they listened closely to every detail.

Mary took no offense over their distrustful looks and continued on excitedly anyway. She told them about weeping at the tomb and speaking to the gardener. It was when she arrived at the part when Jesus spoke her name that Elias' and Samuel's hardened exteriors began to noticeably soften. Then the two looked quisitively at Philip to see if he was approving of what the woman was saying. As he saw them look his way he nodded approvingly for them to see.

Then Philip shared with the two men about that first Sunday when the ten apostles were present in the upper room. He told them in simple but certain terms that when they had gathered they debated if the reports that the women had made were true. He shared about the two men from Emmaus who came to them and reported having seen the Lord. It was following their arrival in the upper room that Jesus had appeared to them alive again raised from the dead. He shared that the Lord had simply appeared out of nowhere, stood in the midst of them and showed everyone his many wounds on his hands, his feet and his side.

The two men listened to him, to his every word but said nothing. They looked around at all the others in the room to see how they were responding to this report of Jesus appearing to the apostles. Their minds and hearts were opening, though slowly, to the reports that they were hearing.

Samuel pushed back from the table they were all gathered and said. "Okay, I am certain that you believe, but I must know more. The Scriptures tell us the truth. We believe that by them we understand that the Messiah has come to us. We believed that he was Jesus of Nazareth. But, we believed that he was coming to restore the Kingdom of David and reign again in power and might.

How is this now fulfilled in Jesus of Nazareth who, though dead, is now reportedly alive? Where do the Scriptures say that he was to be rejected at the Temple, made to suffer and then executed?"

Then Matthew Levi took a turn in sharing with the two men. "You are right. If the Scriptures do not support this then we have to question everything."

The two men somberly nodded.

"Let me share with you from the words of Isaiah." Matthew knew that the disciples of the Baptist were well versed in this scroll and valued it greatly. "Isaiah foresaw by the Spirit that the Messiah would suffer and die. Matthew began to recite from the prophet, "Remember his words: 'Who has believed what he has heard from us? And to whom has the arm of the Lord been revealed? For he grew up before him like a young plant, and like a root out of dry ground; he had no form or majesty that we should look at him, and no beauty that we should desire him.'"

In their strict devotion they had memorized entire sections of the scroll of Isaiah. Now they too joined in with Matthew and recited the text with him, "'He was despised and rejected by men, a man of sorrows and acquainted with grief; and as one from whom men hide their faces he was despised, and we esteemed him not. Surely he has borne our griefs and carried our sorrows; yet we esteemed him stricken, smitten by God, and afflicted. But he was pierced for our transgressions; he was crushed for our iniquities; upon him was the chastisement that brought us peace, and with his wounds we are healed. All we like sheep have gone astray; we have turned—every one—to his own way; and the Lord has laid on him the iniquity of us all. He was oppressed, and he was afflicted, yet he opened not his mouth; like a lamb that is led to the slaughter, and like a sheep that before its shearers is silent, so he opened not his mouth. By oppression and judgment he was taken away; and as for his generation, who considered that he was cut off out of the land of the living, stricken for the transgression of my people? And they made his grave with the wicked and with a rich man in his death, although he had done no violence, and there was no deceit in his mouth. Yet it was the will of the Lord to crush him; he has put him to grief; when his soul makes an offering for guilt, he shall see his offspring; he shall prolong his days; the will of the Lord shall prosper in his hand. Out of the anguish of his soul he shall see and be satisfied; by his knowledge shall the righteous one, my servant, make many to be accounted righteous, and he shall bear their iniquities. Therefore I will divide him a portion with the many, and he shall divide the spoil with the strong, because he poured out his soul to death and was numbered with the transgressors; yet he bore the sin of many, and makes intercession for the transgressors.'"[48]

As they spoke aloud the words of the prophet their reservations about God's intention and plan for salvation by placing the sins of the world on to Jesus melted away. It was their own leader John who had told them that Jesus was the Lamb of God which takes away the sin of the world.[49] But, they had not doubted that he was dead and now they understood God's purpose in his death.

Samuel told the others, "Now we see how in his death that he has set us free from sin and cleansed us. But, this says nothing about this claim of him being resurrected. We do believe in the resurrection of the dead, but we hold that this will only happen at the end of the ages. So how could it

---

[48] Isaiah 53
[49] John 1:29

be that he alone is raised from the dead in this way and at this time?"

Simon now shared with them a few of the prophecies about Jesus' resurrection. "While there are many prophecies about the general resurrection of the dead, we all need to be convinced by the prophecies that are specifically about the Messiah being raised from the dead. On this point I think we are all agreed?"

Elias and Samuel nodded.

Simon went on, "Remember from the scroll of Hosea these very words, 'Come, let us return to the Lord; for he has torn us, that he may heal us; he has struck us down, and he will bind us up. After two days he will revive us; on the third day he will raise us up, that we may live before him.'[50] This not only tells us that it is the LORD who has done this, but that after two days of light, he would revive the Messiah and on the third day, Sunday, he would be raised to life again."

Now the two men nodded but said nothing as they continued to reservedly ponder in silence all that was being told to them.

Simon continue on, "It was David speaking by the Spirit of God who spoke in the Psalms, 'Therefore, my heart is glad, and my whole being rejoices; my flesh also dwells secure. For you will not abandon my soul to Sheol, or let your holy one see corruption.'[51] This tells us that Jesus was fully assured that he could entrust his life into the Father's hands even in his death. Therefore, Jesus was raised from the dead before his body underwent decay."

As Simon looked at the two men for a response, they gave him no indication that they were either convinced of

---

[50] Hosea 6:1-2
[51] Psalm 16:9-10

these things or if they were still questioning their legitimacy. He shared with them one more prophecy that he knew hoping they would be very receptive to it because it was one they had just considered from Isaiah, "Brothers in faith, reconsider what Isaiah said when he proclaimed of the sufferings of the Messiah, 'Yet it was the will of the Lord to crush him; he has put him to grief; when his soul makes an offering for guilt,'"

Now as he came to this next verse the two men perked up and took notice, joining in reciting it with Simon. "'He shall see his offspring; he shall prolong his days; the will of the Lord shall prosper in his hand.'"[52]

These two stone faced men who had sat with so much skepticism that it was seeping out of their pores now had a change in their thinking. And not only did their thinking come around but their lives were being transformed. Their highly conservative ways which lacked much in the way of emotional expression now fell from their countenances.

Samuel looked at Elias and referred to the words of Isaiah saying, "Truly, he is a God who hides himself."[53]

The two men were entirely out of character as they stood to their feet and began to sing in unison with their hands raised up in praise to the LORD.

"'Seek the LORD while he may be found;
call upon him while he is near;
let the wicked forsake his way,
and the unrighteous man his thoughts;
let him return to the LORD, that he may
have compassion on him, and to our God,

---

[52] Isaiah 53:10
[53] Isaiah 45:15

for he will abundantly pardon.
"For you shall go out in joy
and be led forth in peace;
the mountains and the hills before you
shall break forth into singing,
and all the trees of the field
shall clap their hands.'"54

Now as their excitement began to settle down they looked around the room and realized they were not quite in step with the overall mood of the others who were now the more reserved ones. They expected to feel embarrassed because this kind of behavior was far from the ultraconservative norm that they lived by. But they no longer cared if what the others might have thought of them because they were feeling so very wonderful about what they now believed for themselves.

As they returned to sitting Elias spoke out, "How could we have known? We should have known that we could not simply have known by our own reason and effort. As God has said of himself, 'For my thoughts are not your thoughts, neither are your ways my ways, declares the LORD. For as the heavens are higher than the earth, so are my ways higher than your ways and my thoughts than your thoughts. For as the rain and the snow come down from heaven and do not return there but water the earth, making it bring forth and sprout, giving seed to the sower and bread to the eater, so shall my word be that goes out from my mouth; it shall not return to me empty, but it shall accomplish that which I purpose, and shall succeed in the thing for which I sent it.'"55

---

54 Isaiah 55:6-7, 12
55 Isaiah 55:8-11

Elias spoke to the apostles and other followers, "We need to return to our community and bring them this wonderful news about our Lord's redeeming death and resurrection. They are anxiously waiting for us and they need to learn everything that you have shared with us."

Samuel added, "There will be others from among us that will want to come and learn from you about the Lord's life. Shall we send them here to find you?"

Andrew answered, "Yes, send them here to find us. The master of this house is Zechariah and he is a gracious host to all the believers. He will be glad to offer you his hospitality and lodging. If we are not here, do not be put off. He will put you in touch with other believers who will accept you into their fellowship."

Then the apostles and other believers walked with the two men to the city gates and bid them God's speed and they left for their community of disciples.

Chapter Twenty-Five
Prophetic Review

It was later in that second week after his resurrection that Jesus again appeared to the apostles in the upper room. It was shortly after their evening meal and, as was becoming their habit, they were going to begin a discussion about all that had been going on. As before, the Lord appeared in the midst of them. He was dressed in a pure white linen robe that was far finer and brighter than what any of the looms of the earth could weave. He walked among them so they could all see his face, so they could be certain that it was truly him. His face was relaxed and calm. His eyes were sincere, and his presence was a calming one.

He greeted them saying, "May the peace of our God be with you all."

The apostles and all those with them returned the Lord's greeting saying, "And also with you."

Then they gathered around the table and Jesus began to teach them.

Jesus began to instruct them about Moses, the Prophets, and the Writings which foretold of his life, death, and resurrection. "

The Lord stood before the apostles and raised his hands majestically as he looked to his right and then to his left as he gathered in everyone's attention. As he began sharing about the prophecies concerning his life and all that had happened, his eyes grew bright and they revealed the depth of his knowledge. The apostles could see that his wisdom was the wisdom of the ages from before the beginning of creation. And his face was transformed as he began, growing young in appearance but mature by its heavenly nature. The room became silent and all the people settled in to hear his every word with all solemnity.

The apostles and everyone else in the room fell into great awe and he hadn't even spoken a word yet. The Holy Spirit moved among them and they could feel the wonderful sensation of being in God's presence. They all took off their head wraps revealing their kippahs and some of them prayed silently offering praise and thanksgiving to the Holy One.

"I know that you have all struggled to the greatest depths wondering in anguish how I could go from having the blessing of God in my life, performing all miracles, healings, and raising the dead, to being crucified. I know that you do not yet understand why I was triumphantly welcomed into Jerusalem on the first day of that week and then put to death on Passover. But the Scriptures have foretold of these events and circumstances. It was for the very reason that I was born, so that I might die. It was Moses and the prophets who foretold that I would be rejected by the Temple leaders, suffer and die for the forgiveness of sin, and be raised on the third day.

I call on you to remember what had been hidden from your remembrance. It is what I foretold to you three times before it came to pass. I prophesied that I would go to Jerusalem, be rejected by the religious leaders, condemned to die and rise again.[56] This was revealed to you and then hidden from you. This way you were prevented from either fighting to prevent my death or from becoming complicit in it.

It was a great surprise to you when I announced that one of you would betray me. I knew that would happen. I knew who it would be.[57] I knew that he would be given

---

[56] Luke 9:22, 17:25, 22:15

173

thirty pieces of silver for his wages. This was revealed to me by my Father. But before that, it was first foretold by King David when he wrote by the Holy Spirit in the Writings that someone close to me, in who I had placed my trust and had eaten bread with me, would lift up his heel against me and betray me.[58] The Holy Spirit also revealed through a prophecy that he would also return to the Temple and throw the silver back to those who had given it to him as a bribe.[59] But it was Moses who set the price for this and they followed it because it is the price for a slave who was tragically killed."[60] And lastly, regarding my betrayal it was foreseen that the price that was set upon my head would then be used to purchase a potter's field to be used as an indigent person's cemetery."[61]

The apostles and all those with them sat silently and were glued to Jesus' every word as they carefully committed everything to memory. Though the night was going to be long and they were up so very late, none of them tired or grew weary as they sat and listened to all that the Lord was teaching them.

"Though the Scriptures did not foretell specifically that I would be nailed to the cross, it is very well prefigured by David who in the Psalms referred to it saying, 'They have pierced my hands and feet.'[62] And he was not alone in seeing this. Zechariah also foresaw this in the Spirit and wrote, 'They will look on him whom they have pierced.'[63] Then it was Isaiah who gave the reason for it. He wrote that

---

[57] Matthew 17:22, John 13:11
[58] Psalm 41:9
[59] Zechariah 11:12-13
[60] Exodus 21:32
[61] Zechariah 11:12-13
[62] Psalm 22:16
[63] Zechariah 12:10

when my hands and feet were pierced by the executioner's nails and when my side was pierced by the soldier's spear, it was for the sins of transgression that all the world has committed. The offenses and transgressions of the world that were made against the Father were removed from sinners everywhere and transferred onto me this way. I bore them on my body and the punishment that was required by the Law was held against me.[64]"

Jesus looked directly at John, "Do you remember what they did at the cross with my own clothes?"

John took a moment to recall this. It was a very painful memory for him. It brought his thoughts back to when he felt so utterly helpless to prevent his Master's death. "Yes, they striped you and they tore one of your garments into pieces that they divided up so that each man got one part. Then your fine tunic they gambled for it by casting lots. The soldier who won that game of chance got it."

Jesus said, "That is right John, but before you saw that, David foresaw it in the Spirit and he wrote in his Psalm 'They divide my clothes among them, and cast lots for my garments.'[65] And in that same Psalm it is foretold much about my suffering; how my bones would be put out of joint when I was first lifted up, how my heart would fail, my mouth would grow dry, of how when then soldier pierced my side water poured out, and how my enemies would take pride in mocking me. Even David foretold of the sour wine mixed with myrrh that was first given to me, though I refused to drink it, and of the simple sour wine that was given to me for my thirst.[66]"

---

[64] Isaiah 53:5
[65] Psalm 22:18
[66] Psalm 69:21

The company of people there were continually amazed at all that he was explaining. The great number of prophecies that the Lord fulfilled in his death left no doubts in their minds that this was the clear purpose of God. They felt wave after wave of the Holy Spirit flowing over their minds as the truth of all that the Lord was saying enlightened and transformed their thoughts.

Jesus went on, "Isaiah rightly foretold that it was intended that I should be buried in a common grave alongside of where they bury their criminals. However, it was the will of my Father that I would instead be buried in the tomb of a rich man. You all know that this is credited to Joseph of Arimathea who went to Pilate at the time of my death and asked for my body to be released to him for a proper burial according to our traditions.[67]

In my death I was made to be a sacrifice. Just as the lambs are substitute sacrifices for sins committed, so also, I became the final sacrifice for all sins for all of time. As the Lamb of God, this is God's own design.[68] You need to recall how Moses was instructed to make the Tabernacle exactly according to the pattern that he was shown to him on the mountain. This pattern from heaven that was revealed to him was strictly followed because it was fashioned as a pattern of heaven itself. It was a shadowy sketch of heaven.[69] My death was prefigured in all of the sacrifices.

Jesus paused for the moment and then raised his arms high and wide as he excitedly told them, "The greatest prophecies are about my resurrection. David foretold that

---

[67] Isaiah 53:9, Matthew 27:57-60, Mark 15:42-46, Luke 23:50-55, John 19:38-42
[68] Isaiah 53:4-12, 2 Corinthian 5:21
[69] Exodus 25:40, Hebrews 8:5

my body would rest securely and not see decay. Nor would my soul be given over to Sheol.[70] And again, when he saw in the Holy Spirit and he wrote, 'But you, O LORD, be gracious to me, and raise me up.'[71] It had also been revealed to Isaiah that though my life would become a sin offering, God would raise me up and restore my life.[72]

As he finished teaching them he said, "Now, you know that as it was written, the Messiah was to suffer these many things, die on the cross and be raised from the dead on the third day."

The apostles marveled in wonder as their Lord's many words took hold and transformed them from faith to greater faith and knowing the greater depths of the truth of all that had happened.

Jesus paused from recalling and interpreting the ancient Scriptures for the moment. Do you begin to see how at the precise time, all things that were necessary had come together for all the prophecies to be fulfilled? All these things needed to be place, from my birth prophecies to the ones about my crucifixion. At the fullness of that time the Father sent me to you. These things that I share and explain to you do you know that the angels have longed over the eons of time to look upon. Then Jesus blessed the LORD his Father as he recited the Psalm,

*The stone that the builders rejected
has become the cornerstone.
This is the LORD's doing;
it is marvelous in our eyes.*

---

[70] Psalm 16:9-10
[71] Psalm 41:10
[72] Isaiah 53:10

This is the day that the LORD has made;
let us rejoice and be glad in it. "[73]

Following this, Jesus and the disciples shared in fellowship and took time to eat and care for their own needs.

---

[73] Psalm 118:22-24, ESV

Chapter Twenty-Six
Peter and the Sword

Peter's thoughts were just beginning to catch up with the events of this night. His Lord was here and in that he was rejoicing. But still there was a lingering sense of pain that remained in his heart. He was hurt, and he believed rightly so because Jesus had foretold that he would deny him three times before the rooster crowed. To him, though his thoughts were unsettled over it and his feeling not fully solidified, he felt like a dirty trick had been played on him. His belief about that event was further enforced in his mind by what he had wrongly interpreted as a look from Jesus immediately after his denial that he believed shamed him further. The truth was that Jesus looked at him with compassion at that precise moment he made his third denial. And the reason he had foretold this event to Peter was to prove something to him. The Lord wanted to prove to him that he could not by his own strength and will power prevent the things that God had placed in motion. Jesus told him those things on the night of his betrayal to ease his pain and prepare him for the resurrection. His exact words were, "I have prayed for you that your faith may not fail. And when you have turned again, strengthen your brothers."[74]

His eyes looked the room over searching and wondering about all that had taken place in the past few weeks of his life. As he did this eyes came to the place on the wall where two swords once hung, and he let his thoughts lingered there. He remembered Jesus telling him to bring the swords which he gladly did. And as he recalled the sword fight that he started, he felt very hurt that Jesus had stopped it.

---

[74] Luke 22:32

It was at that moment that Jesus came alongside him and spoke, "You are wondering ..."

Peter's eyes had already begun to tear up and he nodded.

"... why I insisted that you bring those swords only to prevent you from fighting for my freedom, aren't you Peter?"

His tears now rolled down his cheeks. He was ready to weep but instead whispered, "I would have laid down my life for you."

"Yes. You would have. And you truly felt in that moment that your spirit was in fact actually empowered to carry out such a great feat. Isn't it amazing that a fisherman should be able to, in one swift sweep of his sword, precisely slice off the ear of a man?"

Peter looked at Jesus and wondered why he said that because that was what he was remembering at that very moment.

"You could feel the Spirit of God in you, couldn't you? Endowing you as a warrior and empowering your body to miraculous feats. Emboldening you before a large number of guards and soldiers and galvanizing your resolve."

"Peter silently wept and said, "Yes. All of that was mine and I know that we would have won the fight. I know we would have if only you had let me." Peter expected that Jesus would have rebuked him for saying that they would have won but he shared that thought anyway.

"Peter you are right about that night. You alone could have slain them all because the Spirit of the LORD was upon you. If I had let you continue the fight it would have been like in the days of old when our ancestors fought. You would have won against the overwhelming and impossible odds of our enemy's strength because of the Spirit's anointing in your life."

Weeping he asked, "Then why? Why tell me to bring the swords and then stop me when victory was assured? Why? Is that too much to ask of you to tell me why?"

"That is not too much to ask of me. And I will tell you why. It was not the right time for you to lay down your life for me, but that day will come Peter. That day will come to you. On that night it was time for me to lay down my life for you. And not only for you but for the world so that by my death I could win your freedom from the fierce bondage of sin. It was my time to lay down my life as a ransom for sin, to pay the terrible price and to win the freedom of all those who will believe in me. If I had let you fight on, then it would have prevented my arrest and kept me from going to the cross according to my Father's will."

These words were very foreign to Peter. Never before had he understood it this way and he shook his head uncertain of what he should believe.

Jesus continued to explain it to him, "On the night of my betrayal, all of the conditions that were necessary for my death to happen in just the right way existed. Everything was in place just waiting to be put in motion like a cascade of sequenced events. I know you Peter. If I had not told you to take the swords, then after my arrest you would have simply returned here to get them. You would have found more weapons elsewhere too. You would have armed everyone of the apostles and sought out my followers throughout the city. You would have called for a general uprising and tried to stop what must, out of necessity, have taken place. If I had simply told you not to fight to keep me from being arrested it would not have been enough. You would have soon forgot what I said. Then you would have lead many of my followers to rise up in the city and riot. You would have tried to storm the high priest's palace. Or raided the governor's Praetorium wherever you might have found me. Then you would have fought to set me free. That fight would have prevented me from going to the cross to die for the sins of the world. It was therefore necessary for you to strike out. That was your nature. Do not take this the wrong way. I told you to take the swords because it was necessary to prove to you the futility of your own actions. This was the best way to keep you and all of my followers from rising up. The best way to prevent you from stopping my arrest was to let you rise up and then stop you in the act. And remember I healed the man's ear that you cut off. There was no lasting injury to him from your hand. It was the will of my Father that I should suffer and die for the sins of the world. I needed to prevent an uprising from happening and this was not only the best way to do that, it was the only way to prevent it from happening. It is through my arrest and being held captive and bound in fetters, that freedom from sin and release to the prisoners of the devil has come to you and all the earth."

Peter listened, and his face was tense as he tried to comprehend all that Jesus was explaining to him. It was all very contrary to his way of thinking and most contrary from what he wanted to believe. "There is so much that you have said about me here. It is more than I can think about right now. I don't know what I am supposed to do with my life anymore. Are you going to abide with us here again? What is going to happen?"

"Soon I will ascend to my Father in heaven. But I have commissions for you and all the apostles to fulfill in bringing the message of the gospel for the forgiveness of sins to all the people of the earth. But first you must return to Galilee where I will come to visit you again. Take all the apostles and go there. Visit your families and spend time with them. Tell them about my resurrection. Visit the towns and villages where I preached and share with them that I was crucified and that I am raised from the dead."

Then Jesus looked at the windows that faced to the east and as he saw that it was first light, he vanished from their sight.

Chapter Twenty-Seven
The Devil's Own Trap

The company of the apostles and those traveling with them were on the road that ran alongside the Jordan River. They were making their way north to Galilee as Jesus had instructed them. The road was not an easy one, but it was heavily traveled by those going between Judea in the south and Galilee in the north. They chose this more difficult road because by it they could avoid the land of the Samaritans. They had reached the place where the road to the north divided. The way to the right lead to Capernaum and the Sea of Galilee. The road to the left lead to Nazareth. The company of the Lord's followers stopped to rest there before they would split into two groups and go separate ways. As they were sitting the Lord appeared to them again.

Jesus said to his apostles, "Two years ago we were further north and traveling to Caesarea Philippi. On that road I asked you, 'Who do you say that I am?'"[75]

Then Peter answered that question in the same words he had first used, "You are the Messiah. The Son of the Living God."

Jesus continued on, "This was first revealed to you Peter. It was not by flesh and blood that you came into this knowledge, but it was made known to you by my Father in heaven. So also, coming to faith in me happens to someone because my Father in heaven by the Holy Spirit reveals the truth to them. Do you remember how you all first reacted on that day when I told you that I must go to Jerusalem and suffer many things at the hands of our leaders? That I would be killed but on the third day be raised from the

---

[75] Matthew 16:13-26

dead? None of you were willing to accept this. That was because you wanted to see me crowned as an earthly king to rule over you. God's plan was one that you could not accept and understand at that time."

The disciples and everyone traveling with them nodded their heads in agreement and wondered what else the Lord would tell them during this visitation.

"Now I am asking you, what do others say about me now?"

Then some of them said, "Some say that you are a fraud. Others say that you have not been risen from the dead. Some believe you are risen but they don't understand anything more about you."

Then he asked them, "What do you believe about me?"

It was Peter who shared, "You have died for the sins of the world and now you have been raised from the dead."

Jesus continued on, "You could not accept this when I first told you and on the night of my betrayal I told you that there was more that I needed to tell you. You were not ready to hear these words then but now you are ready.[76] This is the time for you to understand and believe in the will and purpose of the Father. I was not destined to be an earthly king to rule over the earth as mortal men do. I was not sent to defeat the armies of those tyrants who rule over others in this world. I was sent to live among you and win a great victory over something far worse than any earthly rulers."

When he said this, the disciples looked at each other and wondered what he was talking about.

"Eons ago Satan rebelled in heaven and tried to ascend to the throne of God. In heaven he was cast down like lightning and his rebellion there was defeated.[77] Still he

---

[76] John 16:11

was able to work his evil in this world. You need to know that when Satan put temptation in front of Adam and Eve, he lured them into eating the fruit of the forbidden tree. He lied to them and falsely led them to think that they could be like gods. In my death, by the same temptation to become a god, my Father lured Satan in too. The evil one was led to believe that if he could put me to death on that tree of Golgotha that he could seize my throne and become like a god who would rule with supreme power and authority. Just like Adam and Eve he could not resist so great a temptation. I was the bait that lured him in. He believed that if he killed me, then he would have won the fight to rule supremely over all of creation. In his blind ambition he took the bait. But in my death and resurrection I won supremely the victory over sin, death, the devil and the grave. Satan is filled with pride and in his conceit, he believed that if he could only kill me that then he could seize my place and reign as a god. In his pride he could not resist temptation when the opportunity presented itself. To do this I had to become a mortal man by being born of Mary. Then it became possible for me to die. It was then that he tried many times to have me killed. First by Herod the Great and my parents fled with me to Egypt. Again, when he used the Temple authorities to try to stone me in Jerusalem and also by having his captives try to throw me off a cliff in Galilee. It was the Father's plan from the beginning to let my life be sacrificed as an offering for sin. When all that was needed was in place he seized the opportunity and it was then I laid my life down for the sins of the world.

What he did not see was that I would rise from the dead victorious over sin, death and the grave, and over him. In

---

[77] Isaiah 14:12-20, Ezekiel 28:1-19

my death he believed that he had won the final victory over me. Now he has been defeated by my death and victory over the grave. Just as Adam and Eve fell in sin, so also, he has fallen in his sin and he is defeated. Now the redemption of the world has happened and by it Satan has been disarmed.

And this is my victory that I give to all who believe in me. Remember, that following my baptism, that I was forty days and nights in the wilderness being tempted by him. In those difficult days I was faithful unto my Father in all things. This is my victory for you that the Son of Man won. Adam and Eve fell into sin on that fateful day in the garden. They lived in the best of conditions and even had the direct command of my Father not to eat that fruit. Yet under those ideal conditions they failed and fell in sin. Since then the world has lived under the curse of sin and the Law. It was in the worst of conditions in that desert wasteland that I overcame temptation. I bring you my victory from the desert wilderness. I give you my victory over sin, death, the grave and the devil.

Now you are at this crossroad that will take you to your homes either in Capernaum or Nazareth. Go to your families and resume your lives there. Before long I will come to you again and meet with you there." When the Lord had given these lessons to them he vanished from their sight.

Chapter Twenty-Eight
The First Christian Synagogue

Jairus was a man of faith and that included believing that Jesus of Nazareth was God's Messiah, the Anointed One. His teenage daughter, Elisha, was also a girl of profound faith. They enjoyed hearing reports of the Lord's ministry that came to their town. When Jesus was crucified it took four days for the tragic news to arrive in Galilee. When the first report of it came their faith was absolutely shattered. They, like everyone in Galilee, were distressed and could not reconcile how this man whom God had given such great abilities too could have come to such a fate as this. They were in mourning, but their bereavement was disrupted when the news of his empty tomb and his appearance to others began to arrive in their region. This only complicated things at first. It was an event that continued to shake them soundly and they wondered whatever could these reports mean. Now, they did not know what to believe. Jairus knew that his daughter's life was owed to the Lord because he had raised her back to life in the same hour that she had died. They, along with everyone in their small town, were waiting for more reports from the apostles in Jerusalem about the true fate of Jesus of Nazareth.

Jairus was the Hazzan, the caretaker and a leader of their synagogue and he played a vital role in their community. Galilee had become infiltrated with other Greco-Roman settlements. In many cases these small village sized colonies had grown into cities which were impregnated with very heathen and pagan practices. That lead the people of Judea, and especially those in Jerusalem, to call their region Galilee of the Gentiles. The influence of these foreigners in their lands was unwanted by the faithful people of God, the Galilean Jews. Therefore, their synagogue became an anchor for them that securely maintained their religion, their language, and their culture. Their gathering place was there to preserve their lifestyle as God's chosen people. They were, as Rabbi Jesus had taught them, the salt of the earth. Their building served as a school for their children, all of whom were required to learn to read and write. They were given an extensive religious education and memorized great portions of the holy Scriptures. Their synagogue was their community's place for any kind of social gathering, a festive meal, a townhall meeting, worship, and for disturbing food to the poor.

The building itself was rather simple in design. It rested on a small hill and was the tallest building in their town. That was because it was the most important building there. It was made from stones shaped by a mason's hammer. Inside the doors there were tiers of stone benches for people to sit on along three of the walls. The floor was simply made of stone slabs that had been leveled flat. Many people brought cushions to sit on, either on the benches or on the floor itself while others stood during their gatherings. The walls were plastered and holding up the ceiling were round pillars of cut stones in the middle of the great hall. Up along the ceiling were small narrow windows that let sunlight in. Additional light was provided by a very large menorah which was a large candle that burned olive oil. It was fashioned to look just like the one in the Jerusalem Temple. In the front there was a wooden platform for a speaker to use that was fashioned after the design that the scribe Ezra used in the days when their people returned from their Babylonian captivity.[78] There

---

[78] Nehemiah 8:4

was a chair next to that which was a seat of honor. It was used by the Scripture reader during worship and by the presiding elder of the city during other meetings. The other furniture inside the synagogue was for storing documents. The primary one was the holy ark where the scrolls of their Scriptures were kept, including their prized scroll of the Prophet Isaiah. The other furnishings were simple wooden chests for storing other written records.

Jairus was also one of the local teachers. Though he was not a rabbi he organized the prayer hours. On the Sabbath day he announced its arrival by blowing the shofar which was a rams horn that was used like a trumpet.

On this particular day, as Jairus and his daughter came near to the entrance of their synagogue they stood next to the mikveh. This was a ritual bath that was used to wash in before attending prayers and Sabbath worship. While it was large enough for a person to bath in, most people bathed at home or at the city fountain before coming to their synagogue. As they stood before its waters, the two of them dipped their right hands into the water and touched their wet hands to their faces. This was a symbolic gesture of washing away their uncleanliness and purifying themselves so that they would be acceptable before the LORD in their prayers. While inside the synagogue they fell into their routine of keeping their building perfectly clean. They dusted and swept everywhere. Anything that was showing any soiling was washed down thoroughly. Then a lone man entered and he began to pray silently. Though this was not an uncommon practice it was rare at the afternoon hour of prayer because this service was the least well attended. That was because most of the towns people, especially the men, were busy with their occupations and could not simply up and leave them during the productive hours of the working days. As the man prayed he stood but then he knelt and bowed his head to the floor. There was a certain feeling, an ambiance that emanated from him and it filled the building. It was vaguely familiar to Jairus. He had only felt this way once before in his life. As he sensed it, he stopped what he was doing and remembered that day when he felt that way. It was exactly how he felt when his daughter had been raised back to life by Jesus. He had no idea why he felt this way again. It was not the anniversary of that day and he had not been thinking about it either.

Then his mind made a connection with what he was feeling. Just as his daughter had died so had Jesus and just as she was raised from the dead so was the Lord. At least that is what he had been told. Then he looked at his daughter and a deeply warm feeling filled his heart. He remembered vividly that day when she was deathly ill. The local physicians were able to do nothing to reverse the course of her illness. Then he heard that Rabbi Jesus was near, and he rushed to him. In desperation and falling at his feet he begged Jesus to come to her aid and lay his hands on her and pray for her recovery. Jesus agreed to go with him. As they rushed along people came to him and said that he needn't trouble the Lord any further because his daughter had now died from her illness. That feeling of grief and great distress resurged in him, but it was not over his daughter. He knew that she was perfectly well. His anguish was over the loss of such a great prophet who had visited their community. He struggled within and agonized over the tragic death that Jesus had suffered. It was beyond belief that the Temple authorities and the empire could do such a thing. It was also impossible to imagine how Jesus could have let such a thing happen to him, given the powers that God had worked in his life. His mind remembered how he felt when Jesus spoke those wonderful two words to his daughter, "Talitha cum."[79] The joy of that moment seemed to resurge in his soul and he felt the power of renewed life flow in his again.

Just then, the man who had been praying got up and came over to Jairus and Elisha came to hear what the two were going to talk about. They had not been able to meet him when he first arrived but now they both extended their greetings to him, "Welcome to our synagogue."

Then the man smiled widely and offered his greeting to them as well, "Shalom, my friends. Peace be with you in this place."

As he spoke they recognized that this was the Lord and rejoicing they both embraced Jesus with a warm hug. Jairus' cheek rested against Jesus' face and Elisha rested her head on this Jesus' side as she hugged him tightly.

Jairus said, "Oh, my Lord! My Lord! How wonderful to see you again!"

"And I you" Jesus said as the two now stood looking at each other. Jesus was grinning and Jairus was in awe of his presence and wondering what this now meant for him and the claims of his resurrection.

Then Jesus showed them his hands and his side and said, "It is all true. I was dead and now I am alive. The Father raised me up on the third day. You must believe in me and in God my Father, who brings new life to all who will believe in me."

Jairus nodded and then confessed, "Yes, my Lord, I do believe." Then he and his daughter both fell at Jesus' feet and worshiped him saying, "My Lord and God, you are my Lord and God."

---

[79] Mark 5:41 "Little girl, get up."

Then Jesus took them by the hands and lifted them up. "You must share with your synagogue what you have seen and heard here from me today. Tell them that I am alive, that I am risen from the dead, and that salvation will come to all who repent and believe in me for the forgiveness of their sins."

Jesus looked directly at Elisha and said, "Just as you were once dead and I raised you up to life again, so also, my Father will give eternal life to all who believe in me."

Then Jesus looked at Jairus and said, "After I restored your daughter to life I ordered that no one should be told about it. Now I am saying that you must tell everyone that you have seen me alive here today. Remember how you desperately sought me out and asked me to come to your daughter's side. Now in the same way you must seek out the lost and lead them to faith in me so that they may come into eternal life."

Jairus heartily agreed and said, "Our members will soon be arriving. You must stay and let them see you. You must let them touch you and hear your words! Please stay for evening prayers as well so that our whole town may come and see you too!"

"Blessed are they who have not seen and still come to have faith in me. You two must be my witnesses in your town to all that you have seen and heard from me." Then Jesus stepped back away from them and he vanished from their sight.

Jairus and Elisha looked directly at each other and smiled as then they hugged each other. The confusion they had been suffering under, the sorrow over the Lord's death, and then the reports of his empty tomb were now all clear in their minds. They knew the truth and how exciting it was to them.

Jairus knew what he must to do. He walked over to the wooden chest where the synagogue's shofar was stored and took it out. It was a beautiful ram's horn that was formed with three long spirals from its tip to its trumpet's end. The use of it was for calling the town to Sabbath worship. Other uses were rare, but it could be used to call the town to a meeting or to announce the presence of danger, such as, a fire or a thief. He looked at his daughter and said, "We must call everyone together and share with them this news, it cannot wait for the evening prayers."

Then he went outside and blew the ram's horn long, loud and hard. The normally simple blast of sound carried with it an especially melodious tune. He blew until he could blow no more and then he did it again, three times in all.

Now everyone nearby came rushing over to see what was going on. Those in the nearby fields came as well. Many of them stopped at the town fountain to wash and some returned home to put on a fresh set of clothes. As they arrived at the synagogue, Jairus and his daughter greeted and invited them in. Everyone asked what was going on that he had called them to the synagogue, but he simply told them that all would be told once everyone had arrived.

Jairus continued to greet everyone warmly and once they were assembled he went inside. The elders of the community sat in a row on one of the benches near the front. The room was nearly filled to capacity with many standing or sitting near the front on the floor.

Jairus went to the front and said that he and his daughter had an announcement to make. The assembly was very excited to hear this. She was now fifteen years old and still not engaged. They hoped to hear that she was now betrothed to someone from their tribe. No one could imagine that this big midday gathering was about anything else. Some wondered why they would make this announcement at midday though. It could have and should have waited until the evening or even the Sabbath.

Jairus spoke to them, "Everyone remembers that day when my daughter was taken deathly ill. It was then that I ran throughout our city's streets to search for Rabbi Jesus who was reported to be here. When I found him, he agreed to come to my home and pray for Elisha to recover. It was just after I found him that my neighbors came to me to share the terrible news of her death. We all remember this. Jesus was undeterred and came to my home, and then laid hands on my daughter's body and brought her back to life.

Now in these past few days we have heard the news of Rabbi Jesus' crucifixion and of reports of his empty tomb. Some has said that though he had died he has been raised back to life again. Now in this past hour my daughter and I have been visited by Jesus of Nazareth. He entered our synagogue not less than an hour ago and offered his prayers here. Then he spoke to us both and showed us the wounds on his hands and his side. His message to us is that just as I desperately sought him out for my daughter's life so also, I need to urgently proclaim his resurrection to you. That by faith in him your sins will be forgiven you and you will be given the gift of eternal life."

As he spoke the elders listened carefully as did the entire company of people.

Then the presiding elder, Jesse, stood to his feet and spoke directly with Jairus. "So that we may know the details of your report Elisha, please come to the front and join us." Now this was a rare occurrence in any synagogue for an elder to call on a woman and invite her to the front to speak before the community. Jesse continued, "We all know how Rabbi Jesus came and visited our town in the past. We know that he was a great prophet and about the many signs and wonders he performed here. His death in Jerusalem has been widely reported among us and it brought great sorrow to our hearts. In these last few days there have been reports of his empty tomb and that others, including all of his apostles, say they have seen him again alive. Now please tell us what you saw."

Elisha answered him and spoke to the entire company of people, "When the man entered this place we did not see his face and we did not know who he was. He prayed and then he turned to us and immediately we recognized him. My father and I rushed to his side and he showed us his wounds. All of them. There were scars on both his hands, on his feet and a scar over his heart."

Jesse asked her, "And this was a man was not a ghost?"

She answered him, "No sir. I hugged him tightly and I felt him hug me back. I touched his feet and I worshiped him because I believe that he is the Son of God."

"And you Jairus, did you touch him also?"

"I did. I touched him when I hugged him and I held his hands in mine when I touched his wounds. Then I fell to the floor and I touched his feet when I worshiped him too."

One of the other elders called out, "Where is he now?"

Jairus spoke out and addressed everyone there. "While the man was here I felt his presence before I knew it was the Lord. It was exactly the same emotions that I felt when Jesus had raised my daughter back to life. It was a feeling of greatest comfort and hope, of assurance and a peacefulness that could not be shaken. When Jesus was here, before I knew it was him, I knew that it was him because I could feel his presence. It was unlike anything I

196

have ever know before except on that day he raised my daughter back to life. I urged him to stay so that others could see him too. He told me, 'Blessed are they who have not seen and still come to have faith in me.'"

Elisha then added, "For me I too felt his presence here while he prayed. It was the same as when he raised me back to life. I was dead and when I came back to life I was at perfect peace. There were no cares in the world for me anymore. Though I had been so very sick I was healed, and I have never been ill since then. I know it was the Lord and that I owe him my life twofold. First for raising me from the dead and now again because he died for my sins so that I can be forgiven and go to heaven when death someday comes to me again."

Another elder asked them, "How is it that you are the only two who have seen him here. No one else saw him in our town, did they?" He looked around the room to see if anyone would respond to his question, but no one did.

Jairus looked directly at the older man and said, "I do not know how he came to the center of our town where our synagogue is and no one else saw him. I do know that when he left he stood before us at this very spot and then simply vanished before us."

The elder had a follow up question for them, "You say he was not a ghost because you were able to touch him and hold him. Yet men do not simply appear out of nowhere and then vanish into the air. How is this story of yours is possible then?"

Jairus did not know what to say at first and he shook his head. Then he answered him, "I do not know how this is possible, but I do know that it is real. Perhaps as the Scriptures talk about angels from heaven appearing and vanishing out of sight perhaps the risen Lord Jesus has this ability now also."

The elder simply responded with the sound, "Humph."

Now the presiding elder Jesse spoke again, "I know that among us today everyone here has never disputed that Jesus saved this girl's life. We all accept that, though she died, he raised her back to life. I personally believe that Jesus has been raised back to life too. How these things are possible for the Lord to do remains a mystery to us that we may conclude. I believe and hope that he may even appear among us again at some time."

Then another elder said, "We must make contact with the Lord's apostles and hear from them what all they can tell us about Jesus' resurrection. We must learn more about what this means for us and our lives."

Jesse spoke again, "Yes! I agree, we must seek out the Lord's apostles and meet with them. Perhaps one of them can come to our town and speak to us as well."

Then the elders called on the people to see who they would send to visit with the apostles. They appointed two men from their town to journey to Jerusalem and seek them out. The people of the town then shared in their afternoon hour of prayer and from that day onward they were a congregation that believed in and worship Jesus as their Lord and God.

Chapter Twenty-Nine
The Touch of a Hem

In the same village where Jairus lived there was a woman named Cheran. This was the woman who had suffered from a bleeding problem for twelve years. On that day when she heard that Jesus was in her town she secretly devised a plan to go out into the village and blend in with the large crowds so that she could get close enough to Rabbi Jesus to touch the hem of his coat anonymously. The problem with her plan was that she was not allowed to go out in public because of her bleeding. The Law of Moses prohibited it. It was because of a public health law that was intended to prevent the spread of diseases.[80] If she was to go out into public it was required of her to call out to everyone who came near her saying, "Unclean. I am unclean." For this reason she did not go out into public. She lived a strict solitary lifestyle and because of it she was viewed by those who knew her as being unsocial and a loaner. She preferred being thought of in this way over being know as someone who was unclean. Someone who was unclean in their nation was unclean before the LORD and was viewed as unholy and sinful. Most people viewed them with great scorn and as sinners who refused to repent of their sins. Though this was rarely the cause of these problems, for those unfortunate few the superstitions of the people prevailed against them leaving them stigmatized for a lifetime.

Cheran was plagued with an issue of blood which also caused her to be weak and her face was pale. She had sought out the care of many physicians. None of whom had been able to cure her or even lessen her illness. The

---

[80] Leviticus 15:25

bleeding robbed her of the life she was supposed to have enjoyed. She did not have any friends. Any extra money she had was paid to physicians who treated her in vain. There was little left for her to enjoy in life. So, when Jesus came to town she was willing to risk exposing herself to public shame and ridicule in the hopes of being healed. The danger was that if she was caught she would be exposed and her secret would be known to all. By going out in public if she simply brushed up against or incidentally touched someone they would in turn become unclean. It would become a scandal of the worst kind and the village people would never forgive her of this great offense. Then instead of being viewed as a social hermit, by her own choosing, she would become a community outcast and an untouchable. She had one hope as she told herself, *'if I could just touch his coat I will be healed.'*

As she left home that morning she quietly tried to stay in low profile. She simply blended in with the crowd that had gathered around Jesus as he made his way through their streets. There she encountered some unexpected problems. Jesus was being pressed in upon by everyone in her city. She was growing tired as she usually did when she exerted herself. Such was the effect of her chronic blood loss. She had but only one hope which was that if she could be healed it would be by the power of God that was at work in Jesus. She persevered and pushed inward into the crowd, at times, even using her arms and elbows to squeeze in and move forward. Then as she neared him a well-known man named Jairus and some of the town elders appeared before the Rabbi. Then the crowd around Jesus thinned a little and allowed this community leader to speak with the Rabbi unhindered. Jairus begged him to come quickly to his house because his daughter was near death. Jesus of course agreed, and they began to walk at a very fast pace to the man's home. During that time Cheran was able to move in and get behind Jesus, but he was moving at such a fast pace that she was not sure she could get close enough to him to touch the back of his coat. Then with a final push and the last of her strength she did what she came to do and she touched his coat. A surge of power rushed through her like nothing she had ever known. It was thrilling and so energizing that she was ready to jump up and dance. Her fear was all but gone and she knew that she was healed. As she turned quickly to leave, Jesus also quickly turned and looked at her and everyone who was near to him.

Jesus spoke out boldly and the tone of his voice demanded an answer, "Who among you just touched me?" He said this because he had felt the power of God surge though him and he knew that it had entered whoever that person was who had just touched him.

As he looked around his disciples sought to calm him by saying everyone in the crowd had been pressing in on him. Which was true because many of them reached out and touched him believing that it was a blessing to their lives.

As Jesus impatiently waited for an answer, Cheran's heart sank and her fears rose within her. She was healed but now she was also found out. Jesus looked directly at her and there his eyes stayed. She bowed low to the ground and confessed everything to him. In tears she wept as she fully expected the divine wrath of this holy prophet of God to condemn her in front of everyone because she had gone out in public with her bleeding. Worse yet she had intentionally touched him when this was forbidden by Moses.

To her amazement and everyone else's Jesus did not condemn her at all. Instead he commended her, "Daughter of Abraham! You have lived in fear for long enough." He reached down and lifted her up and proclaimed to everyone there, "Faith in me has made you well! You are no longer an outcast or unclean. Go in God's peace, you are healed, and your life is restored to you."

It was several weeks since Jesus had been raised from the dead that Cheran had gone to the market and purchased fresh food. As she turned down her narrow street where her house was she could see that there were only a few children with their mothers further down the way. Then she felt an ever so slight touch on the back of her coat. She dismissed it as simply nothing. Then she felt that slight touch again and she wondered whatever could it be. Perhaps it was nothing or maybe a breeze had blown past her. Then the third time it happened she prepared to turn around and see what it was that tugged ever so slightly at her. Before she could turn around there came a surge of great power through her body. The tugging at her coat was easily enough dismissed at first. But when it happened the third time she wanted to know why it was happening. But this surge of power flowing through her like this was undeniable. It was that same power of God that had once before touched her when she, in faith, had touched Jesus' robe and was healed. Now her face brightened, and her heart was warmed. She knew that it could be none other than the Lord himself. She dropped her bag of food and quickly turned around to see Jesus standing there right behind her.

"Oh, my Lord it is you! You have come to visit me!" She bowed low to the ground and wept at his feet kissing them without end.

Then the Lord knelt down taking her by the hand and lifting her up he hugged her tightly. "I have never forgotten you daughter of Abraham. I remember your great faith well. Your miracle was the only one of its kind in my life."

Cheran was still in tears as she was being hugged. Then she reached for Jesus' hand and kissed it and looked at the scar that was made by the nail when he was crucified and kissed it again and again. Tears welled up in her eyes and she cried, "My dear Lord how you suffered so." She held his hand to her face and rolled it against her cheek. "Are you well again? Do you still suffer from what they did to you?" She held his hands near to her face so that her tears could fall into the palm of his hands. Tear continued to stream down her face as she waited for his answer.

"I am well. There is no pain for me anymore. You must know that I suffered for you and for all the world. I did it for the forgiveness of everyone's sins. I died to pay the terrible price of the world's iniquities."

"You healed me of my uncleanliness because of my bleeding. On the day of your death you cleansed me of my sins. I know this. Even before you told me that I knew it was true. Somehow your Father has shown me these things."

Jesus smiled to know that this had been revealed to her through the Holy Spirit. Now she invited Jesus to her home which was just a little farther down the narrow street that they stood on. Inside she invited him to sit with her and she poured him some wine and set out bread and charoset for them to eat.

"When you asked who touched your hem that day my heart sank and I thought I would die right there. I feared that my secrets would become known to all. I had lived so many years in misery. All I wanted in life was to be healed. But in the middle of my healing I feared that a terrible thing was happening. I feared that I would be cleansed and then cast out from my own community. You restored my health and when they were ready to condemn me for going out among them you restored me to my neighbors as well. Now instead of being despised I have become something of a renown miracle woman here. You know that I will forever be grateful to you."

Jesus nodded, "Yes, that is true. I had no idea what you were up to on that day. You caught me by surprise. I had no idea that you were suffering so much with your health and in having to live in isolation. I am sure that your life was in many ways unbearable."

Cheran nodded and said, "There was no one I could confide in other than the physicians who tried unsuccessfully to treat me. I could not invite anyone into my home. I went out only when the streets were all but empty. I worried that if others learned about me I would have to go live outside the city and live among the lepers. I did not want to become a mockery to everyone. You changed all that for me. You restored my life to me then and with your death you have forgiven me all of my sins."

"When I heard your confession of faith and what I had unknowingly done for you I was taken by surprise too. Being a prophet, I commonly know ahead of time what is unfolding before me. I worried just as you did, that while by your faith you had been healed, that the townspeople would make you an outcast anyway. I could not live with that especially after seeing how frightened you were. I needed to show the people that you were loved by God my Father and accepted by me."

Cheran replied, "What had become the best day of my life was about to also become the worst day of my life. Thanks to you and your compassion it became better than the best day of my life. I love you dear Lord Jesus for what you did to heal me and for forgiving me of all my sins."

"I love you too and for that reason I had to come to visit you again before I return to my Father in heaven. You are a daughter of Abraham and Sarah. You are a daughter of the promise that God made to them that all the world would be blessed in them. That was because I would be born as one of their descendants. God sent me into the world to be born and to die for the forgiveness of sins. Just as you were cleansed that day on the street and now as you are forgiven your sins you must share with others that by faith in me this can come to them too."

Cheran nodded and looked into Jesus' eyes and said, "Because you have asked me to do this I will share with others what your love has done for me."

Then the Lord vanished from her sight and for the briefest of moments she heard an angelic choir singing the praises of God. She knew peace in her life the day she was healed. Now there was a more profound peace in her life. An unshakable peace. Forgiveness had come to her and that was the greatest healing anyone could possibly know.

Chapter Thirty
Fishing Miracle

Having returned to Galilee in the north as they had been instructed to by the Lord the apostles awaited his next appearing and his instructions for them. Some of those who returned to Capernaum returned to fishing for their livelihood. Included in this group was Peter and his brother Andrew, along with James and his brother John.

It was still very dark outside when Peter rose early and woke the others telling them that he was going fishing. Then they all got up and joined him outside. Together they walked the short distance to the shores of the Sea of Galilee where the vast stretches of its calm waters reflected the night sky. For as far as the eye could see there was above a vision of the night stars. Below was the great sea of Galilee. It was a beautiful and breathtaking view of heaven and earth. It was a sight to behold and the four men cast gazes across the waters and saw the silvery dark image of heaven that was reflected upon the waters.

As they came to the shore, their's was a lone boat resting on the rocky shoreline. They had turned it over to drain all the water out of it and allow it to thoroughly dry. They found their large net just as they had left it. It was laying across their boat and the great length of it was hanging atop their oars they had driven into the ground so that it could air dry. It was old, but they had made many repairs it and it was well able to do its job of catching fish. They had a mast and sail laying under the boat but there was no wind, nor would there be at that hour. Not until the morning sun rose and began to warm the day. Then the wind would rise and stir up the waters of the sea.

In the morning after first light, the people of their community would come to the shore to buy fish from them. And so, they took down their net and loaded it into the boat along with their other equipment. All the men rolled their boat upright and pushed it to the shore and into the quiet waters of the night. As it began to float they jumped in, all put Peter who was last. He gave their boat a final hardy shove out into water and then he climbed in too. They had gotten a little wet as they set out. Peter especially so but that was something they had become accustomed to as fisherman. They lived the better part of their workdays wet and half of those hours were during the much cooler hours of the night. The four of them set their oars into the water and they made their way from the shallows of the shore into deeper waters. They were silent. Not a word was spoken. They knew their jobs. They rowed quietly, slowly setting their oars down and gently pulling them through the water to avoid making a noise that would alert the fish to their presence. They knew these waters well and the star light was all they needed to guide them to a place where they had typically caught fish.

Their early start was necessary because the fish will avoid coming to the surface waters during the hot hours of the day when the sun warms them. It is in the early morning hours when the water has cooled that they come closer to the surface. However, they are less active in the cooler temperatures. That can become an advantage as well as a disadvantage. When they are less active they are not likely to just swim into your net. On the other hand, when you do find them at that time they are less likely get away from your net. Now if they were to go fishing at the most opportune time that would be when the bugs come out. That is during the later hours of the day and evening. Then they could catch large numbers of fish who came to the surface to eat the bugs there. The problem with fishing at that hour is that by the time they got their catch to the shore to sell the sun would be setting and there would be no one at the market to purchase their fish. So, the best time to catch and sell fish was in the morning.

Once they were near to the place where they believed there would be fish to catch they brought in their oars and quietly set them in the boat. Fish cannot see much at night but their other senses of movement in the water and noise are heightened. The apostles did not want to scare the fish away so without a word being spoken they set their net slowly into the water and let its weighted ends drop while the high side of the net was secured to the boat. They let their boat drift with the slow-moving current in the expectation that letting their net drag in the water it would catch fish.

With the coming of first light, they knew that the fish would become more active and come to the surface to find food to eat. All the disciples had to do was wait. The gentle sway of the waters acting on the boat and those quiet hours of the night were very calming to them and they lightly dozed. The two on the left side where they had set their net were Peter and John. They had their hands lightly grasping the waterside of it. They did this to be alerted to a tugging by the net that would come as it began to accumulate fish.

In the still quiet of the night and in the calm waters the disciples drifted deeper into sleep. First light had come and gone and though the sun had not fully risen yet, the day was already bright from the light that was reflected across the water. Peter and John had not been woken by any early indications of fish filling and tugging on their net. When the sun had crested over the waters and warmed the air they woke, and all of them were feeling stiff from having been in the boat for so long. Their necks were sore, their joints were aching, and hunger filled their bellies. Then they took off their robes and tunics because they were hot. Peter and John both tugged at the net and dipped their heads down low to see if they had caught anything. They both looked up and at each other in something of a surprise. Then they looked at James and Andrew and shook their heads with a sad look of disappointment on their faces. Then the four of them began to pull up their net to see if there were fish deeper down in it.

James spoke out, "We have labored here since the early hours of the night and we have caught nothing at all! Not even a single fish. In the morning when the people come here to buy fish we will have nothing to offer them at the market and nothing for us to eat for our own meal."

Peter had a good mind for business and he shared his thoughts, "If we have nothing to sell they will not favor us and our place in the market will suffer."

John was equally disappointed and told the others, "I know these waters have abundant fish in them. It is as if the fish have become smart and are avoiding us."

Andrew tried to put things in perspective, "Alright. Alright. We have had fruitless nights on the water before. This happens sometimes. We all know that." Then he stood to his feet and looked the surface of the water over hoping to see some hit of fish nearby.

John also stood to his feet on his side of the boat and his eyes scanned the water between them and the shoreline. Now as the sun continued to rise over the eastern horizon it shone brightly across the vast waters of the sea. Then John saw a man on the beach who he believed had come to purchase fish from them.

"Children, have you caught any fish for me to purchase from you?"

Peter shouted back to him, "Our net is empty. We have been out here for hours and have not caught anything."

Now the man laughed about their situation and Peter and the others were embarrassed by their lack of success.

Then he called out to them, "Pull in your net and throw it out again. But this time throw it out on the other side of your boat."

Peter thought to himself about how ridiculous that idea was. "What does this man know about catching fish? If there are any fish down there they would be soon caught whether they are on the right or the left side of our boat. If we pull in the net and recast it, we will scare the fish away."

Then his brother Nathanael said to him, "Peter, we have been away from these waters and from fishing for three years. Things change. Maybe this man knows better what the current fishing like."

So, Peter said, "Okay help me drag this in."

But then James and John objected to doing this.

James said, "Let's just steer our boat in that direction. What's the difference anyway? If there are fish there we will still catch them."

Peter insisted, "Let's just do as this the man says. Who knows? This might work. We've been out here for hours and that has brought us nothing. Let's try something different and hope it works."

So, they all labored to pull the water laden net into their boat and together they threw it over the right side of their boat. Immediately the net was filled beyond its capacity with fish and it began to pull that side of the boat down. The disciples even worried that it might capsize on that side because it leaned so much that way from the weight of the fish filled net. Even though there were the four of them, they were unable to pull the net out of the water and into their boat because it was too heavy with fish. Then they all laughed joyously wondering why this apparent lucky catch had come to them.

Now John knew this was far from ordinary and he looked again at the man on the shore very carefully. Even though at first he appeared to simply be a stranger, he now saw that it was his Master, Jesus of Nazareth. Pointing to the shore he excitedly shouted to the others right next to him, "Look! It is the Lord!"

Then Peter became very excited when he heard this. He looked at the shore and he also recognized that it was Jesus and he waved to him with broad sweeps of his arm. Then he put on his tunic and quickly dove into the water so that he could swim to the shore and greet his Master because he could not wait to see him.

The other three apostles on the boat remained on board and labored to bring the boat ashore. The heavy net in the water worked against them because it was like an anchor weighing them down. They worked their oars hard and were able to reach the shore but only with a great effort by all three of them.

When Peter arrived on shore he came up to Jesus. At first, he had run to meet him but as the neared to him he slowed and then bowed low at his feet, "Master Jesus!"

Then Jesus raised his arms and welcomed Peter as they exchanged hugs and warm greetings. As the others reached the shore Peter returned to them and helped them securely land the boat. But the net was so heavy that they struggled to bring it onto the shore. The place where they landed was a stretch of sandy shoreline and the apostles wrangled with their net to drag it in. Their feet found no sure footing in the sand. No sooner had they dug their feet in then the sand shifted against them and the length of their strides were cut in half. But as they labored together they were able to bring in the miraculously large catch of fish.

Peter, whose father owned the boat and net remarked, "I have never known of such a large catch of fish at one time. And look the net has not torn anywhere."

Jesus called to them, "Bring some of the fish with you and come have some breakfast with me."

The apostles came bringing some of the larger fish with them. Then they sat with the Lord who had a fire started with glowing coals that warmed the apostles who had become chilled from being wet. Jesus had freshly made bread with him and he had already roasted a few fish for them to eat. Then he blessed his Father for the food and distributed the bread to the four men and the fish as well. After those early hours on the water and the discouragement they had suffered under not having caught any fish, they were very delighted to be offered this meal. Given the company of their Lord and the food he had prepared, never did bread and fish taste so good.

The four fishermen wondered what the Lord would say to them as they ate. None of them were bold enough to speak first. Then the Lord said to them, "From your nets I called you to be my disciples. Now to your nets you have returned. And from your nets I am calling you again. Soon you must return to Jerusalem where I will appear to you again. There I will tell you what your mission for the gospel will be."

The four of them listened and looked at each other wondering what their future would hold. Not much else was said as they ate their meal. They thought about what they still needed to do to prepare for the arrival of the local people who would be coming to purchase fish from them.

Chapter Thirty-One
Peter and the Lord

When they had eaten until they could eat no more, and their joy in seeing the Lord again was full, James and John got up and tended to the boat and net. They used their oars to prop the net up into the air so that it could dry in the breeze coming in off the lake. Before long some people started to show up to purchase fish for their meals and then Nathanael attended to selling their catch to them.

Jesus invited Peter to take a stroll with him down the shoreline. Peter was silent as they set out and he worried about what the Lord would say to him this time. His thoughts went back to that night, the night of the betrayal. So many things did not go well then and he wondered if he should even bring any of it up. He still felt bad that he had drawn his sword and cut off that man's ear. He had talked about that with the Lord once before, but he continued to ruminate over all of his failings. Though it was very painful for him to think about, Peter's mind touched ever so briefly on that matter of his denial about knowing the Lord. Though he was wrong about at it at the time he thought Jesus' expression to him then showed that he despised Peter. His mind had a hard time thinking about this painful as it was to him. Yet it was also this thought that made his mind freeze in place and he could just not move himself past it. He was numb with the shame and pain of it and stuck on being unable to think of anything else.

Jesus being a prophet and the Son of God knew full well what was going on in Peter's mind and heart. His one desire was to rebuild his relationship with him and make him his chief apostle. He knew how much Peter was hurting and he wanted to bring him healing over this

214

painful episode in his life. So, the Lord led him in the conversation. Looking directly at him, he could not get Peter to look directly back at him as he said, "Simon Peter, son of Johann, do you love me more than your companions?"

Now Peter thought that was something of a strange question. However, it got him to focused on something other than his otherwise unremitting thoughts about having denied Jesus three times. "Lord, you know the answer to that without even asking. Of course I like you more than any of my friends over there selling the fish we caught."

Jesus chuckled that Peter made a reference to them selling fish to feed the local people. He also knew that he had not really gotten through to Peter very well. So, he added this new focus for Peter to think about, "Feed my lambs." But Peter did not make the connection that Jesus was trying to lead him to, that he wanted him to nurture his followers in the faith.

Jesus needed to ask him this question two more times. That was part of the exercise he needed to lead Peter through. So, again he posed the same question to him, "But what I am asking you is this, Simon Peter, son of Johann. Do you love me more than your friends over there?"

Now Peter wondered why he asked that question again and told him again, "Lord, you do know the answer to this without asking me twice. Of course, I like you more than any of my friends that are working for me over there."

Jesus wanted to get Peter to think about overseeing his followers rather than a crew of men who would work for him as fisherman. This time he said to him, "Shepherd my flock." Jesus still had not heard Peter respond to him as he had hoped because he wanted Peter to say that he loved him, but he would not. Jesus knew fully well how Peter felt. He was uncertain and unwilling to commit himself to Jesus' mission again. So, Jesus relented and now said to him, "Simon Peter, son of Johann. Do you truly like me more than all of your friends?"

Now Peter did not care for the repetition he had been subjected to and he was very irritated by Jesus' persistence. He had entirely missed what Jesus was trying to do for him though. He reluctantly looked at Jesus and assertively told him, "You know everything my Lord. Everything. Do I like you more than all my friends? Yes, I do. I like you the most of all, you know that."

Jesus smiled at Peter and then looked at the disciples who were selling the fish he miraculously brought into their nets. He saw them providing fish for sale to the local people. His mind imagined that they would someday soon be nurturing his many followers instead.

It took him a while but finally Peter had an awaking moment. He remembered his three denials of the Lord. He made the connection that now Jesus had him confess and not deny three times that he liked the Lord more than all of his friends. He immediately looked at Jesus who saw that Peter figured out that he had orchestrated this to parallel with his three denials. He feared for the moment that Jesus would give him a look of scorn. Jesus looked at him with loving compassion and this time Peter did not miss it. Finally, Peter made the right connections and knowingly looked at Jesus as he joyously laughed over what his Lord had done for him.

Jesus looked at him too and chuckled with him about it. Then he said to him again, "Feed my sheep, Peter. Feed the sheep of my pasture."

Peter smiled in a childish way to him because he was not willing to commit himself to doing this, that is to return to apostolic ministry again. He looked back at his boat and net, and to his friends selling their catch. He did not want to say no to the Lord either, but the truth be told he had already returned to making his life's work as a fisherman.

Jesus knowing this, gestured to Peter that they should continue their walk further down the shoreline. It had been a mild morning but as the rising sun continued to warm the air, the wind began to pick up. The day was growing bright as the sun's light was reflected back into the sky by the water's surface. After a little while Jesus spoke to him in a reflective way, "Peter, when you were a young boy and begin to dress yourself, you insisted on doing it alone and refused the help of your mother and your father."

Peter wondered where this conversation was going as he nodded in embarrassment because he remembered how insistent and stubborn he was about dressing himself no matter how poorly he did it.

Jesus continued on, "Now consider this Peter. Someday you will become an old man. Then you will look back on what you have done with your life and how you lived it out. When that time comes, what do you want your legacy to be about? What do you want to feel about how you have spent those many years and what do you want to be remembered for?"

Peter thought that it was very strange that he should ask him about this, "Why are you bringing all this up now?"

"Someday when you are old and full of years you aren't going to be able to dress yourself anymore. The best you can hope for is that someone else will dress you in whatever clothes they find for you to wear on that day. They will put them on you whether you like it or not, and they won't care if you do or don't like them, say what you will."

Peter nodding knowingly but showed that he was curious to hear more. He was anxious to see where Jesus was going with this.

"Right now, you can go wherever you want and you can do whatever you want." Then Jesus stopped to lure in his full curiosity.

Peter turned his head to the side and looked at Jesus in the hopes that he would say more.

"When you are old you will do what others want you to do for them. They won't give any consideration for what you want anymore. They will take you wherever they want without even asking you about it first."

"You make it sound so bleak for me."

"This is the way of all the earth. You know that, but you need to be crucially aware of it right now."

"I don't look forward to it but yes I will admit that you are right. That is the way it is now with my grandfather. That is the way it will become with my father and as it will be for me someday too."

"Peter, what I am saying to you is this. What do you want your legacy to be? It is a highly respectable thing to go out on the water every workday and catch fish to feed these many people. You employ a few men, you may someday even have a few boats to do this with. You'll provide a good life for your wife and children. And when you are old and have lost all your powers and what you had been able to do for yourself, all you will have left is your memories. These no one can steal from you. When all else has lost its meaning for you in this earthly life of yours, the memories of your career will carry you forward."

Peter considered what Jesus was saying and he had to agree with him that this would be how his life would go and what it would become in the end.

Jesus went on, "Or when you look back on your life do you want to know that you were my apostle who shared as an evangelist the message of the gospel with the world? Do you want your memories to be that you helped to spread faith in me for the forgiveness of sin?"

"I have to say that I honestly do not know what I will do. Forgive me but I can only tell you the truth. I have to make up my mind about what I will do with my life. Once I knew that I was willing to follow you anywhere and lay down my life for you. That is all gone now. I did not expect that you were going to be the one who laid down his life for my sins. This is all so unsettling. I do not know about the Kingdom of God that you spoke of so many times before. How will it be established?" As Peter said this, he threw his arms up in a show of exasperation. "Will it ever be established?" And again, he threw his arms up into the air.

While the answer to those questions was yes, Jesus wasn't ready to answer that question for him at that time. Instead he said, "Peter, it is time for you and my other apostles to return to Jerusalem. I will appear to you there in the upper room." Then the Lord vanished from his sight.

Chapter Thirty-Two
Philip and Nathanael

In Galilee, in the city of Bethsaida, was the ancestral home of the brothers Nathanael and Philip. It was to these two that Jesus appeared again while the company of apostles were in Galilee. The two brothers were staying with their family there but on this occasion, they were out at the market during a busy hour.

The Lord had concealed his appearance when he came near to Philip, pointed to some bread, and said to him, "How many people do you think five of those barely loaves will feed?"

Philip thought that was a strange question between strangers. He took a quick glance at the man but did not recognize him as someone that he knew. He thought about the question and then he told the man, "Hardly two or maybe three if they are not too hungry I suppose."

Then the man said, "And two fish. How many do you imagine that two fish will feed?"

Philip wondered what kind of questions these were from a complete stranger. He answered him anyway, "That depends on the size of the fish. One that is the size of your hand is enough for a child, three that size would feed a grown man I suppose."

Then the stranger told him, "With that much food I once fed a multitude of five thousand men not including women and children. It was so great a multitude that six months wages would not have paid for enough bread for each one of them to even have a small piece."

Now Philip thought *that is the strangest thing that anyone could say.* He started to make a vague connection to a recollection that he had from when he travelled with

220

Jesus' during his public ministry. Then he realized what was happening. It was the Lord and he was being teased by him. He quickly turned and said, "Rabbi!" and then the stranger's identity was no longer veiled to him alone in that busy marketplace. He turned and embraced Jesus and the two rejoiced together.

Jesus said to him, "Come walk with me while we talk." And the two of them took a stroll down a quieter street.

Then Philip recalled the day when Jesus had fed that very large crowd of people. "I remember how I felt that day when you tested me. I was very alarmed about the situation. I was concerned for the people who had hastily left their homes from all around that part of the country because they heard you were in the area. They were desperate for your help. They had just dropped everything and left their homes instantly in the hopes of seeing you. They had brought no food for themselves and they were famished from their long journey."

"You are right, I tested you that day when I said, 'Where will we find bread enough to buy to feed these people?'"[81]

"Yes, that's right. I failed the test."

"You grew in faith."

"Yes! That I did."

"And now?"

"Since you have been raised from the dead, my faith has grown, and changed and … ." Philip hesitated.

"And what?"

"It is hard to say. My faith has taken on qualities that I cannot quite find the words to describe. Once you said that if I had faith like a mustard seed that I could move mountains. Faith for me was limited by what I could

---

[81] John 6:1-15

conceive of. I think that now what I am experiencing in my faith is that it is only limited by the imagination of God."

Jesus smiled large and nodded, "Yes. That is right. That is faith."

The two had circled around the block during their walk and returned to the market where they spotted Philip's brother Nathanael. The two of them walked over to Nathanael but he did not recognize Jesus because his appearance was veiled to him. Philip looked at Jesus and he understood that he was going to introduce himself to Nathanael in the same fashion as he just had to himself.

Nathanael told his brother, "I have looked everywhere in this marketplace, but the figs here are not fresh. We should just go to the orchards and pick our own."

Jesus said to him, "I could see you doing that, standing under the fig trees and gathering your own. Those would be the freshest of all then. But then you would have to wait for them to ripen."

Nathanael said to him, "Let's go to another market and see what they have for figs there. Did you find enough of the bread you were looking for."

Philip told him, "I imagine that you can find what you are looking for right here, if you are willing to look a little longer."

Nathanael was very pessimistic about that idea, "I don't think anything good can come out of this market this morning. What did you think of the bread here?"

His brother told him, "Oh, the bread here is very good. This man here knows this market and the merchants very well. Why don't you ask him?"

Then Jesus spoke up, "Yes, I do. Come and see what I can show you. I will ask some of the sellers for you for their best figs."

Nathanael cynically told him, "The merchants want to sell off their old stock before they will put out fresh new figs."

Then Jesus told him, "Nathanael, before you came here to this merchants booth I saw you looking at the figs over there."

Now Nathanael recognized Jesus' voice and then he turned to him and said, "Rabbi! You are God's Son! You are the Messiah!"

Jesus said, "See here! You are an Israelite in whom there is no deceitfulness. And when I return to my Father you will see heaven open and the angels of God as I ascend to him."[82]

Then Jesus said, "Do you remember what you did when we first met Philip?"

It took Philip a moment to find his voice and then he said, "Yes, I ah, right away I went and told Nathanael about you."

"Yes, you did. Nathanael do you remember what you said when your brother told you about me?"

"I am embarrassed to say it, but I do remember. I said, 'Could anything good come out of Nazareth.' And I was wrong about what I said about you and your hometown."

"And when I saw you approaching me I said, 'You are an Israelite in which there is no deceit.'[83] Have you ever wondered why I said that about you?"

"I just assumed it was a nice complement that you were giving to a man who did not believe right then that you were the Messiah as my brother had claimed."

---

[82] John1:43-51
[83] John 1:47

"Nathanael you know me. Have I ever made it a practice to hand out compliments to people I do not know something about?"

"Well, no."

"So, imagine now three years later why I said this to you."

Nathanael sighed hard and thought about it. He had been a student of Rabbi Jesus for three years and he was taught very well by the very best. But for the life of him he could not imagine why Jesus had said that about him. Then he resorted to a simple prayer for help. Jesus had promised him and the others that the Holy Spirit would guide them into all truth. Then it came to him and as he spoke the prayer it was revealed to him even before he could give it more thought, "Ah, you said that you saw me before I approached you when I was standing under a fig tree. Then I knew that you were a prophet and that God had revealed this to you. As a prophet you knew more than that about me too. You knew what I had spent my lifetime striving for. That was why you even worded it just as you did. You said, 'Here is an Israelite' because I gave myself to a life of very devout faith, like our ancestor Israel. He was a servant of God and accordingly his name means to walk with God."

Jesus said to him with a certain cunning sound to his voice, "Yes. Go on."

Then Nathanael continued, "Then you said, 'In whom there is no deceit.' And that was because in my devotion to the LORD I have striven to not follow in the footsteps of Jacob the man of deceit who swindled his father and stole his brothers' inheritance. I have striven to be an upright man in all that I do even wrestling at times with God as my sinfulness tried to control my actions. I have striven to treat my father, my brother here and all people with the greatest respect. Like my ancestor I too have wrestled at times with God for his blessing and longed for transformation in my life just as Jacob the man of deceit once did."

Jesus was truly excited about his apostle's introspection and insights he had come into about himself and his heritage, "Exactly!"

Now there was a pause as Nathanael thought about what they had just talked about and he came to see himself in a more exacting way. It was in his interactions for three years with the Son of God that he was changed. When his master died on the cross, all that he was as a disciple died with him too. Now in his Lord's resurrection he was finding a new life for himself as well. One in which he truly was bearing his own cross, dying to himself daily and following after.

"Nathanael," Jesus said to him, "Can you remember from that day what I said to you next."

The disciple thought for a moment and then answered, "You said that I would see great things."

"Yes, go on."

"It seemed strange to me then and I still don't understand it any better now than I did then. You said something about the ascending and descending of angels."

"That's right. I taught you that a disciple is not above his Rabbi but when he is fully trained he is like him in a certain regard. Let your training work for you now."

Now he had to consider all that he had been taught over the course of three years. There was much that Jesus had instructed him in. He was tense at first which only made his memories more distant to him. Then he said to himself that he couldn't simply make those memories surface by trying to force them. He relaxed and told himself that he needed to trust in his memories to sort themselves out and that the right one would simply surface and make itself know to him. That way hopefully the right answer would, by its own accord, come to mind and it did for which he was thankful. He answered, "You taught me that you are the way, the truth, and the life and that no man comes to the Father but through you.[84] Therefore, the angels, though not men but living beings nonetheless, must also mediate their way to and from heaven upon you, the Son of God. Am I right?"

Jesus held off from answering him too quickly. He wanted him to come to trust in the training he had received as his disciple. Then as the moment passed he answered him, "Yes Nathanael you are right and well said I might add. But there is more to this that you must understand."

Nathanael inquired of him, "How so my Lord?"

"Moses wrote that following the fall into sin, God commanded Adam and Eve to be fruitful and multiply. He told them that their children and descendants should spread out throughout the whole earth and subdue it. While some of them did just that, some of the others did just the opposite. They were the ones who built a great city that was named Babel. There they strove against God's covenant with mankind. Instead of spreading out, they built their city to keep the people concentrated there. They made their buildings strong so that they could live there for a long time. But when they set out to build a mighty tower whose heights would reach into the heavens is when the real problems began. They believed that if they could ascend into the heavens in their tower that they would discover the knowledge of God and the secrets of the universe for themselves."

"I remember being taught about this as a child in the synagogue school."

---

[84] John 14:6

Jesus nodded to him and continued on, "Then instead of standing idly by as they went against his will, my Father confounded their speech and they were unable to understand each other any longer. In their difficulties they were forced to separate according to many divided languages and go into the four corners of the earth."

Nathanael wondered, "Why do you bring this up?"

"So that you will know the truth about the way of the earth. Tell me now about Jacob and when he stole his brother's birthright."

"The birthright carried with it the promise of God to Abraham. That promise was that God would bless him and his descendants. That in him all the nations of the earth would be blessed. Jacob wanted that for himself and with the help of his mother Rebecca he disguised himself and deceived his father Isaac who blessed him by giving him the older son's inheritance. Then the first-born son, Esau, wanted to take Jacob's life, so he had to flee from his home to safety. That night in the desert he had a dream. As he slept he saw a vision of angels ascending and descending on a ladder. When he awoke he called that place Beth-El meaning the house of God and he said how awesome a place it was."

The Nathanael stopped to reflect on the story about his patriarch and considered what his Lord had been discussing with him. Then he went on to say, "What Jacob saw in his sleep was a vision of you with the angels. What I see now as we are talking is that Jacob was trying to wrongly accomplish what God alone can do for a person. That was what those people in Babel were also trying to accomplish by their own powers. They were trying to do what cannot be achieved by man alone. No one comes to the Father except through you and through you comes all things from the Father!"

Then Jesus explained to him, "Knowledge and power was what they were seeking in Babel. Jacob was seeking prosperity through possessing the blessing of the first born. The problem is that knowledge and power, or even prosperity for that matter, without out godliness is inherently dangerous. Babel's striving to gain knowledge rather than following the command of God to fill the earth would have given them knowledge without the fear and respect of God. Their effort to discern the higher things of God was going to succeed if they had been allowed to continue. Then it would have doomed them to their own destruction. Their gains would have led to greed, envy, and corruption and their society would have collapsed into godlessness. They were not living faithfully in his covenant and their gain in knowledge would have led to their collapse because every man would turn against the others seeking only his own way and disrespecting the rest."

Nathanael shared some of his insights into the pagan world, "Many people try to understand the creation. Some try to understand God on their own. The Greeks and the Romans have many gods. But I have seen that their gods are fashioned after their own imaginations and in their own image, the image of man. They try to manipulate their many gods through their prayers to them."

Jesus said to him, "That is all true. This is why I will send you and the other apostles into the world to proclaim the Gospel to all men. The world needs to know the truth about their Creator. In all man's own efforts, no matter how noble or well-intentioned they are, no one can come to the Father but through me. That is why you and the others must tell them that God sent me into the world to save them from their sins and bring them faith in the One True and Living God."

Then the two brothers looked at each other and they knew that they must follow their Lord's instructions and bring the message to the world. As they turned to respond to Jesus, he vanished in front of their eyes.

Nathanael said to his brother, "We must go and find the others and tell they what the Lord has told us to all to do."

Chapter Thirty-Three
Brothers in Nazareth

It was in the early days of Jesus' public ministry when he visited the city of Capernaum. This was not far from his hometown of Nazareth, only a two-day walk. He had been touring the region, preaching and teaching the people, and performing signs and wonders among them. Word of his fame had been circulating among the people of Galilee and many of them left their homes to search for him. Soon he returned to his hometown. There his hometown's people had heard about his work and reputation but some of the were very concerned about him and questioned what he was doing. He had been an exceptional student in his youth when he was in the school at their synagogue. However, they did not accept that he was working as a Rabbi and questioned whether he should be doing anything that he was up to. They did not like that he was traveling around Galilee and teaching in other community's synagogues. Some of his family also doubted the reports they were hearing about his miracles and healing.

When Jesus came back to Nazareth it was because it was his turn to read from the Scriptures and teach on the text at his home synagogue. Many people showed up that day. Some came because they always came, others came out of curiosity so that they could hear what his teaching was. Just about the whole town showed up. There were over two-hundred people there. It was so crowded that his siblings could not get close enough to hear him or speak to him. Even his mother was unable to get through to him because the people were so many.

Then someone in the large crowd told Rabbi Jesus, "Master, your mother and your brothers are nearby, and they want to talk to you privately."

Jesus looked at the people who were pressing in on him from all sides and said, "Look all around me here. Who is my mother and who are my brothers?" Then he pointed out his disciples for them to see and he said of them, "Here they are. They are my family, my mother and my brothers! And listen to me. My family is everyone who does the will of my Father who is in heaven. These are my bothers, and sisters, and my mother."

As Jesus taught, some of the people marveled at what he said because he knew the authority of the Scriptures and spoke with certainty about them. Others questioned his teaching and criticized him over it. Included in this group were his own brothers, James, Jude, Simon and Joses. The town's people who did not accept what he was teaching spoke sharply against him, "This Jesus is merely the son of a carpenter and we know who his mother is. He grew up here on our streets and we know him from his earliest years up. How did he come into this kind of knowledge and who gave him instruction in the Law and the Prophets, and taught him these things?"

Then Jesus spoke out loudly to everyone, "In all the world where prophets arise they are not without the honor of a prophet wherever they go except in their own hometown and among their own family. There they are not honored as such." After that he refused to teach them anything further and his prayers for the sick were limited to only those who would believe in him. Then he left Nazareth and visited other villages in the area.

It wasn't until further along in his ministry when the reports about the many signs and wonders continued to make their way back to his family that his brothers began to wonder if any of these were true. Because of their sheer numbers they felt it was likely that the reports were true because of the surpassing greatness of them such as, cleansing the lepers, raising the dead, and walking on water. Then they were compelled to reconsider their position.

Together the brothers of the Lord set out to find him, but they did not travel openly. They did not want to alert their brother to their presence when they arrived. Instead they wanted to see for themselves what the truth was. When they caught up with him, they saw their brother laying hands on the sick and healing them, giving sight to the blind, making the lame to walk, and casting out demons. They had now seen the signs and wonders for themselves. There was no doubt left that he was indisputably a prophet like no prophet ever before him. Now they believed. From then on they all became disciples of their brother Rabbi Jesus. Then James and Jude travelled with him and supported his ministry. Two of Jesus' other brothers, Simon and Joses, did not travel with him. They were both married and needed to remain in Nazareth as they supported their families.

Following their brother's death, Simon and Joses were devastated by the few details about it that slowly made their way north to Nazareth. They could hardly believe that their brother had been so graciously received into the city of Jerusalem, to a palm branch parade and then later that week was betrayed, arrested, and condemned and put to death. Further disturbing their mourning were the reports of his resurrection. They did not understand how he could supposedly appear and then vanish from sight. It sounded to them more like his ghost was appearing which was no comfort to them at all. The two men were together one evening and as they visited with each other, they discussed the things that they had heard.

Joses said to Simon, "I fully expected that Jesus would be anointed and crowned as our King. I hoped that he would have united Galilee and Judea as one Kingdom under his mighty rule. Things seemed like they were all coming together for that to happen. But now what will happen?"

Simon replied, "I didn't expect that he would be crucified. I cannot believe that the Temple authorities rejected him and had him put to death. The people of Judea and Jerusalem showed such overwhelming acceptance to him. I thought that their popular support would somehow have forced the chief priests and even the high priest to accept him too."

"If the reports of his resurrection are true and that he is not a ghost that has appeared to the others, he could still be crowned our long-awaited King. He is the Messiah, or at least so I thought."

"His resurrection from the dead is unlike anyone else's. Look at what we have heard about his friend Lazarus. He resumed his natural life. But people have said that unlike him, our brother appears where he will and then vanishes from sight. He has not simply resumed his natural life like Lazarus."

"That is true. I do not know what is to become of us and all the rest of his followers. Do we simply resume our lives and fade into history like John the Baptist's followers have?"

It was then at twilight as the evening sun was setting into the western sky, that the Lord appeared to them. "You two have too much time on your hands. Isn't that what our father said when we idly talked the hours away?"

Simon and Joses both began to rise to their feet to greet the Lord, but he said to them, "No. Don't get up." Jesus knelt down and sat next to them. "Isn't this like olden times? When we were all in our youth and living at home?"

His brothers were frightened and uncertain of what to think about his sudden appearance. Jesus said to them, "Touch me and see that I am not a ghost. A ghost does not have flesh and bones as I do. See for yourselves." Then Jesus reached out his hands for them to examine.

Then his brothers touched his arms and held his hands in theirs. They looked at the marks of the scars that were left from the nails. It was very hard for them to accept what had happened to him. They would have rushed to his side and fought to protect him. They felt bad that they never had the chance. Instead their thoughts went to carrying out some kind of revenge plot on the chief priest or even the governor of Judea. Somehow none of that seemed to matter anymore. They had come to a certain sense of peace over it. It was a peace that they did not fully understand though.

Simon wasn't ready to simply let the whole thing drop. He was struggling in his heart with all that had happened, "These last few weeks have been something else."

Joses agreed, "I'll say."

Simon continued on, "I was surprised to learn that the chief priests in Jerusalem rejected you as the Messiah. Your miracles and the wonders you performed were testimony enough to convince the world that you are the Messiah. And I certainly didn't expect them to go to such extremes and have you crucified. It was very difficult to comprehend why you suffered and died. Couldn't you have put a stop to it? Loosing you, my brother, in death was one of the worst things I have ever endured. It was like having my own heart ripped out and stomped on. I wept bitterly for you."

Joses was silent but it was clear that his sentiments were equal to his brothers.

"Now, in your resurrection there are certain mysteries that I do not comprehend."

Jesus nodded and showed his brothers that he was giving them his undivided attention.

Then Joses shared, "I remember how sorrow filled I was. It was so very frightening. Now somehow, I do not feel that way at all though the memory of it is seared into my heart and mind forever. Since you were raised from the dead I have somehow been healed of my sorrows. Since then I have a new hope that I live with. The problem is that I don't know what that hope is exactly. And I don't understand how I have been healed. Most of all, I don't know how all this was God's will for you."

Simon did not add anything, but it was understood that he was struggling with the same issues in his life.

Joses said, "Jesus my brother, how is it possible that it was God's will for you to suffer and die?

"To fulfill the prophecies" was his answer.

Joses reacted with quite a bit of surprise, "Where do the prophecies foretell of the death of the Messiah? And why would they say such a thing? What purpose would that fulfill?"

To which Simon added, "If it was only to fulfill them that you died, that would be some very self-serving prophecies at the expense of your life. If they have no greater purpose, then I would say let them then go unfulfilled in your life."

Jesus took to heart what his brothers were saying to him and he understood their concerns were for him as a member of their own family. "The prophecies only foretold it. They do not exist simply to be fulfilled. There was a reason. It was God's purpose and his will that needed to be fulfilled. His eternal plan existed before the prophecies were written."

There was a silence that followed as the brothers waited for Jesus to explain the plan of God for his life to them. Then he went on to say, "Consider Adam and Eve and what they did when they first sinned. From that earliest of days, the day of the fall, God provided a temporary covering for the forgiveness of sins. You remember that it was told to Adam and his wife Eve that on the day that they sinned they would certainly die for their sin? But rather than require their very lives of them, a substitute was provided by my Father which was the Genesis lamb. It was put to death in their stead. Since then, God has patiently overlooked the sins of mankind when an animal was sacrificed following the pattern he showed to them when he sacrificed the very first lamb for them. In his divine forbearance he has been overlooking the sins of the world which were temporarily covered with the blood of bulls and lambs until I came into the world." Then Jesus looked at them to see if they were following his explanation.

Joses spoke asking, "I can understand what you are saying but there has got to be more to it. Tell us more."

"As Moses has written, 'An eye for an eye, a tooth for a tooth, and a life for a life.[85] The blood of bulls and lambs could only temporarily appease God's just demands over the offense of sin. But, because men and women sin, only a human life, their own life, can be sufficient to pay the terrible cost of disobeying and offending God. The righteous and just demands of the Law requires each one to

---

[85] Exodus 21:23-24

be held to account for their own sins and no one can be held responsible for another's.[86] The Father could not simply set aside his righteous judgements. They are absolute and uncompromising as they must be because he is God Almighty. That means that everyone is condemned to die in their sins. Yet God is forever loving, and in his love and mercy he was not willing that anyone should perish for their sins and therefore he had a plan to save the world from its own demise."

Simon was glad to hear this because it clarified concisely for him what he had never before understood so clearly before, "Now we are really getting somewhere."

Joses wanted to learn more and said, "But how? In what way? There has got to be more to it than that."

Jesus summarized what he was saying and he went on to explain, "No one man could die for another's sins. The entire population of the world is condemned in their sins. He sent me to come into the world and die for all the sins of the world, for the forgiveness of all who will believe in me."

Joses was growing impatient and said, "But you just said that no one can die for another's sins."

"I know what you are wanting to learn. God our Father could not die, he is God. However, as his Son, when I was born of our mother, as a mortal man, then it became possible for me to die."

Simon and Joses both dropped their heads and looked sharply at their brother as he explained the rest of God's plan of redemption to them. "As the Son of God, I also became the Son of Man. Then I became mortal and could die. As the Son of God, I could die for all the sins of the world, being his divine Son. As the Son, I could die for all

---

[86] Ezekiel 18:20

237

the sins of the world, for all people, for all of time. Though I died as a mortal man as the Son of God, I could not stay dead. Therefore, the Father raised me from the dead and restored me to life. By my life, death, and resurrection I was able to bring salvation to all who will believe in me for the forgiveness of their sins."

Simon and Joses understood how the redemption worked and their countenances brightened as they comprehended all that their brother had said. Yet that was not without their continuing concerns as the brothers of the Lord.

Simon asked him, "That was all very risky, don't you think? I mean what if it didn't work."

Jesus very confidently declared, "The Father had placed all things into my hands."

Joses countered asking this, "So, because you knew he would raise you from the dead, you went through with it all?"

Jesus nodded and kindly said to him, "Knowing it is one thing. Believing that the Father would raise me up is another. Faith was really the issue. I needed to have faith that he would raise me from the dead."

Simon questioned his brother, "Knowing in advance that even though you would suffer and die, did that make it any easier? Is that why you were willing to do it because of foreknowing that you would be raised from the dead and healed in every way?

Jesus answered him saying, "No, it did not make the suffering any easier, or facing death. No more than knowing it afterword. The suffering, my memories of it, and the scars are still there, but the healing is greater than all of it. The suffering is still very real, real in every way.

But the healing is greater than the wounds they inflicted on me."

Simon wondered, "You said that you needed to have faith in the Father. What is faith to you?"

Jesus simply defined it saying, "Trusting that he would do it as he said he would in the prophecies."

Joses said, "But, for as easy as you make the redemption understandable, how is it that no one has been able to figure that out for themselves before all this?"

The Lord's brothers continued to struggle between knowing and believing.

Then Joses went on to ask him, "But how could you have known these things?"

Simon chuckled and said, "Brother, don't you understand that is the advantage of being a prophet of God, isn't it Jesus?"

Jesus nodded, "That is true. It is a gift to know these things and to have faith and believe these in them. Before you can believe you must know what you are believing in. By which I am saying that you must know the Father and trust in him even though you only know in part."

Joses wondered out loud, "How is it that with all the prophecies that someone or some group of scholars couldn't figure things out like this in advance?"

Jesus paused and then said, "It is the nature of sin that prevents that from happening. It blinds the eyes, twists the mind, and makes the heart corrupt. Therefore, we are dependent on the Father to trust in him for all these things. Somethings he reveals to us, other things remain a mystery to us, but the Father knows all things."

Simon sharply said, "What?"

Jesus confidently explained to his brothers, "Yes, it is true. If we had the power to think like God in this way we might falsely come to believe in ourselves and our earthly abilities rather than trust in him. If we thought that we could live without him and that we could provide for our own redemption somehow, we would only have become self-righteous. The Father holds all mysteries in his hands. Only a few of them are revealed for us to know. Even if we could understand them by the powers of our minds it is not enough to understand them. It could never be enough to simply understand it. Faith, that is the goal for everyone. You must believe in him and entrust the lives of your very souls into his hands."

Their brother the Lord, had given them many things to think over. The greatest thing that he gave them was the challenge to trust in God. As their conversation slowed and there came a lull, Jesus stood up and disappeared before their eyes.

Chapter Thirty-Four
Samaritan Brotherhood

The time came for the apostles to return to Jerusalem and when they had all gathered together they set out for the southern Provence of Judea. The day was perfectly sunny with a clear blue sky as the apostles and all those with them set out that morning. As the day progressed, the sky grew overcast and it threatened to rain as the disciples continued in their journey to Jerusalem. They had been journeying through Samaria and revisiting all the villages that Jesus had visited when he passed through there himself. And as they travelled they spread the news of Jesus' sacrificial death and resurrection. As they pressed on, the sky continued to darken, and they heard thunder off in the distance.

Peter spoke to the other apostles, "That thunder warns me that we need to quickly get to the next village and lodge there until the storm has passed over us."

James, along with his brother John looked worried, as he responded, "I agree but the next town may not be a good place for us to stay in."

"Oh, why is that?"

John cautioned him against the idea, "We only passed through there the one time and they did not receive us then."

Peter was wondering why they were so reluctant to enter the village and stay there because of the storm, and the reason they gave him wasn't telling of the whole story. He said to the brothers, "We've been to so many villages in the past three years. I can hardly remember one from the other. Why is this one different than the rest? Why didn't they provide hospitality for us then?"

James told Peter, "Oh, I remember that all too well."

"Why is that?"

James reluctantly told him, "I'd like to say that I'd rather not say. But then you would just pester me until I got tired of it and then I would have to tell you anyway. So, I will skip being evasive and you can skip pestering me."

Peter picked up on James' avoidance and pointed out, "Good cover James, but you are being evasive by suggesting that you are not being evasive."

"I don't want to tell you, but I will tell you. This is the poor village that John and I offended when we came here looking for a place for the Lord and all of us to spend the night."

"Humm."

James wanted to put things in a certain context hoping it would place what he and John did in a little less bad light. "You remember those days. Jesus had set his face and was bound and determined to go to Jerusalem. He had told us that they would reject him and that he would undergo great suffering and be put to death at their hands. The people of that village could see that we were only looking for lodging for the night and would then push on quickly to Jerusalem in the morning. They took offense at that. They had hoped our Lord would stay on with them for a few days to teach them and minister to them."

There was a silence that followed. James wondered if Peter expected him to fully recall the entire story. Peter on the other hand wondered if James and John would go on to dredge up the dreaded details of that day or minimize them. Moreover, he hoped that they would find a way to make amends with the village's people and bring them healing for their past encounter.

As the silence continued James struggled with recalling the whole story again because he hated the idea of having to say more. Then as he considered other options, he manned up and decided that he and John needed to tell all and make their amends and see about lodging in the inn. "When we came here last time my brother and I were insensitive to the inn keeper. We gave him a reason to be offended with us. To make matters, worse we asked the Lord if he wanted us to call down fire from heaven and consume them because they refused to offer us hospitality. That is when Jesus gave us the nicknames, 'the Sons of Thunder.'"

While James made the confession for both of them alone, John also agreed with what his brother said as he nodded in complete agreement.

After they disclosed the truth to Peter he said to them, "Here is the perfect opportunity for both of you to do things right this time. Why don't you two hurry on ahead of us and make the arrangement for us to stay with them?"

James and John went on ahead of the rest at a quicken pace and made their way to the entrance of the tiny village. As they were arriving the people there wondered if these were two of Jesus' apostles. The reports that Jesus of Nazareth had been crucified and then raised from the dead were now widely circulating throughout the region. These people had also heard reports from Galilee that his apostles had traveled there from Jerusalem. As they came to the entrance to the town, some of their elders were waiting for them to greet them and see what manner of men they were.

As James and John neared closer to them they slowed their pace because they did not want to appear to be rushing or unfriendly. They addressed the elders respectfully and their greeting was, "The peace of the Lord Jesus be upon you."

The village elders and those with them greeted them as well.

"So, you are followers of Jesus of Nazareth?" asked a white haired man.

The two brothers nodded in unison and James said, "We are sir. We are apostles of his. I am James, and this is my brother John. We would be very honored to be received into your village."

Another village elder spoke with them, "We have heard reports from Judea and Jerusalem and from Galilee about your Rabbi's death. We are very sorry for all that he suffered." He hesitated before going on, "Forgive me, but we have also heard reports that he is alive. That he was raised from the dead somehow." It was clear that he did not want to offend James and John by bringing up his death and offering condolences. At the same time, he needed to hear correctly if the incredible reports they had heard about his resurrection were somehow true.

Now other villagers came out to see who these two men were. They stood in awe of them when they learned that these men were apostles of the Lord and wanted to visit their village. They also saw James' and John's humility and how they were very respectful of their elders. It was a rare occurrence when Judeans and Galileans came through Samaria. Most of them looked down on Samaritans with great contempt. Most of the Judeans and Galileans traveled on the eastern route that ran alongside the Jordan River in order to avoid them altogether. The apostles did not look down upon a single one of the Samaritans but rather treated them as equals or even as if they were greater then themselves as they had been taught by their Lord. In turn, the village people felt well respected by these two men.

Now the question of Jesus' resurrection had been brought up by one of the elders and James wanted to share with them all about it. "It is true and let everyone know that Jesus was crucified, died and was laid to rest in a tomb. This happened on the day of the Passover. Then on the first day of the week he was raised from the dead by the power of God's Holy Spirit."

John also spoke out confirming for them all, that Jesus was raised from the dead.

Then James inquired of them, "We are traveling with many others. We are worried that these clouds and the thunder are telling us that there is a storm approaching that will let down rain. We would like to know if you could be gracious enough to let us lodge in your inn until the weather passes?"

Then without hesitation an elder said, "We will provide you with housing, food, and whatever you need since you find us worthy to visit with. Our inn is very small and cannot accommodate all of you. But we will open our homes to you as well. And while you are here please share more with us about your Lord Jesus and all that he has taught you. We would love to hear more about his resurrection so that we may know the truth about his life."

Peter and John looked at each other and grinned ear to ear as they heard these very warm words. They had feared that they might be rejected by these people and told to leave the area. They felt that now if there had been any feelings of animosity between them in the past, that it was now certainly gone. Then as the apostles and all those traveling with them arrived, they quickly settled into the warm hospitality that the people offered them and made plans to continue their stay for several days.

At once the word of their arrival spread throughout the village and into the surrounding rural areas including other villages as well. The people of the village welcomed the apostles into their inn and they brought food from their homes to provide for the needs of the apostles and the others traveling with them. Though the day was growing old, the people of the village very much wanted Peter, James, and John and all the apostles to share with them about all that happened in Jerusalem.

Peter stood before them and announced to them, "All of you have heard of Jesus of Nazareth. He was a man attested to by many signs and wonders, miracles, and healings that he performed. He travelled in Samaria on one of his journeys. He taught the word of God with the people of your nation. He visited Jacob's Well, which is not more than a day's journey from here, and he stayed in the city of Sychar."

Then the people smiled and nodded. They took civic pride knowing that their nation was host to this historic site that was dug by their common ancestor, Jacob the son of Isaac, the son of Abraham.

"It was there that our Master worked to bring healing to the things that in the past have separated our nations. At Jacob's Well the question was put to him, 'Where should we worship? On your mountain of Gerizim or on mount Zion in Jerusalem?'"

Now this was a common point of contention between their nations and Peter worried that as he shared about this topic with them, that they might jump to conclusions and become offended. But the people continued to listen and only desired to hear more from him.

246

"Our Lord shared then what I share with you now. The day has come, according to Jesus' words, that for the true worshipers of God, the place of worship will no longer be such a concern. Those who worship the LORD God Almighty will now worship him in the Holy Spirit and with the knowledge of the truth. This I now share with you, that though we are all sinners equally, Judeans, Galileans, and Samaritan with us too, we may have forgiveness for our sins though the sacrifice of Jesus' life when he died on the cross. It was there that our sins were laid upon him by God in heaven and he died for us and for our forgiveness. Therefore, wherever we are in the world we may freely worship God through our Lord Jesus Christ who has died and was risen from the grave by the power of the Holy Spirit."

Now one of their elders spoke up, "Gentlemen, how can we know the truth of these things that you are making claim to?"

Then Peter answered him, "When I first heard the reports of his resurrection it was by some of the women among us today." Then Peter gestured with his hand to Mary Magdala and the other women. "When I heard what they were saying, it sounded to me like a wild story. To me it was unbelievable and very upsetting. But then on evening of the third day after his death, Jesus appeared to me and not only me but to all of the apostles. Everyone that I am traveling with has seen and touched our resurrected Lord. We are all eyewitnesses to his resurrection and we will all be glad to share with you everything that we have experienced. We can stay with you for a few days if you like. Please ask all of us about how we have seen him and held him in our arms, spoken with him, and eaten with him.

247

Then you will know and come to believe that Jesus is risen from the dead."

During this time the apostles had many discussions with the people about their claims. The people there took joy in knowing that they were accepted by the apostles and they took even greater joy knowing that God's salvation had come to them. When their time with them had passed the apostles left that town where many of the people now believed in their message. Then they continued their journey southward toward Jerusalem.

Chapter Thirty-Five
Lazarus, Mary, and Martha

Life for Lazarus, Mary and Martha had slipped back into their old routine, although, there were changes. They did mourn knowing that their dearest friend Jesus had endured such terrible pain and suffering before his death. They readily believed that he had been raised from the dead when the news first came to them on that very day when it happened. This they had no trouble believing. After all Jesus had raised Lazarus when he was dead four day and sealed in his tomb. So even in Jesus' resurrection they did mourn his absence from their lives. They felt the loss of not hosting his apostles and his followers as they had so frequently in the past. They cherished all that they had experienced in those days and remembered often all that Jesus had said and taught them. And they wondered what their lives in the aftermath of his suffering, death, and resurrection would mean for them.

There continued to be many travelers passing through the village of Bethany where they lived. They wanted to meet Lazarus. That was because they had heard the story of how Jesus had raised him back to life. The three siblings used those opportunities to share with these people the message that Jesus was the long-awaited Messiah and that God had raised him from the dead too. But their day to day lives were for the most part very much the same and they felt a certain emptiness in those days. They felt isolated because they did not live in Jerusalem where everything new seemed to be taking place. They wondered if the emptiness would ever be lifted from them. They hoped that the apostles would have more to share with them about what Jesus' resurrection would mean for them and for all the believers. However, the apostles had travelled to Galilee and there was no further word of them or the Lord for now.

It was several weeks after his resurrection that there came a lone man to their home. It was late in the afternoon. The household servants were all in the kitchen working to prepare the dinner meal and so it was Mary who went to the door when she heard him knocking. She greeted him, "Good afternoon sir. May I help you."

The Lord had not yet shown her who he was but merely appeared to be a stranger to her. "Lazarus your brother is expecting me to visit him today."

"Come in, won't you? Please have a seat."

It was understood that his feet would be washed. That was their custom but as none of the servants were there Mary knelt down on her knees to do this task. Alongside the bench where Jesus sat there was a large pitcher of water and a brass basin. The basin had a lid over it which was used to cover the dirty water and hide it from everyone's sight. Mary knelt to her knees and poured water into the basin and removed her guest's sandals. She lifted each foot in turn over the basin and poured water directly over them. Then she used a soft cloth to wash away any dust or dirt that may have accumulated on them. She did not look closely at his feet as she carried out her task and that corner of the entryway was not well lit. He had scars on both of his feet and though Mary noticed them she was prevented from thinking further about them. Then she took a towel and patted them dry. Lastly, she put his sandals back on his feet. When she was done she returned the lid to the basin to cover the water in it. It was then that she noticed that the water was not dirty, not even in the slightest. In fact, the water seemed to be fresher than when it was first poured out. As she thought about it, she realized that the man's feet had accumulated no dust on them either. Then she noticed an aroma that was familiar to her. She waited for a moment to dwell on it and then she remembered having used a nard ointment to anoint Rabbi Jesus' feet at a dinner party. The dinner was offered to honor the Rabbi for having raised her brother from the dead. First, she imagined that this was just a coincidence that he would have that same perfumed scent on his feet. But as she considered it further she knew that this particular ointment's bouquet was very rare.

Mary quickly stood to her feet and cautiously looked again at the stranger. She did not know what to expect as she gazed at him. Jesus remained seated though and he continued to appear like a stranger to her until he said her name to her, "Mary."

It was at the saying of her name that Jesus' identity was revealed to her. She was a little startled to see him and to learn that this was the Lord's feet that she had just washed. As she collected her thoughts, she quickly bowed low to the floor and said, "My Lord! Who am I that you should come to visit my home or allow me to wash your holy feet?"

"Mary, it was you who washed my feet and anointed me for my burial only a few weeks ago. What you did then was very honorable, and you are remembered well for this service. At the time of my death, they were only able to make hasty preparations to my body for it burial. But you had already washed and anointed me in advance. This was held in your trust and you were the guardian of this service to me until that day came. And now you will forever be remembered for your kindness to me." He offered his hand to her and he stood to his feet.

As Jesus explained this to her, tears ran down her face. She was speechless to learn how she had shared unknowingly in preparing his body for burial. It was like a window into that day and time had been opened to her as she experienced again the tragedy of his suffering and death. Overlaid upon that was the joy of his resurrection and of being in his presence. It was a complex and emotional moment for her that made her want to weep and rejoice in dancing both at the same time. She reached out her arms and the Lord received her into his embrace as she leaned into his side and held him as tightly as she could.

After some time had passed she asked him, "You said my brother was expecting you, my Lord. Is that true?"

"I know that you have learned of my visitations with the apostles. When I said that he was expecting me, I really was saying that I was anticipating that he hoped I would visit him too."

Mary was becoming giddy as she walked with the Lord to the dining room where Martha and Lazarus were waiting for her and the start of their meal. As she and Jesus neared the dining room, she stopped and stood in the doorway and blocked it so that her brother and sister could not see who was behind her. She announced their special guest saying, "We once had a dinner party to honor Rabbi Jesus when he raised you from the dead. Now our dinner tonight has become a celebration as the Lord has graced us with his presence again." With that said she entered the room and stood clear of the doorway. Then as Jesus walked into the room, Lazarus and Martha stood to their feet. They were utterly surprised and were speechless for the moment. They both excitedly rose from their couches and rushed to the Lord as they all shared greetings with him with warm hugs and kisses to his cheeks.

After this, the sisters set a place for the Lord at the table and Lazarus poured some wine for him. Martha lit their candles and they all looked at Jesus to indicate they wanted him to bless the LORD for their food. Jesus lifted up his head and looking heavenward he prayed,

"Blessed are you our Father,
the Maker of heaven and earth.
You have given to us from
the fullness of your creation and
we bless you and praise your holy Name. Amen"

Jesus ate some of the lamb and it was clearly seen that he enjoyed it very much. Then he took a sip of the wine to clear his palate. "I have missed your cooking," he said. "It is very delicious how you roast the lamb here. No one else can do it so good as you, you know."

There was a little pause because the three of them did not know what to say.

The Lord wanted to tell them something very special and so he chose his words intentionally to introduce what he was about to share. "I did not want to leave you feeling abandoned again."

Lazarus, Mary, and Martha understood that he was referring to the time when Lazarus was ill and died. The three of them smiled knowingly and nodded to the Lord.

"There was a plan in place in those days that my Father had designed for all of us to experience."

The three of them wondered it what it was that he was saying to them.

Jesus now took on a very sobering tone as he disclosed this to them, "In all the days of my ministry I prayed for the sick and they were healed. I laid my hands on the deathly

253

ill and they recovered their health. When Jairus daughter died I brought her back to life, just as I did when the widow of Nain's son died. But when you were taken deathly ill, my Father told me to delay coming to you. This was the only time something like that had ever happened."

Now the three sat silently and wondered why that was so. Hearing this rekindled the memory of the pain and sorrow they endured.

"My Father wanted to use your death Lazarus to bring a greater glory to his Name. He wanted it known that you were raised after four days dead in your tomb. This is something that has never before happened in all the earth. This way no one can question if it was a true miracle or not. There is no other explanation for it. It was by the hand of God that you were raised back to life."

Then Lazarus and his sisters smiled to know that it was the Father's plan and that it was not his intention to abandon him to death and the grave.

Martha spoke, "We have all healed and found comfort from our many sorrows of those days. By your coming to us and raising our brother, we found that our broken hearts were healed from those terrible pains and difficult questions we struggled with."

Jesus took comfort in hearing those words and they confirmed for him what he wanted to believe was true of his friends. "Now, my Father has shown me that there was still more to his plan than that. My Father wanted to use our experiences then so that I could feel what he felt when he abandoned me unto death on the cross. Just as it appeared that I had abandoned you by my delay in coming to you Lazarus, he has shown to me from this experience a foretaste of what he would go through when he left me to die on the cross."

Now the three looked at each other in awe because this mystery was now being revealed to them.

Lazarus spoke, "We did not know or realize these things until now my Lord. And now we are honored again to know how we were called upon as servants of the Most High to help you prepare for and face your own death by our experiences."

Martha shared, "When you did not come to us right away we felt rejected and abandoned by you. We did not and could not understand why or how you were treating us this way. It broke our hearts when you did not appear in time. Then when you raised our brother from the dead we found healing. But I have had lingering thoughts about why this all happened that way. Now it is beginning to make more sense."

Jesus added, "When I returned to Bethany it broke my heart to hear you say, 'Lord if you had been here my brother would not have died.'"

Martha suddenly felt very uncomfortable with hearing her words from that day repeated back to her. She felt embarrassed by them and quickly said to him, "My Lord, you do not have to say this. It was a very difficult time for us. Forgive us for our…"

Jesus did not want her to apologize or make light of what had happened, "You were right to say that to me. It was necessary for me to hear it. This was the Father's will. I needed to know and experience the terrible feeling that I had failed you by appearing to have turned a deaf ear to your plea to come and heal your brother."

The three family members silently looked at each other and were deeply touched by what the Lord was revealing to them.

Jesus placed his hand over his heart and took comfort knowing that his very close friends received this news so well. "There was no other way for this to have happened. It was necessary that it be with my close personal friends who are like my own family to me. It was for that reason that you were included in this. That is why, as the Father has revealed it to me, I have come to visit. So that I could share this with you. It is my hope that this can be a blessing to you. By my delay and not rescuing your brother from death I was able to know how my Father felt when he did not rescue me from death on the cross. I could tell when that moment occurred. It was then that I cried out in desperation, 'My God, my God, why have you forsaken me?'"[87]

The telling of this was a very difficult thing for the three siblings to hear. Lazarus spoke for them, "We have heard some of the details about your suffering from the apostles. They told us about that moment when you cried out from the cross. It was a very chilling thing to imagine how you felt. Now we see how you have shared with us in my time of illness on my deathbed. As I felt abandoned to death, so you also were abandoned to death. It is an awesome and fearful thing that you endured on the cross for us."

Jesus took a moment to respond and then said, "It was for a greater glory that these things happened to all of us. So that many would come to believe in me for the forgiveness of their sins."

As the meal came to its end, Lazarus, Mary, and Martha had come into a richly deeper sense of what God had called them to be part of. They were all honored and blessed by their resurrected Lord's presence in their home. The

---

[87] Matthew 27:46

feelings of loss and emptiness that they had been feeling was now forever behind them. They looked with a profound sense of joy at their Master, and as he stood to his feet, he vanished from their sight. By his gracing their home and visiting with them, they came into a new and hopeful vision of what the future of their faith would be.

Chapter Thirty-Six
Great Commission

The number of believers in Jesus and in his resurrection continued to grow in the city of Jerusalem, in Galilee to the north and even in Samaria. The reports of his appearances to his apostles, the ever-faithful women and many of his closest followers, continued to circulate among the people everywhere. His teachings were continually shared in Jerusalem, and in the synagogues throughout the region by his followers everywhere.

The apostles had regathered again in Jerusalem after having travelled to Galilee. It was exactly forty days since the Lord's resurrection. They continued in fellowship with other devout followers of the Lord, including his brothers James and Jude. They all met daily in the upper room as a group. The mystery of when and where he might appear again continued. The apostles and all of those who believed in Jesus lived continually in anticipation of it happening again. There were also many other reports from among the believers of the Lord appearing to them privately, to their families, and among other gatherings of his followers. In all, it numbered over well over five hundred brothers and sisters that the Lord had visited in the five weeks that followed his resurrection.[88]

Now, the time had come for the Lord to appear to his apostles and those with them for the final time. This took place in the upper room. As he had once instructed them in this room on the night before his death, so also, now he gave them similar instructions. As he had so many times before, he appeared in the midst of them and said, "Peace be with you all."

---

[88] 1 Corinthians 15:6

The disciples also returned the greeting of God's peace to him.

Then the Lord spoke to them in a special way because he was imparting to them his final instructions before his ascension into heaven. "The message that I give to you today is the message that you have heard from me from the very beginning. That everyone everywhere needs to repent from their sins and turn to God to live faithfully for their Creator. They need to believe in the good news of the gospel. Tell them all that I came to give my life as a sacrifice for their sins and redeem them from bondage, death, and the devil. Through my death and resurrection, I am able to bring them victory over the grave and bring them into eternal life in heaven."

The disciples were glued to his every word because they did not want to miss a thing that he said. Some of his words were entirely new to them. These words of their Lord were said to give everyone complete clarity in all that they had seen and heard from their Master over the past three years of living with him.

"There is now a new covenant between God and men. Not one that is established by the blood of a lamb or a bull, but one made in the very blood that I shed on the cross for the remission of yours sins. In this covenant you have been given a new commandment which is to love me as I have loved you and given myself for you. In this new covenant you are to love one another as I have loved you and given myself for you on the cross. By this all people will know that you are my disciples if you love me and love one another. This is not like the old covenant in which you were commanded to obey the Law and live by it so that your lives could go well for you. That was one in which obedience was commanded of you. In my new covenant the love that the Father has for the Son is poured into your hearts in such a fullness that it will overflow out of your lives and to the world. God's love will abundantly fill your hearts and overflow from your lives. This will happen as you live in faithfulness to my Father."

Now as Jesus went over this with is disciples the Holy Spirit worked among them and they could feel in their hearts that they were coming into a greater continuity in their faith and understanding of the gospel. These instructions, though repeated to them from the past, carried with them a new lifegiving freshness and transformation that enlivened every one of them and they were not burdensome.

Jesus continued on, "My Father has given me all authority in heaven and over all the earth. And I am sending you in my name to all the people of the earth. I am sending you to preach and make disciples of all the nations. Call on them to repent from their sins and believe in me and the message of the Gospel for the forgiveness of their sins. Baptize those who believe in the name of the Father, and of the Son, and of the Holy Spirit. Teach them everything that I have taught you and lead them in love. Tell them that by the life lived with faith in me they will be saved from their sins. In my name they will tear down Satan's strong holds and cast out demons. In my name they will lay hands on the sick and in my name pray for them to be healed and they will cleanse the lepers. Great signs and wonders will accompany you as a testimony that it is by the hand of God that you do these things in my name. And remember that I will be with you at all times and in all things unto the end of eternity."

It was hard for the followers of the Lord to imagine that these were his final instructions to them. After his death, they had become completely disillusioned with what their futures might hold for them as his apostles. With his resurrection they continued to live in the mystery of what it meant that he was alive again. His appearances to them seemed to come at almost random times, but they always served a purpose. With each visit they were getting a clearer understanding of his intentions for them in the days and years that would follow. As they had hoped before his death they hoped again that Jesus would restore the earthly Kingdom of David and rule as a monarch over their nation. Along with that would come the overthrow of the Roman occupation. Some of them even speculated that the Lord would expand his reign to include the rest of the world. That in their minds would be the fulfillment of the promise given centuries before to Abraham; that in him all the nations of the earth would be blessed. The Kingdom of the Lord was not to be one of this world and of that they had only begun to understand.

Jesus then raised his hands and they imagined that he would give them a blessing before vanishing from them again. Instead he spoke these words, "As Isaiah the prophet foretold of me, so I also commission you and sending you into the world in my name according to his words:

'May the Spirit of the LORD be upon you,
May the LORD anoint you to bring good news to the poor;
May the LORD send you to bind up the brokenhearted,
May the LORD use you to proclaim liberty to the captives,
and the opening of the prison to those who are bound;
and to proclaim the year of the LORD'S
favor to all people everywhere.[89]

---

[89] Based on Isaiah 61:1

Chapter Thirty-Seven
The Ascension

Then Jesus invited them to join with him, "Now all of you must journey with me to the Mount of Olives before I return to my Father in heaven."

Then the apostles and all those with them rose up and stood to their feet and followed Jesus as he left the upper room. Jesus lead the way with Peter, James, and John close at his sides. They were followed by the rest of the apostles, with Mary his mother, and many of the other women who had shared in providing support to his ministry for the past three years. They walked purposefully as they made their way through the city streets and out the eastern gate. This was the last time that Jesus would ascend up to the Mount of Olives. It was on that same road that he had entered the Holy City when he made his triumphal entry less than two months ago.

There was nothing said as they made their way out of the city to the top of the mountain. When they were within sight of Bethany, the village where Lazarus and his sisters lived, Jesus stopped and turned to face his apostles.

The apostles asked him, "Lord Jesus are you going to restore to us the Kingdom of your ancestor David to us at this time so that we may rule in your name? Then all the people of the earth will serve your Father in righteousness and with reverence to his holy name."

The Lord was not surprised by their slowness of heart. He had spent three years teaching them about the heavenly nature of his Kingdom. They had not yet come to fully grasp its nature. He overlooked their lack of understanding and then he instructed them saying, "It is not given that you should know the season or the day that my Father alone has determined for this to take place."

Jesus knew that it would take them some time to understanding the nature of his heavenly Kingdom's reign on the earth. They continued to expect a kingdom like that of David's. This was understandable. Their ancestors had been hoping for the reestablishment of their monarchy for almost a thousand years. This hope was firmly established in their nation and deeply rooted in their culture. The Lord had taught them much about his Kingdom even though he knew they would be slow to perceive that where his will was done, then his Kingdom's reign was being fulfilled. The Lord knew that they needed time and the transformation of the Holy Spirit that was still to come to them. Then they would come to understand the purpose and plans of God. Now as Jesus explained to the apostles that they would not be told the answer to their question, the bright smiles of the apostles gave way to disappointment as their hopes to rule over Israel were dashed.

Then the Lord redirected their attention to his plans for them. "As I have instructed you, this you must fulfill. Wait in the Holy City of Jerusalem until you receive the transforming power of the Holy Spirit who will come to you in a few days. Then you will share your testimony about me with all the peoples of the earth. Until then you all must continue to live in close fellowship together, breaking bread, and living according to the many things that I have taught you. And just as John baptized with water for the remission of sin, you too will be baptized with the Holy Spirit and fire not many days from now.[90] Remember,

---

[90] Pentecost was 10 days after his ascension and 50 day after the resurrection.

I will never, no never, leave you alone or abandon you. I will be with you always, even unto the end of time."

As Jesus spoke to them, their eyes were unwaveringly fixed upon him as he raised his hands to bless them. A light breeze ruffled his robe and blew it slightly about in the air. He had captured their attention so completely that they did not at first notice that he had already begun his ascent into heaven. Slowly their heads tilted back, and they looked upward as he was rising. As he continued his ascent, heaven was opened up to him and they saw the surpassingly beautiful golden clouds that gloriously lined the way between God's creation and his throne. There were bright beams of light that shone down upon them in a dazzling array of golden white colors. In the clouds there was never a shadow, only light upon light in God's glorious presence. From within the clouds their appeared myriads upon myriads of angels all lined up shoulder to shoulder. Some of them were standing on the clouds and others with magnificent wings were suspended in midair flight. They were stationed in rows and columns endlessly together for as far as their eyes could see. Some of the angels were gathered into multiple choirs who sang out glorious melodies never before sung in all the earth. Though each choir sang their own chorus all in different keys and to different melodies, they were wonderfully unified into one voice. Their songs were so grand and glorious that there was no earthly comparison nor could there every be that could match them. And the hymns they sang were in three unified parts:

Most holy: holy, holy, holy is the Lord God Almighty.
This is he, the I AM, who was, and now is,

and who is to come. He alone is worthy to receive all glory,
all honor and all power, forever and ever. Amen[91]

Most worthy: worthy, worthy, worthy is the lamb of God,
who has taken away the sin of the world.
He is worthy to receive power, and wealth,
wisdom and might, glory and blessings,
forever and ever. Amen[92]

All glory: glory, glory, glory to the Son of God.
Amen, blessing, glory and honor,
Wisdom and honor, power and might,
forever and ever. Amen[93]

As the Lord rose further and further from them they saw the likeness of the Father rise from his great white throne and stand to welcome his Son home with a most loving hug. Then the Father sat on his eternal throne and the Son sat on his throne, which was at the Father's righthand side. They saw him in the glory that was his from the before the beginning of time. In awe and wonder, the followers of the Lord bowed to their knees and many of them clutched their hearts in the deepest reverence for him. Others prostrated themselves to the ground and they all joined in with the angelic chorus' and worshiped him singing this hymn:

Give thanks to the LORD our God,
the Almighty who reigns over all of creation.
Make his name known among the nations,

---

[91] Based on Revelation 4:8-11
[92] Based on Revelation 5:12-13
[93] Based on Revelation 7:12

for glorious things he has done.
Sing praises, sing praises to his name.
Glory in his holy name.
Rejoice and be glad, all the earth.
For our God has gone up with a shout,
With the sound of the trumpet he has gone up.
Our God is King over all of
creation and holy is his name.
His dominion is over all the earth,
and as high as the highest heavens.
Be exalted over all,
and let your glory reign over all the earth.
Who rides upon the clouds,
You are exalted above all the earth.[94]

Then, in only a moment of time, the window that had opened for them to see his ascension to his throne in heaven was closed. Awe overcame the Lord's followers again as two heavenly men in brilliantly luminated white robes suddenly appeared to them. One of them spoke with an angelic voice, "Galileans, why are you simply standing there and looking up to heaven?"

The disciples looked at one another wondering what they should say.

Then the other man spoke to them with these reassuring words, "Jesus Christ who has been received back into heaven before your very eyes will return to you in the same way as he was taken into heaven. And every eye shall see him when he comes to you again." Then the two men vanished from their sight.

---

[94] Based on Psalms 47:1-8, 57:10-11, 68:4 and 105:1-3.

266

The apostles and the many followers who had accompanied Jesus out to this place on the Mount of Olives were stunned by the beautiful sight that was opened to them on that day. They stood in silence and wonderment.

DANICA'S REVENGE

DANICA'S REVENGE

QUEENS & KNIGHTS BOOK 2

M KAY NOIR

For those who find beauty in the darkness, and for those who have not yet thought to look

...

(and for my loving husband, who finally found out what depraved things I write)

CONTENTS

A WORD OF CAUTION

This book is intended for a mature audience only. It contains often graphic scenes between consenting adults.

Refer to the www.mkaynoir.com/danica for the full TW/ CW list (on-page and off-page mentions).

If at any point this book makes you feel unsafe, please take a break and consider whether you want to continue.

Mental health matters.

B⦾⦾K
PLAYLIST

Listen on Spotify (also via on mkaynoir.com/danica)

1. *Hayloft II*, Mother Mother

2. *Lonely Boy*, The Black Keys

3. *Indestructible*, Welshy Arms

4. *Freedom at 21*, Jack White

5. *Honey (Are U Coming?)*, Maneskin

6. *Tear You Apart*, She Wants Revenge

7. *This Modern Love*, Bloc Party

8. *Dark Necessities*, Red Hot Chili Peppers

9. *Forfeit*, Chevelle

10. *Lydia*, Highly Suspect

11. *Figure it Out*, Royal Blood

12. *If I Were You,* Nothing But Thieves

13. *Frayed*, The Naked and Famous

14. *Outta My Mind*, Des Rocs & The Cobra

15. *Scared Together*, Silversun Pickups

16. *Nina Cried Power*, Hozier & Mavis Staples

17. *You Are*, Arid

18. *Doing it to Death*, The Kills

19. *This Mess We're In*, PJ Harvey & Thom Yorke

20. *Identikit*, Radiohead

21. *Smells Like Teen Spirit*, Malia J

CHAPTER ONE

CARNAGE

DANICA...

The gates of the Fera mansion are flung wide open when we arrive.

They're never open—not like that. *Fuck.*

I wipe my hands on my pants for the third time since we got the call to hurry back, but they're still clammy. My right knee refuses to stop tapping, restless, like I never commanded it at all.

All the signs of chaos are unmistakable yet I still hold onto some hope that this isn't really happening.

Crunching tires on gravel is the only sound echoing in the silence, amplifying the anxiety knotting in my stomach. "Hurry up, Carlo," I urge the driver. But there is no point; Dante isn't home, not anymore.

The gate guards let us in with a solemn nod, exchanging looks with his colleagues I don't want to interpret. Their

1

faces all say the same thing: we're too late. But I know that. It was already too late when they phoned us.

I wish my last words to Dante weren't "fuck you" as he kicked me out of his office against my will this morning, closing the door in my face.

Regrets won't help me now though, what am I going to *do*?

Focus, Danica.

The unbearable drive finally ends, and I leap out beforeCarlo can fully bring the van to a halt, almost tripping but managing to keep my balance.

"Miss Matthews, please be careful! I have to keep you safe!" the broad-chested Italian with the ill-suited buzz cut shouts after me for the umpteenth time today. They're always telling me how it's their job to protect me. *What about Dante?* Why didn't they protect *him*?

It's all too much. Dealing with a situations like this wasn't exactly covered in my public school education.

Tears threaten to overwhelm me, but I bite my lip to keep them at bay, pushing the emotions down. Crying won't fix this.

New faces are milling about outside the house as I run up to the entrance. They're shouting in urgent Italian and hushed English, but I don't catch any of it. It's been four months since I moved into the Fera mansion with Dante but there is only so much Italian my overthinking brain can process right now—and that amount is zero.

"Fuck," I mutter under my breath as I push past inside. My tough act instantly crumbles in the face of the scene before me. It's something straight out of one of those gangster movies my brothers would sneakily watch when my parents were out.

It's complete carnage in the usually pristine foyer. Two figures lie unmoving on the polished stone floor, separate pools of blood merging into one. I recognize them, unfortunately—it's Marco and Gio, two of Dante's guards. The unnatural angle of their necks and the way flies have already begun to gather tells me everything I need to know. *They're dead!*

"Miss Matthews." A familiar voice turns my attention to the right, forcing me to look away from the bodies I wish I never saw in the first place.

Relieved, I throw my arms around the old man, grateful to see him alive. Alive but not unscathed. "Emilio, thank God. What happened?" I ask Dante's second-in-command, taking stock of his injuries.

A guy whom Dante previously introduced as simply "The Doctor" is preparing to stitch up a gunshot wound in Emilio's leg. He's just like any other doctor except he specializes in discretion, Dante explained once when I watched the tall lanky old man with the receding hairline remove a bullet from Gio's arm. At the time, I remember thinking that this doctor had the longest fingers I had ever seen...

"We tried to stop them, Miss Matthews. But there were too many of them. I don't know how, but they knew about all the security, we—"Emilio flinches as The Doctor pours more disinfectant into the nasty-looking wound. My stomach turns, instantly queasy, and I have to look away for a moment as those long fingers do their thing.

"Where's Dante?" I ask, though I know there isn't much point.

Emilio shakes his head slowly. "I don't know."

"Who did this?"

"I don't know. They were Italian. But we don't know who...Or why." Emilio hangs his head. "We failed to protect the boss; I'm sorry."

It doesn't add up though. "He's usually pretty good at protecting himself. What the fuck happened?" I wonder out loud, wiping my hands on my pants.

"Something was wrong today. Don Fera didn't even put up a fight. He—" Emilio can't find any more words and I'm glad, because I can't hear any more of them. The dread pulses in my chest, tugging at the back of my neck like an unshakable bad feeling.

"Thank you, Emilio. I'm glad you're okay." He's not okay but I can't bring myself to say the word "alive." *I'm glad you're alive.*

Nobody stops me as I head to Dante's study, his sanctuary of power. It no longer looks sanctified—it's a complete mess. Broken glass, spilled coffee, bullet holes in the furniture...there is a puddle of blood on the carpet in front of the large wooden desk. I really hope it's not Dante's but I know it probably is.

It all looks *wrong.* There is no police tape marking the scene of the crime, no forensics dusting for prints. This is not how the Feras deal with their problems.

There are so many questions milling in my mind, but nothing makes any sense. I wish I knew what had been on Dante's mind this morning—what troubled him so much that he sent me away like that, without explanation? He must have known something was up.

I close the door behind me and lean against the heavy wood that, not too long ago, had provided no resistance to the unexpected intruders.

The anxiety pushes up into my mouth like bile, and the knot in my stomach tightens. There is no keeping it at bay anymore, and I breakdown, sobbing. *Oh god, Dante. Please be alive. Please.*

The tattooed god has become my entire world; I can't imagine my life without him. I don't want to. What am I even supposed to do now? This is Dante's territory, not mine. I am just a student.

Until a few months ago, I'd never even held a gun. Sure, Dante insisted I take lessons from one of the guards, and I've fired a few bullets. I am actually quite a good shot—a *natural*, according to Gio. But I am no match for whoever took my knight away.

My back still firmly against the door, I slide down untilI'm sitting on the floor, the same floor I had Dante kneeling before, devouring my cunt like a good boy. But the room is empty now.

Despite the urgency of it all, I don't know what to do with myself, what to think. My 24 years of life had largely been spent in innocence, until the villain himself, the great Don Fera, unexpectedly showed up at my place of work that night, dashing as always in his expensive shoes and dramatic rings, clothes tailored perfectly to his muscular body.

But he's not here now to make a plan, to fight off the bad guys, to swoop in and save me. Who knows where he is, what they're doing to him. I have very few reference points for Dante's life that don't come from dated *noir* movies.

Sure, I play the strict Domme behind closed doors. I take and own every ounce of Dante's pleasure once he hangs up his boss-hat at the end of the day. But in matters of the business, I've steered clear. He's made sure of it. *I can't let you get hurt,* he always said. *I'm not losing you too.* And look now, *he* is the one who's been kidnapped.

Kidnapped. I've never known anyone who was kidnapped.The word feels foreign, jarring. I push it out of my mind; it's too unpleasant. Nothing good happens to people who've been kidnapped. *My poor boy.*

What I wouldn't give to feel Dante's strong arms wrapped around me right now, lifting me up to my tippy-toes and kissing me deeply. To breathe in that musky cologne of his as he begs me to please let him come...But this time, I'm not the one in charge.

As Dante forced me out of the house this morning (so rudely at that), I tried to console myself with the fact that my darling boy always came back to me again. When he was ready, he'd crawl back on his knees (literally), naked except for the beautiful collar that reminds us both he is mine.

What a magnificent sight—a 6'5" tamed King crawling towards you, emerald green eyes dripping with desire and locked on you (and only you) as a curl of his thick, slicked-back hair comes undone over his forehead.

Nobody else sees him like this. *What if I never see him like that again?*

No, shut up. Shut up! Why is the stupid game show host in my head always such a bitch?

There is a gentle knock on the door behind me, forcing me back to the present. It's Carlo's voice that calls from the other side. "Miss Matthews?" he asks cautiously.

I wipe the tears from my face, trying to keep my voice steady. "Just a second."

Before getting up, I take one more look at the mess in the study, the blood on the floor. Somehow, the little zen garden on Dante's desk had escaped the struggle unscathed, its peaceful pebble taunting me with its smooth surface, its tranquil vibes.

Don't worry baby, I'll find you, I vow as I open up the door. Nobody gets to lay a finger on Don Fera's body except me.

Nobody.

Two weeks earlier...

CHAPTER TWO

BUSINESS

DANTE...

I t takes every ounce of self-control to stop myself from tearing the laptop in two with nothing but my bare hands. *Just breathe, Dante.*

For the fourth time, I look over the numbers on my screen, trying to add up the columns that don't add up. *This is not good, not good at all.*

"What's going on here, Luigi?" I speak slowly, my voice straining as I push back the anger sparking at the edges of my extremities, threatening to seep through my skin and engulf me.

The accountant blinks rapidly, the thick frames of his glasses failing to hide the nervousness in his beady eyes. He refuses to make eye contact, clumsily shifting his weight from one foot to another. "I'm not sure yet, *Signore*," he stammers, fidgeting with his hands over his round belly, probably praying to some deity that I don't blame him for this. He knows I have killed men over less.

"Our expenses are way higher than usual. Where did the money go, Luigi?" I ask sternly, closing the laptop loudly as I get up, towering over the little man.

Luigi instinctively steps back, trying to keep his distance. "We're looking into it, *Signore*," he answers, the intonation in his voice betraying his fear.

"This is not very good for cash flow, now is it Luigi?" I sigh loudly, trying to relieve some of the pressure building behind my eyes, but it has little effect.

The accountant shakes his head sideways, lowering his gaze.

"How did this happen?"

"From what I can tell, a large portion of it is the expenditure for the upcoming charity banquet, we—"

Raising my hand to demand silence, I cut him off. "That was budgeted for, no?"

Restlessly, I pace around the large room, running the variables through my mind. *Where did the money go?*

"*Sì, Signore*. It was. To the last cent." It's the truth, I approved the budget myself.

"So, where have the extra expenses come from?"

"We're still trying to figure that out," he repeats.

My morning is instantly ruined. Keeping the books on plan is crucial for the business's smooth operation. Not too much money to attract prying eyes but just enough to keep all the businesses going—those on the books and those off. But if there is not enough cash flow...that is a problem, a very annoying problem.

"I don't pay you to figure things out, Luigi. I pay you—very handsomely, I might add—to fix things. Are we not on the same page about your role here?" I raise my voice slightly, the tension weaving through each word, tighter and tighter, as I struggle to maintain my composure.

"We are, *Signore*. It's merely an oversight, I'm sure. We'll fix it. I just need more time. Please." I know what that whimpering *please* means. It translates to *please don't hurt me*, but the dweeb doesn't even have the balls to beg for his life properly. His weakness disgusts me, almost as much as his incompetence—I can't stand it.

Moving quickly, I grab the switchblade from under my desk. It's always taped there for easy access; I don't take chances. Before Luigi even knows what's happening, I seize the little bespectacled man by his collar, easily overpowering his short, pudgy frame made for the office and not the streets.

"Please," he repeats, barely audible, closing his eyes as he flinches.

"Look at me, Luigi," I demand, sliding the sharp blade over his arm and cutting through the fabric like it is made of nothing but delicate spiderwebs instead of cloth.

Luigi looks close to tears as he tries to meet my gaze. *Fucking coward.* I press harder, drawing a path of blood as the blade slides over his arm.

"I'm sorry. I, I..." he stutters.

"I don't like money issues, Luigi. Don't you know that?" I move the blade to his throat, resting it gently but firmly against his Adam's apple.

"I do, I know...Please..." The accountant holds his breath.

With a sigh, I lower my blade and push him away. He stumbles backward, into the coffee table, and trips, narrowly avoiding hitting his head as gravity does its thing. I don't offer to help him off the floor as he scurries to locate his glasses again.

The cut on his arm isn't deep, but it is bleeding profusely through the once-white shirt. It isn't the first shirt of his I've ruined. For his sake, I hope it is the last.

Counting to ten, I let the air filter through my pursed lips as I push back against the anger that threatens to blur my world into fury like it has so many times before.

For both our sakes, I turn my back on the whimpering accountant, staring out over the lawns as I let my mind wander. The silence is thick and uncomfortable, but I don't care, I need to think; I can't think when I'm worked up like this.

"One week, Luigi. You have seven days to find the answers. If you can't tell me where the money has gone by next week this time..." I don't need to finish my sentence. We both know that actions have consequences.

The relief on the old man's face is obvious. "*Sí, Signore. Grazie*. I won't disappoint you."

"No, you won't. Please leave before I change my mind. Send Emilio in on your way out."

He nods, rushing out in such haste that he almost trips—again.

Leaning back in my chair, I sigh. I've never enjoyed the business side of things; I've never enjoyed any of it really. But what choice did I have?

There's a firm knock on the door, three short taps—Emilio's unmistakable signature.

"Come in."

"Yes, boss?" Emilio asks, closing the door carefully behind him. He is an imposing figure, nearly as tall as me, but his voice is soft, deceptively calm—like Uncle Iroh from *The Last Airbender*, according to Danica (whatever that means). Despite his age, he is still a formidable force to be reckoned with. They don't make men like that anymore.

Emilio has been with the family since I was a kid and he was but a young man with a dark past nobody spoke of. When the others turned on me after I became the head of the family, I got rid of them all except Emilio (and the accountants). His role needed no name. Fuck having a traditional structure; a *consigliere* is no good if he's just going to stab you in the back.

"Have you heard anything from Luca? He was supposed to be here for the meeting with the accountant. It grinds me when he slacks on his responsibilities—" I stop myself from saying more, it's not appropriate.

"I haven't heard from him," Emilio answers simply. He knows me well enough not to add fuel to the fire. Although he's never said anything out loud, I know he's not the biggest fan of Luca himself. Some may find a lack of respect more permissible than others, but in our business, it is unforgivable.

"Such a spoiled brat; I'm getting tired of him not pulling his weight."

My affection for my brother runs deep, yet his knack for inciting a rage within me surpasses that of any other.

Emilio doesn't reply. We both know my brother isn't very reliable—never has been and probably never will be. I shouldn't be complaining though.

"Please send him in when you see him," I order, checking my phone for a reply to my earlier message. It is still unread.

The old man nods.

"And Emilio, nobody gets past that door, understood? I have some urgent things I need to take care of."

"*Sì, Don mio.* Understood."

I dismiss him with a wave of my hand and lean back in my chair, my mind overburdened as I twist the heavy rings on my fingers out of habit. A ring for each of my deceased loved ones, always there to remind me what I've lost. All I have left is Luca, the little shit that he is.

Supposedly, I can't entirely blame Luca for the way he is. What role model did he have?

Staring at the ceiling, I clench my fists, enjoying the satisfying sound of my knuckles cracking. I should work on not getting so aggravated; it's not good for my health—or so my doctor says (and Danica too).

I pick up the little rake on the side of the Zen garden Danica gave me to try and manage my anger issues. It seems so out of place on my desk, yet I've grown so attached to it. Much to my surprise, I like watching the neat paths form in the sand as the rake weaves from side to side in the wavy motions of my design.

It's not enough to calm me today though. Not even close. I smack a little black rock with the tiny rake, sending it flying to the floor like a golfer hitting his mark with a satisfying whack.

Fucking family

CHAPTER THREE

KNEEL

DANICA...

The nightmares jolt me awake more violently than I would've liked—again. They're becoming more frequent, as they always did this time of the year.

The cold sweat clings to my warm body, my breath still caught in a gasp that was supposed to be a scream in my dream. I know none of it is real, but the uneasy feeling remains even after the details start to fade.

All I remember of the dream is that I was nine years old again, running through a field that somehow blended the image of my childhood backyard with a nondescript forest. The twins (my brothers) were chasing me, threatening to lock me up in the shed again.

The rest of the story quickly evaporates from my mind. I'm not mad. The memories from those days are painful enough, I don't need dreams to remind me that my perfect childhood wasn't, in fact, all that perfect.

Picking up my glasses, my brain slowly processing the sunlight filtering through the slit in the heavy curtains that cascades down from the high ceilings. Dante always opens them a little when he gets up.

Maybe he hopes it will rouse me sooner, but he should know by now that I'm not a morning person. If I'm up before noon, it's a miracle. He, on the other hand, has lived a whole life before the sun even rises, starting with his 5 AM workout with Emilio. Rather him than me.

My day starts much slower, usually with a phone in the hand. But today, the notifications contain little of interest—the usual spam emails, a message from my mother asking when I'm bringing my *new boyfriend* home for dinner, and a bunch of other things I swipe off my screen without even looking.

My mother has been nagging me to meet *the new man* ever since I moved out of home. I'd only given her vague details about where I was relocating. The buff men (bodyguards) who had swiftly moved my belongings into unmarked black vans probably hadn't done much to put her at ease either.

But how do you tell your mother you're moving in with one of the city's most renowned criminals? It wouldn't take much digging for her to uncover who Dante really was; what he really did for a living...There would be a lot of explaining to do, especially around why he lied to her by pretending to be a cop that first time he rocked up at my house.

My mother has always been a bit overbearing. Maybe because I was the youngest—a full seven years younger than the twins. Always so overprotective...Yet she couldn't protect me when I needed her most.

Disinterested, I put the phone down again. I crawl back under the fluffy blankets, trying to find the motivation to start the day.

My bladder has no intention of letting me remain in bed though.

With a groan directed at the world at large, I fling the duvet off my naked body and swing my feet into the fluffy slippers waiting beside the bed.

I don't feel like getting dressed properly, I still need to wash my hair anyway (*girl math*). So, I throw on my short black satin gown instead. It does little to cover my hefty cleavage, but who am I hiding it from anyway? Everyone on the property is under strict instructions never to lay a finger on me. Not if they value their jobs (or lives).

The thought makes me smile. Dante's possessiveness is almost cute. Which is bizarre considering how off-putting it was in my ex. But Dante is different…His possessiveness doesn't make me feel trapped, it makes me feel powerful. He's not trying to cage me.

Shoulders slumped, I brush my teeth on the toilet, still slow with sleep. I am under no illusions that I'm nothing like the elegant women Dante is used to having around, the ones with proper breeding and pedigree, the ones who know how to get on a private jet and look unfazed—but I'm not bothered for a second. I know they can't give him what I give him.

Well, all the imagined women. Dante doesn't ever confirm nor deny their existence. Not that I mind. Everyone has a past. He's *old* already, after all. Though I would never call him that to his face.

The gown barely covers the top half of my thighs as I exit the master bedroom, confidently making my way to the study down the hall. I don't even bother with putting on underwear.

Nobody tries to stop me—they're used to me and my night-owlish ways by now.

Nobody except Emilio that is.

He may be used to my ways but he's still under Dante's command.

"You can't go in there, Miss Matthews," he says sternly, blocking the door. I always wonder if he doesn't get tired of standing outside Dante's study all day. Whenever I ask him, he just says that he can sit if he wants to, and that he does other stuff too. Who am I to question?

"Good day to you too, Emilio. Please move."

"I'm under orders to not let anyone in," he maintains, arms crossed over his chest like I'm supposed to be intimidated by him.

"I'm not just *anyone*, am I?" I try stubbornly to shift the brick house of a man more than double my size. An amused smirk tugs at his lips in the face of my growing frustration.

"Miss Matthews," he sighs my name in an exhale. "He's not in a good mood."

"All the more reason to let me in, Emilio." I know he has a soft spot for me. But it doesn't help me much now.

"Not today," Emilio almost pleads, carefully putting a hand on my shoulder to push me away.

"I wouldn't do that if I were you," I say boldly, looking him straight in the eye.

Realizing what he's done, Emilio drops his arm immediately, recoiling like he's touched a hot stove plate. Dante's touch-her-and-die speech must really have made an impression on all of his men.

Seeing my gap, I take my chance and dart under the guard's arm, slipping into the room before he can do anything to block me.

When I barge in, Dante is standing by the window, playing with his rings like he always does when deep in thought. At the sound of the door, he turns around quickly, an angry scowl flashing over his face. But it immediately softens when he sees me.

"I apologize, *Don mio*. I tried to stop her," Emilio says sheepishly, remaining by the door as I waltz over to Dante, victorious.

"It's okay, Emilio. I'm sure you did. You can go now." Dante smiles warmly.

I throw my arms around him as Emilio closes the door on his way out.

"Good morning, darling," I smile, reaching for a kiss on my tippy toes.

"Good *afternoon* to you too," Dante winks, kissing me deeply as he lifts me off my toes, sweeping me up in his strong embrace. As usual, he's dressed like he's about to shoot a fancy cologne commercial where all the men are decked out in dark lines and clean cuts. Today's look features another perfectly-fitted pair of charcoal trousers with a crisp white dress shirt ironed to maximum smoothness. His shoes (Italian leather) are polished to a flawless shine, matched perfectly to his belt.

"I was up all night studying." I pout dramatically but he misses it, staring out the window again.

"You can't use that one anymore." Dante seems distracted, distant.

He's right though—my exams are done already. But it sounds like a much better excuse for my sleepiness than admitting I once again got caught in the social media scrolling trap until the early morning hours while Dante snored softly against my chest.

I glance at his table, changing the subject. "Your Zen garden is a mess. Where's the rock?"

Dante points to a spot on the floor across the room where the little rock had been flung, a sad little dot in an ocean of carpet.

"Again? It's supposed to bring you calm." Shaking my head, I pick up the smooth rock and put it back in its sand pit.

Dante doesn't say anything, so guarded as always.

"Emilio says you're in a bad mood," I say casually as I hop onto his desk, completely disregarding the actual seating options.

"Is that so now?" Dante raises a brow. "I should give Emilio a talking to about what our trust agreement means..."

"Don't be mean to Emilio. You know I'm very *persuasive*."

"Oh yeah, especially when you wander around the house dressed like that." Dante shakes his head but smiles despite himself.

"You said I should make myself at home..." I grin. "So, are we going shopping today or what? I still don't have a dress for the banquet and it's less than a week away."

"I can't today. There's a lot on my mind." Dante sighs heavily, cracking his knuckles.

"That tense, huh?" I ask, trying to hide my disappointment.

"I'll make it up to you..."

I don't reply, letting the silence hang between us.

This is not good. Dante gets nothing done when he's this worked up—I know him well enough to know that. There is only one remedy...

"Lock the door," I finally say, my voice slow and sultry, commanding.

The entire vibe in the room changes.

Dante looks at me but doesn't dare to question me. He knows that look, that voice.

"Yes, Miss." He walks to the door and does as he's told. "Danica, I—" he starts but I cut him off.

"Quiet, *boy*! Stay right there," I instruct, slowly untying the belt of my robe. The look on his face makes me want to smile but I keep up the strict act.

Discipline is an important part of Dante's training. Our contract says as much. It says many other things too, listing all our boundaries, our maybes, our absolute desires. Within the confines of those papers lie the instructions for our entire dynamic...and those confines are not confining at all. He wants me to do whatever I want to him.

Still, I have limits I won't cross.

And Dante respects that.

Keeping his gaze, I drop the robe from my shoulders, the smooth material falling open around my breasts. Dante stands frozen, obediently, practically salivating at the sight. It's been a few days since I've allowed him to come. I know he's easily aroused now, just the way I like him. He is always more submissive when he hasn't had a release in a while.

I slowly uncross my legs, revealing the absence of underwear he should've expected but didn't.

A murmur escapes Dante's lips. I can tell he's burning with desire but does not dare to move without permission. Many painful punishments later, Dante is a better submissive for it. We are both figuring it out—me, how to be dominant; him, how to submit. But with each other, it doesn't feel like work, it feels like a natural journey.

"Come here," I whisper, summoning the tattooed god with my curling forefinger.

Dante starts toward me but I hold up my hand. *Stop.*

"Is this how you approach your Queen? No. On your knees!" I command and Dante instantly drops to the floor, eyes lowered.

Slowly, he crawls toward me, expensive pants on an expensive carpet—everything worthless to him except pleasing me. *What a beautiful sight.*

When he stops on the floor beneath me, I grab a fistful of his thick, curly, dark locks and pull his face up between my legs.

I always wake up horny and Dante never leaves that state. It's the perfect match.

Maybe it is because I can't ever get enough of him, of the pleasure he brings me.

"Look at me, darling." The command drips from my lips, sweet but assertive.

Dante's hungry eyes flicker with lust, with desperation, as he meets mine.

"What do you want? Tell me," I whisper, holding him there, face mere inches from my naked cunt. He dares not look anywhere but my eyes.

"To...to serve you. Please," Dante begs.

I throw my head back and laugh from my belly. How could I ever tire of seeing such a powerful man reduced to a whimpering boy?

The idea that Emilio is just outside the door makes it even hotter. Nobody has any idea that I'm not the one on my knees right now, that their fearless leader is indeed petrified, petrified of never being allowed to come again at the hands of his cruel Queen.

"I haven't showered yet," I say, releasing his hair.

Dante inhales deeply, almost panting at the revelation. I know it drives him mad. The smell, the taste...he loves it when I am dirty, he's told me before.

Dante whines in desperation, gaze focused on my bush. Who knew the great Don Fera was capable of such beautiful sounds?

Nonchalantly, I reach down, unbuttoning the top of his shirt to reveal his beautiful leather collar beneath. Nobody else knows it's there.

Hooking my finger through the metal loop, I yank his face into my pussy.

"Please me, *Tesoro*!" I lock my legs behind his back, pulling him further into me. A loud moan rises from my lips as Dante flicks his tongue over my clit, trained to perfection to make his Mistress come.

Without giving a single fuck that it's the middle of the day, in the middle of his work space, I pinch my nipples between my fingers, grinding my hips into Dante's face in a rhythm I know will send me over the edge in minutes.

Cutting through the moment, Dante's mobile phone starts ringing.

I smack it off the table but it continues to ring.

"Don't you dare stop until you lap up every damn drop, understood?" I hiss between my teeth, gasping between little moans.

The head between my thighs nods but does not slow down. I know Dante enjoys losing himself in my desires; it allows him to clear his mind. A win-win.

"Just like that...Such a good boy," I coo encouragingly in the teacher-voice I reserve only for him; the teacher-voice that instantly gets him hard, desperate.

Oh god! I can't help biting my lip as the pleasure builds between my thighs. My body is on fire!

Digging my heels into Dante's back, I howl loudly as the pinnacle of my climax reaches its crescendo.

But I don't let go.

Instead, I pant my instructions in hurried breaths...

"Every. Last. Drop. Boy!"

CHAPTER FOUR

CONTROL

DANTE...

I t's difficult, but I try my best to walk like there isn't a vibrating butt plug stuffed up my ass.

Danica loves public play, but it always makes my life so difficult.

Oh god, why is it so uncomfortable?

How can I keep up the facade of being the brutal head of the Fera family when all I can think about is licking Danica's feet and begging her to let me come? What has she done to me? But I know it wasn't all on her; my submission has been a willing gift.

The mere thought of Danica roaming around with that powerful remote, ready to activate the plug at any time, makes me instantly hard. The anticipation drips from my sweaty palms. She will be here any second...

At first, I refused to let her come to the auction banquet, but her persistent nagging wore me down. She wanted to wear a fancy ball gown for the first time in her life and she finally had somewhere to wear it to, she said. How could I deny her that?

Besides, despite how dangerous the people in this room were, they operated according to a certain protocol, respect—nobody would be foolish enough to try anything at the auction; it wasn't worth disturbing the hard-won peace among the families.

The lavish foyer fills up quickly with the *crème de la crème* of the underworld, milling about in neatly pressed suits and uncomfortable high heels. It makes them look like ordinary rich people, instead of some of the most sinister figures in this city. In the lavish surroundings of the venue, they look right at home.

Dramatic chandeliers, elaborate artwork on the wall, the marble floor shining without flaw—a certain luxury is expected at these events. I don't care much for the dated decor myself, but I know the families are old school like that, modern architecture fails to impress them.

Not that I have anything to do with choosing the venue. Alicia organizes it all, much like she does my household, buzzing around with a clipboard to make sure things are running as they should. If her hair was pulled any tighter, her cheekbones would stab through her eye sockets.

I make my way over to the door to greet the new guests as they enter. More than a hundred people are expected tonight at this grand venue, excluding the security. No weapons at the auction though: there is a metal detector at the door that everyone is forced to pass through before entering the elegant hotel that was chosen to host the exclusive event this year (and only this year).

The annual Fera charity auction is renowned in all the wrong circles and a secret to the right ones. Large amounts of money exchange hands in the name of tax-deductible charity. Old debts are settled and new contraband acquired at an event that at surface-level appears no different from any other charity galas.

But everybody knows the millions of dollars that flow through the proceedings are not meant for the average-looking artifacts displayed on the stage under heavy protection. No, the real auction happens online through a very secure connection and exclusive access. It is set up long before the actual event, the bounties agreed upon before anyone even checks their weapons at the door.

$1,2 million for an abstract painting for Mister Marino, the paperwork reads. But online, the truth: "$1,2 million for semi-automatic weapons for the Marino

family." Power, weapons, drugs—everything is for sale at the annual Fera charity auction. The family's influence knows no bounds, and everyone makes sure to take advantage of their charity to stock up. It is the only way to keep the peace between the families, or some semblance of peace, at least. That and a truce around keeping the city's ports neutral.

The metal detector beeps by the door and I look up to see Emilio taking a knife off a guard escorting the Antonios. So much for the no-weapons memo. Every damn year, that metal detector goes off like a siren at a techno party.

"Don Antonio. *Buonasera*. Welcome." I nod respectfully, reaching out my hand to the bald man in the dark grey suit hobbling over with his two guards. His limp is getting worse with age, I note, forcing myself to not stare.

"*Buonasera*, Don Fera." The old man shakes my hand firmly, a forced smile forming around his wrinkly mouth. "Good turnout this year," he remarks, looking around the room. I'm not sure if it's a question or a statement.

My face doesn't show it, but I can't stop imagining the plug in my ass. I know I'm clenching but I'm so overly aware of it, I can't help it. Imagine what people would think if they knew. What would Don Antonio say if he knew the head of the Fera family was roaming around with a toy up his rear, completely at the mercy of a 24-year-old brat with a sadistic streak?

"Indeed. We have some desirable items on the auction list this year." Forcing myself to keep my expression firm but neutral, I hold onto his hand a bit longer.

Don Antonio just nods and heads straight to the bar, his guards right on his heels. He doesn't say anything but I know he's secretly judging me, judging the event—he always does. If there's one man who likes to remind me that I'm nothing like my father (as if that's an insult), then it's Don Antonio.

This is going to be a long night.

I snap my fingers at one of the waiters and they bring me a whiskey on the rocks. The familiar burn coats my throat and settles in my stomach, warming me from the inside. It's a welcomed distraction.

There is a sudden shift in energy, and I know she has arrived even before I see her.

The effect Danica has on a room is instant.

Though maybe I am the only one who is this overly aware of her presence...

My body aches for her every second she isn't near. It drives me wild!

It's only been a few months since our paths accidentally crossed, but she has me completely wrapped around her finger—and I don't want it any other way. Some days she is the only reason I don't burn the whole world to the ground.

Like the moon pulls the ocean, my gaze draws to the elegant frame of my Queen passing through the entrance, slowly, almost floating in the long black dress that reaches all the way to the floor. Fully mesmerized by the sight, I can't look away from the neckline that is way too low, her bountiful cleavage hugged tightly in the perfectly fitted dress with the corset-like bodice.

The gown is a symphony of black silk and satin, embracing her like a second skin. It cascades into a voluminous skirt that pools around her feet in dramatic folds, billowing with every movement. The fabric seems to shimmer with a subtle sheen, catching and reflecting the soft glow of the chandeliers above.

Matching diamond earrings and necklace round off the look, complete with dark eyeshadow and sultry dark-red lips that highlight her naturally stunning features. It is the most beautiful I have ever seen her look, and I can't stop staring, waiting for her to get closer.

"You can close your mouth now," she says as a warm hand slips into mine, trapping my gaze in hers. Danica is clearly proud of the effect she has on me, the bemused smirk playing on her cheeks tells me so.

"You look incredible," I whisper, wrapping her in my arms. She's taller than usual. Must be the heels hidden beneath the dress.

"You can kiss me. The lipstick is non-smear," she says with a smile, and I do so quickly, overly aware of the company in the room. I wish we were alone, that everyone was gone already; I want her all to myself.

"You look so beautiful in black." Enjoying the intoxicating scent of her perfume, I hold onto her hand a bit longer. She smells like lemons and lust. It's a new fragrance; she doesn't usually smell like lemons. But it's nice, I decide.

Danica squeezes my hand, and my cock jumps.

Hopefully, nobody is watching. So what if they were? It's not the first time I brought a date to the auction. It has been a while though, admittedly.

Danica shakes her head, smiling broadly. "You think I look beautiful when I'm literally wearing sweatpants and a t-shirt."

"That's true. You always look beautiful. But tonight you look breathtaking."

"Do you want me?" Danica asks as she does so often, her voice a whisper.

"More than I want anything in the world," I tell her truthfully, my other hand resting on the curve of her hips.

"Hmm, such a smart boy. Maybe I'll let you take this dress off me later." Danica winks seductively. Always one for games.

I lean down and whisper in her ear, "Thank you, Miss."

"How's your ass?" she whispers back, the words raising the hair on my skin, warm breath tickling my ears one syllable at a time.

"Nervous."

Around us, some of the most dangerous men and women in the city are enjoying their drinks and making small talk, completely unaware of anything amiss with their host. All they've seen is a beautiful woman entering and the intimate greeting I've given her.

I'm sure the older Italian women will be gossiping about Danica and I like it's going out of fashion. They've all been trying to set me up with nieces and friends-of-friends since my wife died. And now suddenly, a very young beautiful woman appears by my side out of nowhere...

She's young enough to be his daughter, they'll say. Probably not very smart with a rack like that...I don't care about any of that. With Danica by my side, I care about little besides keeping her safe—and pleased.

"Should we see what this button does?" Danica's lips curve into a suggestive smile as she fishes the small black remote from her cleavage.

Oh fuck. I shudder in anticipation, knowing full well what that button does. When she'd first bent me over her lap earlier this evening to insert the butt plug, I naively thought it would be a fun game to play. Bending over her lap is always so arousing to me. Especially when she is spanking me.

But tonight wasn't for spanking. No, tonight she'd carefully slipped a lubed finger up my ass—first one, then two—before guiding the new rubber toy into my tight hole. Instantly, my erection grew against her thighs.

When I'd gotten up, she made me stand against the wall, hard cock out and facing her. I was wearing my formal shirt already, my tie loosely draped around my neck, socks but nothing else on my bottom half. My ears burned in embarrassment, standing there like a little schoolboy before her, plug in my ass.

Danica had wrapped her delicate little hands around my cock and I groaned loudly as soon as she touched me. Nothing could compare to her touch, nothing. It's all I ever yearned for. Still holding on, she'd pressed the on button on the discreet remote. It looked small, harmless, but when I felt the jolt in my ass, I realized it was anything but harmless.

As soon as Danica had pressed that button, I literally jumped, exclaiming loudly as the first vibrations buzzed around the nerve endings in my prostate. The feeling was close to overwhelming. I gasped for air, panting, as I tried to keep my composure. But Danica just held onto my shaft, feeling it twitch and jump as the plug stimulated my hole.

Danica had stopped before I came, leaving me on the edge, pre-cum dripping from my rock-hard cock. She bent down, kissing my erection oh-so-lovingly—before giving it a hard smack that sent me doubling over in pain, crashing to the floor. No coming without permission, she repeated.

"Please, Danica. Have a heart," I whisper now, looking around the buzzing foyer. There is no way I can keep a straight face with that thing in my ass.

She pushes her body against mine, my renewed erection pressing into her. I know that's what she is checking for. She breaks into a grin, satisfied.

"I have a heart." Danica presses the button, putting it on the lowest setting. "But it's a black one."

It takes every ounce of self-control to keep myself together.

Every second is torture, and instant relief crashes over me when Danica finally presses the off-button.

"I should never have agreed to this." My voice is nearly a pant, strained from the effort.

Danica slides the remote back into her dress, between her breasts. "No, darling. You shouldn't have."

CHAPTER FIVE

BROTHER

DANICA...

"**A**ren't you a sight for sore eyes," an unfamiliar voice whispers behind me, too close. I spin around, ready to throw my drink in some asshole's face. But it's not just any asshole.

"Hello, Luca," I stiffly greet the Damon Salvatore lookalike in his well-fitted tuxedo and shiny shoes. He has that same lopsided smile...Not the eyes though, Luca's eyes are dark pools of obsidian that shift around the room restlessly.

"Danica, *cara mia.*" Luca smiles the most charming smile I've ever seen. He takes my hand to kiss it, pressing his lips to my skin for way too long.

Without bothering to be stealthy about it, I look him up and down, studying his intense yet mischievous gaze, the way his short hair scruffs around his ears, the stubble on his cheeks. He is obviously a Fera, the resemblance is unmistakable.

I don't remember him being this attractive. We'd only met once—on his 40th birthday—that chaotic day it all began. That was the night that Dante's story became intertwined with mine. But the faces from that day are all a blur, all but Dante's.

"You look beautiful tonight." Luca bows gently, still holding onto my hand. His hands are soft, warm, almost elegant. I can't help but compare them to Dante's large, rough hands, instantly imagining them all over my body—first Dante's but then, involuntarily, Luca's too.

"Thank you. You clean up pretty well yourself," I reply. "Except for your face, of course." A fresh cut runs over Luca's cheek, down his neck, and into his shirt. It makes him look dangerous. I want to touch it, I'm not sure why. He looks so much like Dante but also so different. He doesn't have that haunted look in his eyes though, the pain Dante carries with him. It is a different pain perhaps.

"You know, this business we're in...it's a tough job." Luca shrugs, smiling broadly like he's laughing off a tear in his shirt rather than his face.

"I've noticed."

He squeezes my hand again, pulling me closer. "Where has my brother been hiding you?"

"Ah, so charming, aren't we?" I tease. "He hasn't been *hiding* me. I'm pretty good at hiding myself. I had exams...plus, you know, reading." I've never been particularly social, not for my age at least. If I could stay curled up in bed with my Kindle all day, I would. Some days I do. It's actually been so nice to have a bit of downtime after the craziness that was my final semester of studies.

I can't believe I actually did the damn thing; finished my degree. Well, I can, because I did. As much as I wanted to just play Dante's Mistress all day, I was determined to not make the same mistake again, to not give up my studies for some guy (even if Dante was way more than *some guy*). Not that Dante minded me keeping busy, he had loads of work to do too.

It was much easier to focus without having to worry about working as well—one of the many perks of Dante beating up my former boss and freeing me from that shitty employment.

Even with the extra time, it was a lot of work to get it all done, and the break has been quite welcome. As much as I wanted to go straight into my Master's degree now, I decided to take the gap year I'd been promising myself since high school. Before, I argued that I couldn't afford to take one. Now, *affording* anything was no longer a challenge. Not with Dante's pretty little black and gold credit cards in my wallet.

Besides, I didn't even know if I still wanted to be a journalist; maybe I never did. It was a good time to regroup and figure out what I want to do with my life, whether this is still me. The more I thought about it, the more I realized I wanted to have my own business some day. I was clearly not cut out to take orders from someone else.

But where does one even start with that?

The younger Fera pulls my attention back to him, almost with force, as his fingers play over my hand.

"I'm glad we finally get to meet properly." He still hasn't let go and I am lost in his gaze; I feel like the only person in the room.

"Luca." Dante's stern voice cuts through the moment. He puts his arm around me possessively. "You remember Danica?" He seems annoyed, his tone clipped.

"*Fratellone mio*," Luca says affectionately, dropping my hand and reaching over to kiss his brother. "I was just telling dear Danica here how lovely she looks." He winks at Dante and I can audibly hear my darling boy clench his knuckles beside me. *Is he jealous?* The thought pleases me.

"Yes, yes she does," Dante says simply. He seems more stiff than usual, but that could also just be the toy up his ass. I smile.

For a moment, there is an awkward silence as the brothers stare each other down.

There is only a three-year age difference between them, but the gap looks wider. Mostly because Luca looks much younger than 40. It's that cheeky smile on his face, almost playful.

Perhaps Dante was a better brother to him than mine were to me. The bar is pretty low though. I was always the outsider; the twins always had each other. Inseparable since birth, born with an instant best friend. The golden boys, everything my dad wanted. A pair of athletic boys who excelled at everything they did—academics, sport, just life in general.

And then I came along, unplanned, inconvenient...female. My family had never had much money, but with a third child, we had even less. I don't know why everyone blamed *me* for it; I never asked to be born.

It was just unfortunate that the boys had hit their teenage years when I was still so young, so vulnerable. Against two of them, what defense did I have? *Wanna play hide-and-seek, Danica?*

Dante speaks first, and I force my wandering thoughts back to the Fera standoff.

"Where have you been?" he asks Luca, his arm still firmly around me, hand resting just above my ass. I feel like the perfect trophy and I can't imagine any arm I would rather be wrapped in. Though, for just an instant, my mind indulges in the fantasy of having both Fera men simultaneously. What it would feel like to have them on their knees before me.

But as Luca rambles off shifty excuses—clearly lies—I instantly realize that the idea of it is way hotter than the reality would be. Luca can never compare to Dante.

Dante replies to his brother in rapid Italian, clearly not wanting me to hear. I don't mind. It's boring when they talk about the business. Dante generally does everything he can to try and keep me out of it; I don't need the details.

Besides, a large part of me never actually wants to hear the details. I know Dante has done bad things and probably will do many more. Still, it is hard to reconcile the image of that man with the beautiful sub who climbs into bed next to me every night, burying his head in my chest as I hold him tight. To me, he is just a lost little boy—a giant-sized lost little boy...but still.

Luca tries to get another word in but Dante cuts him off, silencing him with an assertive wave of his hand. Always with the hand gestures. "We'll talk about this tomorrow. The auction is about to start."

Luca nods, accepting his brother's authority.

"Come, *Tesoro*, there is a seat for you in the front." Dante takes my hand and leads me away. Luca doesn't say a thing, his charm now muted. A frown plays over his face.

When I look back over my shoulder, I can't help but notice Luca is walking with a slight limp. I make a mental note to ask Dante about it later.

For now, I obediently take my assigned seat right in front of the podium where Dante is about to auction off the various items we all know are just for show.

With a mischievous grin meant only for the host at the podium, I slowly pull the plug's remote from my cleavage.

Time to have some fun, Don Fera...

CHAPTER SIX

SCH∞LED

DANTE...

I t is way after midnight already when I slam the front
door shut with more force than I'd planned. It shakes
in its frame. *Stupid thing.*

"Jesus, Dante. What the hell?" Danica asks, trailing
behind me, slowed down by the inconvenience of her
heels.

Without looking back, I march up the stairs. I am
relieved that the banquet is over, and I'm more than ready
to get this butt plug out of my ass. Danica was selective
with her remote usage, but still made my life very difficult
all evening. It was the endless anticipation of her pressing
that button that made me stress more than anything.

"Dante. Stop!" Danica demands as I reach our room.
I freeze in my tracks. When she uses that tone, my body
instantly remembers who it belongs to.

I don't turn around, just wait for her to catch up. A long, resigned breath expels itself from my lips in a sigh.

Danica shoves me into the room and closes the door, all in one move. "What's this about?" With a growing scowl on her face, she crosses her arms over her chest in a stance that I know spells nothing but trouble for me. Danica is pissed off. Once her arms are crossed...

"You've been moody the entire drive back." Her accusation is not unfounded.

"It's nothing," I grumble, taking off my cufflinks and setting them on the dresser.

"Is this about Luca?" Danica asks, perceptive as always.

"No..." I reply unconvincingly, turning away from her again. *It's not about him, it's not.* But it is. I saw how close Luca stood to her, how he touched her. Now that the event was over, the feelings I shoved down earlier were bubbling to the surface.

Danica laughs heartily, a sound so cruel to my ears right now. "You're being a child, Dante. A jealous one at that."

"I don't want him getting his hands on you. You're mine!" I finally turn to face her, fury flashing in my eyes. Luca is such a little prick. He's ruined enough. I'm not letting him near Danica. I've done everything in my power to keep them apart thus far, but tonight had been unavoidable.

"You're so cute when you're jealous," she says patronizingly, stripping out of the heavy dress that falls to the floor unceremoniously and leaving her only in a matching black lace undergarment set. Her large breasts spill over the top of the bra that could never fully contain them.

"I'm not jealous. I don't trust him." I feel like pouting, which is ridiculous—I don't pout. But a nerve has been struck.

"Fair. But you should trust *me*, no?" Danica asks, walking over to me. She looks stunning like that, especially with the heels.

"I trust you..." I lose my train of thought. Danica's swinging her hips as she moves, her eyes locked on mine as I gape at her approaching figure. I want her. No, I *need* her. *Dio mio!*

As soon as Danica is within reach, I shove her into the wall, my body grinding into hers as I kiss her—deeply, messily. I can't help myself. Her mouth feels so good on mine; she tastes of red wine and anger.

Danica puts her palm on my chest, trying to distance me. "Stay!"

"No. You've had this fucking plug in my ass all night, I can't take it anymore." I know I shouldn't disobey her; I'm being bad, but fuck that, she's been driving me mad with lust for too long.

"You'll be punished for this." It's a threat.

"It's worth it," I whisper into her hair between rapid breaths as my hardness grows between us. Her essence consumes me, I can't escape it.

"What exactly do you want, Dante dearest?" Danica fishes my cock out of my pants, stroking her fingers along the side as I forget how to breathe. Just like that, I know I've already lost.

"You," I reply, breath caught in a sentence I'll never speak, frozen, rock hard in her grip.

"Do we take things without permission in this house?" Danica asks in a tone a mother would ask a naughty six-year-old in need of a life lesson. It sobers me up instantly.

"No, Ma'am." I stand up straighter, trying to rectify my outburst with good behavior. But we both know Miss Matthews doesn't tolerate brats, my often-bruised ass knows it too.

She sighs and lets the tension hang between us for a second longer before making her demands.

"Strip, *boy*!" Danica tells me in an authoritative voice that would make me tear the moon from the sky for her if I could.

"Yes, Ma'am," I reply obediently, discarding my clothes in layers until I stand before her completely bare except for my collar, my hardening cock in my hand like an offering, a sacrifice.

"Whose is this?" Danica asks, slapping my erection with the back of her hand.

The instant flood of pain takes my breath away and I gasp for air. "Yours," I breathe when I can.

"Yours, *who*?" Danica demands, grabbing my cock and pulling me towards her, roughly.

Hypnotized by her, bewitched (desperate) I bend down slightly, my face inches from her—humbled. Usually reaching up to my shoulder, in heels she is less than a head shorter than me.

"Yours, *Mistress*," I correct myself quickly.

"There's my good boy. Now enough of this jealousy, okay?" She changes to her teacher-voice. It's sweet yet patronizing, soothing but suspicious, because we both know she has me completely hooked when she uses that voice.

I melt. She called me a *good boy.*

Dio mio, why do I want that so much? To hear her say that, to please her, there is nothing I want more than to make my Goddess proud.

Ready to give her anything she asks for, I nod. It has been so incredible to see her embrace her dominance like this. All it took was a few sessions with Adira to teach her what she didn't know, what she wanted to know...And look at her now, my beautiful Queen, fearlessly in control. Danica was a natural Domme. It didn't take much to refine her power—only a few weeks of private lessons that left us both sticky messes on the floor.

"Care to follow me to the play room, baby boy? It seems some corrective behavior is in order." She's still got my hard cock in her hand, toying with the tip, teasing it slowly. I'm so sensitive, her touch burns on my desperate skin.

Like I've forgotten all my words, I nod again, concentrating hard not to just come in her hand right there and then. As much as the impulse surges through me, I wouldn't dare. Danica would be furious, more furious than she already was.

Like an obedient puppy, I follow my Owner through the adjoining door as she leads me by my cock, pulling me along in a tight grip that makes my hardness throb painfully. I'm about to get what I deserve—the mere thought relaxes me. There is nothing I have to think about, to stress about, to feel guilty about...no, I can just listen to her commands and I will be absolved of all my sins.

Danica closes the playroom door behind us, locking it securely. Not that anyone else would ever come here. The cleaner is the only one allowed in, but only as and when instructed. Vowing them to secrecy, I had them sign a non-disclosure agreement upfront.

The large room is kitted out with every toy, every piece of equipment, every single thing my heart (and Danica's) could desire. The collection has grown significantly since the feisty hellcat that is my Queen moved in, but it had always been impressive—and expensive. Only the best for my Madame.

Danica knows exactly what she wants in the playroom tonight. She is always so decisive, so deliberate in her actions.

Meanwhile, I wait (impatiently) for my fate.

"You know why we are here? Do you accept your punishment for your disrespect?" Danica asks, and I know it's a statement more than a question.

"Yes, Mistress," I answer anyway, eager to repent.

"To the cross!" she orders, making her intentions clear.

I don't hesitate, I just spread my limbs against the padded surface of the seven-foot custom-built St Andrews Cross in the corner, my back to her. The hardness between my thighs press painfully against the cross.

"Such a beautiful ass," Danica says, slapping my naked ass cheeks—hard enough for the skin to burn—before securing me to the cross.

She starts by my feet and cuffs my limbs to the corners: ankle, ankle, wrist, wrist.

Having my back to her makes the anticipation even greater. I am powerless when I'm like this—almost powerless, except for the fact that she gives me *all* the power. No matter what happens, I know I'm safe, that I can stop it all with just a knock on the wood, our agreed non-verbal safe word. But I know that I don't want it to stop; I'm so incredibly aroused!

Danica's delicate hand slips around my waist, between my cock and the cross, and she takes my hardness in her grip, slowly massaging it.

"Was it hard not being allowed to come, baby?" she whispers, breathing into my neck. It's a trap, I know it's a trap, but I can't help but respond to her every move.

"Oh!" I exclaim in surprise as the butt plug starts humming in my ass. She must have had the remote in her cleavage all along—I forgot.

Danica laughs cruelly.

"We're going to make a mess of you today, baby. Just you wait. That pretty little head of yours will soon slow down to insular thoughts." There is nothing empty about her threat.

When she turns the remote off again, I gasp for breath—relieved—even though I know that this is only the beginning.

Danica's heels clink on the floor as she walks to the back of the room. She's selecting her implement, she must be. *Oh God.* I secretly hope it's not the rattan rod—that breaks my skin so quickly.

It isn't the rod. Instead, the leather strips of the flogger tickle over my back. *She's starting slow...*

"You know your safe words, right, darling?"

"Yes, Ma'am."

"Good. Now count with me. Ten strikes."

The flogger hits my ass loudly, stinging painfully. The first one is always the biggest shock, like my skin has forgotten what this feels like.

"Count!" Danica demands.

I grit my teeth, hissing the "one" through pursed lips. It never ceases to amaze me how such a petite woman can manage lashes with such force, such precision.

"Two" burns even more, falling on top of the first one and cascading into a burning sensation. "Three" numbs out everything while "four" completely empties my mind. By the time we get to "eight," there is nothing in my thoughts except the numbers and the blur of pain, the depth of the feeling as I fall through it.

A loud growl escapes my throat as Danica turns on the plug again, my circuits confused between the alternating pain and pleasure. She keeps it on for lashes nine and ten, leaving me so close to the edge that it takes every ounce of energy I have not to spill my load.

"Look at you. What a beautiful sight you are, spread before me like this, so vulnerable, *mine...*" Danica whispers the last word and I pant with lust. "Does someone want to come?" she coos patronizingly, gently running her fingers over my hardness.

I have no words to answer her, just moans. My desire to come for her is complete, whole. There is nothing else I want more, even though I probably don't deserve it.

"Not yet," Danica says, teasing my cock with her forefinger. I know there is pre-cum on her digits, I can taste it when she shoves them in my mouth moments later—I am literally dripping with desire for her.

For a minute or two, she just leaves me there, spread and desperate.

"Okay, little boy, it's time to purge all the bad things from your body, are you ready for me?" Danica whispers in my neck upon return.

The cold leather slides against my back as she reveals her next choice.

I hold my breath. *Fuck.* It's the dragon's tail whip.

"Is this what you want?" Danica asks, sliding the whip down my back and around, gently tapping the tip of my cock with the leather end. My knees buckle but my bound wrists keep me from falling.

"Yes...Miss," I gasp, struggling with the simple words.

"Such a polite boy, I like polite boys...I want you to come for me darling, come all over that cross. Are you ready?" She asks and I consent to the cruel torture I know is about to follow.

"I'm ready, Miss...Please," I beg.

I hardly feel the plug in my ass starting up again, because within seconds a painful thud lands on my rear with impeccable accuracy. It stings! It stings so damn much. The pain is blinding.

I'm in another world as the second blow rains down. My circuits completely flood as pain and pleasure mix in a single fury of feeling.

"I can't..." I try to tell her I'm about to come but I am incapable of even finishing my sentence.

Within seconds, my inevitable release explodes, thick pent-up cum spilling all over my stomach, over the cross. Every single nerve ending in my ass is on fire!

But Danica doesn't stop, no, the vibrating plug keeps vibrating as the next blow of the whip falls on my bum. I know she's broken skin.

Still, I hold onto my safe words. *I want more. Everything. I deserve to pay.*

The blinding pain blocks it all out. For a moment, complete serene bliss. I don't even feel the next blow, or any after that. Nor the plug's vibrations finally stopping.

"You're bleeding," Danica says after an indeterminable period of time. I can hear the concern in her voice.

"...fine," I breathe, the word heavy in my throat. I don't sound fine.

"Enough! Allegro," she calls my safe word herself, putting the whip down. It clatters on the floor, but it sounds far away. "You never use your safe words." I know she's shaking her head disapprovingly. She's not using her teacher-voice anymore, the scene is over.

I don't say anything, just collapse to the floor as she releases my wrists, my ankles.

"My silly boy...Look at what a mess you are." Danica's voice is calm, affectionate, warm.

I don't say anything; I'm not sure I can.

The world is quiet, finally.

CHAPTER SEVEN

AFTERCARE

DANICA...

With great difficulty, I pull Dante's sleeping body closer to me, draping him over me like a heavy quilt made of muscle and tattoos. I love how his skin feels against mine—his fresh, naked skin. If the world would let me, I would stay like this forever, watching him sleep.

Mine. Finally mine. But more than that, I'm *his*. Dante doesn't just want me around, he *needs* me around. I finally have someone to worship me like the Queen I never knew I deserved to be.

To the rest of the world I am nobody, but to Dante—I am everything. And there is nothing I would rather be than Dante's everything. As much as he is my submissive, I am the one who feels completely owned. Owned by his desire for me, his need to make me happy. Is this what it feels like to finally be fulfilled?

Dante murmurs in his sleep, nestling his face deeper into my bosom. Such beautiful little sounds he makes sometimes.

Almost absentmindedly, I stroke his hair, placing a gentle kiss on his forehead. *Poor boy, so exhausted.* I can't blame him. His body took a lot of punishment tonight. I trust him to let me know when he's had enough, but sometimes I worry he doesn't even know his own limits. He's so conditioned to *just take it*, no matter what; endure.

At first, I used to feel bad for punishing Dante, for hurting him. I couldn't understand the appeal of wanting someone to consensually (and lovingly) beat the shit out of you. But now I know why he wants it, the need to atone for his sins, to free himself from the guilt, to take his punishment and be absolved—unlike so many other burdens he carries from his past, things he'll never forgive himself (and others) for.

Whenever I think about what Dante's life must have been like before, I just wish someone would've given him a hug at some point. Many hugs.

There is so much darkness in him now, so much hardened hurt, thick ugly scars over the pieces of himself he has lost, that were taken from him with force. The darkness cannot be soothed by hugs anymore. Not *just* hugs at least. No, the darkness needs to be dragged from Dante's body like a thread of pain that keeps unraveling the more you pull.

I feel hopeless in the face of Dante's hurt, the brokenness he guards like a family heirloom that is no longer precious to anyone, but has to be kept safe at all times. There is nothing I can do that will undo the pain he's lived. But I can give him the opportunity to control his pain now, even if it's a different pain, a physical pain...With a single word, he can make it stop.

If only he'd fucking use that word already when he needs it. It's up to him to define his own limits, I know, but I had to stop the scene; I couldn't bear doing real damage—even accidentally.

Earlier, after helping him down from the cross, we'd just laid on the floor for some time. Dante was breathing heavily, still lost in subspace somewhere. Giving him the space he needed, I just held his hand, waiting for him to float back to me in his own time.

When he'd finally found his way back to me, I helped his exhausted body off the floor and into a steaming shower. Dante had winced when the water touched his fresh cuts. Pain flashed over his face but only momentarily before he pushed it down again. *The things he must have endured in his life...*

71

My immediate instinct was always to try and soothe his pain. I hated seeing him hurt. But it wasn't the physical pain he needed saving from—the closer we grew, the more I realized that.

Studying him closely now, I regard the sleeping giant next to me with his arm wrapped over my waist, holding onto me tightly. He looks so peaceful like this, so content; the dark cloud that normally knits his brow and clenches his jaw is nowhere to be seen.

Even after all this time, I struggle to marry this peaceful image of a sleeping Dante with the way the world sees him—savage, bitter, vengeful. Yet here he is, the kindest person I have ever encountered in my life. I didn't think men could be kind, not until I met Dante Fera. Up until then, men had been nothing but cruel to me.

Sure, my dad hadn't really done anything—but that was the point. I might as well have not existed to him. His twin golden boys, on the other hand, could do no wrong. *What did you do to make them mad, Danica? You must have done something...*

Even when all the facts were on the table, my dad chose their side, everyone did. *Please Danica, it was an accident. Think of their futures. You're okay now, we got you in time.*

Their version of "in time" never matched mine. Their version meant I was still alive. *My* version of *in time* would have been *before* the panic, before the certainty that I was going to die at just nine years old.

We all still meet for family Christmas on the regular, that is the worst part. *Hush now, Danica. Let's just move on. Everything is okay now.* But it wasn't. It never was again.

I am safe now, I remind myself, trying to force the words to sink in, to feel real. Dante would never let anyone come near me again. The twins would be defenseless against his size, his ferocity. That's why I don't tell him what happened back then. That, and I don't want him to see me as weak (or broken).

I sigh heavily, pressing my forehead against Dante's. *My beautiful knight in unconventional armor.*

He murmurs in his sleep and pulls me even closer, hugging me tight like I'm his favorite stuffed toy. His semi-asleep cock rests against my thigh, and I reach down, stroking it like the beautiful pet it is. It instantly reacts to my touch, eager for more.

I smile, running my fingers lazily over his shaft before moving over to my own yearning desire. Slowly, I circle my clit with a single finger, cradling Dante close with my other arm.

Maneuvering myself (and him) a bit, I press the tip of his dick against my clit, rubbing myself on his sensitive head.

Oh god, the shivers! The wetness spreads between my thighs with every bit of friction. Since meeting Dante, my sex drive has been on max! I'm always in the mood now, ready to dish out pain and pleasure with a steady hand. Who knew people like me could also be Dommes?

I'm a far cry from those leather-clad, whip-yielding Mistresses I see on porn sites, but also, who cares? It's not like I'm about to start fitting into boxes now. That's never been me.

Dante groans softly, still lost in a deep sleep but starting to stir. It's a temptation too hard to resist...Even though I'm beyond exhausted myself. It's close to sunrise by now, but it's not like I have to go to work tomorrow.

Not bothering to try and be stealthy anymore, I move my body down, guiding myself onto his erection, finally pulling Dante out of dreamland.

It takes him a second to put all the pieces together, maybe less. The hunger in his eyes instantly flares up, and he tries to get up.

"No darling, don't move." I smile, placing a finger on his lips to halt him. "Go back to sleep. I just want you inside me." It's true, I don't even want to come, I just want to be filled.

Dante watches me intently as I lie down on top of him, his hard cock buried to the hilt inside me. My gaze is locked on his stormy eyes, freshly woken but fully alert. The way he looks at me—like I'm worth more than all the money in the world...I smile softly, pushing a strand of now-messy curls from his brow.

It's Dante who finally breaks our gaze, pulling my face towards his, muscular arms wrapped around my bare back. Neither of us move the rest of our bodies. We just slowly kiss, my lips passing over his eyelids, the corners of his cheeks, the tip of his nose...He takes his turn to kiss mine, the skin between my eye and my ear, my bottom lip, the wrinkle between my brows.

Finally, my lips find his, my tongue dancing around his in lazy circles like a slow waltz only we know the steps to. As I bite his bottom lip, I can feel his cock twitch inside me, but we remain completely still except for the exploration of little kisses.

Content, I place my head on Dante's broad chest, listening to his heartbeat as we drift to sleep together, his cock growing soft inside me again.

Home. I am home.

SERVICE

DANTE...

I wake up still inside her.

My body aches from our session last night, and the sharp pain in my ass is still there. But my body is used to pain, it doesn't bother me.

Instead, I focus on the feeling of Danica's naked body on top of mine. She is still fast asleep, face resting on my chest.

Careful not to wake her, I stroke her hair, inhaling her scent (a hint of lemon persists).

Wrapping both arms tightly around my sleeping beauty, I merge Danica's body deeper into mine.

I want to stay like this, my cock just resting inside her, perfect. But my own body betrays me. I have no control as my erection grows inside her. My desire for her is unquenchable.

Danica mumbles something incomprehensible, eyes still thick with sleep. Mornings were never her thing and this time we went to bed much later than usual.

"Go back to sleep, shh…" I kiss her forehead.

"You're moving," Danica says, slowly rousing from her sleep. She sounds grumpy.

"I'm sorry, my love. I can't help it." My cock twitches as if to betray me even further.

Danica grumbles some more, a drowsy child fighting to remain in their slumber. She grabs a fistful of my chest hair, almost absentmindedly, and tugs.

"Hey, hey, hey, you're starting early this morning." I smile, putting my hand over hers to untangle her fingers from my hair. Bringing her hand to my lips, I kiss each finger individually. So perfect, just like the rest of her.

"You're going to regret waking me this early," Danica groans, her eyes finally fluttering open. She stares up at me with that grouchy look that makes her seem like a spoiled brat sometimes. But the smile teasing at the corners of her mouth is unmistakable.

"Good morning to you too, *Tesoro*." I drop my hands to her ass, resting them on the curve of her behind. Normally

I would wait for permission, but *normally* I don't wake up inside her already, my cock warm and ready.

"You're waking a demon," Danica threatens but smiles nonetheless, reaching up for a kiss. "Good morning, baby."

I know she wants me too, the wetness between her thighs confirms her lust. She always wakes up so feral. Not that I mind. I could never get enough of her. Even when my body is drained of all its liquids, tired, achy, I still need more.

"We should sleep like this more often," I suggest, running my hands over her ass.

"It was a miracle that either of us got any sleep."

"I think we were sufficiently exhausted."

"Hmm..." Danica says, dragging her long red nails over my chest, scraping my right nipple. I flinch, inhaling sharply. My nipples are so sensitive, she knows. "How about now? Are you still exhausted?" Danica winks at me. *There she is. Good morning.*

"It's a secondary concern. I think you can feel how my body is feeling right now." With a wink, I pull her ass down lower onto my cock, fully. We both groan in unison.

"Ah-ha, I see..." Danica pushes herself up into a sitting position, hands on my chest. She gently rocks her hips back and forth, just once. "Is this what you want?" she asks seductively, closely studying my face as my eyes roll back in my head. *Dio mio, yes!*

"More than anything in the world right now," I whisper, arching my hips to feel more of her.

"Who said you could move?" Danica looks down at me with a stern face.

I love how her tits look from down here; they look even bigger. Instinctively, I reach out to them but stop myself before touching.

"I'm sorry, Miss. Please can I move?"

"No, lie still. You are my flesh dildo now; you don't get to move. This is about *my* pleasure, are we clear?"

I nod obediently, arms still outstretched to her as I make little grabby hands. Technically, I'm still moving but she allows it.

"Yes, you may touch them." Danica rolls her eyes, smiling at me like I'm a silly toddler with silly needs. It makes me want her even more. Especially because I know she'll never treat my needs like they're silly.

I eagerly take a breast in each hand. Despite the size of my hands, I cannot contain all of her, she spills over my fingers. Slowly, I caress her breasts, her nipples, exploring the soft flesh as Danica starts to move her hips again, grinding on top of my already-dripping cock.

"I want you to pinch my nipples, darling. You know how I like it. As hard as you can. Play with them," Danica talks me through her desires. I know exactly what to do. She's shown me before, guiding my hands with her own.

I study her face closely as Danica throws her head back, eyes closed, purring like a cat working hard at the biscuit factory. "Just like that. So good..." she encourages me, grinding faster on my cock.

With every movement, it becomes harder to keep my threatening orgasm at bay. But I have to. My Queen comes first.

One hand stabilizing herself on my chest, her other one slips to her clit. I know it won't be long now. Danica can make herself come in mere minutes—way faster than I ever could, no matter how much I studied her movements. She just knows her body so well.

Watching her face contort with pleasure, I am utterly captivated, unable to look away from that side smirk that always forms on her lips when she's close to the edge—how exquisite. My sole mission is to make her plunge from that cliff, shattering into orgasm.

But Danica moves her hand away, she doesn't let herself finish. Instead, she opens her eyes and shoots me a daring look. I know that face, she's just had an idea. *God help me.*

Danica puts both hands on my chest and leans down to kiss me, devouring me hungrily.

"Hold me," Danica breathes and I instantly wrap my arms around her. A knee on either side of my waist, straddling me, Danica keeps her hips rocking, bouncing on top of my cock as I hold our bodies close.

"Please, I'm close...Miss..." I can't take any more, I need to come.

"Not yet," she says, grinding me harder, faster. "Not yet."

"I can't hold it!" I can't. The concentration it takes to keep my body from exploding is immense.

"Almost. Almost...Just like that," she moans. When Danica pinches each of my nipples between her forefinger and thumb, I go insane!

"You have permission," Danica says finally, grinding into me as she pulls my nipples. She knows I love it.

Her words are hardly out before I release inside her, coming violently as every muscle in my body clenches and lets go. I breathe heavily as my cum fills her. Being allowed to finish inside her is a beautiful intimacy I cherish like the magnificent gift it is. Nothing beats that feeling; I never feel closer to her than in these moments.

Luckily, Danica no longer required me to use a condom, not after all our test screens came back clear.

Thanks to her birth control implant, we also didn't have to worry about making little Feras. It's not something either of us wants in our future, we've discussed it in great detail before.

Danica rides me for a moment longer until the overstimulation drives me to loud growls that rip through the room. This time she doesn't choose torture and only lets me suffer momentarily before resting her hips, just holding my post-orgasm cock inside her, sticky and warm—hers.

She gets up, standing over me on the bed, legs spread, as I watch my cum slowly trickle down her thigh. *What a glorious sight.*

"How about giving me some *service*?" Danica asks, winking down at me as she starts to slowly rub her clit again.

I'm riveted, unable to pry my eyes away from Danica's pussy as I watch her pleasure herself.

"There is nothing I want more," I reply. And there isn't.

"But first—you're going to clean up this mess," Danica grins as she lowers her cum-filled cunt over my face.

"Yes, Ma'am."

SEDUCTION

DANICA...

F ingers gripping around the edges, I hold onto the headboard as I lower myself over Dante's face. With a thick thigh on either side of his head, I rock my hips to guide his tongue to the pinnacle of my lust.

At first, I used to worry about whether he could breathe when I was on top, but not anymore. I know he'll signal his safe word if he needs to.

My breasts bounce as I moan above him. What a shame he can't see it. No, his face is buried deep in my dripping pussy, lapping up every last bit of his own cum (and mine).

"Hmm, such a good boy," I encourage him. Like a sleeping predator slowly arising from its slumber, I can feel my pleasure starting to build.

I know he won't stop until I reach a climax, no matter how long it takes. Dante has been lost in my folds for hours before, happily so. But today I get there quickly. The various stimulations have been building since the night before, and in mere minutes I'm screaming his name and that of a deity that means little to me.

The bed rocks as I grip the headboard with all my might, riding his face while his lips bewitch my clit, building it to a point of sensitivity that's unbearable.

"Just like that, don't stop." He doesn't. Dante wants this as much as I do.

I can feel it in my stomach first—the climax that builds and builds until it explodes in tingles that run up my spine and over my whole body.

Without restraint, loudly, I moan as the orgasm reaches its crescendo. I don't care who hears me, why would I?

Dante slows down his movements, flicking his tongue over my pussy lips in broad strokes as he swallows every last drop of my orgasm.

"No more." I gasp, pulling his hair to detach him from my body.

With the last strength I have left, I bring my leg over and collapse next to Dante on the bed, panting heavily, eyes closed, as I ride wave after wave of pleasure spilling over my body.

I try to force my breath back to a steady rhythm but it continues to pant in wild patterns I cannot reign in.

Without having to open my eyes, I know Dante is just watching me, enjoying my orgasm too. But he doesn't touch me. He gives me the space to enjoy the moment. How well-trained he is. *Adira did well.*

At first, I dismissed the idea of getting a professional Domme to guide me as *preposterous*. I could figure it out myself. Why would I let some stranger show me how to please my man?

But Dante eventually convinced me to just come to the club with him once, *just to watch*. I hadn't even known places like that existed. My innocent suburban life had been nothing like the world of dark luxury Dante was accustomed to.

The "club" was more like a private mansion with different floors and rooms for any desire a deprived rich person could have. Dante navigated the halls like a regular; I could tell that wasn't his first time there. *An old friend*, he told the bouncer when asked who we're here to see.

My mouth refused to close as I gaped at Goddess Adira that first time—and many other times too. She is so stunningly beautiful. Not just her physical features (the olive skin, the long brown hair that curls around her shoulders, those breasts, the impossibly tall legs, her plump lips that cast spells without needing words...), it is the grace and elegance with which she conducts herself, the dominance that oozes out of her without a grain of forcefulness. Her movements are almost liquid, smooth.

That first night, I sat mesmerized on the couch with Dante's arm around me as we watched her command two subs. It was a private show. Nobody else had been there. The subs were male, both of them, and had their faces hidden behind masks. I'd felt bad for invading their privacy, but Dante had assured me that they got off on being watched and that we were actually doing them a favor.

One of the subs was a huge man, bulky, ripped—even bigger than Dante. But he crawled behind Goddess Adira like a whimpering dog as she led him around with a leash around his small cock. I had been spellbound, unable to avert my eyes from the scene unfolding behind the glass wall, watching as they obeyed her, desperate for her approval.

The next time we saw Adira, she was standing in our very own playroom, dressed in the highest heels I'd ever seen and very little else—just a harness that covered strategic bits (barely). Her body was perfect, toned, tall. I wanted to *be* her and *fuck* her at the same time. There was something so sensual about her, commanding a secret power that could be felt but not named.

Dante had been a willing guinea pig, letting us use his body as a test subject for my Domme education. Lucky boy. Enduring both pain and pleasure (and often both) as Goddess Adira had shown me how to take control.

She helped us set up the contract too, guiding us in naming our desires and spelling out the boundaries. There'd been a lot of *to be explored* answers on my list, whereas Dante had already been sure of what he liked and didn't. What he *didn't* like was very limited. His green list was far longer, including many things I couldn't see myself mastering—at least not yet.

Adira had come over twice a week for two months. I knew Dante must have paid her handsomely, but money had never been mentioned.

Such a Goddess indeed. There were times when all I wanted was for her to make me kneel before her, begging for permission to bury my face in her cunt. Many times...

I'm pulled back to Dante in the present as his ringing cell phone tears through the sensual memory. He sighs and picks up. It must be very important for him to answer now.

I watch his face change, the frown that gathers above his brow. With a single *sì* he puts the phone down again.

And just like that, everything is different—I can feel it in the air, the way Dante's breathing tenses in his chest.

"You have to go?" I already know the answer before he speaks.

"I'm sorry, *Tesoro*, I—" he tries to apologize but I cut him off.

"It's okay. I know it's already way beyond your usual wake-up time. Go." I smile, squeezing his hand.

In a single smooth sweep, he pulls me toward him again, kissing me hungrily. I can taste my orgasm on his lips and I lick him lustfully.

"Breakfast of champions." I wink.

"Such a crazy woman." Dante laughs as he shakes his head. "Where have you been all my life?"

"Probably under-aged." I grin.

"Good point. I'm sorry I have to go, darling. Trust me when I say there is nothing I want more than to stay here all day with you." Dante gets up and turns on the shower.

"I know, baby. It's okay. I need more sleep anyway."

It's true. By the time Dante is done showering and getting dressed, I'm fast asleep again. I don't even hear him leave, or feel the kisses I'm sure he plants on my face, my breasts too (knowing him).

After all our physical activities, I definitely need a shower for my tired, sweaty body, but I put that on my later-list, my body heavy with post-orgasm fatigue.

Sleep first.

Priorities.

I wonder what Dante's call was about but not for long. The Sandman isn't taking no for an answer, so I let myself drift into an uneasy slumber.

My last cognizant thought is a reminder to myself to feed Dante more cum, but the idea evaporates like mist as I sink into the fluffy duvet, letting it transport me to another world.

CHAPTER TEN

INFILTRATED

DANTE...

Twisting my rings, I pace between my desk and the window. *Fuck.* "Are you sure, Luigi?" I ask, not for the first time.

"*Certo, Signore*...I'm sorry. I don't want to be the bearer of bad news." Luigi keeps his distance, our previous encounter still fresh in his mind, I'm sure.

"How long has this been going on for?" I crack my knuckles, turning my back to the nervous accountant.

"A few months—four to be exact. Since we moved some of the banquet's expenses over to the dealership's account."

"The cash flow was better. It made sense to funnel some expenses through there," I remember.

"Yes, it was a good idea at the time."

Keeping the money moving was always such an intricate process. The complexity of it all used to break my mind; trying to understand all of the numbers and different businesses when I first took over.

I was so young though, so who could blame me? It wasn't about blame though. Nobody was happy to have me in charge, full stop. But they wouldn't dare challenge the will of my father, even after his death. Those who did were no longer in my employ (or on this earth).

Thank fuck for Luigi. As much as he annoys me, he's generally quite thorough. At least my father left me with an impeccable team of dirty accountants who specialized in money laundering (though none of us ever called it that). Luigi had been with me since the start. Just like Emilio. This was the first time any money had gone missing though...

"If it was such a good idea, how did we manage to lose all that money then?" It's hard to keep my temper at bay. No Zen Garden on earth could calm me down now. I am very tempted to draw my knife and finish what I started the last time Luigi brought me bad news. But I need him. Besides, I now know he's not the one to blame, merely an unfortunate messenger.

"Little bits at a time, *signore.* That's why we didn't catch it earlier. They used one of the company credit cards and kept the payments low enough to avoid being flagged. Five thousand dollars here, ten thousand there. Just slowly siphoning it out, paying fake invoices to fake companies, all with the same account number. It got lost in the day-to-day expenses. See here." He draws my attention back to the stack of printed-out statements lying on my table.

As I walk closer to look, Luigi jumps back, out of reach immediately again. So jittery. *As he should be.*

"And you're certain about *who* did it?" I don't want to deal with this. Not now. Everything is going so well.

"*Sì*. He had the card all along. He used it to pay for the banquet's flowers."

I lower my head and sigh heavily. *You can't trust anyone. Fuck.* "And the account? Where all the money was sent to. Who does it belong to?" I finally ask the question Luigi is clearly dreading to answer judging by the way he shifts between his feet, shuffling about like the carpet is made of hot coals.

"It took us a while to trace that one through the various shell companies..." Luigi goes quiet.

"*Who*?" I demand, slamming my fist onto the table.

"It's one of the Ricci family accounts, *Signore*." He's visibly scared of my reaction.

I stare at Luigi in disbelief. "It can't be. Why*?"

95

None of this makes sense.

"I'm sorry, *Signore*. All I have are the numbers. The *why*, I cannot answer."

The sharp intake of breath burns my lungs as I refuse to exhale, trying to push away the darkness coloring my edges.

"Not a word to anyone, Luigi. Understood?"

"Of course. My silence is guaranteed, always."

"I'll deal with it."

Luigi nods.

"Go."

"*Grazie, signore.*" The nervous accountant scatters without any formalities, eager to escape unscathed this time.

Unsure of what to do next, I just stare at the stack of statements on the table, frozen. *Oh, fanculo!* There must be something I'm missing.

I start digging through it all again, line by line. But the evidence is there, black on white, undeniable.

A while later there's a knock on the door. I'm still deep in the paperwork, trying to find more answers than the numbers have to give.

"Not now!" I bark angrily, impatient.

This can't be right. But I know it is. More than $200,000 has been stolen over the past four months. It feels like I've been punched in the gut, betrayed in every sense of the word. It's the deception that bothers me, the lies. Fuck the money—there is plenty where that came from. But once trust is broken, repair is not an option.

The knock sounds again, more urgent.

"I said *not now*!"

The door opens anyway. It's Danica. But even *her* face can't cheer me up today. I'm lost in the numbers, my problem-solving mind desperately trying to make sense of it all.

"I brought you coffee, I—" she starts, smiling sweetly.

"I'm busy," I say simply, eager to get her out of my study. Having her around just makes me more stressed. She's a liability. I can't lose her. That's why I need to sort this mess out before it gets any worse—if it's not already too late.

"You're being rude." She looks at me accusatorially.

"Are you deaf, Danica? Not now," I hiss, hardly looking at her. I don't want to lose my focus; I can't afford to.

"What's wrong, baby? Are you okay?" She puts the coffee down on the desk.

"No," I say simply, stacking the papers on the table together. "You should go."

"Talk to me: what's happening?" Danica pleads but my mind is filled with a singular rage. Nothing exists outside of it. Not even Danica. I don't want her getting messed up in this. Transacting with the Ricci family could only mean bad news. They are the most brutal of all the families. Our on-off feud is a never-ending source of sleepless nights. I still have my suspicions that they were the ones behind my wife's death all those years ago.

"Go, Danica. I said I'm busy." I know she hates being dismissed but I can't tell her what's happening. Not yet anyway. She asks too many questions, questions I don't have answers to.

"What the fuck is wrong with you?" A dark cloud drops over her face. I can hear the angry tears threatening in her voice. But I don't look at her. We have bigger problems than Danica's emotions right now.

Without answering, I turn my back on her, walking over to the window, my gaze fixed on the grounds outside. *Maybe there's a rational answer for everything. Maybe—*

"Dante!" Danica demands, but I don't turn around. "Have you forgotten who owns you?" She can't maintain the authority in her voice, she's too upset. It wouldn't matter anyway. My mind is locked on trying to unravel a puzzle I don't have enough pieces for.

"Not now. Go shopping. Leave. *Please*, Danica. I need to take care of something. Maybe go buy yourself something nice, hey?"

I know I sound patronizing, but I'll make it up to her later. Once I know we're safe.

"Fuck you! You think I'm here for your *money*?" Danica spits, furious. I forgot how angry she can get, the fire that burns inside. Almost like the day we met. I smirk at the memory.

Danica is not amused though.

I sigh. I need to fix this but I can't do it with Danica here.

"Emilio!" I call and within seconds he's by my side.

"Yes, boss?"

"Please get Carlo to take Danica to the shops, I—" I start but Danica interrupts me.

"I'm right here. You can't just treat me like a child."

Ignoring her, I continue my instructions to Emilio. "Please take her to the shop but make sure she has protection."

"Yes, boss," Emilio nods.

"No!" Danica shouts.

"That is an order, Emilio," I say, well aware that Danica doesn't take orders from me.

"I won't go," Danica insists, crossing her arms over her chest.

"You have permission to drag her out if you have to," I add.

"You don't get to do that—"

"Now go," I repeat, waving them both away.

"Argh!" Danica wipes my coffee cup off the table with the back of her hand, shattering it on the floor dramatically. "You dickhead. You're just like my brothers. Fuck you!" She marches off in a huff.

"Please send someone to clean that up, Emilio. I'd like a fresh cup while they're at it."

He nods respectfully. "Yes, boss."

"And Emilio?"

"*Don mio?*"

"I want her out of this house within the hour. Understood?"

"Yes, boss. No problem."

"Good. I have enough problems. Go."

Emilio closes the door behind him.

I can't hold it any longer. The fury boils through my veins as I smash my fist into the heavy wooden door just to hit something. My knuckles crack but I feel no pain.

What a fucking mess.

Chapter Eleven

OUTBURST

Danica...

Despite trying to keep a strong face, I can't help myself—tears stream down my face as I run to our room, slamming the door with all the might I can muster.

I don't want to go anywhere, especially not the fucking shops. If only I could hide under the duvet and stay in bed all day. But within minutes there is a knock on my door, Emilio gently reminding me that we have to leave before the hour is up.

He returns every five minutes, threatening in his gentle manner to break down the locked door if I don't comply. I know he would do it too—Emilio takes his orders seriously. He can go from chill to psycho in seconds if Dante commands it.

Fine! I force myself to get up, to take a shower, to wash the smell of Dante off my skin. I don't want to think of him anymore. Yet everything in this house is his, including me.

As I gather my purse, I secretly hope that Dante is waiting by the door ready to apologize. But he isn't. His study door is firmly shut. *Not this time*, Emilio warns as I try to squeeze past him. I bang my fists on his chest until Carlo drags me into the car. *Assholes, all of you!*

Pissed, I slam the car door shut way louder than anyone can stand, but see if I give a fuck about Dante's cars. I don't remember the last time I was this furious.

"I'm sorry, Miss Matthews. We have our orders," Carlo says sheepishly as he turns around to look at me.

"You didn't have to carry me out of the house," I reply bitterly.

"You left us little choice," the other hunk of meat in the front seat says. He is one of the newer guards. I don't know his name yet and I am not going to ask it now.

Dante should know I hate being told what to do, and I especially hate being bullied by men more than twice my size. That feeling of complete helplessness is so triggering. It makes me feel like a little girl again.

"Just drive, Carlo. Get me out of here." As much as I would rather be alone, I know it's not an option. I am never alone, not after the incident at the sex shop when those attackers almost got me. To be fair, Dante was the only reason my life was in danger in the first place. I didn't need saving until I met him. *Well, that isn't entirely true...*

Carlo wordlessly starts the van, slowly backing out of the large, winding driveway with the rosebushes on the side, lining the paved road like we live in Downton Fucking Abbey or some shit.

As usual, we're stopped at the gate for a full vehicle search and retina scan before the heavy, nine-foot iron gate with the spikes on top begins to roll open.

"Where are the rest?" Carlo questions, pressing his forefinger to the fingerprint scanner.

The guard shrugs. "It's just me today. Two called in sick and the rest are out collecting debts." He walks over to check the boot.

"That seems irregular." Carlo is suspicious as always—it's his job after all. He surveys the perimeter through his dark sunglasses, almost habitually.

"It happens," the gate guard says. "The others should be back by this afternoon."

"Can we go already?" I demand from the backseat, feeling like a bratty teenager more than the Queen of this castle. I don't want to listen to any more business talk, I just want to be away from it all.

How fucking dare he throw me out like that? By now, I was used to Dante losing his cool but never with me, I'd always gotten through to him. Not today.

And to think how our morning had started, with him still inside me. Such a beautiful morning, so perfectly intimate, now all ruined. I feel so far away from him, that is the worst thing about this all. Like it was all just a dream now gone, I'm back to feeling lost, alone...*abandoned.*

What if he never comes back to me? Where would I go? Where would I live? Just the thought of moving back in with my parents again...I don't want to think about it.

Stuck with my increasingly negative spiral of thoughts, I don't speak another word the entire drive. Nor do I answer Carlo when he asks if I want some lunch. Not once do I bother even acknowledging what's-his-name, the new one, in his fancy pants and shiny shoes.

Everywhere we go, people stare, no doubt wondering who I am and why I am important enough to have two giant guards following my short figure through the busy mall. Not that anyone dares ask, not with the guards' gun holsters clearly visible.

I aimlessly wander around from shop to shop. Not too long ago, this would have been my dream—an almost limitless black credit card to buy me whatever my heart desires. Except it can't, because now all my heart desires is Dante.

Emptiness engulfs me, widening the hole inside into a dark abyss that swallows everything up.

So, I spend Dante's money frivolously, almost vindictively, as I buy things I don't need, forcing the guards to carry my designer bags through the shops. It's probably degrading for them, totally beneath them, but I don't care...they might as well be useful.

Despite not being hungry, I know I should eat, I realize when I start to feel faint. I haven't eaten anything since last night. The auction with its five-star buffet feels so long ago now. I stuffed my face with more shrimp than I could afford on a monthly paycheck and then some. But now my stomach is completely empty again with zero shrimp in the tank.

Without bothering to seek out anywhere special, I march the guards into the first coffee shop on our path, ordering them to a separate table so I can have some space.

I get a much-needed coffee and a croissant I can't get down, warming my hands on the cup as I stare out into the small space without focusing on anything. My thoughts are a million miles away when Carlo puts a hand on my shoulder.

"What?!" I snap, shaking him off. He knows I hate being touched without permission. What is it with men thinking they can just touch you?

Carlo is holding his phone, a solemn look on his face. "There has been an incident at home, Miss Matthews...I'm sorry. We need to go at once."

"What kind of *incident*?" I ask, peering at him over my coffee cup. The word *incident* has never spelled anything good. By the time something is called an incident, you know it's actually way worse. "Is Dante okay?"

Carlo lowers his eyes as he shakes his head from side to side—no. I know it must be serious if they're calling us back home.

"Is Dante okay?" I repeat, the cup shaking in my hand.

"We have to go, Miss Matthews," Carlo says sternly.

But it's what he doesn't say that makes the anxiety knot in my stomach.

Oh fuck. Dante!

DOUBLE-CROSSED

DANTE...

As soon as she storms out of my study, I know I've fucked up. I shouldn't have spoken to Danica like that.

But I can't tell her what's going on, not yet. Not until it's all resolved. She would just worry or worse—try to interfere. Keeping her out of harm's way is priority number one.

Still, the guilt sits in my stomach like a brick. Danica didn't deserve to be thrown out like that. I never want to hurt her, she's had enough of that in her life already.

Twisting my rings, I restlessly pace the room until Emilio's familiar knock drags me out of the mental spiral of guilt with a fresh cup of coffee that he places on my desk with a simple nod.

"Taking on new tasks?" I try to smile but the attempt is largely unsuccessful.

"I didn't make it, I'm just bringing it in." The big man's voice shows no humor, it rarely does.

I raise an eyebrow. "Oh?"

"They're too scared, boss."

"And why is that?" I know the answer but I want him to tell me.

"Miss Matthews was quite upset earlier..." he carefully broaches the subject.

Emilio is more than just my guard. He is my confidant, my advisor. In the more than two decades we've worked together, Emilio has been the most dependable person in my life.

"Yes, I suppose so. I have a lot on my mind..."

"You don't have to explain yourself to me, *Don mio*," Emilio says simply, formal as always.

"I should make it up to her though. Will you speak to Alicia please and arrange a special dinner for tonight? Just here at home. It's not safe to go out."

If anyone can pull something together last-minute, Alicia can. My house manager slash personal assistant has only been with the family for three years now, but she's proved a quick learner. Dependable and efficient is a winning combination in such a role.

"Yes, *boss.*"

"And ask her to get some of Danica's favorite flowers too, those dark red tulips. Make it special, you know?" I am trying, but romantic isn't really my style. Not since my wife died...More than six years ago now. I flinch at the mere thought of those days.

Emilio nods.

"And please keep that door closed at all times."

"Of course." Emilio quietly takes his leave without question, resuming his post right outside. I wish I could clone that man; having multiple Emilios would make my life much easier.

Maybe if Emilio had been at home that day, rather than with me, my wife would still be alive. I can't stop the thoughts that drift to the painful past, poking a raw wound that never seems to close. Poking it just to make sure it still hurts. It does. A lot.

Elena.

Sometimes, on warm Spring afternoons, I can still hear her laugh echoing through the rooms of the mansion. She made it all feel so different, the whole house, my life. Things had been dark until she'd come along with those long legs and innocent smile, dark curls cascading down her back.

Elena was made of pure sunshine, beautiful in every sense of the word. A true Italian too, my dad would have been proud. No, my dad was never proud. But he *could* have been.

When I told Danica the story, she just threw her arms around me, crying as she held me. I wanted to cry too, but I couldn't. It was the first time I had spoken about Elena since the day I lost her, more than six years ago now.

I had just turned 32 when we met (Elena was 26). She was Don Greco's youngest daughter, a suitable match. From the moment I'd first laid eyes on her at some social gathering I didn't care for, I couldn't tear myself away from her.

Our attraction had been instant. She wanted me as much as I wanted her. Elena had been used to the crime life; I didn't have to hide anything from her. She loved me as I was. For the first time since taking over the family business 13 years prior, I had found something that was purely mine.

Elena had been the most beautifully obedient sub any man could wish for. The way she kneeled for me, waiting by the door every day, naked except for her collar. The things she let me do to her body, the things she wanted me to do...

Her devotion had known no bounds. And neither had my desire for her. I wanted her all the time, wanted to make her face contort in pleasure as she screamed my name loud enough for everyone in the house to hear.

I had never been a pleasure Dom until I met Elena. But her satisfaction became the only thing that mattered to me. We married within two years in an extravagant affair attended by both families en masse. I will never forget the sight of her walking up in that pure white dress, the smile she wore just for me. We were so happy. So naive too, in hindsight.

I was going to give it all up for her; I was going to get out...maybe move back to Italy, start a family of our own. Luca could take over. He was keen for the power but not so keen to learn. Still, I'd been ready to hand it all over to him, even if he burned it all to the ground. Anything to take my princess away to another castle, to keep her safe.

I'd wanted nothing more than to live by the sea in a modest house, just us, maybe a few kids running around. For a moment, I'd thought I could have it all, that I could be just Dante, not Don Fera.

But nobody gets out alive.

Emilio had been with me the day it happened. We'd gone to bail out Luca again after some or other dumb shit he'd gotten himself into. I don't know if I've ever stopped resenting him, or myself, for not having been there when they took her that day.

Elena had gone to the doctor. A guard was with her, as always. Only much later did I find out she was pregnant. We were meant to have a little boy. I couldn't bring myself to tell Danica this part, not yet.

The guard hadn't been able to defend Elena by himself, outnumbered. They'd taken her.

I still don't know who did it or why. Nobody has ever owned up to the act. I suspect it was the Riccis, but I can't prove it.

It had taken too long to find her. By the time I did, I could no longer save her. They'd left her butchered on the cold floor, naked, bleeding out over the concrete in some abandoned building, her beautiful face desecrated by ugly cuts and bruises.

That had been the first time I cried since my mother died. Elena's body was cold, lifeless, as I picked her up, blood smeared across my shirt, my hands. I cried into her messy hair. Cried for the life we could've had, the life that was lost. Only Emilio had seen me fall apart. But we never spoken about it again.

With a heavy sigh, I kissed the ruby on the ring adorning my right hand. Sweet dear Elena.

Focus, Dante! The painful ghosts of my past won't solve my current predicament. I need to find a way to handle this swiftly and discreetly.

With three big gulps, I finish my lukewarm coffee and check my phone again. Still nothing.

I try to call him again but it just rings. My text remains unread as well.

You fucker. What have you gotten yourself mixed up in now?

I'm still contemplating my next move when I hear a gunshot outside. It's muffled but unmistakable, a dull thud that reverberates through the thick walls of my office. The sudden sound sends a jolt of adrenaline through my veins.

What the fuck?

Instinctively, I open the desk drawer and fish out my gun, the cold metal reassuringly familiar in my hand. My fingers tremble as I try to check that it's loaded, but my vision suddenly blurs. My head feels like it's filled with cotton; I can't focus on the simple task I've performed thousands of times before.

Get it together, Dante! I command myself, taking a deep breath in a desperate attempt to clear the fog clouding my thoughts.

Outside, chaos erupts. Shouts in rapid, frantic Italian pierce the air, and I catch fragments of Emilio's voice, but I can't make out the words.

More gunshots ring out, louder this time, echoing like thunderclaps through the corridor.

I don't know what's going on. *Where are the guards? Emilio?*

Moments later, my door bursts open with the deafening crash of splintering wood. An army of masked gunmen floods into my office, their black-clad forms moving with military precision.

Panic claws at my chest as I scramble to raise my gun, but I'm too slow.

I fire a shot but not before they do. Blinding pain burns through me, and I drop the gun, clutching at my shoulder as hot blood seeps between my fingers. I try to focus, to count the armed men swarming into my study, but my mind is sluggish, unable to keep up with the rapid onslaught.

There are eight of them, maybe more. Their shouts are unmistakably Italian, but the voices are unfamiliar.

They grab me from behind the desk. I try to struggle but it's no use, my limbs feel like lead—heavy and unresponsive. Desperation surges through me, a primal instinct to survive, but it's no use. A blow lands on my jaw, the sharp impact of a pistol butt sending me crashing to the floor.

The world tilts and spins, and I taste blood, metallic and bitter, in my mouth.

I lie there, dazed and helpless, as the one asshole points his gun to my forehead.

No!

CHAPTER THIRTEEN

BLINDSIDED

DANTE...

When I finally come to, I have no idea where I am. My mind races, tangled thoughts grappling for clarity, but one thing cuts through the fog with fierce urgency: I have to find Danica.

Try as I might, I can't see a thing; the blackest of dark surrounds me in all directions. I don't remember being blindfolded, but then again, I don't remember a lot of things.

My head is fuzzy, dazed, like I'd been chasing white lines from dusk to dawn, the sunrises dripping in reckless abandon like they used to do during my youthful Vegas party days. But my nose has been a one-way street for years now, so I know it's not recreational drugs.

Pain pulses through my bruised body as I'm jolted back to consciousness. My face is sticky, warm; the familiar feeling of drying blood clings to my skin, its coppery taste on my tongue. The worst is my shoulder, it's on fire!

I try to wipe my cheek but my arm won't obey any commands. Only when I try again without any result do I realize I can't move at all.

Ropes, it's ropes. Rough ropes are cutting into my wrists. Whoever tied me up did a good job, there isn't even the smallest wiggle room—I am secured fully to what feels like the world's most uncomfortable chair.

My body is too big for chairs like this, those stupid fold-up metal ones that were more for function than comfort. I doubt my comfort was of anyone's concern currently though.

The oppressive darkness presses in, amplifying the silence around me. I strain to hear anything, any sign of where I might be or who might be near, but the void offers no answers. Fear gnaws at me, each minute passing by in a torturous eternity. *It's hopeless.*

But I can't give up. I have to get to Danica before they do. It might already be too late...This is not how this story is supposed to go. Not now. Not when things are finally starting to come together again. I grit my teeth, forcing the pain and fear to the back of my mind. There has to be a way out. There has to be a way to save her.

"Untie me, assholes!" I demand, my voice failing to convey the authority I intended. It sounds weak, hoarse...foreign. *I need water.*

There is no response from the empty room that reeks of sourness, like someone puked on the floor weeks ago and simply left it to dry. The scent is intoxicating and not in a sexy way—quite the opposite.

"You're going to regret this," I try again but my threat falls on deaf ears. My voice echoes back to me in the cold room with the floor that feels like rough concrete beneath my bare feet. Definitely not a luxury accommodation, though I doubt I am here on a social call. You don't just kidnap a Don for *fun...*

Desperate for freedom, I rock back and forth, trying to tip the metal chair, but it's no use—it appears to be bolted to the floor. *Fuckers.* I wish I knew who they were but the assholes are too cowardly to even show their faces, to answer my threats.

I struggle for a few minutes more before my broken body forces me to accept the limitations of my situation. Even the slightest move tugs at my burning shoulder like a knife stabbing through my skin again and again.

How did this even happen? I still can't piece it all together.

I remember sending Danica away. I remember joking with Emilio about the coffee. And then, suddenly, a huge commotion outside my study. Gunshots. So many gunshots—they still ring in my sore ears.

I know I'd jumped up, drawing my weapon, ready to destroy whoever dared invade my home. But my movements had been slow, fuzzy. Too slow. I never stood a chance.

I'd fumbled too long and the invaders got me in the shoulder, a clean shot that went right through me—a small mercy at least. They pinned me to the floor and kicked the shit out of me before I could take out a single one of them.

That much came back to me. But I don't know how much time has passed since I blacked out in a pool of my own blood. Was it this morning? It could have been yesterday too, but I really hope it wasn't.

The last thing I remember was one of the armed men in my study grabbing my hair, pulling my bloodied face off the floor. His Italian had been flawless. Native. *Curse you and your whole family, Don Fera,* he said, spitting in my eye before smashing my face into the floor...

There is nothing in my memory after that, nothing but all-encompassing darkness.

What happened though? The attackers should never have even gotten as far as my study. That has never happened before—not in all the decades the Fera family have lived on that property. We have layers of security, guards patrolling the grounds, and secret access codes that change regularly.

How did they get in? The answer is obvious but it's not one I want to accept. There is no way into the fortress that is the Fera house without insider access. Even then, it would be near impossible to get past the various guards.

Someone in my inner circle has betrayed me. I sincerely hope my suspicions are wrong, and that everything isn't connected. Because if I'm right, Danica is in even more danger than I thought.

The thought of Danica in trouble sends a fresh wave of urgency coursing through me. My heart pounds in my chest, a rhythmic reminder that time is slipping away. I can't shake the image of her in peril, her life hanging in the balance because of a betrayal I never saw coming.

I need to get to her...My beautiful *Tesoro*. I wish my last words to her hadn't been so cruel. She didn't deserve it. She doesn't deserve any of this.

What I wouldn't give to be home in her arms, wrapped around her petite frame, face buried in those large breasts I loved to suck on. She would take her black-rimmed reading glasses off, the ones that made her look like a high school teacher, push her hair behind her ears, and kiss my forehead as she'd done a million times before. She would tell me it's all okay, that we're safe.

But we aren't safe.

We aren't safe *at all*.

Groaning loudly, I pull on the ropes with all my might, desperate for freedom. But it's no use. The only result is the blinding pain in my shoulder damn near knocking me out again.

Oh, fanculo.

CHAPTER FOURTEEN

LIARS

DANICA...

It's been two nights since they took Dante. Two tormented sleepless nights without my *Tesoro*, my treasure.

Trying to keep it steady, I hold my steaming coffee cup with both hands but can't bring myself to drink it. I came to hide out in the library, my usual place of refuge, hoping to find some escape, some peace but all I found was a Dante-sized hole.

Focus blurred, I stare out over the lawns as my feelings toggle between desperate, lost, exhausted, and a million other emotions I don't have the name (or energy for.) Above all, I am sick with worry—it lies heavy in my stomach like a breath I cannot catch; I'm drowning.

This is the longest Dante and I have ever been apart since we met. I don't know what to do with myself, I feel so useless. Emilio and Luca have been out all day, speaking to some of the family's informants, hoping to find something, anything, about who took Dante or why. They didn't want me to come with though—*You'll just be in the way, Danica.* As always.

With Dante away, everyone accepts Emilio's authority—despite Luca's weak demands to be treated like the boss. I'm glad to have the older man in charge. If only there was something I could do to be useful, but I'm frozen, on pause.

I try to keep my mind from the worst-case scenario but it's difficult. Dante has a lot of enemies, enemies capable of things I cannot even fathom. He has shielded me from the horrors of the business as much as he could, but who was there to protect him?

I can't stay in our room. It feels so empty. *What if he never comes back?* If only I could stop asking myself that.

Another thing has been taken from me. *You can't have nice things, Danica, don't you learn?* My inner voice has never been kind. As ugly inside as I am out—or at least that's how I used to see myself. That's what everyone made me believe. My father, my brothers, that fuck-head ex who I gave up my studies for.

But not Dante. In his eyes, I am always beautiful, perfect. He believes it so much that I almost started believing it too. I want to be who he sees me as; I am better with him...no, *for* him. A god like Dante Fera deserves a Queen worthy of worship.

But I am a useless Monarch. I can't do anything to bring my Knight back. I want to cry but I have no more tears left; I'm all cried out.

"You ever going to drink that coffee?" A familiar voice pulls me back to the high-ceilinged room stacked top-to-bottom with beautiful books I should read to distract myself but they hold no appeal when my tumultuous mind seeks only one solace—Dante.

"Any news?" I ask hopefully, turning to Luca.

"Nothing. We've spoken to all the families but nobody knows shit." He puts a hand on my shoulder but I feel no comfort.

I imagine I must look like a complete mess, I feel like one. It's been days since I last showered, not since Dante left, and my hair is tied up in a messy ponytail, my thick glasses pushed over my face. Why bother with the contact lenses now? *Why bother with anything?*

Luca puts an arm around me and pulls me out of the chair, pressing me against his body. His breath reeks of alcohol, a foul smell that hangs heavy in the air, assaulting my senses.

"It will be okay—" Luca starts, letting his hand drop to my ass.

As if stung by a bee, I instantly recoil from him.

"Jesus, Luca!" I exclaim, pushing him back in disgust.

There is nothing consensual about Luca's advances and I'm not here for it, not at all. His touch makes me want to pour boiling water on my skin just to get rid of his slimy fingerprints. How could I have ever imagined him desirable, even for a second, at the auction?

Whatever attractive physical attributes the younger Fera had been blessed with were overshadowed by his shifty personality that became more repulsive the longer you spent in his presence.

Fuck Luca; he could never stand in for Dante. What I wouldn't give to have my darling boy hold me tight again, to hear the word *Tesoro* drip from his lips in that deep voice of his...I just need Dante to come back and then everything will be okay. But he's not here to save me any more than I can save him right now.

Luca grabs my wrist, and I glare daggers into his eyes, desperately trying to shake him loose. "Let go," I hiss. His eyes are shifty, blood red, I cannot force them to obey my commands.

Luca laughs loudly, inappropriately. "You're so cute when you're angry." He doesn't let go. Never mind that he's fucking hurting me with that tight grip, I'm getting very uncomfortable now, overly aware of my personal space being invaded.

"Are you drunk?"

"The alcohol was just the starter," Luca smiles, and it all starts to make a little more sense. He must be high on something, and not the mild recreational stuff—or, if it is, he has clearly consumed more than recreational quantities.

"It hardly seems like the time, Luca," I say sternly.

"Now is the perfect time. When the cat's away, the mice can play." He pulls me toward him again, reaching over to try and kiss me. But I shove my hand up into his face, hitting his jaw. The self-defense classes are finally paying off.

"Go to hell, Luca!" I shout, but I still can't get him to release his grip.

"You're being a real bitch, Danica. I thought you wanted this too?" He is annoyed, touching his fingers to his bruised cheek.

"You've lost your mind. All I want is your brother."

"Well, he's not here right now to protect you, is he? I finally get to have you all to myself." Luca grabs both my wrists to hold me down, pinning me against a bookcase with his body. There is nothing sexy about the move. All I feel is panic.

Squirming beneath him, I scream as loudly as I can. The library is tucked away deep within the house, but one of the guards should be around. *Should be.*

But it's not the guards who hear me, it's Alicia. She appears suddenly in the doorway, staring at us confused. Her expression is not what I expect. She looks angry for some reason rather than alarmed.

"What are you doing, Luca?" she asks calmly, too calmly, as she walks toward us. Luca finally lets up and I pull my wrists free from his grip with force.

"Ali..." Luca's face changes, the fury instantly drains from his eyes, replaced by something pathetic. "I was just—"

Alicia doesn't let him finish. She grabs him by the shirt collar, bringing his face inches from hers. "You're fucking this up, Luca. Do you understand that?"

I might as well not be in the room. *What is going on here?* I'm beyond confused.

"I—" Luca tries to protest, but for the second time today, he gets a hand to the face as Alicia punches him.

"Ali, please. It's not what it looks like," he whines, head in his hands.

"Really? Because what it looks like is you chasing after what isn't yours. Again. Can you just stop making everything worse already?" She is clearly on edge. I am still in the dark as to why, but I'm starting to suspect everything isn't as it appears. Alicia looks like she hasn't slept in days.

"I'm not making it worse. I'm fixing it, remember?"

"Does it look *fixed* to you? When are they going to call? You said it would only be one day. That it's just to get the money and then we're good. It's not one day anymore, Luca."

"Not in front of *her*. Shut up, Ali. You're going to get us in trouble." Luca looks panicked, wild eyes darting between Alicia and me.

"What's going on?" I demand but neither of them look at me.

"Nothing. She's just jealous," Luca covers quickly, nervously. He looks fidgety, guilty.

"Yes, yes I am. Because my asshole druggy *boyfriend* can't keep his addictions at bay long enough to follow a simple plan," she hisses through her teeth.

"Your boyfriend—as in *him*?" I ask, looking at Luca, not all that interested in this part of the story. But they clearly know something about Dante's kidnapping.

"I'm not a druggy," Luca says quietly, shoulders drooping. "Please stop."

But his *Ali* has no intention of stopping. She is furious. And fed up.

"No, Luca. This has gone too far. You said Dante wouldn't get hurt. They would just rough him up. I'm starting to realize nothing that comes out of your mouth is ever the truth."

"Where's Dante?" I beg.

"Tell her, Luca. Tell her what you did. You want to be the bad boy. So own up to your shit. Tell Danica how you sold out your own brother to pay off your fucking gambling debts. Tell her about all the cocaine. About how you promised to help them get into Dante's study so they could blackmail the family for more money and you could pay what you owe. How you got me to help you drug Dante's coffee so he'd be defenseless, how I spiked the two guards' food and gave them all food poisoning. Tell her how you promised this would be the last time, this would solve all our problems and we'd finally be free, done with it all. How you were ready to make an honest woman out of me. Tell her the truth for once, Luca." *Hell hath no fury like a woman scorned.*

"You didn't? Luca? Tell me she's making this up." I look at him in desperation, not willing to accept the words that make sense but at the same time, don't.

"No one was supposed to get hurt..." Luca lowers his eyes shamefully.

"Where is he?" I ask for the umpteenth time, this time to someone who might actually have an answer.

"I don't know. They were supposed to just take him and then demand money. I was going to transfer it to them as blackmail money to pay off my debts and they were going to let him go. Easy peasy. But they haven't even called yet..."

"You're an idiot, Luca. They fucking double-crossed you. The same way you double-crossed your own blood. How *could* you?" I clench my fists, listening to my knuckles crack.

"I had no choice. I asked him for help. He didn't help me. He never fucking helps. It is always just about the business. Or you." He glares at me in accusation.

"You gave your brother to the literal fucking enemy, Luca. He doesn't deserve this."

My desperation is quickly turning to anger.

"I called him, you know. He didn't even bother to answer. Last week. Where was he then? When they were beating the shit out of me? They cut off my fucking little toe, Danica! Did Dante even bother to answer his phone? No!" He is pacing around the room. Alicia stands to the side, leaning against the bookcase, arms crossed over her chest—the look of a woman who is done with this shit.

"Is that why you were limping at the banquet?"

"That's beside the point, but yes. He didn't even answer...he never does."

"You know that's not true, Luca. He's always bailing you out of shit."

"Ha! Is that what he tells people?" Luca scoffs. "I—"

He's interrupted by Emilio's unexpected arrival. "Miss Matthews?" the old man asks, trying to read the room.

"Ah, Emilio. Aren't I happy to see you. Could you please help me with something quick?" My voice is calm to the point of being psychotic.

I'm coming, Dante.

Just hold on.

Chapter Fifteen

CONFESSIONS

DANICA...

"**I**s everything okay here, Miss Matthews?" Emilio puts down the tray he's carrying, nodding at Alicia and Luca in greeting. He's moving slower than usual because of the fresh bullet wound in his leg. I tried sending him home but he would not leave my side. *The boss would've wanted me to protect you.*

"Not really, Emilio," I reply, my gaze locked on Luca. It is far from okay. It hasn't been okay since Dante was taken to who-knows-where.

"I brought you some fruit salad, you haven't eaten all day," Emilio explains.

"Thank you, Emilio. That's very considerate of you." I smile through pursed lips, my voice slow and steady, strained. The tension is so thick you can cut it with a butter knife.

"It's my pleasure. What can I assist you with?"

I take my time in answering, weighing up my options carefully before deciding to just go with my first instinct.

"Please pin that asshole to the bookcase." I point at Luca.

"I'm sorry?" Emilio hesitates, looking at me confused.

"Don't." Luca shoots Emilio a glare.

"It seems Luca here knows where Dante is but has been keeping some secrets from us," I reply calmly.

Emilio has him pinned in two seconds flat. "Is this true?" he demands, slamming Luca into the bookcase again. I've never seen Emilio lose his cool but today is an exception—he looks ready to strangle Luca.

"Get your hands off me, Emilio. Do you forget who pays your salary?" Luca laughs, a cocky smirk on his face.

"Not you." Luca's third fist to the face is substantially harder than the first two. It breaks the skin on his cheek and a bruise instantly starts to swell. It makes Luca look even more deranged.

I laugh loudly, manically almost. The sleep deprivation is gnawing at my edges, making me feel dangerously close to losing it. But the satisfaction I feel from seeing Emilio punch Luca in the face brings me great joy. I wish I could hit someone that hard too. Maybe one day.

"I've always wanted to do that," Emilio admits, stretching out his fingers, his knuckles cracking audibly.

Alicia turns to leave, hoping nobody would see her, but I catch a glimpse from the corner of my eye. "Don't even think about it, Alicia. You're as guilty as he is."

"I'm not going down with him. I told you the truth, you—" she starts to bargain but I hold up my hand to silence her, just as I saw Dante do it previously.

"You have nowhere to run, Alicia. So please sit down and be quiet," I instruct, a newfound sense of power coursing through my veins. The accomplice does as she's told, slumping down into one of the oversized armchairs that would be amazing for reading on a rainy day, not today.

She knows she won't get far. The thing about a fortress is that it's as hard to get out as it is to get in. The guards may have been thinned out severely by this week's massacre but the other two have recovered from their food poisoning and are back at their posts.

I turn back to the men.

"Now. Where were we?" I ask Emilio, ignoring Luca's whining.

"I believe Luca was about to tell us where Don Fera is," Emilio says, pressing his forearm into Luca's windpipe, cutting off his air supply.

"Jesus, Emilio...I don't know," Luca gasps, trying to push the bigger man away. But he stands no chance against Emilio. Even injured, he is a formidable force, a force that is in way better shape than Luca's drugged-up, near-delirium body.

"Hold him for me, please, Emilio," I ask politely.

Without warning, I drive my knee into Luca's crotch and he lets out a loud howl when I make contact with his balls. He doubles over but Emilio holds him up.

"Stop lying, Luca. Enough now. Tell me where Dante is."

Luca coughs, the wind knocked out of him completely. I can't believe I just did that but it feels good, right. No more; I'm done being the innocent bystander, the witness, the victim—fuck that. This dickhead better start speaking if he knows what's good for him.

I knee him again and Luca howls in pain, tears flowing freely now. He's a whimpering wreck, held up not by his own legs but Emilio's strength. His red eyes seem to grow even redder as he falls apart, a drugged-up, sleep-deprived disheveled mess. There isn't a single bone in my body that feels any sympathy for Luca Fera. No, the more he comes undone, the angrier I get. *This was all his fault!*

With a single finger, I tilt Luca's chin up, looking him straight in the eye as I grab the knife from the holster around his waist. Nobody stops me. Quick as lighting, I flick open the blade and press it against Luca's pants where my knee had been just moments before, applying just enough pressure for him to feel its shape.

His whimpering stops as Luca sucks in his breath, keeping it inside his chest. Wild eyes darting from side to side, he looks like someone who needs to take a serious break from partying.

"I'm going to ask you one more time, Luca. Just one more time. And you'd better give me a name or I will cut these clean off, understood?" I press the blade against the outline of his cock, moving it lower down to his balls. My mind has a single purpose—bringing Dante home by any means necessary.

Luca gasps. "No...No. Please," he pleads.

"Where is Dante?"

"I don't know!"

"Who knows?!" I press the blade harder, cutting through the fabric of his pants.

"Roberto! Roberto knows. Please stop!" Luca is howling now, crying loudly. It's a distressing scene but nobody moves to help him. He has no lifelines left. "Please..."

"Roberto who?"

"Ricci," Emilio answers for him, easing his grip and letting Luca fall to the ground. "You absolute twat, Luca." Emilio sighs heavily, rubbing his temples. His neutral face is no longer neutral—he looks concerned.

"Is that bad?" I ask.

"It's very bad, Miss Matthews. It's the worst it could be."

"Is Dante okay?"

"I don't know; I hope so. But he's in a lot of danger if the Ricci's have him." He doesn't elaborate.

"We have to go get him!" I insist.

"We need back-up first..." Emilio seems lost in thought.

"There has to be someone we can call."

"I suppose...We are pretty desperate. The Greco family owes us a favor. But I'm not sure Don Fera would want me talking to them," Emilio thinks out loud, considering our options. I sometimes wonder how he kept so many secrets in his head. But I'm grateful for him. I know Dante trusts Emilio with his life, and so do I.

"Whatever we need to do, make it happen, Emilio. Get me Don Greco on the phone please."

"Yes, Ma'am."

"You don't get to call me 'Ma'am,' Emilio." My voice stern but not rude.

"Apologies, Miss Matthews. It won't happen again."

"No problem. What are we going to do with these two though?" I look at Luca on the floor; Alicia is still sitting quietly on the chair, watching it all unfold, waiting for her lot. The one looks more miserable than the other, though both look pretty bleak—they've been caught red-handed in the worst way, like a teenager trying to have a sneaky smoke and accidentally setting the whole forest on fire.

"I'll get Carlo to lock them in the basement until we decide what to do with them. For now, our priority is to get the boss back."

With new-found determination straining my face, I nod. "It absolutely is, no matter what it takes." And I mean it. I'm done being pushed to the sidelines. *Fuck this.*

I just hope we're not too late. *Bloody Luca!* Why couldn't he open his damn mouth earlier already? But what's done is done. The important thing is that we have a lead, even it is doesn't spell anything good.

Dante has to be okay, he just has to. For the first time in my life, the girl who doesn't belong anywhere has somewhere she belongs—in Dante's arms—and I'm not giving that up for anything, definitely not Luca's gambling debts. There is no home without Dante, he is my home.

*My darling boy...*oh god, please let him be okay.

CHAPTER SIXTEEN

LOST

DANTE...

Time passes but I don't know in what measure. Because of the blindfold, there is no telling day from night. There is just darkness—darkness and increasing discomfort.

Sometimes I forget where I am, other times I forget myself. But the one thing I don't ever forget, is my mission to get to Danica. She is the only beacon of light in the darkness, keeping me fighting.

I'm still tied to this fucking chair, held captive by some unknown enemy for some unknown reason. Though I have my suspicions about what's going on.

They are keeping me alive, but barely. Water only. Not enough. Not nearly enough. The thirst in my throat burns almost as brightly as the aching parts of my body. My shoulder wound needs medical attention, it's pulsating, but the kidnappers pay me little mind.

How long have I been here? I don't know. Long enough for me to piss myself a few times over, any request for a bathroom ignored like the rest of my needs. But that is the least of my worries.

I gasp loudly as the cold water hits my face, another glass that would've been better served going down my throat, but instead, I'm desperately trying to lap up whatever drops I can muster, anything to quench this thirst. But the inadequate quantity only makes me more thirsty.

"What do you want?" I cry for the umpteenth time, swallowing hard.

No answer.

The deafening silence makes the thoughts in my head shout faster as the desperation cycles through my body on repeat.

"Why am I here?" I try again, anything to fill the silence.

Finally, another voice sparks like an ember in the darkness, only briefly—fleeting, but tangible.

"*Chiedi a tuo fratello,*" the man who threw the water in my face says simply, closing the door behind him again before I can even formulate any follow-up questions. *Ask your brother.*

Shouting after him, I want more but there are no more answers to be had. Just silence, again. But this time the silence has new information to process, a confirmation of a suspicion I should've accepted as confirmed way earlier. But I didn't want it to be real; I wanted there to be another explanation.

Fucking, Luca. I should've known better than to let him run the dealership. He's failed me so many times, yet I've always given him another chance. He is my little brother after all. I'd wanted to protect him from the evil of the business, from our father—how naive. There was no protecting anyone.

Our father was never one for affection, especially not after our mother died. I'm not sure he'd ever wanted kids. He did it for her. Nobody had planned for the great, cruel boss to be left to raise two young kids alone. So, he didn't. He brought his parents over from Italy to mind us and that was that, we hardly saw him. He was very much of the children-should-be-seen-not-heard generation.

Luca was too young when our mother died—only seven years old. He doesn't really remember what it was like before, or so he says. I had just turned 10. I remember how it felt to be supported, to be loved unconditionally. She had the most beautiful smile...

Our father hadn't taken much interest in Luca. Sure, he'd beat the crap out of him, out of both us, on the regular. Discipline was very important to him. But other than that, he'd let Luca roam free to get up to any mischief he wanted.

I never had that luxury. There was no time to be a kid. One moment I was an awkward 16-year-old with unpredictable acne and dreams of being in a band one day, and the next I stood by silently as I watched my father stab out some guy's eyes for not paying him on time.

Three years of more fucked-up stuff than I care to remember and then it got worse, then it fell on me to be the guy doing the stabbing. There is no way 19 years on this earth was enough to prepare anyone for that role; no age would be. I may have been born a Fera in name but the blood pumping through my veins was always from my mom's side of the family, I suspected.

Not that it made any difference, it was sink-or-swim and if I let us sink, we'd all sink to the bottom of the ocean with weights tied to our bodies. But there was so much to take on, too much. All the responsibility. The business. The debts. The feuds. The endless power struggle with other families...I wanted to run away but I knew that if I did, they'd come for all of us.

Why is this all coming back to me now? Because fucking Luca. I'm trying to make excuses for him again, trying to justify his unjustifiable actions. Maybe I've cut him too much slack? He's not a kid anymore; he can't blame our father for this.

Luca was 16 when our father died, acne-free and whoring his way through the city with no regard for anyone's authority. He didn't give a fuck. He spent his teenage years setting buildings on fire and torturing small animals, forcing me to bail him out (with Emilio by my side) more times than I care to remember. He always promised it would be the last time, that he learned his lesson, that he'd be good now. What a fool I was to ever believe a word that came out of that narcissistic little cunt's mouth.

Luca didn't know how cruel our father really was. I was only five the first time I saw Don Fera Snr. kill a man with his bare hands—our uncle, the head of the family. Although it didn't make sense to me, I'm sure our father had his reasons. Back then, I could never understand what would make a man want to strangle his own brother. But I do now.

"*Stronzo!*" I curse under my breath. Shit.

Although I don't know who my captors are, I have a feeling it's all connected to the missing money somehow, most likely by the thread that is Luca's aura of selfish chaos.

There is nothing I can do though, I can't move. All I can do is hope someone will come for me, but how would they even start to figure out how to find me? I'm usually the one who comes for others, not the one to be saved. Luca sure can't be counted on...

Maybe I should've told Emilio about the stolen money. But I wanted to be sure, wanted to speak to Luca, first. I didn't know who I could trust. Maybe Luigi will come forward now...But I know it is unlikely. He is paid for his silence.

And so time passes. Not quickly, not slowly. Unmeasured.

I black out from time to time, covered in my own urine and blood that has dried to hard flakes I'm desperate to scratch but can't reach.

Part of me still wants to fight, to get to Danica. But a bigger part of me knows there is no fight left in me.

The Knight has failed his Queen.

With every passing moment, I am slipping deeper into the dark abyss that calls me like a siren to an unfortunate sailor.

I don't know how much longer I can remain conscious. The allure of oblivion is strong—not to feel any more pain, not to have my mind run in endless circles that arrive nowhere; I am Sisyphus, pushing that boulder up the hill again and again, only to have it roll down once more, with no hope of salvation.

The last conversation I had with Danica still plays in my mind, repeatedly, more than the events that led to my capture. I don't even care about solving the entire mystery anymore, about finding the *why*. It doesn't matter anymore *why* my own brother sold me out, or *how*...

All that matters is that I failed Danica...even before they captured me. She trusted me with her heart, with her mind, and I treated her no better than those people I promised I was nothing like.

So many regrets...I should've been more patient. I should've communicated better instead of treating her like a child, taking away her free will, and speaking to her like she wasn't the most precious thing in my life (which she is). Shoulda, coulda, woulda...but it was too late; I couldn't undo it.

The worst is not knowing what's happening outside of these walls. Sometimes, I hear people outside, footsteps...but who is to say whether they are real or whether my mind is slowly dipping into insanity. This room could be anywhere.

But I don't know what happened after they took me, how many of my people were killed. I don't know if Danica got away, or whether she's been taken too. I don't know if we'll ever see each other again, alive—that's the one that skewers my heart like a small child watching *Bambi* for the first time.

This is all my fault. Something like this was bound to happen. How naive of me to think I could keep Danica away from the business part, just wrap her up in cotton and keep her safe. It was never in my control. I should've just burned the empire to the ground ages ago, this empire I never asked for and never wanted. What was the point of it if all it ever led to was more death, more hurt?

Around and around, my thoughts swirl in a whirlpool ready to drown me the moment I let go.

The thought of sinking is tempting, oh so tempting. The bliss, the quiet—it would be so easy.

Oh, Danica. I'm sorry, Tesoro.

CHAPTER SEVENTEEN

PREP

DANICA...

The gothic castle Don Greco calls home towers before me like an imposing fortress as I hesitate for only a second before knocking. It's even bigger than the Fera mansion, and built in a completely different style.

But I'm not here to review their architecture; I have important business to handle. With only Emilio by my side, I lift the heavy knocker, announcing our arrival that was surely already announced by the gate guards.

My heart races uncontrollably as I wait for the door to swing open, the ancient-looking butler ushering us into the foyer with a neutral expression.

I can't believe I'm here. Don Greco has been extremely cooperative. As soon as I requested a meeting, he agreed to see me. Who knows what Emilio told him, but it was enough to get us an audience with the boss, and that's all that matters.

I've never spoken to another Don without Dante by my side. And I've definitely never waltzed into such a powerful figure's private home like I'm just popping over for a casual cup of tea, unarmed, unprotected. But no weapon could put me at ease, not in this situation.

What the fuck are you doing, Danica?

You're out of your league.

This is how you die!

The intrusive thoughts ramble through my head as a guard quickly frisks us to ensure we have nothing on us. Every hair on my neck is standing bolt upright, shivers scattered on my skin, but I stand up straight, keeping my head high.

Just get through the next bit, I tell myself, forcing my mind to compartmentalize. One moment at a time. If I think about the big picture, I will lose my nerve, I know I will. But I have to do this, I have to bring my baby-boy home.

Forcing a fake smile on my face, the one I used to wear during my days in the service industry, I put one foot ahead of the other, focusing on the sound of my rhythmic footsteps on the wooden floor. I don't notice the decor, the color of the carpets...nothing. My mind sees only one picture, one face—Dante.

With a single knock, we're permitted into Don Greco's study. It's even bigger than Dante's office, filled with photographs of his smiling family. It's an intimate touch that sticks in my mind long after I forget all the other details of his imposing office. Dante doesn't have any pictures in his office...

My breath threatens to speed up beyond my control as I survey the dimly-lit space, but I force myself to stay calm. Even as I feel the weight of the guards' eyes on me, their fingers likely hovering near triggers.

Despite my nerves, my voice is steady as I explain our dire situation to Don Greco. He looks like any harmless old man, but I know better. He's way older than Dante, maybe in his 70s already, and his fingers are scarred in crisscrossed white lines that I'm sure nobody ever dares ask about.

"The Riccis are a nuisance," the old man sighs when I finish my tale; he seems almost bored with the topic as he pours himself a whiskey from an elegant glass decanter that's probably older than I am. I decline his offer for a drink; I need to stay clear-headed, focused.

From our brief conversation, it's clear nobody likes the Ricci family. "This has gone too far," Don Greco says simply without bothering to elaborate. You don't kidnap a Don without consequences. "It's sleazy and it upsets the natural order." I can't say I disagree, but I don't say anything.

I don't ask why the Grecos owe Dante a favor or why they care enough to help. All that matters is when Don Greco tells his guard, "Get her whatever she needs," he means it. What I need is manpower, and lots of it.

None of the other families want a war; they all have too much at stake. "War is only profitable for arms dealers," Don Greco explains. But I sense there's more to his willingness to help than wanting to avoid a war. There is a tenderness in his voice when he mentions Dante's name. He looks into the distance, his voice softening. "I promised her..." he trails off. I don't press. My mission is to get to Dante, and fast.

As respectfully as I can, I thank the Don and take my leave. Patience is not my strong point—especially not when I'm fearing for the life of the man who has become the most important person in my life.

After leaving the Greco compound, we move swiftly. We find Roberto Ricci at his usual hangout—the brothel on 7th Street. Cunty little fellow, Roberto—no backbone. All he cares about is finishing inside the woman tied to the bed. That and keeping his genitals attached to his body.

The trembling creep spills everything he knows as soon as I threaten him the same way I did Luca. Dante is at a nearby warehouse apparently, hidden under some fake shell company the Riccis use to launder money through. Roberto can't say if Dante is still alive, he doesn't know.

Luca was a fool to trust the Riccis, thinking they'd honor any deal. They don't care about Luca's debt. This isn't about money; it's about power. The Riccis saw a chance to weaken the Feras, and Luca handed them Dante on a silver platter. *Fucking idiot.*

Before leaving the brothel, I smash Roberto's phone under my boot. It won't stop him from warning his family, but it might buy us some time. And time is a valuable commodity right now.

Every minute we waste is a minute closer to Dante's demise, I'm certain. But nobody speaks it out loud. Who would dare?

We prepare quickly, dressing from head to toe in black. Emilio takes me to a massive arsenal in the basement—a hidden stockpile of weapons and holding cells, currently occupied by Luca and Alicia.

The old guard tries to convince me to stay behind. *Don Fera would want you safe*, he argues. But he knows it's futile. I'm going, with or without his consent. The thought of waiting at home, watching the clock, is unbearable. I need to be there, for Dante and for myself.

As some sort of unbalanced compromise, I agree to stay out of the direct action, hiding behind our army of mobsters. More than twenty men in black suits, armed to the teeth, should be enough back-up, right? *Right?*

Reluctantly consenting, Emilio sighs and lets me choose a weapon from the arsenal. I go for the 9mm, familiar with its weight and grip. Tucking it into the holster around my waist, I feel like a Bond-girl supervillain. I hope I won't have to use it, but I can't think about that now. Instead, I focus on Dante's face, his smell, the memory of his arms around me. If it comes to it, my limited gun training will have to be enough.

Now is the time to be strong, to step up and take control. I'm tired of always being scared, of needing to be saved. It's time I learn to fend for myself, especially if I'm serious about building a life with Dante.

Oh Dante. Every bone in my body aches for him. It's near impossible to think of anything else. The need to see his face, to know that he's okay, overrides everything else—even the exhaustion tugging at my edges, the hunger I should feel but don't...

"We need to go, now!" I shout, rallying our army. We've wasted enough time. The night is creeping on, wasting valuable hours of darkness, darkness we need for cover.

Within the hour, everything is set. Our unmarked black vans pull up a block away from the Ricci warehouse that, from the outside, looks like any other storage facility on the road. The Greco vans are indistinguishable from ours and I wonder if everyone shops from the same shady dealers. (I wouldn't be surprised if they did.)

It's now or never.

The element of surprise may be lost, but we have no choice. Sometimes, you have to take back what's yours with brute force.

Hold on, baby, I'm coming for you.

CHAPTER EIGHTEEN

ATTACK

DANICA...

It all happened so quickly, I didn't have time to question my choices. But now, sitting in the van, about to ambush the warehouse that hopefully holds Dante, the weight of my decisions crashes down on me like a ton of bricks.

My heart is pounding in my throat, my hands trembling like they belong to someone else. *Am I actually going through with this?*

But I have to; I have to save Dante. I have never been more certain of anything in my life.

This is crazy! My current reality is a long way from my suburban upbringing that only prepared me for a life of ignorance. But none of that matters now. Without Dante, I could never be safe again. No matter how you look at it,

I am not the one risking it all; everything has already been put at risk.

On high alert, I look around me for the umpteenth time, trying to relax my tense shoulders but they refuse to budge. Emilio is beside me, in the driver's seat, all dressed in black—same as me, as all of us. It is almost time to move out. *Oh god, I hope we're not too late.*

Carlo and another guard I should remember the name of but don't are sitting in the backseat. Behind us, four more unmarked black vans stand ready in the shadows on the side of the road. The tree-lined streets provide the perfect cover, even if we had to park a block away just to be safe.

"Are you ready, Miss Matthews?" Emilio asks, brows locked in an intense look that has been on his face since we left the library. I'm glad he's the one in control, but I still wish I was following Dante into battle instead. Dante always makes me feel calm, safe. But I don't feel either of those things now.

Staring straight ahead, I nod. I'm not ready yet but I know it's now or never. Dante's coming home with us, that's my sole mission. Nothing else exists. How could it without him? What kind of Domme fails to protect their sub?

I wait as the men file out of the vans as they head towards the warehouse, keeping to the shadows, staying low. As promised, I'm somewhere near the back with three of them behind me to fend off any surprise attacks.

As we cover the distance between us and the nondescript warehouse, I push my nervousness back, forcing my mind to focus. Part of me worries that Dante isn't here, that it is all a trap, but it's the only lead we have.

This is crazy! This doesn't feel real. Am I actually creeping towards a mob family's warehouse with a gun strapped to my body?

Quiet!

Focus, Danica.

This is not the time for thinking, this is the time for action.

Watch your feet.

Counting my breathes, I reach ten before starting over. Treading lightly, I move forward like a cat, each step a delicate balance between stealth and speed. Perhaps doing all those squats with Emilio was worth it. I like how my body moves. *Maybe I'll add some weights next time—*

We reach the clearing where the shadows stop, the part where we're fully exposed in the bright glow of the street light, and my mind goes quiet, listening, watching for hidden threats. It's pure instinct. I may not have been born into a crime family, but I've by no means lived a sheltered life. Watching for threats is second nature.

This time I don't fawn in the face of danger. No, I keep my head low and run toward a warehouse full of mobsters.

There are two guards at the gate but they are dead before they even see us coming. I don't even flinch at the sound of the gunfire anymore, though I'm grateful for the silencers to keep my ears from ringing like a bitch.

We burst through the gate without bothering to try and be quiet, filing into the premises in double lines as chaos ensues around us.

They know we're here. Shots fly past me in every direction, and I keep low like Emilio told me to, hoping it's enough. *What the fuck are you doing, Danica?* the voice in my head chides but I refuse to give it any airtime. There is no turning around now.

Breathe, Danica.

The short distance between the external gate and the warehouse building feels like a marathon. We're exposed, clear targets in the open stretch, but we move quickly, reaching the building's entrance with only one casualty.

Despite the temptation, I don't look back; I never do. Hunched low, eyes locked on the men in black ahead, we barge through the glass door, shattering it with ease.

It was easy up to this point. Too easy. I suddenly realize why. A wall of armed men meets us in the reception area, waiting, ready, guns cocked and ready.

Fuck!

The human shields on either side of me push forward, taking out the Ricci guards faster than they can hit us. What type of warehouse it is, is still not clear. We seem to be in the office side of it; I've seen no actual products or storage pallets. It's probably just a warehouse on paper; what really happens here, nobody but the Riccis know.

Though I know I should stay close to the group, stay protected, the need to find Dante overrides all logic. He has to be here, behind one of the many doors lining the corridor.

Like a single unit, we move through the maze of hallways. The mission is to clear the guards first, then find Dante—I know that—but my need to find him overrides the logic of this simple plan. I can't shake the fear that they will shoot my tattooed god when they realize the building is under attack.

I slow my pace, sidestepping to let another guard pass. He's too focused on the mission to notice me. Gradually, I make my way closer to the back of the group.

The final man in line is distracted by the gunfire happening on the front line, he doesn't notice me, or if he does, he doesn't register who I am. We all look similar in our black gear.

Finally, I'm at the back. There is nobody behind me now. Keeping my back against the wall, I duck into the first room on the left. Immediate disappointment sinks into my belly as soon as the light flickers on—the room is empty. It's just some storage space.

Quickly, I exit again, looking both ways before darting across the hall to the opposite door. It's empty, as are the next two doors. *What if they've moved him somewhere else?*

Anxious to find my good boy, I crawl from room to room, keeping low, as our ambush pushes deeper into the facility. The Riccis have plenty of guns but not plenty of men from what I can tell, but it's hard to gauge from this far back.

There's an orange door coming up on my right. From what I can tell, it's an engine room of some sort. Probably for the building's air conditioning. I straighten as I enter, reaching for the light switch, but a sudden, sharp pain in my arm stops me.

I scream as the knife sinks into my flesh. *Oh god, it hurts!* I struggle to push the hidden attacker away, but I can't see a thing. Blood runs down my arm; the cut is deep. Adrenaline floods my veins, taking over.

With great effort, I flick the switch with my other hand, just in time to see the masked man lunging again, knife in hand.

Hesitating, I pull the 9mm from its holster, a practiced motion. *Can I actually shoot someone?*

But it's not my shot that sends the attacker to the floor; it comes from behind me. Relief washes over me instantly.

"You have to be careful, Miss Matthews," Emilio urges, his large figure blocking the door.

Fuck. That was close, too close. I don't know if I could've pulled the trigger but it doesn't matter right now.

Where's Dante?

CHAPTER NINETEEN

PROTECTOR

DANTE...

The darkness in my mind is pierced by a commotion outside. It can't be a dream, it's too loud. *But what if it is?*

By now, I am just drifting in and out of consciousness, uncertain whether any time is passing or not. My blindfold is still firmly in place, blocking out the room.

I have no idea what's going on. My world has been confined to this uncomfortable chair for what feels like ages, but I suspect it has only been a few days. I can't feel my limbs anymore though—the rough rope ties are too tight.

My heart beats faster as the sounds draw closer.

I'd know that voice anywhere. It can't be though.

"I said—let him go!" the voice repeats, louder this time; closer.

Danica!

It must be a fever dream. She can't be here. My desperate longing has materialized her in this cold, dark room. *Am I finally losing it?*

What I won't give for it to be Danica for real. But she can't be here, it is too dangerous. *Why would she be here?*

The noise outside doesn't die down or fade like the dream I suspect it of being. I hear more shouting in Italian, lots of shuffling, a struggle. For a moment I'm almost sure I hear Emilio.

A gunshot. It brings my drifting mind back to the present.

It's no dream. The sound of the gunshot is unmistakable, and it came from right outside the door.

There is another shot. And another.

Have they come for me? I don't want to get my hopes up.

The door opens and I hear heavy footsteps rushing in towards me. They sound like the same ones that always came in, the ones that threw water in my face and refused to give me any more info.

This is it, I think. *This is how I go. Oh god.*

"If you touch him I will fucking end you!" The voice is loud and clear, unmistakable. *Danica!*

The energy in the room shifts suddenly. The water guy must be close, I feel a tug on my ropes. This is not good.

The next gunshot is very close, too close. The perpetrator screams, collapsing at my feet, his hand brushing against my ankle. I wish I could see, but all I can do is hold my breath, hoping this is real, and if it is, that the right person wins. I'm too weak to help.

"I don't like to be disobeyed, you asshole! I warned you." It *is* Danica. And she sounds furious. It must be a dream. She hates guns. Sure, I forced her to learn how to use one but under great protest. She refused to carry one, even when I insisted.

"You can thank your lucky stars it was just your leg, douchebag," the voice booms.

The man on the floor is pleading for his life in Italian, but I know Danica doesn't understand nor would she care if she could.

More gunshots ring outside, so many more. It's making my ears hurt but I can't do anything to cover them. My body is one with this chair. So, I just wait in the dark and hope nothing happens to Danica. I am powerless to defend her; I can't even defend myself.

And then it goes quiet, eerily so.

"Danica?" I breathe, my voice barely a whisper. *It can't be her, right?*

But it *is* her. I know that scent anywhere, the feeling of her proximity. My body instantly reacts, melting into the chair with relief.

"Dante! It's okay, darling, you're safe now," Danica replies as her delicate hands pull the blindfold from my face.

But I can't see anything. Even the dim light in the room is too much for my sensitive eyes accustomed to only darkness.

"You came for me." I'm in utter disbelief.

"Of course I came for you, baby. I will always protect you."

She kisses my forehead, arms wrapping around me. Winching from the pain in my shoulder, I focus on the part that feels good, the part where I am in Danica's arms again.

I feel like crying, I'm so relieved—not just to be saved, but to feel her near me again. Being away from her was agony. Not only that, I didn't want her last memory of me to be throwing her out of the house.

"I'm so sorry," I say weakly, hearing the tears swelling in my voice.

"It's okay, baby. You did what you had to." She presses her forehead against mine.

I think I am crying but I don't know. My senses are flooded with Danica. It's almost too much to bear.

My eyes slowly adjust to the harsh light and I take in her beautiful face through the haze. She looks so different; transformed. Dressed all in black, hair tied back, thick boots—my Queen looks ready for war. I never imagined seeing her like this, my own G.I. Jane to the rescue.

"You have never looked more beautiful," I tell her, my voice cracking. It's true.

A sad smile tugs at the corners of her lips. "I wish I could say the same." Her grin is fleeting, replaced by a look of deep concern as she gently touches my cheek. Her fingers are warm against my cold, clammy skin. I can't fathom what she sees—a broken, battered shell of the person I once was. How can she still touch me with such tenderness, given the state I'm in?

Behind her, Emilio and other black-clad figures come into focus. I recognize some of my men but the others are unfamiliar. Emilio's limping a tad but it does little to make him look less threatening. His presence is commanding and authoritative—like in the old days when my father used to send us on debt-collecting duties together.

"*Don mio.*" He smiles, nodding in my direction respectfully without interrupting Danica.

"Thanks for rescuing me," I tell him.

"You should thank Miss Matthews, boss."

"Oh trust me, I will. I'll spend the rest of my life thanking her." I rest my head on her chest, closing my eyes for a moment.

"Sometimes the Queen must save her Knight too, you know." Danica kisses my hair. "Let's get you out of these ties, baby."

Please don't let this be a dream.

Chapter Twenty

QUEEN

Danica...

"Everyone, out!" I shout, the adrenaline still pumping through my veins. Nobody dares question the authority in my voice.

Emilio ushers the men out of the room, closing the door behind him to give us a moment of privacy. I know he's guarding the door, just like he does when we're at home.

Carelessly, I drop my gun on the ground. It makes a clinking sound as the metal hits the bare cement that looks like it hasn't seen a mop in a decade. The rest of the room doesn't look much better; the damp patches on the wall spread out like a grotesque Rorschach test. The place is definitely giving *Saw* vibes.

Without the burden of the gun, I'm free to cradle Dante's face with both hands. Tears are trailing down his cheek, cutting through the dried blood and leaving pale trails in their wake. I kiss them away, indifferent to the dirt and gore. His eyes meet mine and for an eternity we just stare at each other. So much to say, but no words seem appropriate, or enough.

With a quick, decisive motion, I pull the knife from my belt and start cutting through the ropes binding Dante's bruised body. My hand falters, the fresh cut on my arm throbbing, but I push through, my focus unwavering.

Dante is a shadow of his usual self. His pants are ripped, his feet bare and bloodied. My heart breaks to see him this hurt, so weak. Protective rage courses through me like wildfire.

But he's alive. That's the most important part.

Still, I'm furious, like a lioness whose cub has been threatened. *How fucking dare they?* How dare any of them? *Fucking Luca.*

After Emilio saved me in the control room, I wasn't stupid enough to navigate the rest of the rooms alone. I made sure to take one of the guards for cover as we barged into the empty store rooms one by one.

The Ricci's men never stood a chance. We were too powerful with the Greco's army behind us too. I don't think they were expecting that. *Thank you, Emilio!*

With every yard we gained, pushing the men back and back until their numbers dwindled to single digits, another door came within reach. But none of them were hiding Dante.

By the time we got to the back of the facility, the Ricci men had scattered, realizing the futility of their defense against our sizable army. I was quickly losing hope of finding Dante here. *We're too late.*

And then, suddenly, just another unmarked door in an unmarked corridor, there he was! Dante. Alive. But oh god, he looked wrecked.

There was no time to think, no time for pity. Some asshole was running towards Dante faster than I could close the distance between us.

This time I didn't hesitate to pull the trigger.

Thank fuck I hit my target. I didn't want to kill anyone, just stop the guy. Luckily my aim wasn't too bad and I got him without accidentally shooting Dante in the process—that was my biggest fear.

Now that the threat has been removed, I can focus on Dante. *Shit, his shoulder looks really bad.* The Doctor better be ready to perform some miracles.

"Can you move?" I ask once the cut ropes are on the floor.

"I don't know," Dante croaks, trying to put some weight on his legs. But he collapses again almost instantly. Who knows how long he's been stuck in that position, his massive frame bent awkwardly around the chair.

Struggling to keep my balance, I hoist him up, ignoring the throbbing pain radiating from my wounded arm. The temptation to call in Emilio for assistance is great, but I'm determined to get by on my own. I don't want anyone touching Dante but me. *He's mine!*

Dante grips the back of a chair to steady himself, his other hand clutching my shoulder. Together, we manage to get him into some semblance of an upright position. His steps are shaky, each one a monumental effort, but he pushes through. He makes it two steps before collapsing onto an old table near the wall, oblivious to the spiderwebs festooning the corners.

The sight of him struggling breaks my heart, but it also fuels my determination.

"My legs need to wake up..." Dante's words are slow, like it's taking a lot of effort to form them.

"It's okay baby, take your time." I wrap my arms around him, hugging him to me despite the sharp jab of pain it sends surging through my arm.

Reaching up, I kiss him deeply, hungrily—feral almost. The rush of emotion is instant. Fuck how vile he smells; I'm just relieved to be back in his arms where I belong.

I never knew I could miss that feeling so much. It's only been a few days but the fear of losing it all, makes it feel so much sweeter.

Dante's cock twitches between our hugging bodies, and I grin, gently petting his growing erection over his torn pants.

"Well, well, well—what do we have here?"

"I missed you," he says, still holding me close.

I look up into Dante's hollow eyes, at his broken face, and kiss him again, devouring his lips lustfully, sloppily.

I missed you doesn't even begin to cover it.

All the emotions—the overwhelming panic and fear of the past few days—is finally freed from the box I've held shut firmly to get me through this mission. *Holy fuck!*

Every sense is on high alert, pulsing with adrenaline; my heart rate still hasn't slowed down.

Dante could've died, *I* could've died. This is crazy! *What am I even doing here?*

But I know what I'm doing here, I'm protecting my good boy, just like I promised him I would so many times.

"Don't ever leave me again," I tell Dante, lacing my fingers through his. Despite the situation, our injuries, I still have an insane urge to pin him on the table and fuck him right here, right now. But there's no time—we need to get out of here—so I resist the desire to make him show me his hard cock; to show me how much he missed me.

Dante kisses my fingers. "I won't ever leave you again, *Tesoro*. You are my everything."

At first, the words catch me off-guard but the sincerity in Dante's eyes quickly soften any reservations I may have had. He means it.

I kiss him one more time, putting my hand on his heart.

"Let's go home, baby boy. You need a bath."

He probably needs a lot more...

CHAPTER TWENTY-ONE

AFTERMATH

DANICA...

We are not out of the woods, not even close. Dante keeps drifting in and out of consciousness as Carlo speeds through backroads to get us home. Emilio already called The Doctor, he'll meet us there.

"Come on, baby, stay with me," I tell Dante, kissing his too-hot forehead. There is nothing I can do to help the situation, still, I nag Carlo insistently to *drive fucking faster already!*

The Doctor is already waiting when we get home, assuring us that there is nothing to worry about, though I'm plenty worried. With a warm cloth, I bathe Dante's face while The Doctor assesses the damage: some cracked ribs, and that nasty gunshot wound in his shoulder.

"He is lucky, there is no damage to his internal organs and the bullet went straight through," Emilio translates for me as the doctor prepares to clean out the shoulder wound and stitch it up.

"*Lucky* would've been not getting fucking kidnapped in the first place, I'd say," I mumble, but Emilio wisely doesn't translate.

It's too gross, I can't watch as the doctor drives the needle through Dante's skin. Dante doesn't even groan much, just takes it. The little energy he had when I first untied him from that chair has long since dissipated after our hurried exit from the Ricci warehouse.

The doctor hands me a bottle of antibiotics with Emilio translating the instructions of three times a day, with meals.

"Is that all?"

"Is there anything else, Miss Matthews?" Emilio asks as The Doctor moves on to fixing up my arm, a considerably less infected-looking wound than Dante's.

"Will he be okay though?" I look over to Dante, fast asleep in the bed. His color is off completely; he doesn't look like himself.

"He just needs to rest, Miss Matthews."

I should've called bullshit. But for two days, I let them tell me it will be fine as I impatiently wait for Dante to get better, to come back to me. Somehow, this is not quite the happy reunion I had imagined. I am glad to have Dante home, but he looks worse now than when we found him.

Try as I might, I can't get him to eat anything without throwing it up again, and the meds have done fuck all to improve the situation. He hardly even has the strength or awareness to recognize me most of the time, and his breathing remains irregular, his heartbeat pounding against my ear whenever I put my head on his chest. *It's fine, Miss Matthews.* Except it's not.

If only I paid closer attention—it's Emilio who notices the expiry date on the antibiotics first. They are more than a year past their effective date. *Fuck!* Shady shit from a shady doctor. "Get him in the car!" I tell Emilio, throwing the blankets off Dante in a hurry. He is sweaty from the fever that refuses to break its grip on him, his complexion as ashen as the grey skies outside.

"Miss Matthews, The Doctor is on his way." Emilio tries to keep me calm, but I can see the worry on his face as he regards Dante's desperate condition.

"No, fuck that guy. Dante needs real help. Get him in the car."

"It doesn't work like that, Miss Matthews. This will complicate matters."

"Dante dying will complicate matters, now get that fucking car, Emilio. I am not asking again!" I know I'm being rude, but I'll seek Emilio's forgiveness later. There will be no forgiveness for anyone if Dante dies on me now. "Please," I add, my voice pleading.

Emilio takes one more look at Dante and nods, calling in some guards to help carry Dante to the car, body limp hanging between them—dead weight. *Oh god, hold on!*

"Get out!" I tell Carlo when I reach the car already waiting in the driveway. He looks to Emilio for direction but the older man just nods and lets me take the driver's seat, adjusting the seat so I can reach the pedals.

It probably would've made more sense to take one of them with me but I don't trust anyone to take me where I need to go. Fuck their secrets and shady doctors, there is only one person I trust with my life.

So, I take Dante to my childhood GP, Doctor Carter—she's been our family doctor since before I was even born, and always treated me with kindness. I know she has many questions but she doesn't ask them. The desperation on my face is as obvious as the vague lies I tell her to spin a cover story. My boyfriend got into a fight, we thought the wound would heal okay.

Skipping past the line of waiting patients, Doctor Carter checks Dante into the hospital herself, sending me to wait in the stupid reception room with the too-white walls and gardening magazines that have been read to shreds.

There are no forms to fill in. Emilio has promised to smooth it all over on the admin side, ensuring the police don't get involved. I know it won't be easy, but Dante getting better is more important than fucking paperwork.

After the rush of the drive—darting through traffic like a real-life game of *Grand Theft Auto* (minus the injury of innocent civilians)—the room feels too quiet, pointless. I pace up and down, restless.

There's only one person I want to see but Doctor Carter tells me that I can't see him yet, she first needs to redo Dante's stitches and clean out the wound properly.

She comes out to tell me that a piece of flesh is already rotten and she has to cut it out. The infection was poisoning his body, he had septicemia. I don't know if it's dangerous but she said it's very. *Fuck, fuck, fuck.*

"Do what you have to," I tell her, continuing my pacing as soon as the doctor disappears beyond the grey swinging doors again.

Googling septicemia does little to put me at ease, it freaks me out even more. *This is bad, shit.*

The doctor's last recommendation is for me to call someone, for me. For a moment I pause, uncertain whether my message will be appropriate, but I send it anyway. There is nobody else I can think to contact.

Despite bracing for certain rejection, they reply with *on my way*.

When Doctor Carter finally lets me into the room where they're keeping Dante, I collapse into the chair beside his bed, burying my head in my hands. *Oh, god!*

He looks like shit, so weak, so pale—like an empty vessel. Various tubes run from his body as the machine steadily beeps beside the bed like I'm on some episode of *Grey's Anatomy*. But it's not TV, it's real life, it's Dante. It breaks me to see him like this.

"Is he going to be okay?" I ask, moving my chair closer so I can hold Dante's hand.

"His body has suffered a lot of trauma, but he should hopefully recover. It's too soon to say with certainty. His organs are still unaffected, that's the good news. You brought him in on time, barely, but on time. Now, all we can do is wait for the medicine to do its thing and for his body to heal. "

With my head hanging low, I let out a strained sigh, fighting back exhausted tears.

"Danica, what have you gotten yourself into?" The doctor puts a hand on my shoulder.

"I can handle it."

"Danica..."

"No, please. Not now."

"Okay. Try and get some rest," the doctor tells me as she exits, and I just nod, no intention of listening to her advice.

When Adira shows up 27 minutes later, I am eternally grateful to see the curly-haired Goddess come toward me with open arms, hugging me close like we are old friends. She was the only person I could think to call, the only one who wouldn't ask too many questions I couldn't (or wouldn't) answer.

"Oh, Danica, darling," is all she says, but it's enough for me to let go, collapsing in emotion that refuses to be repressed any longer.

"I don't want to be alone," I tell her, soaking Adira's shirt with all the tears I've been holding back.

"It's okay, I'm here for you." She sits down on the couch and motions for me to join her. Without saying anything else, I lay my head on her lap, curling myself up into a little ball, my body wrapped around hers.

"He can't die, please, please...I love him, Adira. I really love him."

"I know, baby, I know."

As Adira strokes my hair, I finally allow myself to drift into a restless sleep riddled with nightmares I only remember the feeling but not the content of later.

She keeps telling me it will be okay, and I sincerely hope there is some truth to her prophecy.

It doesn't feel okay.

CHAPTER TWENTY-TWO

REVIVAL

DANTE...

I drift in and out of consciousness, ripped from one world to the other, in no particular rhythm or routine. Sometimes I'm in the hospital, Danica by my side, her familiar scent keeping me calm...other times, I'm still tied to a chair in that dark room, certain my life is about to end.

The only constant is the pain in my body, the sheer stubbornness of my limbs as they refuse to obey my commands. I want to reach out to Danica, to tell her I'm happy to see her, to have her here, but I don't know if I ever say those words out loud. It's all a blur.

The dreams are vivid, so, so real. I know it's all in my mind, but sometimes I see them so clearly, like they're right here.

In my dreams, I'm a teenager again, running through the shiny streets of Vegas, laughing. That face, it's been so long since I've seen (or even thought of) that face, but it's unmistakably them. It's a face I've tried to forget for so many years, but it haunts me in my delirium, taunting me with the future I could never have.

We can't do this, I tell them in my dream. *Tell me you don't want this too*. I can't, even in my dream I can't lie to those beautiful amber eyes.

And just like that, they're gone again, replaced by Elena's kind face, smiling at me with the wind in her hair. But it all soon turns to carnage, like it always does.

Every time the dreams dissipate, it's only Danica's face who remains. I try to smile at her, but my eyes remain closed. Maybe tomorrow.

Finally, after a period of time still unknown to me, the shaky world stabilizes and I manage to squeeze Danica's hand, real Danica, not dream Danica.

"Dante!" She touches my cheek affectionately, her eyes red and tear-stained.

I try to speak but my throat is too dry, but I manage a smile.

"Oh, my baby. Please stay with me." Danica takes my hand and I use all the strength I have to squeeze her fingers again.

It gets easier after that, I stay with her longer. Finally, I manage more than word, later—a sentence. Time is still a blur but reality is starting to settle a bit more. I stop fearing that I'll just drop away into dreamland never to come back again.

Sometimes Emilio is there too. We sit in silence as he does Sudukos in a little A5 book that Danica bought him. Adira comes too. I'm surprised to see her but happy that Danica has someone to support her. Luca doesn't come, of course, but I don't even ask about him, not yet.

Danica refuses to leave my side. I tell her to go home, to rest, but my Queen is nothing if not stubborn. She sits beside my bed with the books and magazines scattered around the room like it's a library and not a hospital room.

At least it's a private room. It's definitely not ideal but Emilio assured me that everything is taken care of; there will be no questions. The one benefit of the many favors due to the Fera dynasty in this town, over three generations of favors, is that there is always someone willing to look the other way, to make things go away. And if not, cold, hard cash helps for the rest.

I don't ask for the details, I don't need them. Emilio knows what he's doing and I trust him fully.

Every day, I whine that I want to go home, recover in my own bed. But every day the stocky nurse with the permed red hair tells me *not yet*.

At least I'm getting stronger, slowly.

It's a Tuesday when Danica makes me scoot over in the tiny bed to make space for her. Keeping her eyes on me, she pulls the curtain shut around us, shielding us with its flimsy privacy.

The bed is hardly big enough for me, let alone both of us, but I don't mind. I miss her body against mine, her warmth; the way her skin feels against mine.

The effect is instant arousal, I can't even hide it—much to Danica's amusement. She wraps her fingers around my untimely erection tenting under the thin green hospital blanket. "Someone is excited."

"I can't help it." I manage a smile, groaning as Danica teases the blood to my cock, fingers teasing my hardness like it was just another normal day in my office.

Even now, with my body broken and my energy levels on reserve, nothing burns brighter than my need for her. When tied to that cold chair in the Ricci warehouse, I didn't think I'd ever get to feel her touch again. The relief is almost tangible.

Despite the aggravating pain in my shoulder, I hold her tightly, breathing her in. Seeing her like that—so fearless, commanding an entire army—I have never seen anything sexier in my life before! Who knew being rescued would be such a turn-on?

I know my body needs many things to stay alive right now. But the primal urge to devour her whole overrides all other needs.

Danica kisses me desperately, chewing my broken lip as she sucks the air right out of my lungs, hand still resting on my cock.

Like an animal, I groan. I want to answer her question but words fail me. All the blood in my body has drained to the hard flesh beneath her hands.

"I need you inside me," she breathes in my neck, affecting me in ways words cannot describe. *Dio mio!*

I'm so painfully hard. The hunger inside had been replaced by a hunger only for her skin against mine. "Please." My plea is barely audible.

Danica moves her hand away from my cock. "Show me how much you want me." We both know what she's asking.

Despite my desperation, the task is harder than I anticipated. The space is way too small to maneuver with ease, especially with only one good arm, but I know the reward will be worth it.

Finally, I manage to pull my cock out from under the stupid hospital frock that ties in the back. It stands proud and erect, ready.

"Such a good boy," Danica whispers, taking my erection in both hands. Shivers run up my spine as she palms me, slowly at first, and then not-so-slowly. "I love seeing how hard you are for me..."

I grunt, my words lost in the euphoria of the pleasure building in my groin. It's been more than two weeks since I came—not since that morning I woke up still inside her, the morning after the auction...the day it all went to shit.

But I don't want to think about that day anymore. What matters is that I'm here, and that Danica is okay.

She doesn't let me finish, of course not. Even in my broken state, my Queen doesn't have mercy. It somehow makes me feel less broken; she's treating me as she usually would.

"Hold that thought," she tells me as she jumps off the bed with agility I only dream of in my bed-ridden state. As seductively as one can in hospital fluorescent lighting, she kicks off her shoes and sweatpants, stripping only her bottom bare. *Fuck, I've missed that perfect ass.*

"Don't move, baby." Danica climbs back onto the bed, planting a knee on either side of my waist. Careful not to touch my shoulder, she lowers herself onto my cock.

Oh god, she is so wet. I bite down hard to trap a primal cry from roaring from my lips as my Queen grinds down on my dick, slowly at first.

The world around us disappears; I don't even feel the aching that has pained me for so long, all I feel is her. Delirious with lust but fully cognizant (for once), I'm lost in the depths of her desire, of mine.

"No coming without permission," Danica hisses at me, staring deep into my eyes. Oh, how I've missed those words.

"Yes, Mistress," I moan, pulling her hair loose from its messy bun. It falls wildly around her face.

"I've been so empty..." Danica gasps as she rocks her hips into mine, the bed creaking beneath us. Someone could open that curtain at any moment! But Danica doesn't let that slow her down. Keeping her balance through some miracle, she reaches for her clit, rubbing it fiercely in tandem with her hips.

I'm bewitched, lost in the essence of Danica as she ravishes my body like the savage I look and feel like, fucking me until I cry her name in a desperate whisper, pleading with tears in my eyes for her to let me come.

And when she does, when she finally gives me permission, I explode inside her, everything I've pent up over the past few days releasing in a mighty climax that threatens to rip my tired body apart.

Although I can't see it on her face, I feel it as she clenches around me; Danica comes seconds later, our fluids mixing in an extended climax, a complete and beautiful mess.

Panting as heavily as I am, she lies her head down against my heart, and I gather her in my good arm, hugging her tight, still inside her. Her body heaves up and down with my chest as I try to bring my heart rate down.

"Don't you ever fucking leave me again," Danica threatens in a light-hearted tone as she lazily traces her nails over my chest, tugging at my chest hairs as she's done so many times before.

I smile, kissing the side of her head.

"No, Ma'am. Never."

"There's my good boy."

EPILOGUE

Two Months Later...

CHAPTER TWENTY-THREE

FOREVER

DANICA...

D ante awkwardly models his new outfit for me, and I nearly fall off the bed, uncontrollable laughter ripping through me. It's so...*different!*

The sight of him in the gaudy ensemble, a pair of neon green shorts and a matching tank top adorned with tropical prints, is both endearing and hilarious.

"I look ridiculous," Dante grumbles, stretching his muscular arms out to display the look fully as he turns around for my benefit. The shorts cling to his well-built frame, and the tank top's loud patterns clash with his usually stoic demeanor. He's smiling though, so I know he's just pretending to be grumpy.

"Yes, baby, you absolutely do. But I love it." I blow him a kiss. "Now show me the Hawaiian shirt."

"I have never owned clothes like this," Dante complains as he digs out the bright yellow shirt from one of the many shopping bags we brought back after this morning's spree. The shirt is a vivid explosion of sunflowers and pineapples, a far cry from his usual dark and subdued wardrobe.

Nothing Dante owned was suitable for our island vacation, but I hadn't noticed until we'd already arrived in Greece. Already halfway out the door, I was donned in my favorite classic one-piece and ready for the ocean. Meanwhile, Dante stood around awkwardly in his jeans and a black t-shirt—his idea of "beach casual."

So, I put on a dress and dragged him to the shop for more *appropriate* attire. Unfortunately for him, it was only a small store and their limited selection had little to offer a man of his size. Now poor Dante has to make do with an overly brightly colored assortment of shorts and vests, much to my amusement (and his horror).

As he pulls on the Hawaiian shirt, the fabric drapes awkwardly over his broad shoulders. The bright yellow material is almost blinding, and the floral print is cheerful to the point of absurdity. He looks like walking sunshine, and I can't help but burst into giggles again. Dante's expression softens as he catches my eye, and he finally joins in the laughter, the sound deep and rumbling.

"Who wears this kind of shit?" Dante asks, inspecting himself in the mirror.

Slipping in under his arm, I hug him sideways, regarding the reflection in the mirror in more detail. It doesn't look like Dante at all, maybe a different Dante.

"People who have lives and go on holiday," I answer his rhetorical question.

"That doesn't sound like me."

"It does now. This is our new life."

"I wish we could just leave for good. Just pack up and move somewhere else. Anywhere. I don't want to risk losing this." Dante sighs, kissing the top of my head.

"We can't leave, darling. You know that. Nobody leaves this business alive, you always tell me. Besides, I don't want to leave. It's my home. My family is there, my friends. I don't want to put them at risk. You know this would never end if we just left. Let's sort this shit out between the families and make peace once and for all."

"You're far too optimistic. But you are right. It can't go on like this."

"Besides, we need to be there for Luca. He's going to have a tough time when he comes out of rehab."

"He can go to hell, he—" Dante clenches his fists, anger flashing across his face.

"He's all you have. We'll look after him." My voice is soothing, patient, as I rest my hand on his chest.

"He doesn't deserve it."

"No, but we'll do it anyway. It's what your mother would have wanted."

Dante's face softens, and he unclenches his fists. "You really haven't chosen an easy life when you picked me, have you?"

"No, but I wouldn't want it any other way, *Tesoro*."

"Forever at your service, my Queen." Dante picks up my hand and kisses it, one finger at a time. "Whatever you want."

"Well, now that you mention it. There *is* something I want..." A grin spreads over my face.

"Don't say it."

"I've been dying to all day."

"I know. Don't," he threatens, but I can see a smile starting to form around the corner of his mouth.

"You know you can't stop me." I stick my tongue out at Dante like an insolent child, teasing him.

Dante sighs, feigning annoyance. "Fine. Just do it. I'm impressed you got this far without mentioning it."

"It's because I whispered it to you in your sleep before you woke up. So many times." I smile victoriously.

Dante shakes his head, smiling unreservedly now. "You're an absolutely crazy woman, you know that right?"

"But you love me anyway?"

Dante just laughs and doesn't reply.

"Happy birthday, baby." I stand on my tippy-toes and pull him closer for a kiss. His lips moved against mine with a hunger that mirrored my own, igniting a fire that burned deep within me. There was just something about Dante's kiss, the way it unlocked my body like no other key in existence.

"How many times do I have to tell you I don't do birthdays?" Dante whispers when we finally part, still holding me close.

"All the times. You still came on this trip, didn't you?"

"You were very persuasive. Still, I can't believe I let you drag me all the way to Greece."

"It's beautiful though. Look at all this." I gesture to the magnificent room around us, the beautiful palms and ocean view through the wide doors of our honeymoon suite balcony. No expense was spared—the Fera way.

"Sure, the view's not bad," Dante admits, pulling me in for another quick kiss. "Thank you for insisting."

I did more than insist, I booked the flights and the accommodation before even telling him. After that hellish two-week period in the hospital, the blur of the days that followed as Dante slowly recovered, we needed this, we *deserved* this.

"So, I got you two things for your birthday..." I wink.

"Danica!" he scolds.

"I know, I know. I promised no presents. But trust me, you're going to like this. One will be annoying to get home but the other one...Hmm..." I tease, disappearing to the bedroom to retrieve the gifts before Dante can protest any further.

When I return, he's seated in the large leather armchair by the balcony door, watching me intently.

"Firstly, for your Zen collection." I pull a small, elegant bonsai tree from behind my back and hand it to him. "I know how much you like gardening."

Dante smiles. "Is this because of my temper?"

"I'm not saying that. But I would like to stop finding those little Zen garden rocks on the floor, hey?" My voice is playful, the wink at the end ensuring he knows I'm just teasing.

"Fair enough. Thank you. It's very thoughtful."

"And then, there's this..." I reveal my other hand from behind my back and hand him the A4-sized black metal case. It has no writing, no indication of its contents, just a simple golden bow on the top.

"What is this?" Dante asks, immediately opening the lid to peek inside, despite his usual insistence that he's not a curious person.

"You asked for it that one time, remember?" I smile as I see him register what it is, his face instantly lighting up.

"You said you'd think about it." Dante is genuinely surprised. And aroused—I can tell by the tent forming in his new casual pants.

"I did think about it." I grin mischievously. "Now that your shoulder is virtually healed, I imagine we can have a bit more fun."

"Seriously? I've always wanted to know what it feels like."

"Be careful what you wish for, darling." I grin, rubbing my hand over his erection.

Dante groans softly. "I want this *so* bad," he confesses, whining as he melts beneath my touch like butter under a warm knife.

"I can tell." I gently smack his bulge and Dante bends over with a grunt, holding his privates protectively.

"You make me so happy," he gasps between hurried breaths as he tries to regain his composure.

"So, what are you doing right now? Want to experiment with your new toys?" Patience has never been my virtue.

Dante doesn't need time to think, his answer is immediate. "It's my birthday, isn't it? I can't think of a better gift."

"Oh, so *now* you want gifts?" I laugh. "Fair enough." I kiss him sweetly on the lips—the last drop of sweetness before the strict teacher takes the reins.

I take the box from him and order him to kneel. Like the good boy he is, Dante bends down before me submissively, handing me his body to command.

It's play time!

CHAPTER TWENTY-FOUR

DESIRES

DANTE...

My heart is beating so fast, it feels like it might pop out of my chest any moment now. The anticipation is killing me, but Danica takes her time.

My cock is painfully hard, but there is nothing I can do about it. My limbs are spread to the corners of the bed, restrained by the cuffs that hold them. Naked and exposed, ready for my Queen to do whatever she wants to do to my body. And what she wants is pleasure, *my* pleasure.

Trust Danica to find an island kink hotel that rents fully kitted-out playrooms. The things money can buy...

The *gift,* though, she'd bought herself. I hadn't expected it at all.

The ocean outside is reduced to a gentle salty breeze streaming through the fully drawn blinds, transforming the grand room into a dungeon. Perfectly dimmed mood lighting illuminates the space and lights up my naked body as a humble offering to my Owner.

Danica stands beside the bed, dressed in thick rubber boots and a leather corset-and-panty set she'd brought for this exact moment. *Oh god, she looks stunning. My little devil woman.*

"You know your safe words, right?" she asks, same as always, switching us both into play mode officially. That question always gives my mind permission to let go, to just float into the safe space we've created.

"Yes, Miss. Tap twice on the headboard..."

"Good boy." She flashes me that million-dollar smile, rewarding my needy cock with a firm squeeze. The combination of her praise and her touch sends me wild with desire!

I groan—a loud, primal sound that reverberates through the room—as I try to arch my hips into her grip, desperate to be touched. But she leaves me wanting more, pulling away too soon. *Fanculo!*

"We'll start slow..."

Danica flicks the switch on the wand, and a light buzzing sound fills the room—the soft hum of electricity flowing. It's not a very big device; it looks a bit like an electric toothbrush (maybe thicker on the handle).

An assortment of electrode attachments lay ready on the table beside her, but for now, Danica's hands are all she needs—*she* is the conductor.

A small metal plate is tucked into the front of her corset, holding it in place against her skin; the other side is strapped to her hip in a leather holster and plugged into the wall. She carefully goes through the steps, making sure she sets it up safely.

"What does it feel like?" I ask as Danica holds her hands up to her eyes to see if she can see anything different. But they look the same as always, normal—just hands. There's nothing normal about the electricity flowing through her body though.

"That's *my* question to ask, isn't it?" She smiles, twirling her fingers in the air like a mad scientist about to embark on a grand experiment, and in a way, she is. "You ready, darling?"

"Touch me, please." I want her to ignite me.

I've always been curious about electro-stimulation, especially with so many new and elegant options on the market; so many attachments to play with. But there'd been no one I could trust—until now. I trust Danica fully, not only with my body but with my mind as well.

The violet wand is on its lowest setting; Danica checks it again to make sure. Such a simple device yet such a world of possibility, especially with the body contact cable turning her into the conductor.

It's nerve-wracking but I am calm, ready. I know Danica has read all the instructions, even watched the tutorials. She'd even tried it on herself before, she told me, to gauge its impact—but it wasn't her vibe, not for pleasure at least. Using it to torture me on the other hand? Well, that she can get behind.

I am desperate to know what it feels like. My cock is virtually dripping and Danica hasn't even touched me yet.

She takes a deep breath before slowly moving her hand closer to my upper arm, trailing her fingers over my skin without ever touching it, just a quick flick.

Sparks, literal sparks, crackle as a sharp bite nicks into my skin. It tickles almost. My heart beats faster but it doesn't help regulate my frozen breaths.

Just like in the tutorial, Danica moves her hand down my arm, never touching me, leaving a little gap between my skin and hers for the electricity to spark into my body.

"Can you feel it?" she asks, briefly holding a finger over my nipple. The current cuts into me with a sharp bite.

I gasp. "It feels amazing." It does.

She turns the device off and increases the intensity slightly. When she turns it back on, I know things are about to get serious.

My leg twitches as Danica hovers her fingertip, just a forefinger, over my feet. She touches my big toe, then the top of my foot, my ankle, little taps following a path up my right leg, my knee, my thigh…

Oh god! I hold my breath as she taps her finger on my inner thigh. It stings. Just a sharp, quick jab. *She's so close.* The anticipation is thick in my throat, almost choking me.

And then it happens. I scream as Danica taps a finger on my erect shaft. The sharp jolt of electricity pinches the skin. It burns! But as soon as her finger moves away, I want it there again. The after-burn is addictive. Almost like getting a tattoo but at the same time, nothing like it.

"Do you like that, baby?" Danica coos, studying the expressions on my face. For her, I let it all show. I don't hide anything like I used to.

She reads my body like a book, reaching out to the tip of my hardness with her electric finger. I don't answer, I just groan loudly as the sensitive skin catches alight.

"Look how you twitch and squirm for me, so powerless." An evil cackle escapes her lips but I know I'm safe.

"Does it hurt?"

"More!" I demand, sealing my own fate as Danica reaches for my balls.

FUCK!

The shock would've knocked me off my feet if I wasn't lying down. My whole body convulses as the incredible shock takes the wind right out of my chest.

Danica gives me a moment to catch my breath, enjoying the reactions unfolding before her. So much power in those little hands, that petite frame. If she wants to, she can end me right now and I would be powerless. She can do with me what she wants, consensually or not, but I know she won't. Still, the thought that she *can* is incredibly arousing.

"Don't you dare come without permission, boy." She smacks my cock with four fingers. The greater surface area spreads out the sensation over my skin, hitting my flesh with a sharp jolt. It's not as much of a sting as the single finger, but the smack itself still hurts.

I growl like a primal ape, roaring as I let it all out, everything I've kept inside for so long. All the anger, all the hurt, the pain, all the times I've had to be the strong one, show no fear, I purge it from my body, one shock at a time, as Danica punishes my body for its sins.

Danica touches a nipple in between her forefinger and thumb and my noises grow louder than I've ever allowed myself before. Like a caged beast, I tug at the constraints around my limbs while she pokes and prods little shocks all over my exposed body.

For a second, Danica pulls away, the reprieve only temporary as she increases the wand's intensity setting. She looks at me and I nod. *Do it.*

Without a second thought, Danica goes straight for my cock and my whole body explodes in pain. I'm on fire! It feels like a knife is cutting through my skin. The sting empties my entire mind with its pulse, closing the walls around my reality to just Danica, just the electricity, the pain, the tingle of the dangerous pleasure...

I grunt, unable to find the words to let her know I'm on the edge, so close to coming. The pain is almost unbearable, but not as unbearable as my need to release.

"Not so fast, baby." She knows my body, its signs. "I've got other plans for that cum." She pinches the tip of my cock in a move that sends me into an oblivion of pain. *Oh god.*

Then Danica turns off the device, her fingers instantly just fingers again.

She grins. "Now a little gift for myself..."

CHAPTER TWENTY-FIVE

GIFTS

DANICA...

W atching him intently, I let Dante cool off for a minute. He clearly needs it.

As I unclasp his ankles and wrists, they drop to the bed, limp. His cock is still twitching, so close to orgasm, but left unsatisfied just before its big moment.

How beautiful he looks like this, a beautiful mess—*my* beautiful mess. Lovingly, I stroke Dante's cheek, and he instinctively flinches, expecting electricity. But my skin is no longer electric.

While my darling boy figures out how to breathe in a steady pace again, I fetch a box from my suitcase, a smaller one. It is already open. I'd tried it on earlier, just to see what it was like. It had worked *exactly* how I'd hoped.

I throw the lube down next to Dante before climbing onto the bed, standing over my hungry Knight as he regards me with those awe-filled eyes. He keeps my gaze while I discard what little clothing I have on my body, finally freeing my breasts from their tight confines. They droop over my waist slightly, resting against my body—right where they belong.

Dante still doesn't know what's in the second box. Without breaking eye contact, I take out its contents and drop the box on the bed. Slowly, I sink fingers into my cunt to feel if I'm wet enough—I am.

As I hold Dante's gaze ransom, I slide the short end of the expensive silicone vibrating dildo into myself until the front stands out like a cock of my own. A ribbed bit on top rests perfectly against my clit. Carefully, I slide the custom panties over the dildo, harnessing it against my body to keep it all in my place—just like I'd practiced.

With newfound power, I stand over Dante, letting him admire my new purple cock. It's bigger than the one I usually peg him with but not bigger than his own.

"Do you like it?" I ask, looking down at him.

"You look magnificent." He looks at me in wonder, like I'm the only person in the entire world. It makes me feel brave, powerful.

"And how magnificent will I look pounding your ass into oblivion?"

"Please…" Dante virtually whimpers, his own cock still ready and close to release.

I kneel over him, lowering my new dick to his face. "Why don't you start by wetting this for me, darling?"

Without question, Dante takes me into his mouth as I thrust my hips forward, fucking his face as he gags on my length, almost choking.

"Slowly," I urge, pulling Dante's hair and moving his face.

He nods, sucking on the 7-inch strap-on that is so much more than just a strap-on.

"There you go, such a good boy." I kiss the top of his head, then pull his face off my cock and kiss him deeply, sloppily, as he gasps for breath. "Come here," I order, and Dante shuffles his body down the bed until his ass is on the edge. Making him comfortable, I slip a pillow under him.

Spread in a power stance, I stand between his thighs, resting my cock next to his. I rub them both together, feeling Dante grow to full hardness again.

"Let's warm you up, darling."

Dante gasps as the cold lube hits his hole, even more so when I slip my finger inside his ass to prep him, stretch him. Then two fingers. I wiggle them, finding my way to the nerve endings around his prostate, activating them with the mere flick of my fingers.

I love it when he groans like that, melting into the bed under my touch.

"Are you ready, baby boy? Ready to take my cock?" I rest the tip of the purple member at his hole, letting the anticipation sink in as I draw out my sentence seductively.

"Fuck me, please. I'm ready."

There is something so mesmerizing about seeing such a powerful man so desperate for my touch, something I can never grow tired of.

I push Dante's legs against his chest, lifting his bum into the air so I can guide my strap-on into him, slowly, carefully.

"Relax, darling. Just breathe," I coach him through all the steps he always instantly forgets when we get to this point.

Dante takes a deep breath, unclenching.

"There you go, look how exquisitely you open up for me. Are you going to take it all?" I coo encouragingly, almost patronizingly.

Dante nods, groaning loudly as I push in all the way. For a moment, we just stay like that, unmoving.

He locks his legs around my hips, behind my back, holding me against him as I reach for the remote, turning the dildo into a vibrator, pulsing inside us both—and over my clit. We moan at the same time.

"Now you listen carefully, my darling boy." I lean down, whispering. "Here's what's about to happen. I'm going to fuck you senseless and you're going to blow your load over my breasts like a good boy, is that understood?"

"Oh god," Dante moans, his cock jumping at the mere suggestion. A beautiful flutter of surprise slips from his lips before he composes himself again. "Yes, Ma'am."

"That's what I thought." With a smirk, I slowly pull out until only the tip is left inside his ass. Time for more lube. Holding onto Dante's thighs, I push back in, all the way, vibrating inside him.

The stimulation on my clit is so powerful, as is the vibration inside me. Every time I plunge back into Dante, it pushes against my clit harder, buzzing pleasure into my body.

He doesn't last; he's been on the edge too long. "I can't. Please..." Dante cries, clenching to try and keep the cum from exploding all over himself.

I lean down, pressing my breasts around his cock, rubbing it up and down slowly. "You have permission, my love. Come for me. Let me have every last drop of you."

I wrap my hands around his throat, squeezing with every ounce of strength as I continue thrusting inside him. Dante gasps for breath but I hold on, choking him, riding him until, moments later, he exclaims loudly, swearing in Italian as he releases his spunk all over my chest.

The orgasm between my own thighs quickly builds and I keep fucking him through his cries of overstimulation, riding him until my body contorts in pleasure over him, my skin on fire as the orgasm rips through my veins.

Wave after wave of pleasure crashes down on me. I struggle to find the remote to turn the dildo off as we both become too sensitive to continue.

It finally stops vibrating and I pull out carefully, collapsing into Dante's arms, our bodies heaving up and down together as we try to catch our breath.

Content, I weave my fingers through his, holding his hand as I close my eyes.

"Happy birthday, baby," I tell him but Dante can't speak yet, he just holds me close as my fingers tap against his chest in the rhythm of his heartbeat—my favorite sound.

CHAPTER TWENTY-SIX

INSATIABLE

DANTE...

"This is torture," I complain to Danica, pulling her naked body closer to mine. Her skin is the only blanket I need; we haven't even gotten dressed yet after her glorious birthday present surprise. Not that I mind the lack of clothing, it sure beats the ridiculous clothing she made me buy.

"This? I've literally shocked your balls with electricity today and you think *this* is torture? We're only on the second episode." Danica laughs, playfully hitting me with a pillow.

"I thought aftercare was supposed to be soothing to me? There is nothing soothing about *Parks & Rec*, I'm sorry." I cross my arms over my chest the way Danica always does when she's upset, pushing a pretend huff through my lips.

"You silly man, you should get us more snacks!" Danica laughs heartily, nestling her head in the pit of my arm. "And more water. Hydration is important."

"What happened to it being *my* birthday? Aren't *I* supposed to be the one who gets service?"

"Didn't you get enough service? Besides, I thought you don't do birthdays."

"Okay, fine. If they're always going to be like this one, maybe I'll reconsider," I tease, pulling Danica closer for a kiss.

Absentmindedly, I run my finger over the jagged scar forming on her arm, the one she got that night of the warehouse ambush. I hate that it's there, that she carries this mark, that someone dared to lay a finger on my Danica. But, at the same time, I love running my fingers over the permanent reminder that she came for me, that she cared enough to risk her life for me.

I press my lips to her broken skin, holding it in a soft kiss.

Hopefully, this saga is all behind us now. Don Ricci personally apologized for his son's disrespectful behavior in kidnapping another Don, vowing to punish him accordingly—and proposed a truce between the families, once more. He says he had no idea, and considering everything my own brother hid from me, I can believe him.

Just in case, I've asked Emilio to upgrade our security at home while we're away.

Having Emilio run things a bit while I recover has been so nice. My brain needed the break as much as my body did. For so long, I've been on autopilot, pushing through the days, the weeks, the years like they were endless, empty.

But I don't want to waste any more of my life, not when I can spend it with Danica. She gives me a reason to get up, to carry on. No matter how much time we spend together, I still can't predict what she'll do next, and it's the most exciting thing. Who thought I'd have so many firsts left to explore at the ripe old age of 43? *You're 44 now*, I remind myself.

"I already know what I'm getting you for your birthday next year." Danica grins mischievously as she tugs at my chest hair like it doesn't hurt. But I like the sensation. "And I'm not telling you, so don't even ask," she adds quickly.

"You're going to make me wait a whole year? You cruel woman."

"I thought I was your Queen?"

"You are. My evil Queen." Too quick for her to get out of the way, I jump on top of her, pinning her body beneath me as I cover her in tickles. Danica squirms around, laughing so hard that she can hardly breathe.

But she quickly gets the upper hand, grabbing my sleeping dick and calling me to order. "I've been called worse."

Throwing my hands up in the air, I surrender, rolling onto my back. But she doesn't let go, oh no.

"I wouldn't want you any other way. You're perfect." I kiss her nose.

For a moment, we just lie like that, her hand lazily playing with my half-sleeping cock like she's petting a dog. There is nowhere I have to be, nowhere I'd rather be, than right here.

Everything around me feels light, breezy almost—not just the temperature but the tension in my shoulders, the pressure at the back of my throat…This unexpected state of contentment is warm in my belly.

How effortlessly Danica waltzed into my life, merging our completely different worlds like they were always meant to intertwine, two puzzle pieces finally interlocking. I didn't have to change myself to fit her, to overthink my next move to be agreeable to her—I could just be, and I was exactly who I needed to be.

"I love you," I whisper into her hair, breathing in her scent.

My unexpected confession catches us both by surprise. But I don't regret it.

Danica pushes herself up onto her elbows to look at me intently. She is pensive for a moment, searching my eyes for the sincerity I know she finds.

I smile almost sheepishly, feeling even more vulnerable in this moment than I did spread out naked and tied up on the bed before her.

She touches my cheek affectionately as she smiles, telling me with her eyes as much as her words: "My darling *Tesoro*, I love you too."

Overwhelmed by emotion, I kiss her deeply, taking her face in both hands as I bite her bottom lip gently.

"So many birthday presents. How lucky am I?"

"Care for one more?" My not-so-soft-anymore cock jumps to attention as Danica flicks her fingers over the tip, trailing her long red nails over the skin carefully.

"You're insatiable, woman!" It's a statement of fact more than an accusation.

"Is that a yes?"

"Oh god, yes. Please, Miss."

Danica drags a sharp nail over my shaft, over my balls, and I hold my breath. She smiles mischievously, reaching for the lube on the bedside. "I thought as much, baby boy..."

A loud grunt bellows from my insides as she pinches my cock between her fingers in a move that is both painful and incredibly arousing. *How does she do that?*

"Hmm, I have this thing I want to try. Hold on, let me get my phone. I saved a screenshot somewhere." Danica jumps off the bed without waiting for a response, determined as always.

"As long as it isn't more *Parks & Rec*," I call after her, drawing an annoyed grunt from Danica in the other room.

Smiling, I put my hands behind my head like a pillow and lie back, waiting for my Queen to return with whatever treat or torture she has in mind.

Perhaps I can learn to like birthdays after all.

Want more Danica & Dante content? Read Book 3 (*Valentine for Dante*), or unlock the free *Domme vs Don* short by joining my monthly newsletter via mkaynoir.com/newsletter

THANK YOU

Thank you for reading my book.

If you enjoyed it, wouldn't you please take a moment to leave me a **review** at your favorite retailer? It helps more like-minded people to find this very niche content.

Do you want more stories with this vibe? Then carry on reading...

To get bonus content and fresh releases, join my **newsletter**(via mkaynoir.com/newsletter) or follow me on **BookBub**.

Kay

MORE BY M KAY NOIR

Valentine for Dante

Queens & Knights Book 3

***

Torn between desire and duty, I'm frozen.

Danica and I are so happy together.

So, why now? Why are you here?

This won't end well...

I can't want this.

I shouldn't.

But I do.

***

More info and links via mkaynoir.com/dante

About the Author

M Kay Noir is a queer romance author and journalist obsessed with moments of desire. Most of her stories are kinky, queer-friendly, polyamorous undertakings with neurotic characters who are often their own worst enemy. If you expect any regard for traditional gender roles or power dynamics, you will be disappointed.

Kay has been penning steamy moments for more than 15 years now, from fanfics to ghostwriting and now finally her own stories. Her day job also involves a lot of writing, albeit a different kind—mostly sustainability things. When she's not writing (or reading), she enjoys making her husband look at yet another sunset and watching live music concerts.

**See mkaynoir.com for the long version.